MW00616991

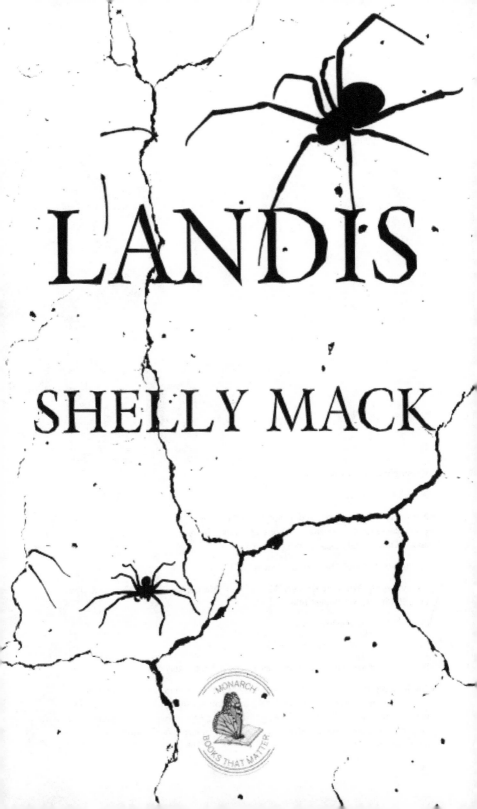

LANDIS

SHELLY MACK

MONARCH
BOOKS THAT MATTER

Praise for Shelly Mack

"Fantastic read full of faeries and friends with fledgling powers and romances forced to battle an evil princess for control of their kingdom. I could not put it down!"

AMY CHRISTINE PARKER, AUTHOR OF FLIGHT 171

"LANDIS is a beautifully-written YA fantasy that is sure to be a huge hit. The prince and his friends must try to understand and develop their unique abilities and work to save their world from evil forces, all while navigating friendships, family relationships, and romantic interests. This exceptionally compelling novel includes themes of loyalty, bravery, and being true to one's self and others, and it's filled with magic, fairies, and brilliant world-building."

SYDNEY DUNLAP, AUTHOR OF IT HAPPENED ON SATURDAY

"Lyrical and awe-inspiring, LANDIS is a captivating story of a visionary prince and vengeful princess and the class that takes place when light meets with darkness."

ASHLEY WHITE, AUTHOR OF THE IMPOSSIBLE GIRL

Praise for Shelly Mack

"What an imaginative world of magic, fairies, and an evil princess I couldn't help but root for even as she threatened to destroy friendships and a kingdom."

ANGELIQUE BURRELL, AUTHOR OF A MARK IN
THE ROAD

"From the first page, Shelly Mack's Landis plunges you into a mesmerizing world that holds you captive until the end and leaves you craving more. You meet Alunattra, the Dark Princess, who longs to escape her 'shackles.' Her plight sparks your curiosity, and as you read on, you find yourself asking: "What is the hidden truth behind Landis?" This magical island has a mysterious order, governed by the Immortal Hosts, and no one dares to challenge them. But when Prince Benjamin receives his Sovereign Dominion on his 16th birthday and awakens his magical powers, he starts to unravel the secrets of his realm. Along the way, he forms unexpected alliances with a colorful cast of characters, each with their own unique perspective and voice, who keep the story flowing at a breathless pace."

STEPHANIE COTTA, AUTHOR OF THE IRON
KINGDOM SERIES

"Within those first few pages, it became evident that I was privy to something truly unique. I image it's how the first readers of Harry Potter felt: we were witnessing the beginning of something that deserved to be huge, globally. The it factor is strong with this one."

ELYSIA NATES, AUTHOR OF WRITTEN & DIRECTED
BY ME, MACKENZIE

To my husband and girls,
my world and inspiration,
this is for you.
With all my love forever.

Landis Lots

Castle Landis

Valor Rock

PURE BAY

Purity Creek

The Forbidden Vale

The Crying Caves

The Tree of Vulnerability

OBSIDIAN CREEK

Alunattra's Tower

The Perimeter Seas

Two Hundred Years Ago

Mileah laid her hand on the windowsill and a spider scuttled onto her palm. It crept up the length of her bony, bruised arm, and she sighed in contentment as the creature buried its way into her dark, matted hair.

As she peered over the castle grounds, the white shutters swayed, tapping the flawless brick walls beside her. It was like a perfect picture of a place she would love to visit but was out of her reach. She clenched her jaw, surveying the row of stone homes stretching out in the distance. Thatched roofs decorated with trailing sprays of rainbow-laced flowers glistened like prisms beneath the moonlight.

Thoughts from different people in the village forced their way into her mind like an insect weaving through the cracks of a wall.

Let's gather around the fire.

Would you like a bedtime story?

Children were laughing somewhere, an action that stung her insides. The longing locked up tight, banged inside, but bitterness vied to retain her damaged heart. It won.

I hate that they're happy. What kind of people are they to allow me to rot? You're evil. All of you.

The warm breeze from the night sky danced over the hollows in her cheeks, yet she shivered with internal frostbite.

I have never been a princess. Only a prisoner.

The need to escape the alien bedroom she stood in consumed her.

This was supposed to be hers—the wrought iron bed, the writing desk with the flawless feather quill, and the wardrobe of untouched silks. She bristled, thinking of the cold dank floor her cheek was so used to now, and a bitter laugh bellowed out in a strangled cackle.

Where was Ebba? Her beautiful fairy—the only friend she'd known—was usually there in the moments she hadn't been put in the dark place.

Maybe she doesn't know I escaped.

Like a spark in the darkness, she remembered.

There is no one here to tell me what to do and no one to block my call. I can be heard.

"Ebba!" Her dry throat croaked out the summons for her wishing fairy who burst forth before her. Ebba's skin was originally cobalt blue, with the brightest white wings. Now, her once sparkling exterior had been replaced with shards of patched-up clothing that hung the way wet rags do. Mileah swallowed the painful lump trying to attach itself to her windpipe. Ebba had been imprisoned too, and only Mileah could save her with a summons.

"My princess, you're here. Are you okay? Let me check you. What do you need?"

Mileah gave a rare smile. One that was reserved for the only person that cared for her. "I am now. I escaped, and I need you to gather the villagers."

Ebba stared at her in awe before fear clouded her features. "But the king and queen—they won't allow that."

"I took care of the king and queen. They are not here. Things are going to change now, Ebba."

With me as queen, Ebba will be my equal, as it always should have been.

The tattered blue-gray of Ebba's dress flexed and the tiny threads began to repair themselves as her skin burned brighter. Her wings went from sagging to vibrant white and pointed like a flower blooming after a rainstorm. She sparkled and buzzed in a circle around Mileah's head, leaving speckles of white fairy dust in her trail. She stopped to face her, and Mileah saw tears in Ebba's pale blue eyes. Against her tiny cheeks, they looked as big as raindrops as they fell, each one landing with an audible thud that added a new dimension to Mileah's soul.

They will not take anything else from us.

Ebba may have been the size of Mileah's hand, but she was mighty and loyal.

"I tried so many times to rescue you, but the dungeon is impervious." Ebba wailed out her words.

"Ebba, hush. It is of little importance. Now is the time for the king and queen to experience dungeon life and for us to rule."

Ebba's brow unfurrowed and her eyes lit up. "I will meet you at the castle entrance then, but before I go..."

Mileah watched in fascination as Ebba swirled her delicate fingers and the oak-carved wardrobe doors burst open. Out flew an ivory-flowing satin gown encrusted with pearls over the bodice. A sheath of opalescent lace hung from the shoulders and ran down the length of the dress, creating a diamond shaped train.

Ebba blew a kiss and disappeared, leaving the magnificent gown suspended mid-air.

Mileah discarded her dirty rags that no longer resembled clothing. Her eyes brightened as she pointed to the pile; she stood tall as her new power blazed through her. Flames spun from her fingertips and the tatters turned to ash.

Every dirty pore of her body rippled clean, and she stepped into her dress. The material caressed her skin, but the dress was too big for her malnourished body.

Now I can eat what I want—as much as I want.

Her eyes fell on the square glass box that she'd never been close to. The crystal clear lock buzzed with invisible protection, put there by the fairies at her mother's command. What lay inside made her fingers twitch as the crystal blue diamonds sparkled in the moonlight. She felt the power of the enchantment, and with an absentminded flick of her wrist, the padlock shattered, and the door popped open. A rush of adrenaline brought a smile. Her weathered fingers delicately lifted the solid gold crown from the violet velvet pillow.

I will never take this off.

Power surged through her as the weighted crown sat upon her head.

She left the room and the hallway outside was deathly silent. The only sound was the swish of her train behind her. She passed the nursery and hovered. She wasn't supposed to know that she had a brother.

I can't think about him now.

She reached the walkway and crouched, trailing a finger over the ornately carved spindles.

This castle is mine.

The encased stairwell stood out—a stone pillar that ran from the north to the south wing. She entered the arched doorway and looked down the steep steps.

My moment has finally come.

She clicked her fingers and the staircase lit up on her descent.

No longer will I live in darkness.

Her bare feet did not feel the cold of the marble floor as she left the last step. She had grown accustomed to numbness.

Never again.

Ebba curtsied between the open wrought iron doors. Mileah hesitated for only a second before gliding over the hidden spot far below in the castle that had caged her all these years. The dark, dank dungeon. The corners of her lips curved at the thought of her parents there.

Now you both will know what it means to suffer.

Ebba straightened Mileah's gown but couldn't contain her horror. "My lady, I have a potion that can heal your bruises."

No amount of self-cleaning could hide the ugly wounds that decorated her wrists like the cuff of a garment. "Leave them. I want everyone to be held responsible."

Mileah saw that her fairy understood and visible pain reflected Ebba's scars too. "As you wish."

Ebba took her place at Mileah's side but before they moved further, another fairy appeared. Bishop. The head of the king's fairy guard. He looked flummoxed, and the buzz of his irate wings echoed in the lower wing of the castle.

Mileah bit the inside of her lip till the blood flooded through the cracks in her teeth.

He will not spoil this for me.

"Get. Out. Of. My. Way."

Mileah's eyes blazed into the dots of Bishop's, stunning him into submission.

Finally, I can have control over you.

Fairies' minds were not easily manipulated through gifts, but it seemed this didn't apply to her. Yesterday, she saw it. The fear that radiated from the fairy line. This only strengthened her determination.

All thoughts of Bishop vanished as she strode out toward the expectant faces. The collective sound of voices amused her.

They all want to know why they are out after curfew. You're all in for a shock.

The crowd grew silent, but the people's questions screamed at her. Mileah singled out a few of their thoughts.

She wasn't so thin yesterday…

Why does she have all those marks?

Why are we here?

Where are the king and queen?

Mileah acknowledged them with a slight curve of her lips. The maintained lawn where they stood shined like emeralds beneath the glittering night sky. The people were nervous, not like the previous day at her coming-of-age ceremony when they watched her receive her power—jubilant from the flowing wine the fairies circulated. Her mother's power of Illusion had them all fooled, but these faces wore tight expressions.

You're all on edge. You should be. Now you see the real me, not the version that was created by the people who gave me my birthright.

The bitterness started dissipating as possibility took hold.

This world is mine now to mold. My power can stand up against all of yours combined.

As she drank in the crowd's growing fear, she locked eyes with the dark-haired girl who had freed her from her prison. Mileah had an unexpected window of time yesterday to find someone to control, and the girl had been the perfect pawn. She used her gift to call out to the girl who was, as it were, at the wrong place at the wrong time, but at the perfect place at precisely the right time for Mileah.

The girl held Mileah's gaze, looking with curiosity, not fear.

She has no idea what she did. Good.

Mileah seared her eyes into the girl. *You will be my servant from now on.*

Her power responded and swelled within as the girl nodded.

I don't even know your name and you did exactly as I asked. So easy.

A loud rumble from the sky above snapped her back to the task at hand, and she saw the clouds part. Warm air turned to ice as it breezed through the castle grounds, making everyone shiver.

He was coming, and Mileah was glad.

In the blink of an eye, he stood in his blistering white robes.

Vallore. The High Host. The immortal being who controlled their world. The entity that gave Mileah the gift to control minds. The one responsible for creating powers she couldn't begin to fathom. The power of All Transcendence. Never more alive, she couldn't wait to explore her capabilities. Mind control was only the beginning. These people would be like clay to the potter.

Mileah gained so much insight yesterday. Vallore had no power over the gift she'd been given. Mileah manifested it herself. He only possessed the power to trigger what already lay dormant. He'd been brainwashed by the queen like everyone else. How the queen had managed that, Mileah did not know. Vallore towered with swirling hatred in his blackened eyes.

Mileah lifted her chin and met his gaze with a pointed glare.

"I am the new queen."

Vallore's beaded black irises flickered in panic. It was so fleeting before they expanded and bore into her like liquid tar.

Mileah ignored the urge to squirm and held strong, searching behind his eyes.

She saw everything then. Vallore. His life. It flashed before her. Snippets of him, hidden. Not here but somewhere else. Outside of their world. He flinched and tightened his jaw, pulling his inner wall back up.

We are not alone in this world. We are mere pawns in a sick game. I am not the only one who has been imprisoned. Every person here is.

Vallore's jaw twitched.

He can hear my thoughts.

Vallore spoke through her mind. Each word stung like the heat from a molten poker. *"You will never share what you know. No one can ever know."*

Vallore lifted off the ground until he towered above her. Mileah surprised herself by rising off the ground to reach him.

"You dare to challenge me?"

Mileah's body twisted hard at his words, and every bone and muscle tautened. *I will not let him beat me.*

Vallore took advantage of her hesitancy and surrounded her in a band of circular light. Mileah tried to move but was trapped inside the ring. Vallore descended, touching the ground without sound as though weightless. His hand flexed and sparks flew from his fingertips as an invisible force pulled her to the front of the stage. Some looked at her in disgust, some with pity.

He's shaming me.

"You are a descendant of my creations. You cannot beat me. You cannot escape. Ever. Instead, you will writhe in the dirt where you belong and be forced to live a pitiful existence with nothing but time as your friend."

Vallore raised his bony white finger and drew a stitched line over her lips. They closed, and she was silenced.

This is not the end, Vallore. The only reason you're not killing me now is because you can't.

Vallore perceived her thought, and a spark of rage burned in his irises, but it left as quickly as it came. The High Host was working to guard his thoughts—a needless endeavor.

I already know your mind, Vallore. You can't save yourself from that.

A strange expression dulled the white sheen of Vallore's creped skin, then he stepped to the side and summoned Bishop.

In desperation, Mileah tried breaking free from the invisible chains, but it was useless. The command part of her power was sealed. When she looked up, Ebba was taken by the Fairy Guard. *Vallore, don't do this to her. She was assigned to me. It's not her fault.* Mileah pleaded for the first time, but Vallore smirked, basking in her obvious pain. For one so small, Ebba's screams were piercing. Sorrow filled Mileah's heart as the only constant in her life was removed.

The wave of despair turned to boiling anger. The small spider crept out of her hair and skittered onto her shoulder. Soon after, hundreds of spiders appeared from the earth, scurrying over every inch of the stage. They moved their way up the length of Mileah's frame until they covered her.

The crowd gasped and then started chanting Vallore's name. In an instant, it was just the two of them hurtling through the sky. Vallore's inflamed hands weaved her contorted body through the mottled clouds. The sparks from his fingers flinched her skin, and the roped band of light around her waist crackled, sending shards of pain through her body. The smoky gray clouds parted and Vallore landed at the Tree of Vulnerability, slamming Mileah into the ground. Her spiders remained stuck to her skin.

Mileah fought to fill her lungs with breath as she took in her surroundings. This was her first time seeing the fabled tree. For a moment, its reverent beauty left her awestruck; the leaves glistened like they'd been sprinkled with fairy dust. The shaft of the tree was knotted together like it had been hand-crafted with the roughest bark. She gulped. Her spiders crawled over her skin and fueled her purpose.

All types of fruit flowed from the branches and the bright green leaves highlighted the red in the apples and the orange in the clementines. Her stomach churned.

How long has it been since I've eaten?

"You don't deserve food. Your body does not require it to live. From now on you will be in solitude to decay in the sins of your making, and you will be known to this world as Alunattra. The Dark Princess."

From the tips of Vallore's fingers, he produced what resembled a rippling wave of water. It rose right through the center of the tree. Mileah heard the crack, but the tree remained grounded. The water-like wall sprang high till it disappeared into the heavens above and stretched out to the edges of her world.

Mileah was on one side of this barrier. Vallore the other.

Mileah screamed, breaking apart the seal on her lips. The skin ripped, and the taste of iron in the warmth of her blood was the only element of heat on her skin. The circle of light wrapped around her waist dispersed, but the barrier in front of her did not falter. She felt it —Vallore's infused power. It was impenetrable.

He is stronger than me. For now.

She stamped her feet into the ground, and the soft green grass turned black, spreading like a disease until everything around her lay shrouded in darkness. The rose bush hedges around the tree shriveled and every red petal turned to ash. The pearls on her gown exploded, leaving jagged protrusions in the once delicate gown. The Tree of Vulnerability on her side crumbled and the branches snapped, hanging dead. Rotten fruit festered into the earth as Mileah hammered her fists into the black soil.

Her crown never left her head. Instead, when she touched it, her fingers felt the heat of her rage, transferring pieces of the metal into her skin.

Her dirty nails dug deeper into the ground. "My power is strong, Vallore. It will take more than this to stop me. I have been in captivity my whole life."

"My magic is untouchable. You can try, but you will fail." His breath misted the barrier in a taunt.

Mileah slammed herself into the barrier and its shock floored her, dropping her to the ground in violent convulsions. She shifted her head, the only movement she could muster, and tightened her eyes toward the High Host.

Vallore sneered into her soul before disappearing in a hazy mist.

The spiders smothered her body, setting up home until all that could be seen were burst vessels in her bloodshot eyes. The moment she rose her body responded.

One thing he cannot take from me is my power.

Mileah looked out over the landscape, hatred destroying the last shred of her humanity.

You are right, Vallore. Time is my friend.

One day...

CHAPTER 1

Ben

S ixteen. *I'm sixteen.* Ben bit the inside of his lip. His ceremony was the day everyone had been waiting for and now that it was here, was he ready? His stomach churned, a prequel to the nausea that followed. The toilet lid was cold on his chin as he heaved. He needed Tweek.

His robe clung to his clammy skin. Just another day of weighted responsibility.

The drag of his feet to the sink was the only sound breaking the silence. Ben turned the squeaky tap on, letting the water rain over his hands, and then he blotted his face with his fingers, in the hope it would wash the anxiety away as well.

As he wiggled his fingers dry, his stomach performed a nauseating sequel. He winced, walking to the window. What would be best—fast-forwarding this day or staying in the safety of the unknown?

I just wish I could be like everyone else.

The shutters creaked open as he looked over the village. Not for the first time, he wished he lived like his friends, in one of the beautiful stone homes encased in flowers. They all lived in "The Row"— the only street in the village that ran down the hill from the castle. He wished he could walk to the square and go to the shops at leisure time. To be normal. Not a prince.

I'm too in my head. Keep control.

He counted random numbers until his hammering heart slowed its pace. The smell of the flowers from the gardens below blew in with the breeze, grazing his moist face—*that's better.* The view from his room was spectacular. Pure Bay—the largest part of Landis Lots—was blanketed with the most lustrous green grass, sprinkled with every imaginable flower, and speckled with towering trees. Ben took in the village shops then cast a glance farther north, to the lofty blue mountains known as Valor Rock. They were home to The Crying Caves and rippling streams flowed from the mouths of the caves. Waterfalls cascaded into crystalline pools that weaved into rivers and intersected, meeting in a central reserve known as Purity Creek. Like droplets from a tap, sweat trickled down his back.

I could do with an ice pool right now.

Ben sought the calm of Purity Creek. It shimmered in the distance. The prisms of light reflected off the sky as rainbow colors beamed from the clear lake. The only body of water the people were authorized to visit. Farther out lay the Perimeter Seas, teetering around the edge of the island. Nobody was allowed there. Always for safety reasons.

How would I even get there anyway? How long would it take?

Ben closed his eyes. Wafts of freshly cut grass filled his nostrils.

What would happen if I didn't turn up today?

Not an option on an island with nowhere to hide. Landis Lots was all that existed. Or so he'd been told.

But could another land exist beyond the Perimeter Seas? The bizarre dreams disrupting his sleep lately flooded his mind with questions; something wasn't adding up. It seemed possible that they were not alone. His dreams were far too real. He'd come to look forward to sleep, to the circle of vibrant light that pulled him in. Someone was there, always waiting for him. A silhouette, not from his world, reaching out to him. Each time closer.

Who are you? Are you there now?

Nothing. No response when he was awake. After these dreams, the helpless distress was so raw. It was like reading a book with no end.

He shivered. As always, his green eyes flickered across the terrain, past fields of daisies and poppies, and focused on the far side of the island where the beauty abruptly ended.

Obsidian Creek.

Like an insect bite that caught him off guard, his skin stung.

A familiar tickle on his ear brought him back. "Tweek, how many times have I told you? Don't bite!"

His wishing fairy giggled, and pink fairy dust swirled around her. "I prefer to think of it as a pinch of endearment. I just wanted to wish you a happy birthday," she said, blowing him a kiss.

He held his hand out for her to sit on. "Thank you."

"You better hurry up. It's almost time," Tweek said, burling off his palm. "I've laid out your clothes. Shout for me when you're ready."

As Ben moved from the bathroom, he discarded his brocade robe and changed. He summoned Tweek back. She floated his gold crown set with diamonds and rubies toward his dark short hair. Tweek, with a snap of her tiny fingers, used her magic to place the black, gold, and lilac threaded cape over his navy tailcoat and breeches.

"Perfect, and I was right. The cravat matches your eyes. That's you, my prince. Are you ready?"

That's a loaded question. I don't know the answer.

His cravat felt like a noose.

"I guess I better be."

Tweek looked him up and down. "Don't take this the wrong way, but you look awful."

Only Tweek could say something like this to him without offense. Her gold-veined wings sagged.

"I'm okay, Tweek, honestly."

She hesitated before dropping a tiny kiss on his nose. "For luck."

Ben loved her. People moaned about their fairies, but Tweek had his back, and he trusted her more than most. She was as close to a sibling that he would ever get, and although he was only supposed to use her for general amenities and clothing, he suspected those boundaries could be pushed with some nudging.

"I'll take some luck. By the way, love the dress."

Tweek spun for him, and the pink of her long satin skirt sparkled as it plumped like a parasol. Her pale pink skin brightened as she twirled, complementing the gold flecks of her wings and the twinkle from her bare toes.

"On you go, I'll be down in a minute," Ben said, tenderly shooing her away.

She winked, and after a dramatic twirl, she disappeared.

Sporadic beams of morning light pushed through the stained-glass rafters above him, lighting his path as he walked along the corridor of bed chambers. The walls were decorated with old tapestries made by his great-great grandmother. Interspersed were portraits of the royals to date. Ben quivered at the space in the hall that remained blank. Princess Mileah's portrait was never hung; instead it remained a dark, empty space.

Don't think about that now.

At the staircase, Ben hesitated. He lived in the north wing, the highest point of the castle's interior. Opposite him was another stairwell—iron, open, and corkscrew in shape. It led to the tower, which boasted an expansive veranda. Ben had never been up there—it was just another restricted area of the castle. He stared up at the corridor's sprawling skylight, and a crackle sparked its way into the clouds. The vortex swirled above. He asked his grandad once what it did.

"Keeps our climate pleasant and keeps us safe."

All a bit vague if you ask me. Why does nobody ask more questions?

His thought process was interrupted when Tharmus, his father's head guard, emerged from the shadows, like always.

Tharmus could be spotted a mile out in his magenta woven wool trousers and a long lilac overcoat. On his lapel, he wore the Landis Lots crest—a black circle with gold stitching and "LL" sewn in lilac thread that matched his coat. It was pathetically oversized, and Ben wondered if Tharmus had his fairy make it this way. Ben had run out of reasons to think him ridiculous.

"Everyone is waiting for you. The prince can't be late," Tharmus said.

"Just as well, that's the direction I'm going in then, isn't it!" Ben bristled as he stomped away from Tharmus, but the man remained close behind Ben. He detested the head guard and was sure his father had appointed this annoying mound to torment Ben. Why did he even need a guard when nothing bad ever happened?

I may be a prince, but that doesn't mean I asked to be.

Tharmus and the Fairy Guard were the unseen eyes of the island. Spying was one thing Ben would change when he became king. It caused tension within Landis, which was obvious to him, but of course, that couldn't be voiced.

I just want to get through this day so I can enjoy the party and maybe speak to Vara. Vara, the girl from his physics class who had captured his attention. *She is something special.* His heart missed a beat.

"Ah, Tharmus, don't you have a job you need to attend to?"

Ben smiled as his grandpa's voice echoed behind him.

"Absolutely. Thank you, King Father." Tharmus bounded off.

"You should give the guy a break. He's not so bad," Grandad said, his authoritative voice softening.

Grandad Baylor always saw the good in everyone, but truthfully, he wasn't ever wrong. At 102 years old, the man was still sharp as a tack. He was always there. Whenever Ben needed him, he would appear.

Maybe that is part of Grandad's power? Ben's grandpa Bay had the gift of Guidance. *I've never asked him about that. I should.*

"Anyway, fancy helping an old man down these frightful steps? My knees would thank you if they could talk." Grandad Bay offered his arm, the twinkle in his eye matching the glint of his snow-white hair as the sunlight beamed from the large stained-glass panes behind them.

A ruse. His grandad knew him better than his father did. It was Ben that felt *his* legs could give at any moment.

"Sure," Ben said, squeezing his grandad's arm.

"Not long now. How are you feeling?"

"Like I ate a bad round of chicken." Ben could almost taste the bile.

"Understandable but make your nerve work for you. After you receive your gift, your life will take a turn down a lane full of revelations. Your new aspect will be part of you, like an extra limb. You must embrace it warmly."

Ben swallowed. *How did Grandad handle the pressure when he'd been king?* He shook off the thought.

By the end of this day, he would have his gift. His Sovereign Dominion. His Verdo.

What if I can't control it?

"Grandad, where does the term Verdo come from?"

"Your Sovereign Dominion is like an inevitable verdict. Verdo is a more casual way of saying that. It stuck as many words do."

"What determines the kind of power I'll get?"

"Nobody can answer that. I don't even think the Immortal Hosts hold that knowledge. It's predetermined. As you know, many have lower-level gifts, some moderate, and then there are the top-tier gifts."

As they left the stairwell and exited the castle onto the lawn, Ben's legs wobbled. His grandad steadied him.

"You have nothing to fear, Ben. I'm going to take my seat, but one more thing, my boy, have fun today."

The sudden warmth from his grandad's embrace filled him like a warm drink on a cold day. *How long has it been since someone hugged me?*

Ben blinked and was gladly distracted by his mother's waving hand. She mouthed "happy birthday" from her place at the back of the line-up. He missed her. She wasn't quite herself these days, and the castle was so grand, it sometimes felt like months since they'd seen each other.

The last bell chime sounded, and the other expectants were already in place to walk onto the stage.

This is happening.

Ben tapped his foot and withdrew his handkerchief from his pocket to mop the moisture from his forehead. He wished he was back in his quarters where he could throw up in private.

A sudden kerfuffle around his mother caused a new panic. His parents' fairies, Aristo and Perial, were dousing her with a watery mist.

Why is she that ashen color? Why won't my feet move?

Ben's father was immediately at her side after casting a solemn glance at him. Ben felt the force of his father's gift of Command lock him in place. He didn't use it often but the gift meant, "I say, you do!"

Why is Father keeping me back?

"Not to worry, Master Benjamin," Perial said. She was so close Ben could smell her floral scent. "Your mother hasn't eaten well enough this morning. Just focus on your special day."

Ben liked his mother's fairy, but he didn't appreciate being patronized. The irritation brought his fingers to his lips and he peeled at the skin.

"Ouch." Tweek was nipping his finger.

"Stop picking," she said.

"Stop sneaking up on me!"

Her bossy pointed finger was the constant he needed, and he sighed as her wings tickled his ear from where she hovered on his shoulder. His mother's vacant look was gone, but Ben didn't miss the mutual worried glance Aristo and Perial shared. His suit felt tight.

His father barely acknowledged Ben's presence as he thundered past him. "Benjamin, take your place. It's time."

Typical. His father was trying to pass this off as nothing. Control was slipping and he wouldn't like that.

Ben walked over the bridge and down a set of stone steps, onto the crisp green grass to begin his Walk of the Red—the official opening to gifting ceremonies. This was the most extravagant yet. Each white chair was wrapped in ivory lace on both sides of the red carpet. The ground was rough under his black buckle shoes, and he welcomed the grip. The air thrummed with incoherent words. Every face studied him. He gulped.

All thirty village families and extended members were eagerly waiting. The younger ones yet to reach sixteen seemed the most curious. They waved miniature flags to match the large one that flapped in the breeze above the tower. It was striking with its three stripes—black, lilac, and gold, with the circular crest in the middle. Floating bunting swayed in time with the choir as the students chanted the most captivating tune. One by one, the room quietened.

Vara's looking at me. Ben tried to be casual. *I have to look.*

She was on an aisle seat, turned towards him. Her dress alone made her stand out—mint green ropes weaved around a fitted basque and a long, flowing, satin skirt of dark emerald. Like his cravat, *and my eyes.* But it was the chocolate brown warmth of her eyes that caused him to lose his footing.

"Hold it together," Tweek whispered.

The other three expectants were already seated on the staged deck. Walking toward his throne, Ben acknowledged them with a slight nod.

He hesitated to look at one of them—Gabriel. His new friend stood out with his shoulder-length brown hair that took on a life of its own. Gabriel was shrinking back in his seat. *Maybe he feels like I do.* Ben remembered the day they'd been paired together during a science experiment; the day Gabriel had caught a glimpse of his soul. Ben had blacked out. Gabriel, not drawing attention to them, had nudged Ben's arm. A spark from his fingers brought Ben around and he saw loneliness in Gabriel that didn't sit right. Since then, Ben looked forward to physics, although he hadn't spoken of the incident. Gabriel had a quiet confidence about him, and when relaxed, even showed signs of a good sense of humor.

I'm sure Gabriel's birthday was this week too.

These zoning out episodes were becoming more frequent, and not just when Ben was sleeping. If only he could control it. After the dreams of the girl, the moment of connection faded like a dream he desperately wanted to hold on to but slipped away from his memory.

Gabriel must have felt Ben's stare as he looked up with a jolt then relaxed his shoulders. Gabriel gave Ben the tiniest eye roll. Surprisingly, a wave of calm fell over him, and he swallowed down his nerves.

He sat down quickly, scanning the crowd for his best friends. Severo stood taller than everyone and shot Ben a goofy smile, then he caught Niall's eye—his oldest friend since their first day of school. A chill feathered through him. For a fleeting second, a hint of something off lingered around Niall's aura.

I need to get my act together!

He looked again and Niall was beaming at him.

I'm losing it.

The bell chimes rang three times to mark the beginning and would ring again, thrice at the end of the line-up. Ben's father strode to the podium. All eyes were on him as the sun kissed the golden threads of his royal cape. He raised his right hand. Silence veiled the crowd. Ben had to admit, his father having an element of mind control was to be envied, not that he used it much, though.

"Greetings to all on this extremely special occasion. I always feel nostalgic on ceremony days as it takes me back to when I first received my Sovereign Dominion. Today, I'm as proud as a father can be as Queen Moline and I witness our son, Prince Benjamin Landis, receive his. On his birthday no less. Let us all celebrate together afterward." He turned and smiled at Ben.

Funny, that's not what it feels like to me. Clearly, this is to keep up appearances.

"Now, may we all be still as we say our sacred words." At this, everyone in the crowd bowed their heads.

"Landis for the people. Landis for the free. We honor our king and queen and the powers that be. We will be brave. We will stand tall. Protectors of the realm, we live by our call."

"All rise for our Land Anthem," his father boomed.

This was sung before the ceremony in acknowledgment of the Immortal Hosts. The people of Landis rose from their chairs at the king's instruction and the choir led the crowd in song.

"Landis Lots,
come one, come all.
We live, we grow,
we wait for our call.
May the land be blessed,
may you keep us in health.
We thank you for family
and our blessings in wealth."

THE CROWD TOOK TO THEIR SEATS; THEIR EYES TRANSFIXED ON THE STAGE. Everyone seemed on tenterhooks today for the same reason Ben was.

"Without further ado, I present our four expectants, all of whom are now sixteen." His father appraised each one as he worked his way down the line, stopping to linger for a second upon Ben's face. "I now invite our Immortal Hosts to join us and bestow this honor to our beloved sons and daughters. We remain ever thankful to our creator for the peaceful world in which we live. Long live Landis." The king placed his hands together as whispers fell from his lips.

A hush settled upon the castle grounds. The hosts were respected but inspired uncertainty and fear. Aside from these ceremonies, they were absent from their world. Ben could cut the tension with a knife. Then, like a spark of magic, they were there.

Holy though they may be, Ben thought their appearance other-worldly. Each one had the same translucent skin that appeared as strong as marble yet breakable like glass. The only mark of difference was in the chief Immortal Host, Vallore. His square face was sculpted in such a way that the sharp edges looked like they could draw blood. Black halos rimmed Vallore's eyes, and when they locked on, it was impossible to look away from the gray haunt that held one captive. The other hosts' eyes were the color of milk with the same black rim, and oval faces.

Nobody knew how many Immortal Hosts existed or any of their names, aside from the chief. There were four here today, one for each expectant. The hosts hovered into position, their floor-length robes gliding like tail feathers, and the chief took his place before Ben.

He gulped, staying stock-still.

Vallore flicked his wrist, and the Domain Cup took form, resting in

9

his hand. Liquid silver bubbled from the ice goblet, signifying the commencement of the first stage of this ritual. Upon first taste, it would alter a person immediately. Power would emanate from them, and viewers would watch, like reaching a pivotal point in a novel. This sacred act was as much a part of the ceremony as the anointing was.

All four expectants drank from the goblet, one by one. The chirp of hoppers, a bug that lived in the grass, offered the only sound to the long-awaited moment.

Vallore began, "Today you will hereby be granted your Sovereign Dominion. The age of sixteen marks the seed of your power. The cup and the seal will root your seed for growth and your power will continue to ripen from its implantation. Your training will begin thereafter."

Ben swallowed.

Vallore's steely gaze landed on him. "You must nurture your power, but it MUST not be used recreationally. You have this gift for the sole purpose of defense should it ever be needed in battle. It is our hope, you will never need to use your gifts. You are answerable to us, and you will be monitored by the leaders of Landis. If found in abuse of your power, it will be presented to us and consequences will be severe."

Ben had heard this all before, but this was the first time it hit home. He'd never understood why powers were given at sixteen if they weren't allowed to be used. He also knew that people did use them on the fly but somehow were never caught.

"Let us begin," Chief Vallore said and raised his right hand in the air. The sky weaved and crackled. A beam of the brightest light connected in and through him like a prismatic conduit. As Vallore lowered his face to the crowd, the Domain Cup disappeared and was replaced with the Seal Staff—the next item in the ritual. It slid into his firm, creped hands. He drifted to the first host and gave the wood-woven rod to him.

The first host moved closer and spoke, "Blessed are thee, Clara Waits, on your day of anointment. Please kneel and hold out the palm of your right hand." He held out the Seal Staff and placed the tip on Clara's open palm. The Seal Staff blazed sapphire and threads of light engulfed her, making her shine brightly. She stiffened, and her eyes burned azure. She was vested, and as she rose, the host offered his hand.

"Your Sovereign Dominion will be the gift of Healing."

Ben watched the host—his face showed no expression.

What a great gift. To heal the injured at the touch of your hand. Brilliant.

Ben applauded along with the crowd. Clara was one of Vara's friends. He didn't know her well, but she seemed pure. The sun pinked her cheeks and made her straight black hair glow.

Next up was Gabriel.

Ben watched with fascination as Gabriel went through all the same motions. The dodgy look in his eyes suggested he would rather be anywhere but here.

"Your Sovereign Dominion will be the gift of the Mask."

Ben wasn't the only one to gasp at this declaration, but again, Gabriel's host stood stoic. This gift was top-tier and highly coveted. Who wouldn't want to pick their moments to be invisible?

I wish I could.

Gabriel looked overwhelmed yet strangely at peace.

As the next host approached the third subject, Ben observed him with a tight lip. Elias was someone he knew too well. Ben had gotten on his wrong side after intercepting an attack on one of his best friends, Niall. It only got worse when his other best friend Severo left Elias's circle to join him and Niall. Funny how Tharmus had not been around to intercept that attack. Ben loved the relaxed feel of his home and school life but hated how some things were not seen. Elias, unbeknownst to him, was revered by the adults of this town. Evidently, ignorance was bliss.

Ben twitched. *Please don't get a good power.* Ben gritted his teeth, watching the red-haired school bully crack his knuckles. The last thing Elias needed was more opportunity.

A subtle smirk curled the side of Elias's mouth as he waited for the host to speak. Ben wondered if the host noticed, but his gaze gave nothing away.

"Your Sovereign Dominion will be the gift of the Inner Ear."

Ben reveled in Elias's obvious disappointment.

I can't remember this power.

The cessation of sound inspired goosebumps. Ben was next. The chief host stood before him.

Please legs do what you're supposed to do.

"Blessed are thee, Prince Benjamin Landis, the blood of the royal, on this your day of anointment. Please kneel and hold out the palm of your right hand," Vallore said, slowly extending the Seal Staff.

Is it my imagination or is Vallore hesitating?

The power of the Seal Staff was unreal. The moment it touched his skin, it felt like warm fluid trickled through his veins. The strength was immediate, palpable, and all-powerful. His eyes scorched with heat and locked on the chief. Something lay deep behind his eyes, a hidden truth.

What is your story, Vallore? Why are you never around?

Ben had the urge to peer closer, but pain hit him like a red hot poker, and he flinched.

Ben rose, accepting Vallore's icy, wrinkled hand. Vallore pursed his lips to the point his face almost absorbed them.

Have I made him angry?

The sky above swirled around the visible vortex, and a chill breezed through the crowd. *Something feels wrong.* A crackle appeared from the deepening blue sky, and a drizzle of rain tittered down over those watching. An air of uncertainty seeped its way through the people of Landis. The chief remained unperturbed.

"Your Sovereign Dominion will be... the gift of the All-seeing Eye."

Stunned silence fell upon the crowd. Time seemed to stand still before an eruption of applause resounded throughout the castle grounds.

Then the skies opened.

Ben let the rain soak through to his skin. The most sought-after gift had just been given to him.

CHAPTER 2

Niall

No, *no, no, noooooooooo.* Bitterness took hold and squeezed Niall's insides. He gripped his coattails, wanting to tear his jacket from his body.

I need to be on my own. What does this mean for me?

He ripped his gray silk scarf from his neck and trampled over it as he ran from the castle grounds. The inside of his mind tingled as new threads of his power surged through him. His gift of Perception had reached a new height. *I made my parents think I was standing right beside them. I shouldn't be able to do that yet, but it felt good to deceive them.* Especially his father, who brought a new meaning to self-righteousness.

All that mattered now was getting away, and the hammering rain aided his escape.

Your gift might be strong, Ben, but mine is getting stronger.

They weren't boys anymore; a wall had been slotted between them. Ben was no longer the friend that rescued him from Elias years ago—Ben was a potential threat. His skin itched.

Niall ran through the flowered gardens and left through the iron gate. His body knew where it was going as he strode over the sandy creek path trying to keep a grip on the ground. The wind was aggressive and the long grass on either side of him swayed like it was in pain. He reached Purity Creek and the water moved in a panic as the waves rippled up to the pebbled shore. He sensed a shift. Something was wrong, but to him it felt right. He kept running. The trees scattered around the edge of the lake offered no shelter from the rain as water droplets from their leaves pelted his back. His legs didn't tire, and he gained a second wind when the arched caves that formed an "M" came into view. The Crying Caves.

They dazzled in invitation.

He reached his hideaway, the largest cave that lay off to the right of Purity Creek. Winded, he entered the cave and screamed, knowing it would never be heard. The Crying Caves received their name because they were soundproof, safe he wasn't sure, but at least it was a place he could take out the frustrations of his life. The dank mixture of earth and water breathed familiarity into him.

His black wool suit clung to him, and the buttons from his cummerbund popped as he pulled it from his body.

Who cares? Does anything matter anymore?

Furious, he slammed his fists into the dark rock and let the numbness have him. Blood slid under his nails as he clawed his hair in agitation—he clawed harder. He flicked several spiders from his body and swallowed the disgust they prompted. All Niall wanted was to tap into what had awakened in him. In answer came the voice. One that had niggled his mind for months.

Niall, come to me.

He wasn't sure if it was real or not. He brushed it off as he always did.

Going back now and keeping up the pretense of being the loyal best friend was a nauseating thought. He wanted Ben's new talent. He already knew everything about it and how it should be nurtured.

Ben's immature and careless.

Niall would be a better suited king, yet Ben had been born with that birthright. What a waste. Niall got stuck with a father who was obsessed with work and a mother content with the simple life. He did not feel connected. How could he when he knew he was destined for more.

Niall surveyed his bloody knuckles and smashed his fists again into the jagged rock. The possibilities this would offer Ben crippled Niall.

I hate that your power makes me feel weak, Ben.

As Niall sat in his own personal wrath, the dew seeped into his skin. The cold perked his senses. He wasn't alone.

"Who's there?" On the surface his words were stern, but they didn't conceal his undertone of panic.

Niall crept around the cave—there was no evidence of anyone. But a presence was undeniable. A strange pull tugged at him. His legs started moving of their own volition. He left the cave and was running again, not back home but toward The Forbidden Vale.

A tingle scaled his flesh. He stopped and silenced every part of himself. The voice sounded again, clearer like a bell chime.

"*Niall, come to me.*"

He woke in an unnatural way, yet it was as real as breathing, like a flame light on a wick. He needed to find the source of this voice. It felt like he was walking on a cloud, guided by the ominous force.

In no time at all, Niall neared the edge of The Forbidden Vale as if he had been airlifted. The dark loom of the trees was sinister and menacing, spiked and ready for battle, unlike the horse chestnut trees in Pure Bay.

For years, all he'd been taught was this stern warning: "Don't go near the forest. It's dangerous; it's prohibited."

But the coiled tree branches unfurled and created a path for him. The smell of rotten tree bark filled his nostrils, and he tensed.

What is happening?

The eerie noises were like nails scratching down a squeaky surface.

Should I turn back?

Deep inside, a hunger tore at him, leaving exhilaration and a new notion... absolution. Finally, he was where he belonged, not back at the castle living the long-suffered life that had grown so tedious. Pretending, always pretending. This. Now. He was meant for more.

He came to an abrupt stop. The impenetrable barrier—as legend told—was filmy, iridescent. His legs wobbled as he crept toward the rippling wave extending all the way to the murky clouds. Soaring above him stood the Tree of Vulnerability. The autumnal leaves glistened with sparkling dew and stood out of place in the darkness. The tree's thick roots sprawled between the two sides. Even through the glaze of the forcefield, Niall saw the contrast.

What existed opposite crept into his lungs like the smell of death. Long, withered branches with ashen leaves pointed at him like the tip of a knife.

Niall flinched as the inner workings of his mind warned him not to get too close.

Legend said, anyone who entered this forest would surely be granted an early death, yet there was no sense of this. A ruse to keep everyone out. Clever, yet despicable. Niall studied the tree further, comparing both sides, and longed to be on the other side. His mouth became dry, like a thirst he couldn't quench.

His obsession consumed him as his brain surfed on tangents he'd had for years. Obsession was a familiar friend, driving him to study every written word of the limited information available about Alunattra. He wanted the voice to be *hers*. Nobody on this island possessed a power like hers, and Niall craved more. He'd read once that her power of All Transcendence could be received if she chose to share. He wanted it, although he didn't know if it was possible because of the barrier.

I need to know if it's her.

He stood there for what felt like hours—frozen and then something moved in his peripheral vision. Niall searched the forcefield for any sign of life, but there was nothing other than a deeper ripple and a strange buzzing. He drew closer and trembled, sensing another sharp movement. He fixated on a perfect coal-like speck, then something smacked the barrier with a thud. He collapsed onto the ground, shaking in fear as searing pain coursed through his veins.

Niall stared, stock-still, and his breath came short. Dark, flame-like shadows writhed in spirals on the side he couldn't reach, the side where he knew she roamed. Each caress felt like it could punch a hole in his soul. These flames caused the barrier to bulge, but it did not break. A sickly-sweet smell shot up his nose, and he choked on his vomit. The flames cocooned him, and the heat prickled his skin.

Intoxication clouded every part of him, and he lay immobilized. Her power. He felt it.

The smoke evaporated and was replaced with a mass of remnant charcoal. The barrier vibrated like rocks thrown at a puddle. The ground underneath him quaked. When the smoke transfigured, taking form, Niall was near hyperventilation. A dark, womanly figure materialized, clad in torn, dirty garments that were sculpted to her haggard frame. What looked like black tar spiraled around her like a cape. Her face may have been beautiful once, but now only her haunting, soulless eyes and twisted sneer were visible. Veins bubbling with blood protruded all over her ancient gray skin. Nothing could tear his eyes from the tarnished crown that seemed woven into her skin like an addition to her anatomy.

A tight, villainous smile broadened, splitting the skin on her face until it reached her shriveled ears. Niall flinched as pain stabbed at his temples. He had to look away. It was her; his knowledge was absolute. She faced him and ran her claw-like nails down the screen that separated them. They did not pierce the shimmering veil. How could she touch it at all?

Words were unable to take form. The ceremony. The weather. The shift.

Alunattra.

His studies waned in comparison to what stood before him.

He tried to see behind her eyes but all he got was a jabbing pain in his temples. Was the barrier between them flawed? His pain intensified.

He always knew she must be quite powerful, but not on this scale. Her hair flowed like elastic, springing and recoiling. Her eyes had a black solidity—soulless, empty—yet danced with something close to intrigue as she focused on him. Her fingertip trailed over her unnatural purplish lips that looked starved of heat.

When she spoke, her voice gripped like a vice. She held him in his own personal, wonderful prison. He was paralyzed. He was taken. He was hers.

"Niall, for years I have waited for you."

He was right. It was her inside his head.

"You were not ready, but now your time has come to live in subservience. You are my soldier. Bound to me. Change has been coming gradually, and today it has accelerated. It's a matter of time before I reclaim my throne. You will be my vessel, my converter, and I charge you this day to be my eyes and ears. You are mine to shape and you will be the one to lay the path for my resurrection," her raspy voice said, mesmerizing him.

She placed her long bony fingers against the barrier and channeled herself deeper into him. He screamed. It felt like his innards were being ripped and pulled. He crumpled to the ground. At once the pain subsided. He stood, no longer wet, his bloody hands restored, and not a hair was out of place. Not even a crease in his suit.

I've been chosen.

This too had been a day of anointment for him. His brain swelled, accommodating the knowledge she'd given him.

In the distance, three bells chimed.

"From now on, I'll be watching and listening. Wait for my instructions. You're mine," she said.

"I'm whatever you need me to be."

The blackness around her broke apart like an intricate puzzle. As Niall peered closer, tiny, long-legged creatures approached the barrier and circled their mistress like a deadly protection detail.

Niall's pores opened as fear became his sidekick. So many spiders.

Then, without warning, he ran toward the castle. Speed owned him. His hands worked of their own volition, tidying his suit, and fastening his silver buttons to hide the missing cummerbund.

She's doing this.

He wasn't sure how he knew, yet he did. The castle stood before him as if no time had passed, and Niall wondered if he had experienced a delusion.

Alunattra's voice coursed through him.

"Do not fail. I can give and I can take away. From now on, you and I are connected as one."

"Yes, my queen," he relayed back, striding into the crowd.

Niall searched for Ben and seethed when he came into view. It was time to fix the mask he'd worn for years. His teeth crushed the skin inside his mouth, and his forced smile curved as he lifted a hand to his friend. Ben had never known the real him. Nobody did, and with that thought, Niall pulled from his new well of strength and walked, primed with his power.

Here we go.

CHAPTER 3

Ben

T *here he is!*

"Where've you been?"

"I ran for cover from the rain, then held back so the crowds could get in first," Niall said. "So, it appears we are officially the dream team. What do you intend to do first with your newfound power?"

Ben gave his first chuckle of the day. "I can't believe it—it's like a weird dream. I'm trying not to think about it too much. I'm glad I could dump those heavy robes and look like the rest of you. We better find Severo. He's been like a caged animal wanting a three-man high-five to mark this moment."

Ben remembered back a few months ago when Severo and Niall had their ceremony and how he'd wished he was up there with them. Now they were all in sync.

They remained silent as they walked.

The All-seeing Eye. Ben's heart beat faster. *Will I really be able to know and understand everything?*

Ben had avoided learning about the gifts whenever he could. His skin felt damp as he tried remembering what the power meant. Why had he not been focused like everyone else? He tried to distract his mind and noticed Niall fidgeting.

"Niall? You good?" Ben stopped to face him. "And where's your neck scarf? I don't think I have ever seen you without one."

Niall squinted.

Did something flash across his eyes?

"Ha, true. It got soaked in the rain. Ben, to be honest, I'm not sure what to say. You know I don't do emotions, but I guess I'm... proud of you. You deserve all good things."

So that's it. Makes sense. Niall has been an introvert his whole life.

Ben swallowed. Since their first day of school, he couldn't remember much in the way of compliments from his friend. This was high praise. It felt good. Ben shoulder-bumped him.

So far so good today. What was I worrying about?

His grandad had been right. Earlier he'd embraced Ben the way he wished his father had.

"This, today, my Benjamin, is every grandfather's dream. I wish your grandmother had lived to see it." That was the first time Ben had seen sadness cloud his grandpa's countenance. The late Queen Mother, Liora, died in childbirth.

What must it feel like to lose someone you love?

His grandpa hugged him before hoarsely telling him he was leaving the party for the younger generation to enjoy.

Grandad saw Ben more than his father did. Each expectant was allowed to choose one person to be a training mentor to help learn about their gifts. Grandad had offered, but deep down, Ben wanted his father.

Maybe if I ask Father, it would give us a chance to have some time together.

Ben saw Severo's huge physique tower above everyone like a beacon.

Of course, he's at the buffet table.

After Severo received his power of extensive strength, it seemed no amount of food could satisfy him.

The kitchen fairies had covered every inch of the table with steaming roast beef, herb and butter-covered potatoes, and honey-glazed vegetables. Ben's eyes landed on the desserts, and the sweet smell of treacle sponge pudding made his mouth water. He wanted to take a handful of strawberries and drench them under the flowing chocolate fountain. There were hot and cold drinks and plenty of wine on a beautifully crafted stall behind the main feast table. He watched in fascination as the tiny fairies waved their hands under the wine barrel taps for the adults. Magically a flute appeared below the tap, filled the glasses, then the fairies guided these flutes toward waiting hands.

Ben wished he could have some food but it was impossible to eat; he was too pumped with adrenaline.

As he and Niall maneuvered their way over to Severo, a hint of dazzling green caught Ben's eye. Severo was standing next to Vara.

Are they talking?

Jealousy hit Ben like an unpredictable storm, and he picked up his pace.

"Ben, Ben."

Ben turned to Niall, almost forgetting he was there. "Sorry, what's that?" he asked.

"What about meeting tomorrow? I have been meditating with the Fairy Guard in my internship, and I have exercises I could teach you. Our powers could be an asset to one another."

His friend's offer got under Ben's skin, pricking his annoyance. Niall had been recruited by Ben's father because of his perception skill, and the guards were hoping to nourish his power to perceive if the island was under threat. A nerve-racking thought formed.

Maybe I could help Father now?

Ben pursed his lips. "Niall, look around, we're at a party. Let's enjoy ourselves for once. Maybe next week, though." Ben needed a breather himself. Niall sighed but nodded in agreement.

They arrived at Severo's side as Vara departed into the sea of villagers.

I wonder what they were talking about.

Severo looked flushed, but not in a good way. Irritation bubbled within Ben.

Severo, now aware his two friends were there, reverted to his usual goofy grin. "Yee-haw and all is right in the world now." He slapped them both on the back, then waved his hand in the air for the long-awaited three-man high-five. Severo did this with the biggest, proudest grin.

"Right, our first task as a tri-pack is as follows: A covert mission if you may. Come with me," Severo said with over-exaggerated hand gestures. As he took off, Ben and Niall followed.

They walked through the open terrace at the back of the castle. Instead of going in the back door, Severo turned left and kept walking towards the extensive gardens. Ben turned his head back. The white bricks of the castle looming above shimmered like they were watching him.

I hope Tharmus isn't around.

One thing he loved about his father was how he tried to make everyone equal, yet Ben knew Tharmus was tasked with reporting back. He had never needed a bodyguard, and Tharmus was less than subtle. What could honestly happen in this peaceful existence anyway?

An icy breeze slapped his face.

Doesn't mean anything. Doesn't mean anything.

Ben strained his eyes, hoping something else would burst into his thought process. He scanned the rainbow-colored flower beds that lay before the rising, expansive vineyards. Each vine flowed with round, succulent, green and red grapes in a polka dot maze. The highest quality wine was produced here, and no household was without its own supply.

I will never understand why I have to wait till I'm married to try wine. No chance of getting any with Tharmus the wine guard always there!

Severo stopped at a row of vines.

"I smell a Severo scheme," Ben said.

Severo ignored this and turned to Niall. "Niall, do your perception thing and tell us if there's anyone lurking."

Ben watched closely. *I wonder how Niall feels when he's doing that. Can he sense everyone around him?*

Niall closed his eyes in concentration. "Nobody about," he said, his eyebrows tight together. "Everyone's either drunk or about to be."

"Excellent news. It wouldn't be fair not to have our own party!" Severo's eyes twinkled as he pulled out a flask.

"Sev, do I need to remind you of all your previous bright ideas?" Ben said.

"This, my friend, is the best one yet. I hold in my hand a never-before-seen, bottomless flask. I've aptly named it, the Omless. Made by the ever-talented fairy, Striker. It can contain an endless amount of liquid, and as you can see, it's tiny enough to be concealed. Perfect for the job."

How does Severo get his fairy to do that? Jealousy was kicking Ben from every angle. *I'm definitely trying something out with Tweek.*

Severo ambled further into the vineyard and stopped at the end of the row. Behind him loomed a wooden chalet that seemed to go on for days, and this was one of many. In each window crevice, a barrel protruded with its very own tasting tap, and several cabins had theirs missing due to the celebrations. Severo looked around, then opened his flask and placed it below the tap. Plum-colored liquid poured into the Omless with no sign of it reaching the brim.

The fruity scent wafted through the air, making Ben's nose twitch. "Wait, don't be stupid. If you get caught, you'll be home-schooled for a month, not to mention all privileges taken away. Do I have to pull rank?"

"Ben, lighten up. Every fairy is at the party. I'll just take a bit. Please? C'mon, you can't say you don't want to try it?" Severo waved the flask under Ben's nose.

Ben breathed in more of the scent and let his guard down. "Well, I suppose a few sips won't do us any harm. Niall, you in?" Ben asked, prodding his friend.

Niall jumped. "Sorry, I'm on edge. I don't want to get caught."

"Ni, you've never lived a day in your life. I love you but come on, man, let your hair down," Severo said with an insistent grin.

Niall grabbed the flask out of Severo's hand and took a big gulp.

"Thata' boy." Severo followed, doing the same. "Wow, Ben, this is the tweets. Try it."

Tharmus isn't here for once. I'm doing this.

The sweet liquid warmed his body, energizing every part of him. Ben felt like he could conquer anything and took another swig.

Severo swiped the flask from him. "Save some for the rest of us!"

"I think with a bottomless flask, and the amount you poured in, you're safe," Niall said.

Ben giggled uncontrollably. *I feel awesome.* He loved when Niall and Severo got into it. He couldn't remember the last time he'd laughed. All the tension left him like a freely flowing river.

What was in that wine?

"Right, boys, let's get back to the party." Ben felt his cheeks warm.

I'm buzzing.

"Okay, if you lot need any more, you know where it is." Severo tucked his flask inside his suit jacket whilst tapping his finger to his nose.

Ben's feet swayed beneath him, and he suddenly felt weightless. *Why can't I feel the ground anymore?*

Ben looked down, and his mouth flung open.

I'm not on the ground anymore.

Panic set in. Something else felt wrong, like his body was trying to split in two. His feet craved the ground and his spirit felt like it was trying to escape.

Awareness quickly dawned on Severo and Niall. Wide eyed, they pulled the bottom of Ben's breeches in haste, bringing him back to the ground.

"How did you do that, Ben?" Niall's eyes darted up and down Ben's form, scrutinizing every inch.

Ben's jaw was sore from clenching. "I have no idea."

"That was wild." Severo whistled, holding Ben in place. "Let's see if you float again!"

As his friends took their hands away, Ben started to rise in the air.

This is just what I need. How am I going to explain this?

"We can't go back to the party. What should we do?" Niall said, rubbing the back of his neck.

"Stop panicking. I know how to fix this. Striker." Severo called for his wishing fairy.

Ben wished he had his friend's confidence. Fortunately, wishing fairies—when sought out by their charge—could materialize instantly.

"Yes, Master Severo, I'm at your service."

"Eh, we seem to have gotten ourselves into a bit of a fix." As Severo spoke, he nudged Niall, and they both let go of Ben.

Ben darted up again like a stray balloon, and his friends grabbed him by the ankles. The three boys looked at Striker sheepishly.

"How did this happen?" Striker fluttered his wings and directed his flinty stare at Severo. "What did you do?"

Severo didn't look Striker in the eye. "Erm. You know the flask you gave me? I sort of used it to have the tiniest taste of wine. Niall and I are fine, but Ben has been… affected differently."

Striker's wings were translucent with silver threads and crimson edging that stood out more when he was angry—like now. His red skin glowed like a tiny fireball. He stiffened and buzzed as he made his way onto Severo's nose. "That was supposed to be for hydration juice. One of these days, Severo, you're going to get yourself into a situation that not even I can rescue you from. Rules are there for a purpose!"

"So, you'll help us?" Severo said.

"I'm not exactly sure what's happening. This incident, as far as I can tell, is the first of its kind. There is a reason wine should not be touched till you are older and wiser. In this case, I'm not sure I'll live to see that." Striker ignored Ben's grunt and continued, "These wines, after fermentation, can be rather potent. Prince Benjamin, how much did you drink?"

"Only a few gulps."

Striker rested his fist on his chin and tapped a finger to his lips. "Has anything like this ever happened to you before?"

"No, I swear I've never even had the smallest sip of wine! It must be something to do with my Verdo. I don't know how to control it yet. I feel sick." Nausea rippled through his stomach like a surging wave.

How can this be happening so soon? What will my father say?

Striker sighed. "What you need is a concoction to eliminate the alcohol, and luckily, I happen to know of the very thing. We fairies are aware of some of the shenanigans that take place on this island, and I have some in stock. I'll be back soon. DO NOT GO ANYWHERE!"

If a fairy was asked for an object, their magical ability allowed them to locate the item and shrink it—no matter the size—ready for transportation.

Thank Landis for on-demand teleportation.

"How much do you know about your power?" Niall asked Ben.

The pounding in Ben's head did not get better with Niall's intense stare. "As much as anyone else does when they get their power. How was I supposed to know this would happen?"

"Maybe if you actually studied, you'd learn something. Not everything is fun and games," Niall chided.

"Calm down, buzzkill. We're not all as blessed as you, now are we?" Severo said.

Niall stared Severo down, a maddened gleam in his eyes.

"Look guys, it is what it is, and we'll sort this out. Thanks to Striker, problem solved," Ben said.

I sure hope so.

Niall's small, deep-set eyes shifted back to their nonchalant leaf green.

Why is he letting this bother him so much?

"Clearly this wine has got the better of us tonight," Ben said. "Not one of your better ideas, Sev."

Severo rolled his shoulders. "Ach, you win some, you lose some."

Ben tensed. "Did you hear something?"

Severo put a hand on Ben's shoulder and opened a space in the vine to peek through. "Nope. Nothing there to see. You're freaking out, Ben. Don't worry, it's all good."

Striker reappeared and retrieved something from his tiny pocket, then clicked his fingers. He asked Severo to hold out his hand. A speck evolved into a tiny vial. The mini bottle was transparent and contained the brightest blue liquid labeled *Settle Serum*.

"One drop each should be adequate," Striker said.

Severo handed the bottle to Ben. "Do the honors."

Ben unscrewed the wooden lid till it made a popping sound and brought it to his mouth.

Disgusting.

Ben held his nose and drank. A cough followed as the burn lined his throat. The result was instantaneous, and that clouded feeling lifted like a veil. "Wow, Striker, that's good stuff. Thank you. Try letting me go now."

Severo and Niall took their hands away and watched him closely, but he stayed grounded.

Niall took the vial next and drank, then handed it to Severo.

Severo held out his palm for Striker to sit on. "Thank you, Striker. As always, you have saved my perfect hind."

Ben and Niall rolled their eyes.

"I'll see you back home. Thanks again, little bud." Severo flexed his hand, and Striker sighed but fluttered a body swerve into it. When their rescuer was gone, Severo clapped his hands. "Right, let's get back to the party."

"You two go ahead. I'm right behind you," Ben said.

Niall remained still. "I'll wait with you."

"I kinda need a minute. I'll catch up with you," Ben said.

Looking perplexed, Niall nodded. "Of course, see you soon."

Severo draped his arm around Niall, gibbering away, and off they went—their previous squabble forgotten.

Ben sank into the muddy sponge of earth, not caring if he dirtied his suit. The freak incident that just occurred proved his new power needed to be handled carefully.

Great, something else I need to get a grip on!

He closed his eyes.

Darkness.

Ben breathed in slowly, and the familiar circle of light formed in the blackness.

Am I asleep?

A shadow moved through the light, but he wasn't afraid. As the shape became clearer, his insides hurt. A girl. Wispy hair danced over her shoulders as she drifted toward him in a sea of blurriness. His heart rate calmed and was replaced with a sense of peace.

I can't move or speak.

"I can hear you," the girl told him. "I was waiting for you. I can only come to you in my dreams—I can't control them. All I know is, I had to come. Something inside keeps leading me here, so I can tell you…"

Tell me what?

"You're in danger. You're all in danger."

CHAPTER 4

Alunattra

T he sky crackled, and Alunattra's talons twitched. Her time to
reign again hung on the precipice.

The boy. Niall.

Finally, he heard my call.

His seething frustrations had sung to her. She'd bit back her shock
when she saw him for the first time. He looked identical to the girl
who'd freed her all those years ago.

This world hadn't changed. His heart, so full of hate, had called to
her. She saw no trace of humanity in him—no qualms about doing her
bidding.

He's just like all the others.

She licked her scabbed lips as if tasting the oncoming destruction.
A treacherous laugh bellowed from her gut, and the translucent forcefield quavered like sea waves.

She touched her brittle nails to the barrier. It rippled, sparking
every known color to race its length. There was no pain, just a mere
tingle through her fingertips.

The events of the ceremony had weakened it once again.

Soon.

She clicked her fingers, and a scuttle announced her spider spawn.
Their long legs softened as they curled around every inch of her like a
blanket.

She imagined the descendants of the weak ones who had stolen her existence falling before her as they screamed her name.

"Alunattra!"

The young prince. Her descendent. He would pay.

CHAPTER 5

Severo

'*ve got this.*

Severo wiped his hands on his fitted suit trousers, undid the buttons from his jacket, and tidied himself up.

If only Striker hadn't emptied my Omless. I hope she likes my suit.

Severo stopped fussing with his attire and glanced around the large marquee.

There she is. Round two. This time I will actually form words. I've got this. I've got this.

Vara was with her friends near the buffet table. Her flawless skin looked as soft as flower petals.

What would it feel like to touch her?

The green satin of her dress rippled over the ground as she walked, and the lace sheath she wore as a cape sat perfectly over her shoulders.

Wow. Severo stared at her, itching to say something. Every day was the same, he would go to make a move, then bottle it.

I'm doing this. I need more food anyway and a drink.

A small but strong hand pulled him back.

"Ah-ah, no you don't," his sister said, coming up behind him.

"C'mon, you know this body needs food. Let me go, Cece."

"Yeah, but you don't have food on the brain, do you?" Cece swatted away the tendrils of orange hair that had escaped from her bun. "Just hate to see you crash and burn. That girl is not interested."

"Honestly, I've no idea what you mean," he said.

"Sev, I know you better than you know yourself. Don't be pathetic." Cece gave Severo her famous all-knowing head tilt.

Nope, there is something there with Vara, I feel it.

"Where's Mimi?" he said, using the childhood name Cece had used for their mother since she was an infant.

"Changing the subject won't wash with me. Mimi is fine, she's at home." Cece's meadow green eyes darkened.

He knew why. Their mother always struggled on ceremony days.

I can't go there now.

"I'll check on her as soon as we're back, but my stomach is hanging here."

"Yeah, you're going to be hanging." Cece chortled, highlighting the sprinkle of freckles that decorated her alabaster cheeks. She shooed him away in amusement. "On you go. I'll get some sweets. Could use some entertainment."

Why does Cece pick up on everything?

Ten months between them and sometimes she seemed like she was older, not younger. Severo stared her down.

"I'll be over there." She wagged her finger over her shoulder. "Call me if you need a hug."

Cece went to sit at one of the large antique tables, and Severo pretended not to notice the smirk. The boy from the ceremony was sitting at the far side.

Gabriel was it?

He stood frozen in place, staring at Cece. Severo suppressed a laugh. His sister could be scary. Cece sat down and Severo thought he must be seeing things because when he looked again, the boy was gone.

Refocus. Good, Vara's still there. I'm like a hunter after its prey. Maybe Cece's right. I'm pathetic.

Severo inhaled the delicious smell of roast beef and his mouth watered.

Why am I never full?

As luck would have it, Vara came to stand beside him. Her chocolate brown eyes stole a peek at him, and her slender eyebrows furrowed.

She's checking out my suit. I knew the gray damask silk was a good idea.

Other girls had told him he had beautiful, blue-green eyes. Severo hoped Vara agreed but he never could tell with her. She was a total mystery at times.

He gulped the last of his steak baguette and wiped his greasy hands on his trousers. And there went the suit. Not the best first impression.

"Hey girl, what's up?"

Vara stared at him for three seconds before she answered. The longest three seconds of his life. He loosened his mint green scarf and pulled at his linen shirt that suddenly felt tight.

"I've never understood that phrase. But if you're asking how I am, then the answer is very well, thank you."

There it was, her infamous I'm-better-than-you speak. Severo picked up a piece of cake and began eating again, unsure how to answer. Instead, he gave her a thumbs up and then picked up a glass of hydration juice.

What is wrong with me?

She gave him a quizzical look. "Have you seen Prince Benjamin? I've yet to give him my best."

Severo tried to read her face; it was blank as usual. Why did she want to see Ben? Was it to congratulate him or for some other reason? The heat crept in as his temper climbed. When he didn't answer, Vara probed further.

"Severo, it's only polite to answer when you're asked a question." The patronizing comment rolled off her tongue.

"As you can see, it's a busy place, Vara, and Ben has many hands to shake. You must've been overlooked in the masses."

She looked at him with a twinkle in her eye, and Severo didn't know what to make of it. It only deepened his confusion.

Vara smirked and gave him a thumbs-up. "I'll do another turn then. I can't have Ben missing out." She turned and floated away.

Who does she think she is?

The tension in him built, and the goblet shattered in his hands.

Stay cool.

Cece's fiery red hair bounced into view, but she didn't look smug, just concerned. *That's worse.* He also didn't miss the stares toward his sister. Her simple, floor-length, white satin dress didn't look plain on her, and everyone watched her walk as her long kimono sleeves trailed in the breeze behind her.

Great.

"Let me see your hand," she said, reaching for his arm.

Of course, she'd seen that. He waved her off. "It's nothing, just an accident. You know I can't get hurt."

Technically not true, but I won't remind her of that.

Severo held out his hand, showing Cece he didn't have a scratch on him.

"What if glass got in your eyes?"

She's been reading up on my power.

"You need to be careful, Sev, and while you're at it, figure out how not to destroy everything you touch," Cece said, her eyes soft and pleading.

As always, she was right. The number of things he'd broken in the last six months was ridiculous. He wasn't great at controlling his power of extensive strength—yet.

"I'm heading back," Cece said. "See you at home?"

"Yeah, I'm right behind you, just gonna catch Ben and Niall for a bit. Was that guy Gabriel sitting with you?"

"Oh, him, yeah. Not with me but at the same table." Cece's neck started forming a red patch.

"I've honestly never seen him before today," Severo said.

"How typical of you, brother. How can you not have seen Gabriel? He's in your year."

Severo shrugged.

"Anyway, I better check on Mimi," Cece said.

Severo watched his sister walk away and hoped his mother was okay. Days like today were hard for the three of them. Eight years since his father went missing. Danyall Arison had left for work without his ID tag one day and was never seen again. The rumor mill thought he may have drowned in the Perimeter Seas or got lost in The Forbidden Vale, but no trace had ever been found.

The thoughts Severo kept locked up threatened to spill.

Where did Father go?

CHAPTER 6

Ben

I don't want to wake up.

Something close to soft velvet slid over his cheek and his eyelids flickered.

Where am I?

He saw the vibrant green of her dress first.

Vara.

"This is starting to become a habit of ours."

What does she mean?

Then Ben remembered. Another blackout recently. He'd collapsed at the coffee cart, and she'd been the one to pull him out of his trance. They'd locked eyes and something sparked. They'd connected.

This time though, he didn't have amnesia.

The girl in my dream. She's gone. But there is another girl right in front of me. And my ability to speak has left me.

"I was hoping to run into you," Vara said. "I never got a chance to congratulate you. The gift of the All-seeing Eye. Well deserved, Prince Benjamin. You must be so pleased."

As usual, he was struck dumb and highly aware that this was the first proper conversation they'd ever had. Vara had the gift of Preservation—beauty, self-healing, and a sharp mind.

Is that why I can't get my lips to do what they're supposed to do?

Vara waited, her eyes twinkling with amusement.

"Oh, right, yeah. That." Ben rushed to stand and dusted himself off. "It's still to kick in, I think. You enjoying the party?" He didn't want to talk about his gift.

"Not as much as some of the others." She laughed.

It was the sweetest sound; he was rattled again. "Maybe we should get back." Ben said this more like a statement and she seemed a bit taken aback, hurt maybe. He wasn't sure. "Would you like to take the long route?"

Her smile glowed like a radiant moonbeam. "It would be an honor, Prince Benjamin."

"Only if you call me Ben." He laughed to break the tension. "Have you ever walked through the gardens here?"

"I've only seen the view from the castle classrooms. I always wanted to though."

Vara was right next to him. Her long, slender fingers grazed her dress. Her hand was so close, he could reach out and hold it. He didn't. The two of them made their way into the gardens. Ben stopped when they arrived in the central area. A circular fountain stood there. Four different openings, comparable to a compass, faced the flowing water structure and led down arched pathways. His parents came here on dates. Ben remembered them speaking of how they would escape here to meet, which made sense now—the thundering water was a perfect smokescreen. An abundance of hydrangeas in rainbow glory lined the edges of the walkways. A captivating sight, even for a boy who wasn't interested in flowers.

"I don't think I've ever seen anything so beautiful," Vara said.

Words tumbled out of his mouth before his brain could rein them in. "I have."

Ben noticed her green dress perfectly complemented his tie and navy-blue suit.

She's biting her lip.

Ben took the plunge and reached for her hand, but a pest of a voice interrupted, "Prince Benjamin, are you out here?"

Oh, come on!

Tharmus stood covered in smug.

Ben turned quickly to Vara. "I have to go. I'll see you back at the party." The curve of her lips barely created a smile as he left.

"Prince Benjamin, where've you been?" Tharmus lifted his head to appear taller, but Ben was now at his eye level.

Ben didn't respond.

"Your absence has been noted. Your father, the king, requests an audience with you immediately."

"Right away, sir," Ben replied with a mock bow, not sticking around for a response. Tharmus was on form today, chasing Ben's heels. For the longest time, it had been like that, and it was just like his father to send his servant to find him.

Filled with bitter thoughts, Ben wanted to find Vara and say goodnight. Thinking of her, turned his mind around. If only fate hadn't intervened right at the point of potential.

At least we got to talk.

Ben blended his way back to the party. Some people were sprawled on the fresh grass, others dancing inside the marquee. *Niall was right.* The result of wine consumption was evident in the older people. *Funny, I'm not so curious now.*

Fear trickled in as he considered what the future held. Wine might be absent from his future unless he could learn to nurture his skills. Responsibility continued to gnaw into his flesh.

The food was gone, and a sparkling dance floor had replaced the chairs. Many people were swaying to their old folk dances.

Glad I missed that.

He brushed past the tables that edged around the dance floor, every person bowed, and each voice was lost in a sea of congratulations. He spotted his parents sitting in their delicately carved wooden thrones and speaking with Gabriel's parents.

Yes, I need to find Gabriel. I can't believe he gets to be invisible. What a cool power.

Tiredness threatened again. Maybe he would meet the girl again tonight in his dreams.

Should I be thinking this? What about Vara?

He felt Tweek before he saw her.

"Hi, Tweek."

"My prince, I missed you. I won't lie, I've been gloating all afternoon." She covered him in little fairy kisses.

"Cut it out!"

"Okay. Okay."

Tweek flew off to join her friends.

She's like the sibling I've always wanted.

As Ben reached his parents, Tharmus was at his father's side with a sneer.

He's like the brother I never wanted.

"Benjamin, I'm so proud of you. Come here." His mother embraced him and kissed both of his cheeks. She didn't look right. Her eyes were glassy.

His father rose from his chair. His frown lines deepened. "You have received a gift many yearn for. Most do not get the opportunity to wield a power like this. Be sure it's not abused."

Not the words Ben had hoped to hear from his father.

Not even a "happy birthday."

"We've been talking with Clark and Leah," his father said.

Ben moved in to shake hands with the Johns' as they both bowed their heads to him. With princely duties occupying much of the time, he rarely saw anyone other than his friends. This was the first time he'd spoken with Gabriel's parents.

"Well done, Prince Benjamin, you are truly worthy of this honor," Leah said.

Now there's a compliment.

"Thank you, Mrs. Johns."

"It was a lovely ceremony," she said with a thoughtful smile. "We're so proud of Gabriel as well, and he only turned sixteen yesterday."

"You must be. What a gift! Mrs. Johns, do you know where Gabriel is? I'd like to give him my best."

"Now you mention it, I haven't seen him. He's no doubt working his way around everyone."

Yeah, not likely.

Gabriel was not one to mingle. "I'll go and look for him. All the best to you both." Ben turned to acknowledge his parents. "May I go?"

"You can go to your quarters, yes. The party is over now," his father said.

Ben bit the inside of his cheek and turned from his father. He squeezed his mother's hand. He hadn't forgotten what he'd witnessed earlier. Her alabaster skin was still pale. "Mother, are you okay?"

"Oh, yes, of course, son. I'm tired from the day. Now on you go and finish off your goodbyes for the evening."

He wasn't sure what to think as he moved through the crowd.

It isn't anything serious. It can't be anything serious. People don't get sick here unless you count natural death. My mother has at least another 150 years.

Ben quickly started wishing everyone well and the people continued to say for the umpteenth time, "Blessed be your Sovereign Dominion."

He found Severo and Niall. They were sitting at the last table near the tent exit. "I hope you managed to stay out of trouble on the short walk back?"

"Whatever do you mean?" Severo said.

Niall laughed along with Ben.

"I've been given my wrap-up orders. I'm turning in. I'll see you at school. Have either of you seen Gabriel?" Ben asked as an afterthought. They both said they'd not. On leaving, Niall grabbed his arm.

"Ben, I think we should meet tomorrow. I could help you with understanding your Verdo," Niall said as he scratched his arms.

"Well, being Seven, I imagine I'll be confined to the castle."

The days of the week were defined by number, as were the months of the year. Weekday One to Five were school and workdays. Evenings had some leisure time, Six was a social day, and Seven was a rest day to be spent at home, reflecting on the past week.

Strange that Niall would ask this?

"I know, but if you need help, I'm sure for study purposes the king and queen could let that slide."

Ben's body tingled, then stiffened, like it was working without his permission. Niall's unblinking stare filled him with new and unsure feelings. He felt very protective of his new-fangled power, and his head tightened. "Thanks, Niall, but I want to go over everything myself. Have a good one tomorrow, and I'll catch you at school." Ben walked away in a wave of confusion. Far too much for one day.

I'll find Gabriel on weekday One. I need answers.

He discreetly left the party and entered the castle from the rear side. The protection detail shimmered like a clear waterfall as he approached and activated his bracelet for entry—a requirement for everyone entering the castle. The veil separated for him to enter. He glanced back at the gardens in the distance. Butterflies multiplied in his stomach as he imagined kissing Vara's full, perfect lips. He had never kissed a girl and hadn't thought about it much before today, but she stirred up a swirl of new and unexpected emotions in him. It took a while getting through the castle, but adrenaline had him pumped.

As Ben walked through the south wing lobby, he buzzed again and the sparkling sheath that separated the upper and lower castle parted to let him through. Ben bounded up the never-ending stairwell, two steps at a time. After one more buzz at top, Ben ran the long corridor to his room. Tweek was there waiting with his cotton drawstring trousers and buttoned nightshirt laid out.

"Master Ben, I'm so proud of you." She flew around his head, ruffling his hair, and he smiled at her. "I've finished fluffing your pillows, do you need anything else?"

"Not now, but I have a favor to ask in the morning."

"I will be here. Goodnight."

"Thanks, Tweek. For everything."

Tweek, the ever-obedient fairy, understood and asked no questions. She burled away in a burst of gold flecks.

Ben discarded his clothes and welcomed the comfort of his drawstring trousers. He almost tripped on a search mission through his integrated bookcase. He retrieved the book he was after and opened it to the chapter entitled *Sovereign Dominions*. He scrolled down the list until he located his Verdo.

There it was, listed under primary top-tier gifts, of which his and Gabriel's took the top spot.

The gift of the All-seeing Eye.

Book in hand, he drew the heavy curtains. The sky above the forest broke with shards of lightning, and murky smoke crept out from the coiled trees. A definitive shift was present. Ben shivered; his home didn't feel like his anymore.

CHAPTER 7

Gabriel

y mission this morning—find Ben.

Gabriel tucked his flyaway hair behind his ears and slurped the last of his strawberry mixer—a combination of fresh strawberries, syrup, ice, milk, and cream.

"Would you like another?" Lila, the treat fairy, asked with a smile.

Gabriel looked at her from his hidden booth at the back of Furio's Fancies and smiled. "No thank you, Lila, but while I'm here, might as well make myself useful." Gabriel shuffled out of his seat and made his way through the swinging door to the kitchen and washed his dessert glass in the sink.

"Master Gabriel. Stop that. That's my job. Let me." Lila tutted around him, her rainbow skin brightening.

"Too late, it's already done. Nobody knows I'm here so don't worry." Gabriel winked at Lila, and she slumped her shoulders before fluttering over the tables, sprinkling something on them—a product he'd never seen that made them shine like a new coin. Furio's Fancies was the first shop in the village square and Gabriel, for a while now, had a reserved table before opening hours. They didn't offer coffee, which was his go-to, but mixers were a close second—not to mention this was a perfect place to hide from Elias on his way to school. For the last two years, the school bully had made Gabriel his favorite torment piece. Most mornings, his hair smelled of toilet water.

He left some Minty Waves—a sweet he discovered was Lila's

favorite—on the table in a cloth drawstring bag with a red ribbon. His way of payment. He didn't have a job yet and no way to save revils.

Gabriel watched Lila hum as she danced over the tables. The fairies were next in command after the Immortal Hosts, but he often thought about how hard they worked, especially as they didn't require sleep. He knew they got to choose their life, but he hoped they were appreciated by everyone.

Lila beamed when she saw the sweets, and as he waved goodbye, his heart lightened a bit.

Gabriel sighed as he ducked out the back entrance, keeping to the shadows, but it was still early. No sign of anyone, but Elias always seemed to be one step ahead. Gabriel moved behind the cobblers, blacksmiths, and the dress shop, stopping to check if he was in the clear. The castle was now in view as he marched past the Bank of Landis to the gravel dirt path. His feet took on new life as Elias could be anywhere, ready to attack.

My skin is tingling. This is new. Did I make this happen?

He shook away the thought. A niggle of guilt poked at him.

Should I tell Ben I was spying on him and his friends?

What unnerved him the most was the fact that Severo had looked right through the vine.

I was standing inches from him, and he never saw me.

And Elias. His tormentor was oblivious as he'd walked past Gabriel on his way home from the party. That was the first time he had experienced the tingling sensation.

Did I will that?

Gabriel could get in trouble if found using his powers, but it was happening outside of his control.

I'll just have to watch who I tell.

One thing he'd always been good at was keeping to himself. The gift of the Mask, the power to be invisible, made a lot of sense. For years, it felt like nobody saw him anyway.

The starched school shirt cut into his throat and the heavy coat got his pores working. Thankfully, the bottom half of his uniform was short breeches. He preferred his wardrobe of neutral linens.

A deliberate buzz stopped him in his tracks as a bright yellow spark appeared before him. Fritzi, his wishing fairy, fluttered his red dusted wings.

"Master Gabriel, you snuck out again before I could bring your coffee."

"Fritz, I'm good. I'll get some at school." Gabriel hated asking his wishing fairy for anything he could fix himself.

"Oh okay, could I get you something else?"

"No, I'm fine, but how about a game of Shriek later?"

Fritzi spun and his flamboyant, tomato-red wings left a trail. Gabriel smiled. He respected Fritzi. He found it odd that the fairies were at the people's beck and call, yet they could pull rank.

"Have a good day, Fritz. See you this afternoon."

Gabriel continued on his way. The bright white bricks of the castle shone like a beacon laced with glitter.

Something feels different today.

It had been two days since the ceremony, but the air held uncertainty. Gabriel shivered.

He stopped at the castle's entrance. A bright green circle flashed on the left side of the iron door frame. He held out his identification bracelet, waiting for the beep and the veil to lift.

"Gabriel Johns recorded," said an automated voice. "Would you like any beverage tokens today?"

"Yes, three please."

Three gold tokens formed in front of him and dropped into his waiting hand. Three was the limit and he didn't compromise on coffee.

The coffee cart stood off to the right of the south wing in the marble-floored entrance. It was made of hand-crafted wood, and it sat on four wheels, but it never moved. Canisters of plain and flavored coffee beans hung from the back wall with floating syrups ready to add to any beverage. The entire cart glowed like morning mist from the surrounding fairy dust.

Gabriel favored the plain bean—straight black to hit the spot. He put his order in with Fairy Nilla—she was one of his favorites.

"The usual, Master Gabriel?"

"Yes, please, Nilla, but first"—he reached into his satchel—"I have something for you."

"Is it something for my collection?" Nilla clapped, reminding Gabriel of the flutter of a butterfly's wings.

Gabriel winked in answer and handed her a tiny, hand-crafted, wooden chest.

"Master Gabriel, thank you. It's perfect. I know just where to put it."

Gabriel smiled at her as her little hands clicked and circled, causing the coffee beans to crush and ground. He had been crafting items for her fairy home for a while in his favorite class—Art and Design. A thank you for all she did. Nilla was a castle worker and seemed, like him, a bit of a loner.

He gazed around the castle's ground floor. There was the familiar buzz of the fairies as they prepared for their many jobs of the day. He saw the king and queen's fairies in the distance, no doubt comparing lists.

They look like a couple. That would be nice.

His steaming hot coffee hovered before him, and the smell brought him out of his daze. He thanked Nilla and took a sip. The rich scent was like a hug in a mug. He crept to the side of the spiral staircase, past the pillars, and moved to a corridor spanning the length of the castle. Evenly spaced thinking benches lined one side of the hallway and opposite was wooden paneling with deep-set carvings. A few months back, Gabriel discovered that they were hollow inside. After a bit of poking and prodding, he managed to pry a panel loose. The interior was wide and spacious with sporadic wooden beams running along its length. Although intended to support the upper levels of the castle, it made an excellent purpose-built hideaway. Every morning he would go to his secret spot to drink his coffee in peace. The hut was now kitted out with a few large velvet cushions and some of his latest library books. This place was where nobody could bother him.

Moving aside the loose panel, Gabriel dipped inside his hideaway and settled onto the red-velvet cushion. He didn't mean to watch the goings on, but the small crack in the wood gave him a direct line to the coffee cart. He couldn't help it, especially as *she* would be here soon.

He wrapped his tie around his finger, causing the tip to turn purplish, and tapped his foot. He always noticed her hair first. The orange curls were in a braid today, bouncing down her back as she walked. Strands had already escaped with a life of their own. Somehow, her hair reflected how free her personality was. Cece. The girl who had his heart.

I can't believe she sat near me at the party. I wish I had the nerve to talk to her.

He watched as Severo gave her a quick hug before they went in different directions.

Severo's a good guy.

Gabriel couldn't imagine talking to him though. He would come off as a prize fool. He already felt like a fool the more he watched her, sipping his coffee in the shelter of his hidden hut. Part of him wanted to approach Cece right then.

What would it feel like to hug her?

His stomach flipped, and he nearly dropped his coffee. Elias strutted in with his two cronies, Norris and Clive. Gabriel squirmed, gripping his cushion, white-knuckled. They snatched a satchel from an unsuspecting student and emptied the contents all over the marble floor. Papers flew everywhere. Severo got the lad to his feet in seconds and fixed him up. Kindness wrapped up in the largest package Gabriel had ever seen.

Elias started scouring the crowd, a nasty scowl distorting his features.

He's looking for me.

Gabriel winced but was glad to have escaped today's torment.

Niall arrived and met Severo at the coffee cart. A tiny piece of Niall's shirt hung outside of his shorts and his hair was unkempt. Unusual for Niall.

The caffeine tickled Gabriel's temples as he expected Ben to arrive, but he didn't. Where was he?

Niall and Severo walked to the south stairs, heading to their classes.

I better go too.

But a shuffle of movement outside his hut stopped Gabriel. He peeked through the crevice. Someone was there.

Ben.

The prince sat on the bench opposite the hut, raking his hands through his hair. Something was stressing him out, and Gabriel could guess what. He popped off the panel. Ben jumped up, dropping his books.

"Gabriel, man. Where? What?"

"Hi, Ben, sorry, I didn't mean to sneak up on you," Gabriel said, sheepishly holding the wood panel in his hands. "If it's okay, would you mind not mentioning this to the king? I'm pretty sure this doesn't cut it in the rule book."

Ben relaxed, much to Gabriel's relief, and smirked. "You're not wrong."

Gabriel bit the skin around his nails as Ben shuffled over to have a look inside the hide hut.

Ben whistled. "Very cool. I won't say anything." Ben stepped inside and gasped.

"This place is huge!" Ben couldn't stop shaking his head in wonder. "I looked for you at the party but didn't see you anywhere. Great Verdo. Oh, and happy birthday." Ben's eyes kept flitting to the hide hut.

"Cheers and happy birthday back." Gabriel hesitated then took a deep breath. He still had a few minutes before class. "I wanted to talk to you. How much do you know about Sovereign Dominions?"

"Funny you should ask," Ben said with a tight smile. "Not all that much. My parents don't talk about theirs. My father is constantly reminding me of how training and development are so we don't *have* to use them."

Gabriel didn't miss the sore look in Ben's eyes.

He's not close to his father.

Ben rubbed his chin. "The one I know most about is Severo's, as he's an open book, and it's impressive. He's shown me things, although, technically, he shouldn't have. Anything that hits him bounces off him like a rubber band. Niall doesn't say much, so I'm not sure of his. I tried asking my father once, and all he said was, 'Gifts are only to be used if authorized for safety measures, and don't forget, Benjamin, we answer to Vallore and the fairies. Someone's always watching.' That's pretty much it. I sort of feel like my gift has other ideas of its own, though." Ben's eyes held a faraway look as he whispered the last part, almost to himself.

Gabriel's mind latched onto something interesting Ben said. If Vallore was always watching, how could he not detect when powers were used inappropriately?

"Yeah, I know what you mean," Gabriel said. "Look, we don't have much time before class. Something happened to me, and I couldn't stop it. Things are not making sense. I wanted to run it by you. Can we meet? Maybe this week after school?"

Ben nodded. "Something happened to me too. We definitely need to meet. Come for a study session on Four this week so it's not suspicious. I'll arrange it."

Gabriel didn't mention he already knew what happened to Ben but felt relieved as they both walked towards the stairs. Sooner would've been better, but they had assigned study days, and Gabriel knew Ben was always with his friends. That would make their conversation impossible. They parted as they reached the top of the southside stairs.

Ben turned back and called out to Gabriel, "Don't mention this to anyone."

"Of course not. I'll see you in classes throughout the week and we can talk properly on Four."

"Don't be a stranger. Come sit with us at lunch," Ben said.

"Eh, sure," Gabriel said, not sure what else to say, then headed towards his first-class—Music and Song. He arrived as the bell chimed and beelined to the back of the class. As usual, nobody took one bit of notice.

At lunch, Gabriel got his tray of food and went to his table in the corner. He couldn't see Cece. He stopped walking when someone hollered his name.

"Gabriel, over here. Come sit with us," Ben called from the hierarchy table.

Gabriel could've heard a pin drop as everyone stared at him. Embarrassment colored his face as he tried to make his legs remember how to walk. People were whispering, but Gabriel could not hear what they were saying. *Oh great.*

Ben indicated the free chair at their table. "Grab a pew. How's your morning been?"

Gabriel looked at the other two faces at the table. Severo's mouth was open with food falling out and Niall looked like he'd been bitten by a stinging plant. "Em, yeah, fine, thanks."

Ben smacked his forehead. "Severo, Niall, have you met Gabriel?"

They remained silent and Gabriel quickly said, "How you are?" He froze. WHAT HAD HE DONE?! Intimidation trumped the ability to articulate his sentence. Prize fool was right. He immediately wanted to disappear.

Severo bellowed a laugh and more food tumbled out of his mouth. *"How you are?* That's a good one. I may even steal that." Severo reached over and slapped Gabriel on the back.

Gabriel heard a stitch pop in his blazer. That he hadn't expected.

Gabriel coughed to counteract the chortle forming as Severo packed more food in his mouth.

Niall was very careful and polite. "We've not had the pleasure."

He's very formal, like the king and queen.

Niall reached across the table to shake Gabriel's hand, all irritation now gone, and he looked pleased to be speaking with him.

Gabriel's heart was hammering, and he wondered if they could hear it. He flicked his wrist to dry his clammy hand.

"I was impressed with your gift, Gabriel," Niall said. "Have you had many chances to study it?"

Gabriel looked at Niall, unable to stop his eyebrow from rising. How strange. Being so open about gifts. Arrogance was written all over Niall's flawless skin. Gabriel lowered his eyes, twisted the blue lid of his hydration juice, and watched dark purple droplets infuse into the water. He drank to give himself time to answer. "I've not. I know as much as our books tell me. I'm keen to start Verdo training. Have you found the classes helpful?" Maybe Niall would enlighten him more.

"I did in the beginning, but I'm sure you know of my gift. There's not much left for me to learn."

Yup, sheer arrogance.

Niall's eyes didn't leave his. Gabriel savored another mouthful of his blueberry juice and looked away. "Yes, I've always envied your Verdo."

No, I haven't, but what else can I say to that?

Severo interjected, "Gabriel, man. Ben reminded me we have Weapons and Devices together, is that right?" Without waiting for an answer, Severo draped his arm around Gabriel. "I'm bumping Elias out of his seat and replacing him with you. I needed a new study partner anyway. That guy is the worst."

Gabriel breathed a sigh of relief. "On that, we agree." Severo clearly hadn't realized they had two other classes together.

This semester might be okay after all.

For the first time in school, Gabriel found himself in a much lighter spirit. Still a bit wary of Niall but Severo was easy company. His intention to sit and read the *Landis Tribute* at lunch was long forgotten.

Gabriel left with them after lunch and went straight to VDS—Verdo Development Skills—for the afternoon. Outside the hall,

Gabriel saw Elias indisputably waiting for him. When Elias saw Ben, his eyes narrowed in annoyance. Gabriel exhaled.

At least today I'm safe.

The VDS classroom screamed intimidation with its high iron walls, long stained-glass windows, and sterile light. Professor Longwind strode toward them, and the loud clack of her heels on the marble floor sounded like warning chimes. Her steely gaze made Gabriel squirm.

Professor Longwind pointed to a small elevated gallery with several desks protected in a glass casing. "New starts in there."

Gabriel shuffled inside and sat down. The glass door to the gallery closed. All the other students with established gifts sat at desks in a square zone facing a bigger area with a giant floor mat.

"Today we welcome four new additions," Professor Longwind said with a stern voice that resounded from one end of the classroom to the other. "You may be sitting there expecting to learn all the knowledge about your powers, but no two powers are the same, and what you have gained will be very personal to you. Patience is a virtue of old and you will be learning no more than what you should have already memorized in your books for the next few weeks. You may meditate at home with supervision. What you will see today are examples of how your peers can use their gifts and testimonials on how they have been cultivated."

Professor Longwind's eyes roamed till they stopped on Gabriel's. "You, come forward."

The glass door opened on its own. Gabriel almost tripped walking toward his new teacher. She was tall and her plum robes enveloped her like a sealed piece of parchment. Her straight gray hair sat rock solid on her shoulders and her cold gaze could intimidate an ice cube. He bit his lip and followed her signal, stopping before her.

"Look at me," she said.

He didn't like looking at people directly, but when he did, he saw a hidden warmth behind her cold front. It eased him.

Professor Longwind held out her palm and pursed her lips. She let out a breath like she was blowing a kiss.

Gabriel stumbled and fell backward onto the floor. He rubbed his eyes in confusion.

Where am I?

Elias snickered and it was enough to bring Gabriel around. The students in the square zone were looking at him with knowing smirks. Severo lifted Gabriel to his feet and turned to fire a warning glare at Elias.

Great, now I look like I can't fight my own battles.

"That was a little taste of my gift. It's a defensive skill designed to render an opponent useless. It doesn't last long but it allows for enough time to escape," Professor Longwind said.

Escape from what?

Gabriel went back to the gallery and thought about what was hidden on the dark side of the island. Questions abounded. Did Professor Longwind know something they didn't? Gabriel cringed. His whole life had pretty much been a peaceful one. What if that changed?

Professor Longwind clapped her hands. "This is where you will be free to practice your skills as they develop. However, today is for observation. We do this in the form of defensive duels. Severo and Erik, you're up."

Both boys stood and moved to the large mat, bowed, then started circling each other. Erik held out his palms and Gabriel watched, fascinated, as two perfect balls of ice formed on his palms, swirling till they picked up speed. Without warning, he hurled them at Severo. They landed in the center of Severo's chest, and the ice spread over him until he was frozen.

So, Erik's the winner?

Gabriel thought it too soon. Severo flexed his hand and then touched it to his body. The ice shattered and Severo sprang into a roll, wrestling Erik to the ground till he had him in a headlock.

Impressive.

The gossip girls, Eloise and Lottie, were up next. Lottie screamed and Gabriel covered his ears. He noticed the others beside him had done so too. The stained-glass windows shattered—everything outside of the matted area bounced off an invisible forcefield. As shards of glass spiraled through the air, Eloise disappeared.

Where did she go?

Gabriel blinked and spotted something crawling up Lottie's leg. She cried out, falling backward. Apparently, Eloise could shrink herself.

That is so neat!

Eloise grew back to normal size and pinned Lottie flat on her back.

Although they weren't allowed to do much but watch, it was cool to see the skill in the room.

"Remember, class, meditation is also just as important as practice. It will allow you to connect with your gifts. Please ensure both are carried out in a controlled environment. Never forget, we must always be ready for an attack, as you never know when your abilities will be needed," Professor Longwind said.

Why do I feel like that could be sooner than we think? Gabriel shivered.

After demonstrations came a reading hour. Gabriel noticed small beads of sweat drop on Ben's textbook. Gabriel squinted at the page. Ben was studying the gift of the All-seeing Eye. His gaze seemed transfixed on a singular highlighted line that read, *this power needs the utmost control.*

Gabriel returned his attention to his textbook, reading the same page as Ben. The first four Verdos featured on this page, including his and Ben's, were under Primary Gifts. Strangely, the first half of the page was blank with no explanation as to why.

"Ben, do you know why this page is blanked out?" Gabriel whispered.

"Hmm. I never really thought about it. Probably an oversight."

Gabriel nodded but the hosts and the fairies were not known for mistakes. They all had their jobs, and Vallore used them to run a tight ship.

"Okay, books down, please. Now it's time to witness a more mental-based gift. Niall, please take a book from the shelf," Professor Longwind said. "Have you read this book?"

"I think you will be hard-pressed to find a book I haven't read, professor." Niall smiled at her, and she nodded in agreement.

So arrogant.

"Very well. Can you give the book to Clara, and can you follow the text as Master Niall recites it?"

Clara nodded and Niall began to read.

After a few pages in, the professor asked Niall to stop. "Clara, did Niall read this verbatim?"

Clara nodded with her eyebrows raised. "Yes, he did."

Everyone gave a round of applause.

Niall came to life talking about his gift, albeit in a pompous way. He could figure out any problem on demand and had the answers.

Niall's power had developed quickly, and it also appeared there was more to it than anyone knew. Clearly he'd been holding out.

How can I know this? Is that part of my power?

From what Gabriel understood, Niall was able to make others see only what he wanted them to see. The gift unnerved him.

The bell rang. Ben stiffened beside Gabriel as they left the gallery, and he followed Ben's eyes as Elias expertly sailed a sharpened quill in Severo's direction. It shattered off his hard clavicle but not before Severo's white shirt got spattered in ink. If it had been anyone else, the quill would have pierced the skin.

"Just checking. Wow, Severo, you are impressive," Elias slurred.

This wasn't just about Gabriel.

Severo and Elias must have history.

Gabriel swallowed. Outside the classroom, he said to Ben, "Is Severo going to be on the warpath now?"

"Possibly. He has a pretty short temper but is quick to forgive. However, Elias is different, and Sev has been at odds with him for years."

So, I'm right. I hope it doesn't come to anything.

Gabriel wasn't sure what else to say so left it at that. Ben was quiet as they walked and kept rubbing a hand over his hair.

"I was kind of looking for some enlightenment on our gifts. No such luck, eh?" Ben said, changing the subject.

"Exactly what I was thinking."

Over the next few days, Gabriel ate lunch with Ben, Severo, and Niall, and this normalized the routine for everyone. People started talking to him in the halls. Gabriel didn't know what to think—all of it was so new to him, but it kept the bullies away.

I guess who you know makes a difference.

Each day his guard came down a little more, and Severo's zest for life was infectious. Even Niall, at times, seemed bearable. Gabriel didn't see Cece as much, but when he did, he went in for the smile first. By day Four, she even said hi to him between classes. She had the power to make him forget his worries as more wistful emotions took over.

My nerve is growing.

The best thing to come out of the week was getting home each day unscathed. Elias hadn't been able to get anywhere near him.

At the start of Four, Gabriel's body seemed to have developed an involuntary twitch. In physics class that morning, Ben whispered, "Did your parents say it was okay to study after school?"

Gabriel answered under his breath, "Yes, my mother gleamed like her polished silver." He laughed. "Meet you at the coffee cart at the last bell?"

"Yeah, ideal. I found something out in the last few days. We've lots to discuss," Ben said, his fingers trembling.

CHAPTER 8

Ben

Ben lifted his hand to the brass door knocker of his mother's chamber. Perial hovered before him in a sea of fairy dust.

"Master Benjamin, why are you not in class?"

"I have a study hour. I want to see my mother."

"Your mother is resting. Can I pass on a message?"

"No. I'll speak to my mother on my own." Ben moved to open the door and Perial blew something onto his hand. He shook his stinging fingers.

"Perial, come on. Let me in."

"I'm sorry. She is resting."

Ben glared at her, and she flinched.

What kind of life was this for any of them? Does Perial know what's wrong or is she conforming like everyone else?

"Fine, but I will be here every day until someone tells me what's going on," Ben said through gritted teeth.

He fidgeted through his classes and loosened the barrel knot of his purple embroidered necktie. Sweat dampened the cotton material of his shirt as thoughts of his mother and what Gabriel might have to say ate away at him.

How will I ever be a king? It's too consuming.

The permanent boulder in his stomach refused to budge. His body felt disconnected to him, like it was forcing itself to host an imposter.

When the final bell rang, he squirmed so much in his seat his pores were begging for refreshments. Vara was at the coffee cart, and he moved toward her, but the new alter ego within had other ideas for where to walk. Ben exited the rear of the castle instead and welcomed the breeze that whispered hello. He walked to the curved white bridge, identical to the one at the front of the castle, and rested his weighted arms, peering at the water below. He stood in a trance, taking in Rainbow Lake—the expanse of water that rippled around the castle's perimeter and flowed under the bridges. A pearlescent glow beamed from below and reflected prisms of every color. Ben followed the threads that traveled to the skies above.

Is there anything else up there? Vallore is up there somewhere. Hiding? Ben didn't think so. *Does Vallore have a clue about what's going on?* He shivered at the thought of summoning the High Host for help. He took a breath and exhaled.

As he scanned his world, pressure began to build behind his eyes. They were drawn to the darkness. The Forbidden Vale. He tried so hard to ignore its existence, but it beckoned. Swirls of smoky tendrils swarmed in and out of the forest like weeds prepped to smother.

Ben dragged his mind back, fighting the internal battle within.

If I ignore it, it'll go away. If I ignore it, it'll go away.

Gabriel would be waiting. The sun beat down on his back as he made his way back inside. Beads of sweat performed a sequel, but despite the warmth, the hairs on his body stood at attention.

Ben's head snapped back to The Forbidden Vale as if a set of hands had moved it. His eyes felt like they had projected from their sockets. He remained rooted but at the same time was at the entrance to The Vale. He watched as an array of branches twisted together to create an opening, willing him to walk through.

Hyperventilation threatened as he pulled himself back with all his strength. His legs gave way, and he toppled onto the cobblestone.

What was that?

His skin hurt, like pins and needles puncturing his flesh. He scratched his arms. Despite his fear, his inner strength fought off the darkness. The new part of him screamed through a series of vibrations in his body as the two parts separated—one grounded and one spirit-like.

He saw himself and felt his capabilities race through his body like electric shocks. Unlike a mirror image, what stood on the other side was filled with urgency and panic. His time to act was coming soon, and he needed to be ready.

CHAPTER 9

Gabriel

G abriel checked the grandfather clock. Ben was late. He walked through the foyer but turned when he heard footsteps clopping behind him. Ben was walking back through the rear castle doors. He looked pale.

"Sorry to keep you. Just buzz your bracelet. I arranged clearance." Ben stood at the other side of the filmy barrier to the upper levels, not meeting Gabriel's eyes.

Gabriel was used to requesting access to the library—another favorite haunt of his with endless stacks to get lost in—but never to the royal quarters. The red circular light turned green and the screen that looked like clear plastic sprang open to let him through.

Something's wrong.

They entered the stairwell and Ben chatted like he was reading from a rehearsed script.

Hopefully, he will tell me what's going on.

For a bright castle, the curved staircase was shaded and bricked in, and the only way to get to the other levels. Gabriel leaned into the wall as there was no railing—he always did this. They bypassed the first exit that housed the library, the hospital where his mother worked, and Weapons and Devices where his father had a supervising role. Ben stopped to buzz again, and another invisible forcefield within the stairwell shimmered and separated like oil and water. He followed behind Ben, and the shimmery barrier sprang back into place.

The royal quarters were all new to him. Gabriel whistled. White walls with intricate gold patterns curved above him and intermittent skylights paved the way along a corridor that seemed to have no end. The entire first floor of his home could slot inside Ben's bedroom. Ben closed his heavy door and sprinkled a powder around the circumference of the room.

"Tweek, my ever so sound and intuitive fairy, made me this. It's called 'Conceal Dust.'"

"What does it do?" Gabriel never asked Fritzi for anything.

"It will keep what we say totally private. You may not have noticed, but my life is not my own. Tweek gets that. After I wished for my room protection, she concocted this so I can use it anywhere. It will keep the spies at bay. With Tweek, we have what could be called a mutual understanding. That and I keep her in a supply of Tweetles."

Light and dark chocolate swirls with a caramel center—Gabriel's favorite too.

He treats his fairy well. I like that. Tweetles are the way forward.

"Tweek sounds great. I'm not one for asking Fritzi much. I kind of hate that the fairies do so much and don't get recognized for their hard work."

Gabriel hadn't meant to say that but was glad he did. *What will Ben's reaction be?* He wiped his hands on his trousers.

"I've been thinking about that, actually. I agree, although some fairies see it as a power trip, others do far too much. Tweek told me once that there's a fairy rule book and fairies are not supposed to have close relationships with their charge. They are solely in place to keep order and report." Ben huffed out a breath.

Gabriel rubbed his chin, taking this in. "Huh, well, that was a fool-proof plan."

Ben laughed. A lot. Gabriel thought it seemed like Ben was letting more than laughter out.

Ben stopped and cleared his throat, a little embarrassed. "To be fair, it would be nice to acknowledge how much the fairies do, if it's allowed, that is. Maybe I could talk to my father."

Gabriel sighed. *Good.* Fairies were higher beings, after all, and shouldn't be taken for granted. "So, what's up?" He wasn't sure how else to get the conversation going.

Ben slumped onto a large sofa that faced his window, and Gabriel took a second before sitting alongside him. "I'm not sure what's going on with me. It feels like I have to make room for an extra body part or something. I can't get my head around my gift, but I know it's doing something in here." Ben pointed to his heart and head.

"I feel the same, and on some level, I knew you'd get it. Doesn't make it less confusing though." He was glad Ben nodded in agreement.

"I know you saw something in me that day in physics. I have visions, and they've become more frequent this last week—today even. My body keeps wanting to be elsewhere."

Gabriel remembered that day well. It had freaked him out when Ben collapsed. He rubbed his temples. "I wish we knew more about our powers. Do you think Vallore is always watching?"

Should I be asking this?

"I've been wondering that. Something in me is telling me no." Ben got up. "With the Conceal Dust, maybe we could try and access our gifts without being caught?"

Gabriel wasn't one to break the rules, and he guessed neither was Ben, but things were getting out of control. "I'm in and I'll keep quiet."

"Thanks. The visions and dreams I have... sometimes someone is there with me. I think it's the shadow of a girl. I can't reach her, but I know I'm the only one who can help her. I mean, is it an illusion or could there be a place outside our world? Gabriel, it feels so real, and I've no idea what to make of it. There's something else. My dream from last night. When I woke, I was outside."

This was a lot to take in. *Why do we know so little?* Gabriel pulled at his shirt collar. "Weird. I've never thought about a world beyond ours, do you think that's possible?"

"I really don't know, but if she's real, she must be from somewhere else. She told me we're in danger, and because of something that happened to me, I'm inclined to think she's right."

He watched Ben pick his lips, and a chill touched Gabriel's skin like the trail of a feather. *If an outside force is somehow aware of this, then we're in trouble.* He gulped.

"I've not shared this with Niall or Severo. Niall seems stressed, and Severo, well, he's Severo. I'm not used to having a serious conversation with him." Ben paused. "And don't take this the wrong way, but

I'm not sure why I'm telling *you*. I guess you could say it's a gut feeling."

"Sometimes we can't tell the ones we're close to the things that haunt us the most. Perhaps it's because I'm kind of impartial?"

"Hmm. Perhaps."

Gabriel bit his lip. "One thing I'll say is, you *can* trust me."

Who would I have to tell anyway?

"I believe that," Ben said.

"I need to own up to something. The night of our ceremony, I followed you all, and I saw what happened." Gabriel lowered his head to avoid Ben's eyes. "I was on the other side of the vine, but Severo looked right through me."

Ben's eyebrows lifted. "How? You'd only just been given your Verdo."

Gabriel wiped his hands on his breeches. "How is it that you rose from the ground when you drank the wine?"

"Touché. Clearly, the rule book is different with us. It must mean something. I've been trying to tap into my power when I'm awake but nothing. It seems to be more responsive when I'm not able to think about it."

"That's it, exactly. I managed to completely shield. Like I *made* it happen."

"That might explain why nobody saw you at the party," Ben said.

"I'm not so sure. It's almost like, on some level, I've always had a form of this ability. When we finally spoke this year, it was because I let my guard down. I let you see me and then I guess I mirrored that action. What you saw felt as real to me as it does to you, but I don't know what it means. What I do know is, you were having these visions before your Verdo was given and that should be a statistical impossibility."

"Good point..." Ben's brow furrowed. "Gabriel, why were you spying in the vineyards?"

"I-I'm sorry about that. I didn't mean to spy, it just kind of happened. I hope that's cool?"

"It is, but I have enough spies around me, so next time, ask."

"I was looking for you. I was a bit overwhelmed. No two people have received Verdos like ours for decades, let alone in the same ceremony. Was it due or was it for some other reason? We need to find that out."

Although their conversation was protected, Ben whispered, "We do. Ever since last weekend, when the skies changed, I felt a full-on shift."

A knot formed in Gabriel's stomach. "I've had the same feeling. I keep wanting to look at the other side of the island like something's happening there."

"So do I. When Tweek was making the Conceal Dust, Bishop came in and she had to hide. She overheard that someone on the night of the ceremony breached The Forbidden Vale, and they haven't a clue who it is."

"Really?" Gabriel shivered. This was getting too real. "That's worrying. Would Tweek not have been told this anyway though?"

"Nope. She gets told nothing, but she has her ways. Only the Fairy Guard knows what's really going on. For all this time, we've been living oblivious. Tweek tells me a lot. She's my family."

This made Gabriel smile, but he noticed a tone of resentment in Ben's voice. "That's good we have her on our side. It might help."

"I agree. I don't know how to get more information. I don't think we'll be told anything. We're just teenagers after all. We'll need to find answers ourselves."

"You're right. I second that. Do you think meditating could work?" Gabriel asked.

Ben nodded. "It's a good place to start, and at least we're safe from spying eyes."

But are we? Gabriel didn't know if he believed that. It was as if the Fairy Guard had multiplied.

They got into positions opposite each other on the hardwood floor.

"It seems when something happens to me, it's brought on by some kind of emotion."

Gabriel thought about that. "Yes, you might be right. Well, I'd say we're both pretty freaked right now, so it can't hurt to try."

They both closed their eyes at the same time.

Gabriel breathed in and out, trying to connect to his power. No tingling occurred. He was about to say so, but when he opened his eyes, Ben was gone.

His skin prickled as he stood. A noise above made him look up. Ben floated. His eyes were open but white with no iris visible.

Is he unconscious?

Ben's body spun fast, then lost control. Ben hit the ceiling and landed with a thud at Gabriel's feet.

CHAPTER 10

Vara

O n day Five, Vara kept to the shadows on her climb to school. Severo and Cece were up ahead. Severo made her nervous.

Why does he make me feel like that?

She didn't need an answer. She knew. Their ceremony had been the same day, along with Niall. When the sky crackled and they were given their gifts, something sparked.

Ignore it. Ignore it. Remember the princess plan!

She jumped back behind some shrubs when Severo and Cece stopped. She tried listening to what they were saying but couldn't make out much through the prickly bush. Cece looked tired and her eyes were red. Severo was comforting her. *He cares about his sister.* Her stomach clenched seeing this soft side of him.

Stop thinking about Severo. Go and find Ben.

She had tried for days to find an excuse to slip her hand in Ben's and finish what had almost started in the gardens. She wanted to know him better.

He seems so nice but so closed off sometimes. Not to mention, hard to find.

Distracted between classes, Vara rounded a corner and collided with Severo before falling to the floor. As she slid, her skirt swept the floor like a mop. Severo tried to help her up, but she shrugged him off.

She knew her cheeks were flaming. "Watch where you're going, you big fool," she spat, smoothing her now ruffled hair.

"Ooh. Excuse me for trying to help you up. Let me get out of your precious path," he drawled. His look held confusion.

Why are we so mean to each other?

She felt even more conflicted at the last bell. It was Buzz Ball tryouts—not her thing— but it was the sporting event Landis lived for. Two tournaments a year and the school captains were looking for new recruits. Severo was one of them, and Ben would be in the audience.

The arena was gargantuan. The bleachers curled around the open-air field with two gaps at either side for the entry and exit tunnels. In the central grassland, two separate black marks in the shape of triangles were inked along the length of the pitch, each one facing opposite sides of the field. They connected to form a diamond with a thick black line through the middle. Each triangle had nine white dots.

The sun pinked her cheeks as she found a seat in the bleachers beside her friends. After she sat, she tried to catch Ben's eye, but the mound of muscle she was intent on ignoring forced her head to turn.

I like Ben, not Severo. I like Ben, not Severo. Guilt tickled her at how rude she'd been earlier. *What's wrong with me?*

Severo was staring at something. She followed his eyes and saw Gabriel, the boy who she'd never noticed before the ceremony, walking towards Severo on the other side of the pitch. Elias was thundering towards Gabriel as if rage owned him.

Is he possessed?

What happened next was nothing short of amazing. Elias hurled himself at Gabriel. It was like slow motion as Severo intercepted Elias with inhuman speed. With one hand, Severo lifted Elias off the ground like he was a grain of rice and tossed him to the opposite rows of bleachers. The crack of the collision against the metal railings made Vara squirm and her friends screamed.

Where are all the teachers?

There was a split second of silence, then chaos ensued. Everyone got up from their seats and ran to the middle of the open-air arena. The collective voices hummed in her ears. Elias had a group around him. Ben and Niall ran to Severo and Gabriel. Ben seemed to be talking Severo down. Vara noticed Cece hanging back. Her eyes were wide and darting around nervously.

Will Severo be suspended for this?

The Fairy Guard swarmed the scene like flies. She'd never seen so many. Come to think of it, they were everywhere. The professors would arrive soon. As if this thought summoned them, they burst through the stone tunnel that opened onto the pitch. The principal was with them.

"Order, order!" the principal shouted throughout the arena. His voice carried in the afternoon breeze.

His authoritative voice stopped the incessant chatter at once. Vara worried for Severo. Nothing like this ever happened. Fighting was against the rules. Severo was too young for the dungeons.

The professors will only see what Severo did. Why can't they see Elias for what he is? It's not fair. What if Severo's punishment is homeschooling for months?

She realized she didn't want that.

"I demand to know what's happened here," the principal commanded.

No one spoke. The professors rushed to Elias and helped him to his feet. He was doubled over, his face contorted. His arm was twisted unnaturally.

Vara stood. "Principal Gaines, it was an accident. Elias attacked Gabriel out of nowhere. If it wasn't for Severo intervening, Gabriel may have been hurt."

People were gasping in surprise.

Where did that come from?

The principal looked at her incredulously. "Now, Miss Vara, that sounds very out of character for Elias. It will do no one any favors to speak untruths."

Ben came forward. "Principal Gaines, that is an accurate account of what happened."

Ben looked at Vara, and the appreciation in his eyes almost made her lose her footing.

The principal paused, pursing his lips. He swiped a hand over his forehead. "Well, we will discuss this in private. Elias, let's get you to the hospital wing. Severo, report to the confine office immediately. In light of current events, Buzz Ball tryouts will be postponed. If you all can make your way to your homes."

Elias winced, sauntering to the entrance with the help of one of the professors. On his way, he looked at Severo, Vara, Gabriel, and Ben. If his jaw was any tighter it would shatter.

She felt like she was having an out-of-body experience. Her mother's voice rang through her head. *Remember, Vara, never speak before you think. It doesn't make for good queen etiquette!*

She moved weightlessly, contemplating what she'd done, and stopped when she felt a light touch on her shoulder.

Ben.

"Thank you for the backup," she said.

"No, thank you. I've known about Elias and his behavior for years. Everyone has, but nobody ever says anything. Well, except you." His lip curved up at the side.

Vara stared, then hung her head as she felt her cheeks warm. Gabriel walked over. He smiled, reserved. She took him in for the first time. He had the kindest and most unusual eyes. They were a rich brown with tiny green flecks that twinkled in the sunlight.

"Thank you, Vara," Gabriel said.

Vara returned the warmth of his gesture. How had she never noticed him before? "Hey, Elias had it coming, didn't he?" Laughter bubbled out like a bath about to overflow. Ben and Gabriel joined in.

She turned to Ben. "I better find my friends. I'm coming to the castle tomorrow with my mother. Maybe I'll see you?"

Vara was dumbstruck when Ben beamed.

"Yes, that'll be great. I'll look out for you. Maybe we could do a private tour?" he said, waggling his eyebrows.

Just the two of us?

She gulped but recovered with a smile. "Can't wait. Till tomorrow, then." She felt his eyes on her as she walked away, and elation pumped through her. Vara spotted her friends. They were at the other side of the arena. As she approached them, she saw they were talking to Elias's two friends.

Norris pushed his way forward and spat, "Here she comes, the spinner. Did that feel good? You have a mark on your back now. Be warned."

Vara had judged others in the past with this exact term. She didn't want to be tarred as one to cause a disruptive flow.

Too late now.

Norris and Clive fist-bumped, and as they walked past Vara, they pushed her so hard she lost her balance. Strong, delicate hands caught her mid-fall, and she looked up to see Cece.

"Are you okay?"

"Yes. Thanks, Cece."

"I was hiding at the back from Sev. I could tell he was angry I was here to try out. When I saw you coming this way, I wanted to thank you. I'm hoping he won't get into as much trouble now after your help."

"Oh, not at all. It was the right thing to do."

Cece smiled, tucking a fiery red curl behind her ear. "Listen, I know we don't know each other very well, but if you ever need a friend, I'm always around."

Vara swallowed.

"I best go find Severo. Wish us both luck."

Vara felt lighter as Cece danced off. She was like a warm, unannounced breeze and had an intensity that was not obvious from distant observations.

I wonder what made her sad this morning. Maybe she needs a confidante too?

Gabriel and Cece were so kind. They didn't know her, yet it came so naturally to them. It struck a chord within her. As she tried to process this, she absentmindedly greeted her three friends.

Clara's head was low. "Hi, Vara."

Eloise and Lottie stood like mirror images, glaring at her.

"We don't talk to spinners. You think you're better than us. You always have. The news today is, you're not. Find new friends, *princess*," Eloise said, storming off arm-in-arm with Lottie.

Vara looked at Clara and held up her hands. It was like a dam had burst and the water washing away hit her with a harsh dose of reality.

Clara took a hesitant step toward Vara and rubbed her shoulder. "Eloise and Lottie have something going with Norris and Clive. They were all vocal about what you did. Don't take this the wrong way, but you do tend to be a stickler for the rules. If you want my opinion, I think it was brave."

"Well, let them think what they want. This life is exhausting sometimes. Why should we walk on eggshells and not stand up to bullies? Landis help us if we talk about our feelings. Myself included. What kind of life is that? I feel like everything has built up inside me and now I'm ready to explode." Vara slumped her shoulders.

"Power to you, Vara. I knew you had it in you. Don't worry about them. If I'm honest, I stuck around because of you." Clara threw her arms around her, hugging her tight.

Vara stood like a statue, not used to this kind of physical affection. It was a real comfort. She gave her friend a light pat on the back. Clara was right.

Why worry about girls that behave that way? That's not me. I need to be better. Like getting a sudden answer for a test paper, she was seeing Clara for the first time. *I'm glad I have one good friend.*

Vara waved goodbye to Clara as they parted in the castle foyer. She edged behind the coffee cart and caught wind of a conversation. Eloise and Lottie were deep in gossip. She crept further back.

"Severo has got off with an admonishment. Can you believe that after the way he threw Elias? Apparently, Elias didn't put up a fight about it either," Eloise said.

"How big of Elias. Severo is lucky Vara took his side. We knew she had to be flawed. Goes to show, being beautiful is not everything," Lottie scoffed.

Their giggles echoed and trailed behind them.

Vara felt numb on her walk home until footsteps approached behind her. She stiffened as they crunched the gravel, drawing closer. Instead of looking over her shoulder, she slowed and waited for the person to reveal themselves.

Severo.

Her mixed feelings churned as he sauntered past her without a backward glance.

What? He's not even going to acknowledge me?

"You are WELCOME by the way."

Severo halted, then turned with a glint in his eyes. "Excuse me?"

"You heard me. I saved your neck today. Has that bypassed you completely?"

Severo casually strode toward her, holding her gaze. "And what exactly do you think deserves thanks or makes you so special? Because you have the gift of Preservation, or is it the way you strategically plan every word? You've never looked my way or bothered before, therefore what can be your motive for what you did, I wonder?"

His words were harsh, but she saw a visible softness there.

Is it a defense mechanism?

He stood so close now, his sweet, whispered breath feathering over her face. Stunned, she studied every inch of his chiseled bone structure then back to his eyes where they lingered.

That was a good question. What was the answer?

They continued their stare down. Vara was scared to breathe.

"I-I…" she said.

He stared at her full of intensity, and as he stepped closer, the footstep was like a horn in her eardrum.

"You what?" His voice brimmed with whispering hope. Severo transferred his weight and raised a hand to caress her face. Large soft fingers traced her smooth skin, sending shivers through her. When Vara stared into his eyes, the anger was gone. He stared back with gentle determination. She waited.

I don't think I could move if I tried.

Severo inched closer. "I'm sorry for being harsh. You unnerve me."

She took a deep breath as he laced his fingers through hers. She watched in freeze-frame as Severo's lips lowered until they were inches from her waiting mouth.

Vara's skin tingled, and her heartbeat came to a standstill. Her eyes closed, anticipating the inevitable kiss, but she jumped when something hit her, hard and fast in the arm. They both turned, and the trance was broken.

Who did that? Did someone see us? What if they talk? What if they tell my mother?

Vara edged closer to the sprays of rose bushes between homes and swore she heard them rustle. Confusion took over as her fingers touched the spot that now felt sore. She looked at Severo. His eyes held a wounded glint.

The plan. Ben. What have I done? I need to go.

The weight of Severo's towering gaze poked holes into her helpless frame and followed her home. The loss of control was too consuming, and her feelings were all mashed up. Emotionally, she had been ransacked and now everything was changing.

When she arrived home, she mounted the stairs and flung her bedroom door open so fast it retracted back in a slam. Then she lay on her bed and cried.

CHAPTER 11

Niall

Niall ducked in behind the rows of homes and fled down the alley of flowered hedges. He got away before Vara saw him. Alunattra had told him to spy. Human emotion, *love*, was not something he understood. It irritated him.

Why live with feelings you could survive better without?

He slipped in through his back door, unaware why Severo and Vara warranted any kind of attention. He searched his mind. No more words came to him. *She* was no longer there.

"Hi, son. Dinner will be ready soon. Go get washed up," his mother said.

He smiled at her in the way a son should, but a face he felt no connection to was all that stood before him. His parents were never the kind to put a foot wrong. It had always been that way. He was built for more. And now, the most powerful person on the island had sought him out.

He scratched at the red welts on his skin that kept appearing. A reminder that he wasn't close to where he wanted to be. Ben. *I need to understand his power.* Niall ground his teeth.

He climbed the stairs, ignoring the smell of gravied beef. His stomach churned. All around his bedroom were integrated bookshelves. He'd read everything. Not for pleasure. For knowledge. He located his Verdo textbook. He knew it inside and out but checked again.

Niall slammed the book shut and started pacing. Nothing from the book. Nothing from Ben.

His brain tingled, like fingertips tapping his temples. Someone was there.

"Niall, can you come down, please?" his father shouted.

Aristo, the king's guard, was waiting at the front door.

"Ah, Master Niall. May we speak in private?" he said.

Niall's father bowed and retreated to the kitchen. Niall led Aristo to his father's study and took a seat behind the crowded desk. He was interested in what the fairy might have to say. He folded his arms and waited.

"I have checked with your father, and I have something to ask."

Well, ask it then. Intrigue trumped his frustration.

"Can you be at the castle tomorrow midday? I have a summons from the king."

Why ask when I'm not allowed to refuse?

"Yes, of course. I will see you then. Can I ask what this is regarding?" Niall leaned forward, looking into Aristo's eyes.

They flickered before Aristo answered. "The night of the ceremony, our intel detected a breach. Someone visited The Vale that evening, but that's all we know. For years, Landis security hasn't had to act, and we need to keep it that way. We have been impressed with your skills, and the king would like you to help us in our investigation." Aristo rubbed his eyes. "This is not my place to say; however, the king will go into more detail tomorrow."

Niall saw Aristo out, feeling much lighter on his feet. *Did I just blindside a fairy? That shouldn't be possible.* It was like the walls of his mind were expanding. It kept happening each day.

"Interesting, Niall. Good. Things are falling into place. Just as I wish."

Alunattra was back. Her voice gripped his mind like a vice. This was all her doing. After dinner, he retreated to his room and called for his fairy. Pixel didn't look him in the eye. She hovered before him with her arms crossed. Time for another experiment.

Niall perched on the edge of his bed, focusing on Pixel's eyes. She drew closer. His mind was sparking again, like a brainwave of pins and needles. He could almost see a line of connection linking them together.

"Pixel. Look into my eyes. What are you thinking?"

Her voice changed, like in a trance. "Well, I know it may be out of place to say, but I've not felt needed these last few weeks, and seeing you talk with Aristo accentuated that for me."

Niall reveled in her confused expression when she realized she had said too much. He shared a calming look with her, and she relaxed. The power of persuasion worked on his fairy. A test he'd been carrying out all week at school with his peers. It had worked like a charm with Elias, although Niall had asked him to watch Gabriel, not attack him. Seeing more into Elias's mind was like reading a book page on repeat. The boy was shallow, uneducated, and always looking for a fight. But his gift was interesting. That, and Niall enjoyed the dislike Elias had for Gabriel. It seemed this had been ongoing for a while, and all because Gabriel had a liking for Severo's sister. *Idiots, all of them.*

Even more interesting than that was the prospect of a wishing fairy that could be controlled. That would provide much better outcomes. He had assumed it wouldn't work as fairy magic was not to be toyed with.

"How about I put a list of things together that you could help me with?"

"Oh, yes, please. Anything, Master Niall."

The side of Niall's mouth curved into a sneer. He had fairy magic on tap. Whatever Alunattra was doing to him, it was working. His power was mutating.

I wonder if my power will work on the king.

CHAPTER 12

Vara

Vara chewed the skin at the side of her nail until it hurt. When she pulled her hand away, the redness faded away to reveal the perfect half-moon of her index finger. She couldn't eat, but the hustle in the kitchen distracted her thoughts.

"Darling, is everything okay? You've barely said a word to anyone since you came home last night," her mother said, concerned.

Prine, her wishing fairy, circled Vara's head, tutting in agreement.

"Yes, Mama. Prine, I'm fine. I didn't get a good sleep. Did you hear about what happened at the Buzz Ball tryouts?"

Vara waited, not sure she wanted to know the answer. Prine joined the other fairies in clean-up duty.

"Yes, we did. You know how the fairies gossip. I can't quite understand it. Elias is such a good boy and from a respectable family. I can't believe he would have harmed that boy. Gabriel, is it? I'm struggling to place him. He was the one at the ceremony who received the gift of the Mask, yes?"

Vara nodded.

"All we were told was Elias attacked this boy and Severo intervened. Your father and I wanted to ask you last night, but you never came down."

So, her parents didn't know her part in this? That was a relief. They would prefer her to be the "princess in training" they were preparing for. Not this new speaking-without-thinking mess. Up until recently, she had one goal: to be princess. But it was like a veil had been removed from her eyes. Severo had changed things for her.

Stop thinking about Severo.

"Vara," her mother said firmly. "Will you answer me, please? Your behavior is really out of character. I don't know what to make of it."

"Mama, I'm tired. Please don't fret. Let me go get ready. Are we still going to the castle today for your photo shoot?"

Her mother relaxed a bit. "Yes, absolutely. This will be a good move for your future. Be quick. We don't have long till my appointment."

When Vara returned to her room, she summoned Prine to help her get ready. Her relationship with her fairy had never been overly personal, but she felt the budding urge to change that. She was starting to care about different things and other people. Her emotions were deeply stirred, and today's experience surpassed anything she had ever felt before.

How do I begin?

She was out of her comfort zone, but she still tried.

"Prine, can I talk to you in confidence?"

Prine's gorgeous pale green wings expanded in a surprised flutter, and her puffy skirt looked like an umbrella as she hovered. Her teal skin brightened, and her eyes sparkled. "Why, yes. Can I help you with something?"

"Lately I've been embracing my inner self and all sorts of emotions are getting mixed up in my mind. I feel like everyone is acting differently and out of the ordinary. I don't know who to talk to about it."

Prine's face turned pensive. "I believe it's normal for a girl your age to struggle with emotions, after all, you have a lot to consider these next few years, especially if you marry the prince. Even at that, you might want to undertake a working post, or I could teach you to cook. We fairies always feel working keeps us on our wings, as life can be tedious sometimes. Anyway, I think it's an incredibly positive sign that you feel this way," Prine said.

Vara wished she had spent more time talking to Prine. This felt good to share. "I feel like it's more than that. My problems up till now consisted of what to wear or getting a good grade in class. I never worried about boys. I assumed I would get what I wanted. I now understand that is far too presumptuous. On the day of the ceremony, when the prince was given his Verdo, something deviated in the air. I can't explain it. Please, Prine, I know the fairies talk. Has anything seemed unusual to you? You can trust me, I promise."

Prine disappeared and was back again instantly. "I needed to be sure we were free to speak; there is one thing. You know I help at the castle?" Vara didn't know this but indicated otherwise. "Well, one of the fairies overheard the king speaking with Tharmus. It seems that someone has breached The Forbidden Vale. The Fairy Guard don't know who it is, and I don't know how they know but they do. I think the king has his guards working around the clock. That's all I know, and I'm sure everything will be fine. It might even be a mistake."

I doubt that. I'm glad I asked. Best keep this to myself.

"I'm sure you're right. Thanks, Prine, for trusting me with this. Now, on to a more important topic. My outfit."

Prine's giggle was like a soothing wind chime. "Of course. I was thinking understated but with staying power."

"Sounds perfect."

Prine pointed to the wardrobe doors and, with sharp hand gestures, lifted out olive-green slacks and a three-quarter length, ivory satin jacket in cream lace with gold buttons. Vara wore her hair down, and Prine clapped, waving big loose curls through her expanse of hair, leaving a bounce of tendrils cascading down her back. She opted for no jewelry today and went with a more natural look. Her father was the fashion designer for the village and had designed a delicate brooch to give to Ben's mother. Her parents thought it would score points for Vara. They had planned this from birth, but Vara becoming princess wasn't their decision to make.

Can Ben see me by his side?

She tucked the ribboned box into her satchel.

VARA BREATHED IN THE SCENT OF FRESH GRASS AND SWEET FLOWERS. Every thatched roof resembled the top of a wedding cake—frosted with yellow roses and pink pansies, which drizzled down the sides like ribbons. She sighed as her curve-heeled shoes dug into the soles of her feet—a new design of her father's.

Her mother muttered her interview notes under her breath,

although with the gift of Presence, and adoring fans at her feet, Vara wondered why she needed to. Her mother almost always made the front page of *The Landis Tribute*, especially as Vara's father designed all the gowns she advertised. Vara did welcome the silence, though. As they walked past Severo's home, her gaze lingered on the upstairs bedrooms. Ivy and clematis plants framed the rims of the shuttered windows and spilled out over the shades of brownstone.

Which room is his?

She blinked and swallowed the hurt.

Vara heard a subtle sob coming from Severo's garden, and she did a double-take. Cece was sitting on a hand-carved bench tucked in behind rows of sunflowers. The anguish was unmistakable. Vara wanted to help in some way. Her mother hadn't noticed, and they continued walking over the bridge.

Her over-crammed mind longed to be emptied.

The castle exterior had several guards in place at the entrance. Vara and her mother waited as their bracelets were activated for entry through the castle's sprawling levels. The Fairy Guard had a much more intimidating quality—gray skin, white eyes, and gold hair that stood in a dramatic point. Their translucent wings were also larger and more teardrop shaped. They may have been small but they exuded order.

Her mother got two tokens for them, and they made their way to the coffee cart. It was in full motion, beans grinding in mid air and pots whistling. Nilla prepared two hot cinnamon swirls—a mother and daughter favorite for them, which they sipped as they entered the doorway to the stone staircase. Vara often visited the library in the lower west wing, but other than that, the upper castle remained a mystery. A current of excitement raced through her.

As they approached the east wing, Vara put her hand on her mother's shoulder. "Do you mind, Mama, if I have a look around? This is the first time I've been in this part of the castle."

"Absolutely. This is a perfect time for you to shine." She stroked Vara's cheek. "This castle suits you well."

"Well, let's see if the prince agrees."

"Don't be negative. It's not becoming. Nobody has your beauty."

She wanted to tell her that beauty wasn't everything, but it would fall on deaf ears.

"Tell you what," her mother said, "Come to the newsroom with me and that way I can let them know you are here. I don't want you to get into trouble roving the halls without permission."

They exited the stairwell to the right and moved onto the walkway. Vara looked up at the skylight.

This castle is ginormous. How would it feel to live here? My family would love it.

Would I?

The newsroom was opposite the library. The news fairies and some of the townsfolk were hard at work finalizing *The Landis Tribute* for the coming week. Tharmus was there to greet them both.

"Welcome, Mrs. Beautelle and Miss Vara," he said, shaking their hands.

"Good morning, Tharmus, and call me Celine. My daughter was hoping to have a look around. Would that be permitted?"

"Yes, of course. Miss Vara, I'll give you a tour shortly. Feel free to wait for me right outside. Celine, I'll escort you through."

Vara had no intention of waiting. She wished her mother luck and left to have a look around. It felt exhilarating to do something out of character. She left the newsroom and stood on the bridgeway of the second floor. The interior looked like a square-tiered cake with the inside scooped out. Each level boasted a balustrade walkway with ornately carved columns threaded through the banister. She couldn't see much beyond that. Crystal chandeliers hung from the high ceilings above; they tinkled like an instrument as she moved.

Wow.

The desire to see more of the castle thrummed inside her. Could her clearance stretch to the upper west wing? The hospital had always held intrigue. There was no point in checking out the Weapons and Devices department—it was too heavily protected. At the staircase, Vara held her buzzer to the scanning device, and lo and behold, it allowed her access. Ben must have cleared her already. She felt safe to go to the next level.

I'll check out the hospital.

Vara could have heard a pin drop; it was that quiet. A lady at the reception desk looked up at her in surprise.

"Hello, can I help you?"

"Hello, I'm here for a tour. I'm waiting for Tharmus, so I thought I would have a look around. I'm Vara."

The receptionist held out her hand. Vara struggled to place her.

"Yes, I recognize you. You go to school with my son, Gabriel. Call me Leah," she said. "There's not much to see but on you go. I'm here if you need anything."

"Very nice to meet you, Leah. Thank you."

Leah smiled warmly then returned to charting.

There were several rooms on the right. Vara opened the doors to take a peek, discovering all were identical, each one white and clinical with an empty bed. Several chairs sat perfectly positioned on either side of the wrought iron beds, eerily waiting to be occupied. Flowers festooned the windowsills in a spray of varieties, adding vivacious colors to an otherwise sterile environment.

A locked room, with a tiny window midway down the corridor, homed an abundance of different creatures of all shapes and sizes. Most, upon quick glance, were unidentifiable to her.

This must be where they study the medicines and serums. I'm glad my body is self-healing!

On a central island was an all-glass concave vat with a large overhead fountain. Vara had heard the water from the creek was harbored here as it possessed the power to heal. If people could get to the hospital or Purity Creek in time after an accident, all damage could be repaired, with no evidence of injury. A sight her generation had yet to see.

Opposite this was another room with a notice above. Secured area.

No glass in this one—I'll just see if it's open. It wasn't. *Yeah, no career in medicine for me. What a letdown.*

As she turned to leave, a voice stopped her in her tracks. Vara tiptoed closer to the sound, and it was coming from an isolated room at the end of the hall. The voice belonged to Elias.

Why is he still here?

Usually, hospital visits were minutes at most, not hours. She listened closely.

"I'm getting out today. Yeah, I know, Severo has it coming. He shattered my lower arm and hip bone. The incompetent staff are clueless and thought they would try out their new discovery. My parents won't be happy. I swear some people are going to pay. They fight me, they get double in return."

Vara peered through the hospital room's door crack. Elias was on his own and talking to thin air.

How is this possible?

"Clive, get Norris. We have things to discuss. Don't tell him you've talked to me. I'll deliver this news."

It went silent.

"Okay, come by later when I'm home."

Her mind scrambled to remember what his Verdo was, but her brain failed to muster the knowledge. Maybe Ben would know what to do with this unsettling information. In a daze, she made her way back to the reception. Tharmus was standing there waiting and tapping his oversized foot.

"You, come with me. One thing I cannot tolerate is young people not abiding by the rules." Tharmus escorted her through the hospital doors and Vara tried to smile in thanks at the now-confused Leah.

"What were you doing exactly and how did you get up here in the first place?"

Vara was distracted by Tharmus tapping his foot again. It seemed independent from his body.

She was about to tell him but didn't have time to answer.

"Nothing for you to strain yourself over, Tharmus. Vara's my guest. She was looking for me, and I authorized the clearance. Off you go, don't let us interrupt your day of wreaking havoc on the lives of others," Ben said, appearing with Niall at his side.

Vara choked on a giggle.

"The king will hear of this." An echo sounded as Tharmus stormed away.

When Ben turned to Vara, they looked at each other and burst out laughing, as did Niall.

"I'll leave you both to it. I was heading out anyway. Ben, I'll see you this afternoon." Niall looked at them both and nodded. It seemed Niall was happy about her being here.

Had they been talking about me?

"A tour, my lady?" Ben bowed.

His lady. Yes, that's the plan.

Vara curtsied. "That would be lovely, Ben, thank you."

"How about we head to the other side, and you could be one of the first to see Weapons and Devices?"

Vara couldn't stop staring at him. He was wearing a V-neck cream shirt that emphasized his upper arms. His muscles were subtle—not bulked like Severo. Heat crept up her neck, making her fingers tingle.

Ben waited for her to answer. A slight curve of a smile formed on his lips.

"Oh, yes, that sounds wonderful. I have something for your mother." Vara reached down to her side. She didn't have her bag. "Oh shoot, I must've left my satchel in the newspaper office."

"Why don't we head there now? I'll inform the department and wait for you."

Vara assured him she would be right back. This day was heading in a great direction, and maybe they could get their walk. She just had to keep Severo from creeping into her thoughts.

The dance. *I hope Ben asks me*. Yes, that kept Severo out of her mind for a good ten seconds. As she left the staircase, a dark head of hair led her eyes to the ground.

Niall.

Something about the urgency of his body language was all wrong. He was heading out the back entrance of the castle. The opposite way from his home.

CHAPTER 13

Ben

B en rubbed his shoulders to soothe away the pain. He was covered in bruises.

This meditating business is not getting any easier. At least Gabriel is there to stop me from flying around my room like a balloon.

He waited at the Weapons and Devices department opposite the hospital. The indented doorway was made of indestructible cold steel. *Very intimidating.* Not surprising though, it held many explosives, right down to neat gadgets. The inner sanctum was protected in case of malfunctions, so it had to be strict. Ben raised his bracelet to the activation panel and waited.

"Master Benjamin Landis recorded. Who do you require?"

"Procter Smart, please, and access for Vara Beautelle."

"Access granted."

Ben expected Niall's father to open the door—he was the floor supervisor—but instead was warmly greeted by his grandad. His grandad's fairy, Bishop—the oldest out of all the fairies and head guard since the beginning of Landis Lots—hovered with irritated wing movement.

"Ben, what a pleasant surprise. Come in, come in," his grandad said.

"I'm waiting for someone. Someone I want you to meet. What brings you here anyway? No, let me guess. You wanted the new inventory lowdown before everyone else," Ben said.

His grandad's laughter echoed off the cold walls, creating its own kind of warmth. Bishop whispered something in Grandad Bay's ear before departing. Ben barely knew Bishop. He didn't look anyone in the eye or speak to them. He also wore a constant scowl on his face. Bishop respected Ben's grandfather, though. Ben could sense their unique bond.

"It seems we have some very exciting prospects indeed, but firstly, Ben, how's your mother? I've been here all morning." Concern reflected like mirrors in his grandad's eyes.

Two days ago, Ben had been on his way to meet Gabriel in the north wing when his mother suddenly fainted. Gabriel had got to her before her head hit the floor. Ben had stood helpless, too stunned to do anything. His father and Tharmus arrived thereafter and rushed her to the hospital wing. Dr. Lovett and several fairies laid her in an isolated room while Ben and his father waited, unable to talk.

Gabriel stayed, which Ben had been grateful for.

"She's fine, Grandad, she's fine. With the dance coming up, she was busy with Perial. The doctor said she was dehydrated."

"Ben, I can see you're worried," Grandad Bay said, placing a hand on Ben's shoulder. "Bottling things up will only cause an explosive exit. If you can't talk to me, always have someone on your side to confide in."

Ben nodded. He would have talked to Gabriel at the hide hut, but they never got to meet yesterday.

Maybe Vara could be a confidante?

With this thought, the scent of lavender flexed his nostrils. There she was. The picture of beauty. His hands were clammy.

"Ahem."

"Oh, sorry, Grandad, this is Vara. She's visiting today and I thought I might show her around Weapons and Devices."

"What a lovely idea. Miss Vara, nice to formally meet you."

"The pleasure is all mine, King-Father." Vara curtsied in respect.

Ben watched the exchange, eager to have his grandad's approval. His grandfather had abdicated in his eighth decade to make room for his parents when they were crowned king and queen but a king he would always be.

They walked in together and the whirring of machinery was over-powering. Ben side-swerved a look at Vara. Her mouth was slightly ajar as her eyes swept the room. *She's impressed.* Striker waved a clipboard around and passed out orders. Striker made the most amazing things, always reaching new levels.

No wonder Severo is so proud of his fairy.

"Now, I'll leave you both to it as I have work to be getting to. Procter will come and give you the inside scoop," his grandad said.

Bishop was back on his grandfather's shoulder as they left the department.

"Thanks for showing me around, Ben. This place is... intimidating. It was nice to see Niall too. He looked like he was in a hurry," Vara said.

"Yeah, he's off for a walk before we meet later. Sev's declared a boys' day. Here. Come with me. Have you seen one of these?"

Ben clutched her hand, and she gripped it as he led her to a large cubed see-through box. The structure was made of substantial shards of glass. Nothing was inside but on the outside were two buttons.

"Give me something out of your satchel."

Vara retrieved a mirrored compact and with the slightest hesitancy handed it to him.

"Watch."

Ben opened the door and threw the compact in the air. It floated effortlessly and moved to the center of the box. Ben pressed the green button and Vara's compact disappeared.

"What, where did it go?"

Ben didn't respond. He pressed the red button and the item reappeared. As he opened the door, it flew straight into the palm of his hand.

"Amazing," Vara said, her eyes big and bright.

"I'm not sure if you know this but the fairies can shrink things down for transportation and resize them again. They've perfected the development that it's now invisible to the naked eye. Striker is designing it this way, so nobody is unarmed in an attack."

Ben always imagined this ancient castle would stand the test of time. It had been around longer than anything documented but there was an element of haste in the air and more guards were being placed around the castle. His flesh pimpled.

"Hopefully we never have to use them," Vara said. "Ben, while I have the chance, I heard Elias in the hospital. He was talking to his friends, but they weren't with him. I think he was communicating with them somehow. After what happened yesterday, I thought I should tell you. Do you remember his Verdo?"

She's confiding in me.

Ben laced his fingers through hers again but this time more intimately. He enjoyed the flush it brought to her cheeks. Her lips looked so inviting, he forgot they were in a room full of people.

He never got to answer as Niall's father arrived.

"Nice to see you, Ben, it's been a while. You must join us for supper one evening. Deta and Niall would be delighted," Procter said, bowing.

Niall's mum, Deta, made the best roast dinners.

They fell in behind Procter as he worked his way around, much more animated than Ben had ever seen him.

"Yes, that would be lovely. I'll fix something with Niall," Ben said.

That was the only sentence Ben uttered. Procter spent an hour showing them everything, without stopping for a breath. All through their childhood, Niall and Ben favored the castle as Procter was kind of awkward to be around. Ben had asked Niall about that once and he'd said he had nothing in common with his father.

Ben had to interrupt.

"Excuse me for the intrusion, Procter, but I have plans today. Thank you for showing us around."

Procter returned to his working station, scoffing under his breath. Ben was still holding Vara's hand. They passed the wall of swords; thirty in total hung from metal hooks and were covered by a glistening screen that looked like a glittering waterfall—protected by magic. Ben wished he could hold one. His father's was at the top—made of the finest steel, with a stealthy leather handle and the Landis crest weaved into the material. He heard they were heavy.

"What's that?"

Vara was pointing at a glass cabinet. They walked closer, hearing the drone that surrounded the lock. More weapons fused with safety magic. "These are enchanted catapults."

"Enchanted?"

"Fairy made. I'll get someone to show us." Ben went to get Striker, who was happy to assist.

"Now, Ben, place the stone in the sling and aim for the iron wall that faces you."

Ben had never done this before. His stomach churned and he wiggled his fingers. *Don't come across as nervous.*

He pulled the sling back and watched the small boulder sail through the air. When it hit the iron backdrop, it punched a hole right through it, then sparks crackled as the metal mended itself.

"Wow," Vara said.

Ben shuddered at the thought of using this.

"Well done, Prince Benjamin. I'm needed back at my station." Striker flew off.

"Ben. Do you ever wonder why all this is necessary? It's just, I've been feeling different lately. Like something is changing. In a bad way. I've never thought about my power much and I'm wondering if my mind is trying to tell me something."

Ben wanted to hug her. She was worried too. *Is everyone feeling like this?* He was overwhelmed with a feeling of protectiveness. For her. For his island. *I want to take her fear away.*

"Vara, our world is strong. You don't need to be afraid."

"I'm not afraid. I want to be prepared."

She's strong. I like that.

"Thank you for telling me about Elias. He's rotten to the core. I don't know much about his gift but after what you said, I think we all need to be careful around him! I'll see if I can find out more."

Vara smiled. He felt more connected to her than he ever had. The time flew away. Could that really have been two hours? It felt like five minutes. "I wish I didn't, but I need to go. I'll walk you out first. Maybe soon we could go for a walk to Purity Creek and finish off with dessert at Furio's?"

Then I could give her the private time I promised.

Ben saw a flash of disappointment in her eyes and wondered if she was thinking the same.

"I'd like that." Vara kissed his cheek before walking away.

His skin tingled as he touched his warm cheek. *I want more time.*

In a daze, he made his way to the coffee cart. Coffee would be good.

I'll go to the hide hut.

As he turned the corner, he saw Bishop beckoning to two of the fairy guards. He could tell by the hushed whispers that something was up. He followed behind.

He knew every shadow of this castle. He had to with Tharmus

watching. He crept closer to the voices as Bishop led them to the school's confine office.

He strained to listen, but their words floated right under the doorway.

"We've been ordered to The Vale tonight as a matter of urgency by our informant. We need to check security and extend our search to the barrier."

CHAPTER 14

Niall

*S*o the king has sent me on a mission to find out who breached The Vale. *Priceless.*

That was what the meeting had been about. Niall had tried to work his mojo on the king. It didn't work. It had been the same with Ben.

And Gabriel. He was a problem. Always in the way.

Niall stopped and leaned into a nearby tree, pulling at the cuffs of his loose white shirt. Hives were appearing regularly now. He fixated on the distant forest, biting the urge to claw at his skin. A buzz sent his fist striking without any needed focus. His fingernails dug into his palm. What used to be a Glow Pinion—a long teal-winged insect that lit up in the night—lay disembodied inside the hollow of his hand. Unrecognizable.

Niall tried to call out to *her* in his mind, but she either wasn't there or wasn't listening. The irritation festered through him. After their first encounter, it seemed like they would be sharing one mind but that was not what happened. She crept in and out like a spider maneuvering through the cracks.

Can she hear all my thoughts? I hope not.

Eagerness drove his feet forward. His insatiable thirst needed quenching. When her voice did come, it stabbed, inciting bristles of fear. The main issue was Ben; she wanted to know about his gift and Niall sensed her growing disappointment.

There was a sudden presence but when he turned to check, nobody was there.

Was it her?

Her voice was there, screeching in his mind. "Someone is with you. Who, I cannot determine from where I am. Keep going. I'll guide you. I have strengthened your power so your whereabouts can go concealed from here. Close your eyes," Alunattra said.

Niall felt a shield of protection. He was no longer walking but moving toward the inside of The Forbidden Vale, the eerie darkness welcomed him like an old friend. Relief and desperation flooded his senses. To be so close to her again—the want for more power consumed him, yet something else was brewing. Obstinance toward her. He shoved this back down into his depths.

If I could get through to the other side, not as a servant but as an equal. He salivated. *Where is she?*

In the distance something—someone—was standing there, like an apparition. He looked closer, but he must have been mistaken.

And then, there she was, in a similar duplicitous form. Her veins poked prominently from her skin as she neared him. If it weren't for the barrier, he could reach out and touch her. Her head leaned to one side, beguiling him.

"Do not be troubled. Some things do not require answers, and do not focus on what I see and what I don't. It's irrelevant."

Niall gulped. He clawed at his itchy wrists.

"Instruction will always be given to you when it's deemed necessary. For now, be as you've always been. It's imperative you do not raise suspicion. The prince's power is strong; however, he's unaware of how to use it. It'll not be long till he figures it out. You must do better."

Niall seethed. *I can be as strong as Ben.* His eyes flicked to Alunattra. Did she hear that? *I don't think so.*

"I need you to find out more about Gabriel as well. He's an interesting one."

Not to me.

"Niall, you will listen and undertake my will."

Niall cringed at her scathing hiss.

"I'm trying, my queen, but it's hard to come between him and Ben —they're never alone. I'll try to make them talk this week."

"Yes, be sure you do. The girl will open up new doors for you.

People are weakened by what they think is love. Concentrate on encouraging that!"

Understanding had arrived. So this was her plan. Distraction. Throwing that stone and causing Vara to wince brought a thrill.

How would it feel to do something else? Something to cause more pain? To Ben. Or Gabriel?

His brain primped, filled with ideas.

"Pay attention, boy." Her long, skeletal hand stretched through the barrier and encircled his head. She looked deformed. All-powerful. No part of her ever touched him but a hum radiated through him in a helpless state.

How was she able to do that?

"Use this afternoon with your friends to gather information and draw close to Ben and Gabriel so I can gain insight. Suggest to the prince that he should ask this young lady to the upcoming dance. I need you to act as you always do. I'll be removed from your thoughts this coming week. This is a test and I expect results. Do not come here again unless I request it."

Alunattra didn't explain why. She was gone and he was back at Purity Creek, refreshed and absent from sweat patches. The red patches on his skin healed.

"Master Niall, did you find anything?"

And where did you come from Tharmus?

"You can tell the king I sensed a presence. I will be paying close attention to this, and I hope to find the person who's risking the safety of our island soon. And Tharmus…"

"Yes, Master Niall."

Niall walked slowly toward Tharmus. Niall's eyes bore into the underwhelming blue of the king's head guard. "You will do as I say when I say it, and you won't remember a thing."

Tharmus stumbled, walking away like he'd had too much wine.

"Very good, boy," Alunattra purred.

She had armed him once again with her dark energy. Niall realized two things. Firstly, the barrier was wavering, and secondly, some of his thoughts today he'd managed to shield.

Tonight would be interesting.

Tharmus and Pixel are under my control. How many more can I bend to my will?

It was time to build his army.

CHAPTER 15

Gabriel

G abriel put down his book and glanced up at the sky as he rocked on his porch swing. He considered Ben's words. *Could there be a world beyond our own?* The blue sky was without flaw and filled with puffed-out, snow-white clouds. They were almost too perfect to be real. It seemed impossible to know the answer.

Still an hour till I need to meet the boys.

They were going for milkshakes at Furio's then to Severo's house. He gulped. Would he get to see Cece? He could feel the perspiration form at his neck, and he tugged at his shirt.

I'll go to Purity Creek.

Gabriel didn't have clearance, but he started walking in that direction anyway. Lots of families were out in their gardens. People were laughing, children were playing.

Oblivion rules this world.

He walked onto the smooth green lawn that paved the way to the castle. The landscaped grounds resembled a tucked-in bedsheet, sprinkled with flower bushes bursting into bloom. As he moved to the high brick wall that enclosed the gardens, Gabriel saw Tharmus in the near distance. He was guarding the arched iron gate that led to the creek. The buzz of guard fairies was also in the air.

He tensed. He hadn't asked permission for this walk. Sometimes that took days to approve.

I don't want to get caught.

His body responded in a strange way. It was like it had the ability to produce threads. Every pore was heightened as these strings seemed to spring from his body.

My power. I feel it. He wiggled his fingers, loving the sensation flooding through him. When he looked up, Tharmus was focused straight ahead. *He can't see me. Emotions are definitely my trigger.*

How will I open the door without him noticing?

His body willed him to try something. He stretched his hand out toward the metal door. His hand disappeared in front of him like he was missing a limb. Next he tried his leg. Same thing. Half of his body looked erased. He fought the urge to laugh. He pursed his lips, scrunched his eyes, and took a full step through. Scared to look, he did it one at a time.

I'm on the other side. He patted himself down. *I'm intact. I can move through things. My body has its own intuition.*

What a buzz!

A bit dazed, he walked the sandy path, taking comfort in the field of daisies on his left and poppies on his right. He breathed in the peaceful silence and exhaled as the clear blue water sparkled before him. Gabriel slid off his new, dark brown brogues and let the warmth of the flawless sand encase his feet. He reached the water's edge and dangled his toes into the transparent water, basking in the icy trickle.

Something tickled his toes. It was the new creature they'd been studying, an Ortho. He lifted one out and was surprised at its sturdiness—long, slim, and eggshell in color, running the length of his hand. A bit slimy underneath but with a rough shell of protection on top. Whilst gently putting the creature back, a flash of dark gray reflected over the water. He turned.

Niall.

The left-hand side of the lake wasn't lined with trees but open, revealing The Crying Caves in the near distance. Where Niall was headed. Gabriel had always been reluctant to go there: They were too close to The Forbidden Vale. For years, school lessons taught that the whispers could set in beyond the caves and lead to the darkness.

Gabriel hurried, light on his feet, and crept behind the sporadic trees leading to the caves. When Niall's pace picked up, Gabriel shirked back but Niall caught him, or so he thought. The same springing feeling took over. His shield was up again.

The next thing Gabriel knew, he was crumpled on the ground, muddled in a blur. He opened his eyes and colored stars were circling his head.

I don't think Niall saw me.

Confusion swirled in his mind and fear took up residence. Something wasn't right. Niall had disappeared, and a roaming sensation of dread filled him. The contents of his stomach threatened to make an appearance. As he stood, Gabriel almost toppled back into the grass. Wherever Niall was now, he was not visible.

I need to go.

On wobbly legs, Gabriel started walking back towards the castle.

I'll try and ask Ben about this, but where to start? Will he listen? How strong is his friendship with Niall?

He wished they'd agreed to meet at the hide hut. It was kind of their place now.

Would Severo understand?

He had no idea. He stumbled, still a bit woozy.

All too quickly the castle was in view. He would try to stage a talk with Ben later. Niall—he wasn't sure what to do about him.

Gabriel was the last to arrive at the coffee cart. Walking towards them, he discreetly studied Niall's demeanor and there was nothing out of the ordinary. If anything, Niall looked better than he had in days and seemed relaxed.

"Gabes, my man. How you are?" Severo said with a teasing grin.

Gabriel laughed it off. *My one-liner will never be forgotten.*

"So, how would you feel about an epic-style games marathon at my place after Furio's?" Severo suggested, like an excited toddler.

Gabriel gulped at the thought of seeing Cece and self-consciously eyed his clothes, not something he usually did. He'd asked Fritzi this week to make him some new clothes with a bit more appeal. Fritzi had taken it seriously. Gabriel sported a beige drawstring shirt that hung over his breeches. Not his style at all.

Would Cece like it?

His thoughts were equal parts panic and elation. "Sure, that sounds good. How are you, Severo? After yesterday?"

"Grand, Gabes, grand. I got off with a warning, and Elias did too, unfortunately. Enough about that. Now we have a four-man pack, let's trek."

With Ben and Severo taking the lead, Niall fell into step beside Gabriel. "How's your week been, Gabriel?"

The question gave him a welcome distraction from thoughts of Cece. "Good, thanks, Niall. Yours?"

"Yes, the same, busy. Today's been the first time in a while I've switched off. I'm just back from a walk to the caves, and I'm glad to spend the afternoon with little to think about. Mindless fun is needed."

That was not the answer he was expecting. *So, it wasn't a secret where Niall was today? But where did he disappear to?* Gabriel second-guessed his hunch that Niall was the one who breached security.

"Gabriel, is everything alright? You seem lost in a world of your own," Niall said with genuine concern.

"Oh, sorry, yes, I suppose I'm getting used to being around people. It's all very new for me."

"To tell you the truth, I still feel like that now. I'm grateful for my friendships, and if it hadn't been for Ben all those years ago, I think I would've been fine on my own."

Gabriel was getting more confused by the minute. This was a Niall he could be on board with. "Maybe we're two of a kind, Niall?"

"Exactly what I was thinking. Gabriel, I wanted to ask you something." Niall stopped and stared at him.

Gabriel shuffled his feet.

What could he want to ask me?

"Could you tell me more about how your power works?"

Gabriel's skin tingled as pain shot through his eyes like a red-hot poker.

Ouch, my brain feels like it's separating.

He rubbed his forehead. When he forced his eyes open, Niall was bent over, throwing up in a bush.

Okay. This just got weird! I felt my power again. Was it protecting me or did I cause that?

Everyone was way ahead. Nobody was around to see this strange occurrence. Gabriel walked towards the bush and tapped Niall's shoulder. "Em, Niall, are you okay?"

"Sorry. Not sure what happened." Niall swiped his hand across his mouth. "That'll teach me not to overeat at breakfast."

Niall didn't catch his eye again, and Gabriel fidgeted with his now sweaty palms. His suspicions were back in full force. Gabriel quickened his pace as they navigated through the narrow lanes between houses. The village square thrummed with activity. The market stalls were open on Six and most of Landis was there, shopping the latest trends.

They arrived at Furio's. Gabriel wasn't used to seeing it from the front entrance. Large flower boxes decorated the tall windows. A bell chimed as Severo opened the door, and they all followed behind.

Severo stiffened, and Gabriel followed his eyeline. Norris, Clive, and several others were eyeballing him.

"Let's take our shakes to go, boys," Severo said, glaring back.

Gabriel sighed in relief.

I'll stick to my morning visits.

They took their seats at the counter, waiting, and he watched as Severo handed over several revils for payment. Lila buzzed before them, preparing their orders. She clicked her fingers and flexed her wings like she was doing a dance. Gabriel watched, transfixed, as ice cream, fresh fruit, and flavored syrups weaved through the air into their cups.

As they left, Gabriel was sure he heard Norris say, "I hope they're ready for what comes next."

Gabriel shivered and kept close to Severo on the way to his home.

They entered the large stone house. He couldn't believe he was walking into Cece's home. He'd almost spoken to her this week but bottled it at the last minute. He was surprised to see her at the arena yesterday, and he'd been taken with how she looked in her tryout gear. She didn't come across as the sporting type.

Please don't be going to the dance with anyone.

Severo shouted, "I'm home, family."

Gabriel's heart walloped, and he touched his chest. Cece danced into the living room as they entered. She was wearing a cotton house dress that grazed below her knees and was belted with a pastel blue belt that shaped her waist. He gulped. Her hair was twisted up on the top of her head, with her various shades of red curls fighting to be free. She was prettier than he'd ever seen her. Gabriel gaped, and she gave him a shy smile before turning to Severo.

"So, you're here for 'boys day'? What exactly do you have planned, brother? I'm on the edge of my seat." Cece anticipated Severo's response and ducked before the cushion hit her.

"Very funny, sis. You be good and run along. This is strictly boys only."

Gabriel struggled to get his words out. "You don't need to go. Join us if you want."

"Gabriel, you're too nice for your own good. Cece is busy. Isn't that right, Cece?" Severo said with a hint of pleading.

Cece hesitated and looked between Severo and Gabriel then sighed. "Yeah, Sev is right, but thanks Gabriel for showing us what it means to be polite."

Gabriel looked away but bit the corner of his lip to contain his smile.

"If you guys need someone to show the rules of Shriek though, give me a shout." Cece caught his eye and winked. Gabriel almost choked.

Severo was looking at him with squinted brows.

I better fix this.

The last thing he needed was for Severo to figure out he had feelings for his sister. "Would your mother like to play?" he asked Severo.

At this, all the boys lost it, and laughter filled the room.

"Gabes, man, you're too much. Come on, grab a seat. I'll set up," Severo said, then called to his fairy, Striker.

Twinkling fairy dust breathed into the room. Striker bumped Severo's fist with his body then flew onto his hand, relaxing his red-rimmed wings.

They act like best friends. Gabriel smiled.

"Can you help provide us with some tasty treats this fine afternoon?" Severo asked his fairy. "I will owe you one."

"Yes, I would be delighted, Master Severo, and at least I can keep my eye on you."

Striker fluttered his wings and tapped his fingers. One by one, the wooden dining table filled with some of Furio's signature delights: cream cheese vol-au-vents, plum duck pastries, and broccoli and cheese pastry cups. At the far side were the sweet treats: Tweetles, Minty Waves, and a new creation.

Striker clapped his hands. "Furio wants reviews of this new product called Crumble Cake. It has crushed biscuits and meringue laced with coconut and cherries and topped with fresh cream."

Severo moved toward the cake and Striker buzzed in front of his face, pointing his finger. "Let your guests have some first!"

Gabriel smiled when Severo held up his hands. The cake was enough for a crowd of twelve. It looked tasty and he took a piece. His stomach churned.

After eating, Severo set up Shriek.

Good, at least I know how to play this game.

Gabriel hated the boobie traps though, as they were situated all around the enchanted board. Each one gave a shock through the fingers. During the first game, Gabriel came close to winning. It came to sudden-death at the tip of the tower. A face-off with Niall. Niall won. Gabriel flinched. Niall held more than a competitive edge in his eyes.

Ben distracted him by shaking his hand at the end. "Impressive, Gabriel."

When he pulled his hand back, a square of crinkled paper sat in his palm. Ben looked at him knowingly, and Gabriel slipped it into his pocket.

As the afternoon continued, Cece didn't come back down, and Niall kept winning so they got to talking.

"So, gentleman, have you decided who you might ask to the dance?" Niall asked.

A baffled silence followed that uncomfortable question.

Severo was the first to speak. "Well, what do you know: Is my boy Niall finally on the level? This most definitely calls for celebration. More importantly, are *you* planning on going to the dance?"

"Well, yes, I believe I will." Niall's eyes lit up.

"Who are you going to ask?" Ben wasn't even trying to hide his disbelief.

"I thought I might ask Clara Waits. She has a quiet, studious countenance that would suit me well, I think."

Severo laughed and said, "Quiet and studious? Come on, Ni, tell us the real reason. That girl is all-out cute!"

"Yes, of course, I like her looks. I've still to ask her. I'll speak to her at school," Niall said, looking pleased with himself. "And what about you three? Who are you planning to ask?"

Ben and Severo shifted in their seats, avoiding each other's eyes. No way was Gabriel mentioning Cece. He didn't want Severo to hurt him. And he knew why *they* hesitated. Vara.

If it's obvious to me, it must be obvious to them.

Vara was playing them both like instruments, although he didn't think it was intentional.

Gabriel jumped to rescue his friends. "To be honest, I haven't thought much about the dance. Are you the same, boys?"

Severo coughed and Ben wiped his brow.

Ben downed his drink and redirected his focus. "Yes, there's still time to sort that but good for you, Niall."

"That I can concur. Hey, who says we need to ask anybody? We can all go together with Niall and his girlfriend." Severo nudged Niall in the shoulder.

Gabriel got up for a bathroom break and noticed Niall scratching at his skin. Niall sharply turned his face toward him, and Gabriel rubbed his eyes again. They stung.

What is he doing to me? It's nothing. It's nothing. He hoped more than he believed and shook it off.

It looked like they were all going to the dance. This was a first for him. After closing the door to the bathroom, Gabriel took the note from his pocket.

> *Sorry, I've not had the chance to talk much today. I wanted to let you know my mother is completely on the mend. Thank you again for your help, and my mother wishes you to have her thanks also. Something happened today. If you can, meet me at the fountains in the garden tonight, at hour ten. I'm going to The Vale. Destroy this letter.*
> *Ben*

Gabriel flushed it away. Anxiety was playing its very own drum-roll in his chest.

I will talk him out of whatever he's thinking.

He splashed cold water on his face and took in his appearance. As he closed the bathroom door, he found Cece standing there in the hall-way. He grabbed the doorpost and smiled. His hand was shaky.

"Hi," she said, grinning.

"Hi."

"Hi," she said again.

"Hi."

Oh brain, make my mouth work.

He noticed her neck was turning redder than her hair and unpracticed words escaped him. "I like your... your slippers." He wanted the power to reverse time.

Cece laughed. What a glorious sound. His heart hammered against his chest.

"Thank you. I like your belt."

His cheeks warmed, and they both burst out laughing.

Cece took the reins. "Are you trying out for Buzz Ball again this week?"

He needed a ventilator. "Yeah, your brother kind of forced me but in a nice way."

It was happening—his first conversation with her. He was sure if someone stuck him with a needle, he would be none the wiser.

"Yes. Severo was born with the power to persuade," she said.

Gabriel didn't want her to go. "Are you trying out? It seemed like you were going to last week."

"Would you like me to?" Cece held his eyes, and he wondered if she was flirting. His legs were seriously about to buckle.

He was about to answer when a distinctive knock came from the front door. Cece reluctantly walked away to answer it. Severo beat her to it. Gabriel hung back in the hall; he wanted to keep talking to Cece. When Severo opened the door, Vara was standing there with a strange look on her face. Pain? Sympathy? Gabriel wasn't sure, but these emotions seemed directed at Severo as she was looking right at him. She tore her eyes away to address Cece.

"Hi, Cece. I wondered if you'd like some company this evening?" Vara looked around the open-plan living room. "I can see you already have some. Maybe I'll come back another time?"

"Not at all. V, in you come. This lot is having 'boys night,' so come on up with me. We still have an hour till curfew." Cece grabbed Vara's hand. Gabriel noticed Severo and Ben couldn't take their eyes off their mutual love interest, but Vara kept her head low as Cece bounded to the stairs.

When Cece walked by him, she brushed her silky soft hand against his. All thoughts of Niall and the evening ahead became hazy in his mind until he caught sight of Ben.

Determination was etched into the prince's frown lines.

CHAPTER 16

Ben

en stood at the fountain, sheer force of will partnering his adrenaline rush. It was thirty minutes past curfew. The sky was a dark, velvet canopy, and the only source of light came in the form of hover clouds—clusters of fairy lights woven together that lined the pathways and gardens of Landis. He shifted from foot to foot, the sound of trickling water masking the quiet. Tweek had told him that his father and the guards were meeting tonight, so Ben waited until most of them had left their post before exiting the castle. He wished he knew more.

Ben wasn't waiting any longer. Something had changed in him. He knew his power could help.

I may not have asked for this, but I can't let anything happen to my people.

He crept over to the tall hedges but stopped when he heard someone panting. It was Gabriel. His friend bent over to catch a breath.

"Ben, wait. Sorry for the delay. My parents were late to bed. I think we should head back. It's too dangerous."

Ben gritted his teeth. "Gabriel, I want to know what's going on. My father doesn't tell me anything. If I'm to be king one day, I need to see how it's done. I'm sick of waiting around when it's obvious something serious is going down."

"Well, I'm not letting you go alone."

They walked in silence. Ben sensed Gabriel wanted to say something, but he didn't encourage anymore chatting. His head was too jammed full. They hurried past the fields to Purity Creek. Both kept to the shadows of the trees, hiding behind the branches. A threatening presence hung in the air like a taunt, stealing the night's warmth.

As they neared The Vale, they crouched low. Ben knelt, studying the ground. What should've been a stretch of luscious grass was now dull and weathered with streaks of black like a rotting infection. He hadn't been out this far before, but Pure Bay had always been a picture of beauty.

Maybe it was because they were so close to The Vale? No. He knew the truth. Evil was festering.

They scampered from tree to tree, then pulled back. A group of the Fairy Guard were at the perimeter, conferring.

"I wish we could hear what they're saying," Ben said.

"Look, four of them are moving in. Ben, this is a bad idea."

"C'mon, let's follow them." Ben moved with purpose, zigzagging between the trees until they reached the forest. Gabriel was panting but kept close behind.

Ben turned, pointing. "There's a gap in the trees. If we tread quietly, we should make it in without being seen."

All credit to Gabriel, it was clear he didn't want to do it, but he followed.

He has my back.

They entered the forest. The cold slashed his skin, stripping every ounce of heat. Ben pretended the determination he felt was enough to squash the fear that prickled every one of his pores.

"Ben, turn around."

Ben turned but couldn't see Gabriel. "Gabes, where are you?"

"You can't see me?" Gabriel said.

"No."

"Ben, my shield is up. I know what it feels like now. I think it taps into my emotions. I'm pretty freaked right now. It just popped up, and it's stronger."

"Keep it up, in case anything happens to me," Ben said with a nervous swallow.

Gabriel didn't say anything else. They walked further, and the air grew so noxious, Ben imagined it was what death smelled like. Damp and rancid. The roots of the trees slithered like snakes beneath Ben's feet.

This forest thinks I'm its next meal.

Ben raised a hand for Gabriel to stop. They were at the barrier. This was the first time Ben had seen it. It quivered in front of him, and although he could see through to the other side, it rippled in brownish tones, like a muddy puddle. "Gabriel, do you see what I'm seeing?"

Gabriel gasped.

A mirage in shadowed tatters floated across the barrier, then stopped. What looked like a finger was indicating to the fairies to step forward.

Bishop took the lead.

Does Grandad know his fairy is here?

Ben and Gabriel wavered as the ground rumbled and the sky above thundered. Lightning perforated the horizon, and Ben watched in horror as the shadow monster somehow projected its hands out through the barrier. Threads of charged sparks zapped from its nails, and four tiny specks tore out of the fiery forest. Ben looked up just in time to see sharp branches sailing through the air, straight for his heart.

He closed his eyes, but nothing happened. He looked up. *Did I imagine that?*

"Ben, are you okay?"

His heart thumped and his breath came short. "Gabriel, I thought I was going to die."

"I jumped in front of the flying debris. It bounced off my shield. Instinct spoke to me, if that's possible. I know, it sounds crazy."

"You saved me," Ben said, focusing his eyesight on where he heard Gabriel's voice.

"Technically, my shield saved *us!*" Gabriel rematerialized before Ben's eyes.

"I feel like 'thank you' is not enough, but thank you." Ben got up and brushed himself off. "Gabriel, we need to check on the fairies. I saw them forced out of the forest at some speed."

They dashed from the forest as quickly as possible, and Ben was immediately drawn to a plume of colored smoke rising high into the night sky.

The guard fairies.

Their once translucent wings were singed and smoking. Their light now dull as they lay void of life.

As Ben walked forward, he stiffened. At his feet was Bishop.

A siren blared. Ben grabbed at his ears, and Gabriel did the same.

"What should we do?" Gabriel said.

Before Ben had time to answer, an automated voice boomed through the darkened skies.

"PLEASE, DO NOT BE ALARMED. THIS IS A TEST, I REPEAT, A TEST. DO NOT LEAVE YOUR HOMES."

This announcement must have been heard in the village. Ben suspected most people would let it brush over them. His father would be here soon.

Ben gripped Gabriel's shoulder and pulled him up from where he had slumped. "We need to go."

Gabriel didn't budge. "We can't leave them, Ben."

Ben stared at his friend, and for the first time, he saw Gabriel battling with his emotions. Trails of a few fallen tears interrupted the soot glazing Gabriel's skin.

Something in Ben took charge. "We have to. My father will be here soon, with more guards and Tharmus. He can't see us."

"Ben, do you get what this means? Something has managed to kill part of our world. And since history tells us that the only being on the other side is Alunattra, I'm guessing it's her. That shouldn't be possible. How long before she comes for the rest of us?"

Hide my panic. Hide my panic.

"You need to calm down. My father will already have a contingency in place. Believe me, there is a lot that goes on that we don't know about. I'll find another way to get more info. I promise."

Ben saw the hope in his friend's eyes and wanted his words justified. What Ben didn't tell Gabriel was, he agreed.

Who else could it be? And if it was her, how long would it be before she pierced her way back through?

CHAPTER 17

Alunattra

You got what you deserved, Bishop. Yet, why do I not feel satisfied?

The girl she once was would never have harmed a fairy, but Bishop was different. Conniving. He had been the one to cast her in chains.

The boy, Niall, had carried out everything she had asked.

He is too strong, though. I don't like it.

Bishop had faced her, smug and self-righteous, and still had no idea of what she was capable of. It took her back to all those years ago. Nothing was better for the fairies and her Ebba. Where was she now? The fairies were, and always had been, prisoners. Slaves to Vallore.

I hate this world; I want to be free.

Alunattra punched her fist into the barrier, and it shuddered.

And soon I will be.

CHAPTER 18

A Notice from The King

It is with great sadness that I must inform you of the loss of four of our Fairy Guard during a routine check of The Forbidden Vale.

As a mark of respect, I declare a day of silence as we lay our precious fairy workers to rest, and I want to take this opportunity to thank the fairies for their continued service. We appreciate all that they do.

Please do not be alarmed. Regarding our current security measures, the barrier has been checked and reinforced by Vallore.

Please keep the Fairy Guard in your thoughts at this time.

Regards,

King Vardez

CHAPTER 19

Ben

Where am I? *Definitely a dream but not a familiar one. His feet were not on the ground.*

His body moved of its own volition. His skin started to prickle. The edge of darkness was near.

"Ben. Ben, I need you. You are the only one. Follow my voice."

A new, unfamiliar voice, but it didn't scare him. The desperation left him with the same helplessness his other dreams did, though. He bypassed Valor Rock and The Crying Caves and traveled towards The Vale. The voice pulled him.

The sinister creep of smoke enveloped him as he entered The Forbidden Vale, but oddly enough, he was encased in a protective bubble. Evil fought to find its way in and screamed in defiance. He wanted to wake up, but his body had other ideas.

"You are almost there; do not worry about the evil you fear. I have silenced it, but we don't have long." *Angst seeped from the unknown voice.*

He urged closer.

"I'm coming," *he whispered.*

BEN AWOKE FACE DOWN IN A POOL OF SWEAT, ACHING ALL OVER. HE RAN with unsteady legs to his bathroom and let the shower drench him. He shuddered as the cold water pelted his skin, opening his pores. This was new. Who was that guiding him?

"Are you still there?" Ben waited but got no answer. He dried off and slumped on the cold floor in defeat.

One more thing I need to add to my growing list.

"Master Ben, are you decent?" came Tweek's voice a few minutes later.

"Hold on, Tweek. I'll be right out." He hadn't seen Tweek yesterday after what happened, and he hadn't called on her. He was glad to hear her lyrical voice.

Ben's robe clung to him as he pondered the notice to all citizens. His father had lied. *Maybe Grandad could help me understand?*

Tweek's eyes were red and puffy.

"You doing okay this morning? I missed you," Ben said.

"To be honest, no." Tweek stared at the ground, her face somber. "The fairy village is in turmoil. We didn't know the guard fairies well as they kept to themselves, but the funeral was hard for all of us."

Ben knew Tweek. There was something else. "And?"

"Since you mentioned it, I'm a bit put out."

"What happened?"

"Did you know that Aristo and Perial have a day off today? A day off? Never before has a fairy had a day off, my prince. Yes, we are in charge, but if Vallore is allowing the king to hand out days off, it needs to spread evenly! Can you believe the absurdity of this? We were all affected by what happened, but this is special treatment." Her voice was so high now, the crystal chandelier on the ceiling swayed with a tinkle.

"Tweek, I'm sure it's all surrounding the current situation. There must be a reason, and it's only one day. Try not to let it upset you so much."

This response made her wings vibrate so fast, they looked fit to explode.

"Just one day! I admit, it never crossed my mind before, but if it's not that much of an ordeal, then why has no other fairy ever had a day off?" She flew right to the tip of his nose and stared him straight in the eye. "Why have you never given *me* a day off?"

"I've been thinking about this a lot lately, and you're absolutely right. You all deserve more. Would you like me to put a suggestion forward to my father?"

Tweek beamed and buzzed in circles around his head then stopped to drop a kiss on his nose. "Oh, would you? You are the best prince. Wait till I tell the fairies. This will give everyone a lift. A day off. This is so exciting." She flitted around with glee, and her colored trail made Ben dizzy.

"I'll ask, but don't get your hopes up, just in case. Tweek, now maybe you can do me a favor?"

"Yes, of course, my prince. Anything."

"I was wondering if you might know more about the breach of The Vale?"

Tweek darted back and forth, stopping, starting, and then stopping again. "Master Ben, please, never let it be known that we have spoken of this."

Ben put a finger to his lips.

"I don't know anything else aside from the fact your friend Niall is investigating this matter for the king. Although I'm sure you must know this already."

Ben pulled his robe tighter. He felt like something had just socked him in the stomach. He knew Niall interned with the guard sometimes, but this was not usual for a sixteen-year-old. *Why?*

"Oh, right. Yes," Ben replied.

"I've left your clothes out. The king and queen are just about to take breakfast. I'll inform them you're on your way, and thank you again."

Ben was barely aware Tweek had gone.

Niall's helping Father? I could have helped Father. The feelings he'd been trying to ignore bubbled to the surface. *Niall is Niall, don't overthink.*

He left his room. Tharmus stood outside his door.

Oh, great. He's back.

Ben wasn't in the mood for this. "Is it necessary, Tharmus, to walk me to the breakfast room?"

Tharmus didn't say a word, though. If anything, he looked a bit dazed. Ben walked in silence and didn't offer any conversation either. He heard more buzzing as they left the bedroom chambers and moved across the walkway. At the staircase entrance were three new fairies in black overcoats with crests of purple and gold—new guard recruits—not official Fairy Guard but guards in training. Ben shivered.

As he entered the breakfast room, his stomach growled. He hadn't eaten yesterday. His mother and father were at the table and looked up as he took his seat. It had been months since they last shared breakfast together.

"Good morning, darling, did you manage to get a good sleep?" His mother smiled at him, but her eyes were downcast.

At least her overall color was brighter. Ben still felt that he was missing something regarding her health, but he turned to his father when he spoke. "Yes, I guess. I hardly know what to say about the fairies."

"I know, son. It was a terrible loss. If anything, the Fairy Guard will need to take more care. There's a reason we're not allowed into The Vale. I hope it'll be a lesson for the people."

Ben studied his father, and his anger bubbled. How could he shift the blame when he ordered this? It was clear he had no intention of voicing the truth. Even his mother was fooled.

His mother nodded at his father's words. "Yes, my dear, I agree. How about a night off this evening? Perhaps a walk in the gardens?"

"Sounds marvelous. I'm looking forward to it already," his father said.

Ben watched them with envy as he ate. They were lost in each other. His stomach wasn't the only thing that felt empty. His mother and father didn't show much affection, but every now and then, he picked up on their intimate connection. Everyone knew how they met —Moline had been interning at the paper. It was the annual courting month, and she had given Vardez a letter from another girl who had been his intended wife, but the two of them had looked at each other properly for the first time, and that had been all it took. It was part of Landis' history. They married at eighteen after two years of courting. Shortly following their wedding day, they were crowned king and queen.

Ben wiped his hands on his linen trousers. *Will Vara be my princess or does she like Severo?* He hadn't missed the weird tension between them over the weekend.

"Grandad told me you had a girl—Miss Vara I believe—visit with you?" His mother winked.

It was like she'd read his mind. He blushed. "Yeah," was all he could think of to say.

"Well, for what it's worth, I approve. Do you think she might be the one to send you letters at courting month?"

Ben didn't have time to answer as his father interrupted their conversation.

"Now, Moline, leave the boy. He's the prince and will have many options. Plenty of time for all that. So, Benjamin. What are your plans for the week ahead?"

Ben blinked in surprise at the soft gleam in his father's eyes. "The usual. I have VDS training today. Nothing much has happened in the class yet, but I'm looking forward to it, and of course, we have the Buzz Ball tryouts on Five."

"Yes, that reminds me. I heard what happened, although I'm confused. Severo injured that boy, Elias? Benjamin, I don't want you mixing with people who behave in this way."

The hard look was back. Ben gritted his teeth. "Severo was not at fault. He was helping Gabriel. My friendship circle is one I'm proud of." Ben looked his father in the eyes.

His father mirrored the look and waited a moment before speaking. "Very well. I have no time for childish nonsense, so let that be the end of it. Are you trying out for Buzz Ball, son?"

This was a new bag of mixed emotions this morning. His father never asked about these things. "No, I'll be spectating, but I think Gabriel's trying out, so I'm rooting for him."

His father chewed thoughtfully. "Gabriel, yes. I was impressed with him. Please thank him for his assistance the other day. He's welcome here anytime."

Ben's surprise continued. He didn't want this breakfast to end. It was nice having a real conversation with his father. His thoughts shifted when his mother sprang to her feet.

"I have things to attend to this morning, but have a great day, Benjamin."

Ben watched her leave.

Is she okay?

She looked better at least. Ben searched his mind for answers but was rewarded with a headache.

"Father, am I right in saying, Perial and Aristo have the day off today?"

His father raised an eyebrow. "Yes, that's correct, but it's not something you need to concern yourself with."

"I merely wanted to suggest a fairy day off... regularly. They work with no reward, and I think they deserve it." He bit his lip.

His father swallowed the last of his buttered loaf. "Benjamin, I don't imagine you have ever seen the fairy quarters, but let me tell you, they live well. Vallore makes sure of that. They are his creations and don't want for anything. However, that may be a nice way to commend them after recent events. I'll take it under advisement and speak to Tharmus. Let me get back to you. Have a good day. I must get started."

Tweek would be pleased with this outcome.

Let's hope Tharmus doesn't spoil it.

It was still early when Ben finished breakfast, leaving time for a visit he wanted to make before school started. Concern filled him as he knocked on his grandad's bedroom door. He answered disheveled, still in his robe.

"Grandad, I'm so sorry about Bishop. Can I come in?"

His grandad nodded and led him to his chamber's sitting area, handing him a coffee. Something Bishop would have done.

"Can I do anything?"

"Thank you, Benjamin. I wish you could, but this is one of those times where feelings need to be felt, and healing will only come through grief."

Ben wondered what it felt like to grieve. He'd never lost anybody.

"This must bring back memories of my grandmother."

"Yes, it does. Your grandmother was a wonderful woman. I felt helpless when she died, and I feel helpless now. Never take loyalty for granted, Ben. Bishop was not only my fairy, he was my confidante and friend."

That I can relate to.

"Grandad, I have a confession to make." He stared into his coffee cup before meeting his grandad's eyes. "I went to The Vale two nights ago, and I saw what happened. I know I shouldn't have, but things are happening to me, and I need answers. My mind tells me I'm built for more but at times... my heart is not on the same page."

Ben jumped when Grandad's fist hit the solid oak table. His coffee spilled onto his china saucer.

"Don't ever be reckless, boy. I thought you were smarter than that."

Ben gulped. "I see that now. I just want to help. Something in me is taking over."

His grandad rubbed a hand over his forehead. "I suppose I can't condemn you for that. If I had been a lad, I might have done the same. One of life's gifts is finding your way. You have more responsibility than most, but you mustn't be spontaneous. There is only you who is next in line. Your safety comes first." He rose from his chair and went to the far wall. He synched his bracelet and pressed a button. A brick popped out, and he pulled out a metal container from inside the wall.

Ben couldn't move.

"I want you to have something." Grandad Bay handed Ben a pristine leather book. There was no title but on the inside page, it read *Book of Sovereign Dominions*.

Ben flicked through the gold-trimmed pages. This wasn't a book he had seen before. *There is so much writing in it*. He itched to read it.

"This is the only one of its kind. At the time of Alunattra's imprisonment, all these books were burned. I was fascinated to have been born of her line, and I managed to obtain one as a boy. How, is irrelevant. The information is somewhat cryptic, but reading between the lines will come. The government felt after Alunattra was banished, they must ensure no other person would abuse their powers, so they removed all temptation. Guard it carefully, and I must stress how serious this would be if put in the wrong hands. I hope it will help you."

The wrong hands? But who's?

"Thank you, Grandad. Can I just ask one thing?"

Grandad Bay sat back down and crossed his legs, waiting patiently.

"Is Alunattra the only person in Obsidian Creek?"

Grandad gave him a strange look. "Yes. She once had a wishing fairy, Ebba, but she wasn't cast out. In fact, nobody knows what happened to her."

Grandad didn't meet his eyes.

I wonder if he's telling me the truth.

Ben wanted to ask more questions, but his grandad said nothing else. They finished their coffee, then Grandad led him back to the cold corridor, parting with a kiss on his forehead.

Ben couldn't resist a quick look, so he found a shadowed alcove to sink into and opened the book. It smelled of mothballs, like old books do, and he shivered as the presence of old magic sang from the pages.

Ben located his Verdo in the table of contents and zoomed in on the subsection. Astral projection.

A difficult skill to master. An out-of-body experience that will separate your soul from its physical essence. Your divided soul is still fully connected to your body but can travel. If not truly grounded, injury can occur unless control is maintained. Meditation and mindfulness must take precedence to procure this ability.

This was good to know, and something he could control. Ben kept reading. Another point jumped out.

After practicing meditation, your mind can evaluate situations and create a way out. Therefore, manifesting the answer.

What on Landis did that mean? Ben didn't have time to read anymore, so he tucked the book into a zipped compartment inside his satchel. This book was a game-changer. He would keep it to himself for now.

As he descended the stairs, he heard the smallest of whispers. Aristo and Perial were heading out the front doors together. They were holding hands. Now it all made sense. Love was everywhere. Their annual courting month was coming soon, during which suitors wrote letters to the people they wished to court.

I'm already laying the groundwork with Vara. Will she choose me? Am I ready?

"Good morning, Nilla. May I have a coffee, please?"

"Yes, of course, Prince Benjamin."

Ben got his drinks on tap. His taste buds tingled as his coffee floated toward him. He made his inconspicuous way to Gabriel's hide hut, now quite the expert at popping the panel. Gabriel was waiting for him.

"Hi," Gabriel said, putting his book down.

"One of these days, I'll beat you here!" Ben lowered onto his cushion. "How are you holding up?"

"I don't know. Has your father said anything about the fairies and what really happened?"

"No, nothing. It's been swerved. I doubt we'll ever know."

Gabriel slumped on his cushion, looking defeated.

Ben racked his brain for a distraction. "I'm glad we at least had a good laugh at Severo's."

"Yes, that's true. How's your mother?"

"Fine. I think." *I hope.* "I've yet to tell you thank you, and by the way, you're in with the family. I also forgot to mention the other night what Vara found out. Elias apparently can communicate with other people without being near them. She overheard him in the hospital. I'm not even sure what this means. It must be part of his Verdo which could mean Elias is also experiencing escalation with his skills. Do you think that's why Elias looked at us when we were here last week?"

"That makes sense," Gabriel said. "At least we have the Conceal Dust now."

"Yes," Ben said, bringing out the dust and sprinkling it around the hut. He rubbed his chin. Something triggered in his mind. "So, for our powers to be on fast forward means something has changed. This shift we feel could be responsible for it, and our bodies are taking on a defense mechanism."

"Then danger *is* coming," Gabriel said. "I think the teachers know more than they're saying, and what about Clara? Do you think she's also affected? Is there some way you could ask Vara about it?"

"Just what I was thinking. I'm hoping to arrange a walk to Purity Creek with her soon. I'll bring the subject up." Ben picked a loose bit of skin from his lips. "I was also thinking of asking Vara to the dance. Are you asking anyone?"

"Oh. Um. Eh. I don't know. I was thinking we could all maybe go as a group. Like Severo suggested?"

"Do you want to ask Cece?"

Gabriel's jaw tightened. "How did you know? Is this part of your power?"

Ben laughed. "No. Don't take this the wrong way, but it's pretty obvious."

Gabriel's complexion resembled fresh milk. "Do you think Severo knows?"

"No, I don't think so. Severo doesn't always pick up on things. Thankfully." Ben sipped his coffee. "Maybe you should talk to him. You don't want him to find out after something happens."

A tinge of color appeared on Gabriel's cheeks. "So, you think something could happen?"

"I honestly don't know, but I definitely picked up on something with you guys." Ben was finding this conversation so odd. It hadn't been as hard as he had envisioned, though. "Let's do the group thing. Plus, courting month is soon, so maybe a group date would work? It would take the pressure off."

Gabriel sighed. "Yes, I think that'll be best."

Ben took another sip of his coffee and switched the topic. "This morning when I woke, I was on the floor this time." He filled Gabriel in on his weird dream. "I think it was real that I was there—at The Vale."

"Was it the same person you've been seeing in your dreams?" Gabriel asked.

"No, it was something else. The voice was in Landis, and it sounded trapped. Whoever it was told me that evil had been silenced but not for long. I woke before I got any more answers." Ben massaged the sides of his head.

"Here, take these." Gabriel pulled out a bottle from his satchel. "I had Fritzi source them yesterday. I've been having headaches when my invisibility catches me off guard. The weekend didn't help." Gabriel handed Ben a little bottle containing bright yellow bouncing balls.

"What are they?"

Gabriel shrugged. "Not sure exactly. They take away a sore head almost instantly though. They're called Pina Drops. Try one."

Ben unscrewed the lid and helped himself to one.

"Ben, something happened before we met over the weekend. I'd been for a walk to Purity Creek, and I saw Niall. I followed him, on instinct, and I thought he'd caught me. My Verdo kicked in, 'cause he didn't see me. I think he knew someone was there. Then he vanished without a trace."

Gabriel wasn't looking at Ben but staring at his lap. Anger bubbled inside.

Where did Gabriel get off?

Ben pushed down other thoughts itching to break the surface. "Are you planning to continue these covert operations? I thought I made my feelings clear on this."

"Ben, I don't know what happened. I felt compelled to do this. I wanted to tell you, but the other night didn't seem right. I'd wondered if Niall might be the person who breached The Vale."

Ben narrowed his eyes. "What makes *you* the expert on Niall?"

Gabriel winced but continued to rub salt in the wound. "Ben, maybe you don't know him as well as you thought you did. I had to be honest."

"Honesty with a side of sneak. I don't like double standards, Gabriel!" With that, Ben left the hide hut and stormed back into the south wing. His headache was gone. Deep down he knew he'd overreacted, but the agitation wouldn't leave. He couldn't help wondering if Gabriel was right about Niall.

CHAPTER 20

Ben

Ben slumped in every class for the next three days and avoided his friends. He didn't need anyone asking why he wasn't talking to Gabriel. The walk with Vara had been forgotten with everything else cramping his mind. All the gossip about the guard fairies just kept reminding him that he watched them die as he stood by. He was going around in circles, and the loss of control was like nausea that never left. His lunches were spent in the library, avoiding everyone, and the fight with Gabriel was on constant replay. Like a graph, his emotions were a ride of rise and fall, caught between anger and remorse. The one person he'd planned to confide in had the ability to get under his skin, and he felt like his life was crumbling.

The book was complicated. So much information about everyone's Verdos and other things too, like how the fairies came to be.

How we came to be.

Ben zigzagged through the rows of bookshelves until he found his recent spot—an archway between two bookshelves that created an alcove for him to hide. Behind him sat a stack of unfiled hardbacks. He sat with them, tucked away like a dusty, unread book. His eyes just wouldn't stay open.

His grandad still managed to find him though.

"Ben, you missed your meditation this morning, and why are you hiding from your friends?"

Grandad's head popped into view out of nowhere, and he sat cross-legged in the aisle opposite him.

"Where did you come from?" Ben said with a hint of bitterness.

"I'm worried about you. Meditation will only help you get a grip on your skill. My gift of Guidance will help, but you must practice. Now is not the time to stray from your friends."

Ben folded his arms. "And what if my friends are not what they seem?"

"Look closely at your friendships. You already have the answers. Trust your instincts. Relationships are not supposed to be easy. You have to navigate the curves. To halter at a bump is to divide, to move over it is affirmation." His grandad got up to leave.

"I'm due to meet your mother, but be at the meditation chamber tomorrow before breakfast. One more thing. I want you to have these." A small, metal circle with a heart etched in the center dropped into Ben's hand. When he touched it, he noticed it was made of two parts. Magnets that slotted into one another like a jigsaw.

"What's this, Grandad?"

"Affirmation."

Ben slipped the iron disc into his pocket. Sometimes he wished things could be spelled out, but that wasn't the way in Landis. He wondered what his grandad and mother were meeting about. He'd noticed them together a lot recently. At least she had color back in her face and seemed well.

He sighed and dragged his feet along the walkway to the stairwell. Three days had passed.

Enough is enough. I need to make things right with Gabriel.

Ben arrived in the lunch hall and placed food on his tray. His usual table was empty. He sat, picking at his choices. He'd barely spoken to Severo and ignored Niall's many attempts to talk this week. He waited. Niall was first in, and Ben couldn't shift the guilt when Niall took a spot next to him.

"Hello, Ben. I haven't seen you in days. How are you?" Niall asked.

"Yeah, fine," Ben mumbled. "I've been busy studying. I was disappointed after VDS, but it was cool seeing everyone's powers. I hope it gets better."

Niall stared at him with a piercing gaze. "Tell me what you know?"

Ben blinked his lashes and streams of water poured from his eyes. It felt hot on his cheeks. He splashed some water from his bottle into his palms and brought them to his eyes.

"Ben, are you okay? What happened?" Niall said, appearing concerned.

"You tell me? What did you do to me?" Ben said under his breath, rubbing his eyes. The sting blurred his vision.

"I don't know what you mean. I simply asked, 'Do you really want to know?' I was trying to tell you not to expect much from the training. I never do."

But that's not what you asked.

Niall seemed worried for him. Ben was confused and was not sure if this had been a trick of the mind. Severo and Gabriel were making their way over. Gabriel looked sheepish and reluctant, so Ben nodded to him to let him know they were good. Gabriel let out a sigh.

"Ben, my man, what's with your eyes?" Severo said, taking his seat beside Ben.

"No idea. I suddenly felt them get hot. I think I need more sleep at night. You boys set for tryouts this week?" *Safe territory.*

And there went Severo, lost on a mission to tell Gabriel the techniques of Buzz Ball.

Ben looked up as he felt her presence. Vara and Clara had entered the hall. He felt like the last few days had blended together with no sense of achievement, and he missed her. Ben was compelled to go to her. She may have looked confident, but he saw deeper. Her usual friends were now sitting with Clive and Norris. Ben scanned the lunchroom for Elias.

I heard he was back at school this week, fighting fit, and no doubt armored and ready.

Ben couldn't see him.

Vara held her head high and went to take her seat. Elias appeared from nowhere, put his foot in front of Vara, and she tripped, falling face-first to the ground. The lunchroom erupted into a mass of calculated laughter—all but Ben's table.

Ben leapt from his chair and saw Clara and a breeze of vermillion hair intercept the scene. Without warning, Cece took her fist and clocked Elias right in the nose. Ben heard a *crack*.

"Your nose needed improvement, and hey, I'm all about the greater good!" The room laughed again. Elias glared at her as blood streamed from his nose. He sprinted off, leaving a trail of blood spots behind him.

Ben watched Vara's burst lip heal itself before his eyes. "Vara, are you okay?" he asked. Severo was right beside her now too. Ben took a step closer to Vara and touched her shoulder. Severo glared at him.

"I swear, Vara, that creep will get what's coming to him." Severo clenched his fists.

"I'm sure your sister has that covered," Vara said, touching her lip.

"Cece, I believe you are entering my turf here," Severo teased with clear admiration.

Ben was impressed too. "That was a thing of beauty! Cece, how is your hand? I've never hit anyone. I heard it hurts."

Cece shrugged, waving her hand like it was no big deal. "I'll live."

"Why don't you ladies come and join our table?" Ben took the lead while Severo's beefed-up torso lifted an empty table with one hand to extend their seating area. Ben led Vara to a seat and sat down next to her. Severo went to take the other chair beside her, but Cece got there first. Severo gritted his teeth, and Ben avoided smirking at him.

What am I doing? This is pathetic.

Niall stood at this point and said, "Clara would you like to sit by me?"

Ben watched as she blushed and took a seat beside Niall.

He's so strange. Niall didn't follow suit when they'd all gone to check if the girls were okay, but he stood now. *I guess Niall must really like Clara.*

Gabriel leaned in. "Are we cool?"

"Yip, all good. I needed to wind down. Sorry I overreacted. Hide hut tomorrow?" Ben whispered back.

Gabriel nodded, and they both sighed in unison.

An awkward silence fell among them. Ben looked at the new seating plan.

There are girls at our table.

Cece broke the tension. "So, this is the infamous lunch table where it all goes down!" She remarked in a rhetorical way, taking them all in. "Fit for a king, Ben."

Even though Ben and Severo had been friends for years, he hadn't been around Cece much. She was usually scarce when Ben visited their home.

I'm not sure how to take her.

Most people either walked on eggshells around him or ignored him. Only his friends ever called him *Ben*. He liked that Cece was so bold.

Ben locked eyes with her, and there was a hint of a twinkle in them. It was clear her statement had been meant in jest. Ben grinned at her, and she did the same back. Just as he had her pegged as bracingly confident, a glimpse of something in her eyes awakened in him like a spark. It was well hidden.

What is happening to my brain?

It was like an out-of-body experience.

His mind transported him elsewhere. Cece was dreaming, and distress was written into every crevice of her face. As Ben peered deeper, he heard her say, *"How can I save you? Please, tell me. I'll do anything."* She was clawing at the air and her tears were falling in helpless desperation.

"Ben. Ben. Ben!"

Ben jumped when a roll hit him on the forehead. Severo was giving him a pensive stare.

"Sorry. I zoned out for a second. What did I miss?" Ben rubbed his cheek, aware everyone at the table was staring at him, and he could feel the concern flowing from Gabriel. He didn't want to look at Cece.

"I was talking about tomorrow," Severo said. "It turns out Gabriel's not the only one trying out, but the youngest Arison is too. Of course, I've advised her against this, and I'm looking for backup."

Ben blinked, recentering himself. "Sev, you know I have your back but in this particular case, I reckon Cece can hold her own."

Severo growled. Ben gave him a pointed look then welcomed Cece's winning smile.

She has no idea I just saw into her mind. That's good. Ben rubbed his tight chest. *Out of all the gifts, I get one that invades my friends' minds!*

Ben felt like he'd crossed a boundary. His power was growing in new aspects again. The book—maybe it could help. He had forgotten it was in his bag.

"Ben. You okay?" Gabriel whispered.

Ben grunted a quick yes back. *But am I?*

He still hadn't told Gabriel about Niall helping his father or the book and now Cece.

Can I even tell Gabriel this?

This situation was like a woven piece of material blending into intricate patterns.

If only I could switch my Verdo off.

He braved a peek at the face that always distracted his mind, but Vara didn't look happy. Ben tried smiling at her, but she looked away.

Is she mad at me?

He slipped his hand into his satchel and groped for a Pina Drop.

Girls should come with their own rule book.

Ben tried a different tactic. "So, what does everyone have planned for the weekend?"

Severo, as usual, took front and center. "We've a Buzz Ball meeting on Six so that's pretty much my weekend mapped out."

Clara timidly said her first words since sitting down. "Cece and I are meeting at Vara's dad's shop to sort our outfits for the dance." She gave Niall a side glance, and he inched closer.

Ben caught Severo staring intently at Vara.

Before he knew what he was doing, Ben said, "I was doing some thinking, how about we all go to the dance together? Safety in numbers? Clearly, Elias has us as targets now, and hey, it might be fun."

I just don't want Severo asking Vara.

Gabriel sighed in relief. Severo shrugged his shoulders and Niall squinted. Clara frowned, as did Cece, and Vara looked positively hostile.

Ben needed to lie down.

"How about aperitifs at mine, and we can all head to the party from there?" Severo said.

Ben watched as Severo and Vara shared a mutual glance. It was like a vise was pinching his brain.

As the bell rang, he hoped to catch Vara, but she was too fast on her heels. Gabriel fell in line with Ben on the way to History—his favorite subject.

"What happened at lunch? You blackout again?"

"I'm not sure. It's all a bit hazy. If it comes back to me, I'll let you know." Ben fiddled with his bag strap. "Is that cool about the dance?"

"Yeah, I think it's the best idea. I haven't really mentioned this before, but this business with Elias is my fault. I've been his target for years, and now he's expanding his net. I'm sorry I've brought you all into it."

"Gabriel, this is not on you. That guy has been a nightmare ever since Severo left his little group eight years ago, not to mention Elias is always making cracks at Cece." Ben remembered the brewing rivalry all too well. That and everything else was like a ton of weight. He had no energy left and craved rest.

That night, he collapsed into his waiting bed as sleep fed his soul.

It was her again. This time she was clearer, her multicolored hair framed her heart-shaped face, and her gray eyes showed contentment. She held her hand out to him. It felt like the most natural thing to grasp it and never let go.

He still couldn't form words.

She said, "You don't need to. I hear you. I wish I could hold your hand too."

Then, in the blink of an eye, she evaporated, and he was back on familiar turf. Flying, this time. He was at The Forbidden Vale, and the voice awoke his spirit within.

"Keep going, you're almost there."

He descended into the depths of darkness. A familiar feeling of safety kept him going—it guided him. He sauntered to the ground, facing the Tree of Vulnerability. It was majestic. He could not move as he stared, enchanted. Ben waited for what was to come.

"Prince Benjamin, my spirit has been lost in here for years, and I have been fighting for so long to be heard. We have little time. She is absent when I'm here, but very soon she will silence me again. You are the island's only hope. Please listen carefully…"

CHAPTER 21

Severo

I t was the day of tryouts, and Severo was more on edge than ever.

Please let it go without a hitch.

He kicked at the gravel on the way to school. A feeling of déjà vu accompanied his walk to the castle along with an unwelcome blanket of unease.

What a weird week it's been.

He'd kept to himself a lot, but so had everyone else. Even his sister Cece seemed preoccupied.

So much for old times. Everyone has someone else they would rather be with. I wish I could switch my feelings off.

He was pretty sure what he was feeling for Vara was love or the start at least. The chemistry they shared couldn't be denied.

But Ben likes her too.

Severo didn't want to be locked in a standoff with Ben, but he wasn't going to sit back either.

During his free period yesterday, he had gone to the common room in the lower south wing to see if his friends were there. They weren't, but Vara was. Having her so close ironed out all his tension.

I want to kiss her. She turned to him, and her eyes brightened. *I knew it. She feels it too.*

Niall had appeared then.

"Severo, just the person I wanted. I'm just about to meet with my chess club. Do you want to join?"

Severo gave his friend a blunt stare. "Niall. Do you know me at all?"

"It would have been rude not to ask," Niall said.

"Actually, I'd say it's the opposite. Later, Ni."

Vara had already left with her friend, and Severo had missed a chance again. Aside from VDS and Botany—which was his new favorite subject—their schedules never intertwined. Severo's dimples dented. Botany was later today.

At least we are going as a group to the dance. If Ben and Vara had been going together... Severo gave his face a slap to bring his current world into focus.

After getting his raspberry hydration juice, he slumped against one of the cool marble pillars. He shivered and welcomed the icy wave of his drink. Severo heard a scraping noise coming from what he thought were the wood panels. As he squinted into the corridor, Gabriel was removing a panel. Confusion flooded Severo. He faintly made out Gabriel's words, "So, you finally beat me to it."

This was followed by an all-too-familiar laugh. *Ben.* His instinct was to go and join them, yet Severo held back. He crept forward, pressing his ear to the wood, hoping for some clarification.

As he listened, it became clear only Ben and Gabriel were there with no sign of Niall. Niall was all about his chess club now.

But where do I fit?

"I just walked past Severo, but he didn't see me. I must have been cloaked again. I really wanted to tell him. I feel bad leaving him out," Gabriel said.

"I know. I do too, but if we tell him then we'd have to tell Niall. And I wanted to tell you why I don't think that's a good idea, but first, the Conceal Dust. I have something to show you."

Ben's voice faded out, and Severo couldn't hear anything else. It felt like something heavy was weighing him down. He could feel the fury building. The exclusion had not been his imagination, and he was clueless as to what Gabriel meant by *cloaked.* Niall wasn't in the loop either. Was this the way things were going to be from now on? Severo was not enjoying it.

Severo marched to the end of the corridor, unsure how he wanted to play this. That was when he saw Vara walking in with his sister, and his insides started to party.

Vara's so beautiful. He wanted to take her hand and run away from everyone. *But where would we go?*

The emotions swirling in his chest were incarcerated. "Hey, girls, how are we this fine morning?"

"Hello, Severo." Vara avoided his gaze.

At least there were no insults. He wanted to hold her. Severo forced himself to look away. "Cece, are you ready for battle today?"

His sister wore her game face. "As you would say, brother, I was born ready. I don't think the team is prepared for the goods I'm going to bring."

"You got this, Cece. Clara and I will be there cheering you on," Vara said.

"Well, I'm off to the library for my study period. See you guys at lunch." Cece danced off, light on her feet.

That left Severo alone with Vara. He'd forgotten how to stand. He squirmed, intaking breath as he prepared to start a conversation with the girl who had hijacked his heart. However, Vara beat him to it.

"Aside from lunch yesterday, I haven't seen much of you or Ben this past week."

Why did she have to mention Ben? Now Severo was irritated. "I'm sorry, is that a question?"

Vara sighed. "I'm simply making conversation. You know, passing the time till class."

"Well, here's your friend coming. She can take my spot." He stormed off without looking back.

I've done it again. Hurt the girl I care about. Ego, get out of my way.

He sat tight-lipped in his first class—Creatures of the Ancient—as he waited for Gabriel. This mysterious club and his friends' duplicitous behavior made Severo want to break something.

Gabriel arrived just on the bell.

"Cutting it tight this morning, Gabes. Where were you?" Severo watched him to gauge his answer.

"I didn't think I would make it. I just lost track of time." Gabriel fidgeted with his satchel.

So, Gabriel wasn't lying, but he wasn't owning the truth either. Class was ready to begin, so Severo didn't push it, but he would the first chance he got.

In Botany, he automatically looked for Vara. She was lost in conversation. The guilt was already building after the way he'd behaved this morning. He took his seat next to his lab partner, Walt. Walt was a brainiac, and Severo always sat with him in this class because of his intellect. Severo had aced every project as a result. Sometimes Walt droned on a bit, but today, Severo wanted someone to distract him.

"Walt, my man. How are you?" he asked, slapping his lab partner's back.

Walt started choking and stumbled on his chair. Severo flicked his own chair back into position. "Oops, sorry about that. I don't know my own strength. You good?"

Walt gave a nervous giggle. "That's quite alright. I'm fine. Thank you for asking."

"So, are you going to the dance?" Severo asked him, not sure what else to say.

"I don't think so," Walt replied without a flicker of disappointment. "They've just discovered some new plant life at Purity Creek, and I've started an internship. I'm helping with deciphering its qualities."

Severo wished for some of Walt's enthusiasm. "What's your Verdo again, Walt?"

"Plant Insight."

"Fantastic. Tell me more about that. Sounds interesting," Severo said.

Walt's eyes brightened behind his horn-rimmed glasses. Clearly, nobody had given him the opportunity to speak of his gift before. Severo was glad he'd asked now. He tried hard to listen and not switch off.

"This new Necal Dust will be used to instantly sanitize a room. Naturally, goggles and protective gear will be needed as it's potent and particularly dangerous if it were to get in the eyes. The test results have been astonishing, and it's almost ready to be released. We're just waiting on Weapons and Devices to finalize the product. It's fascinating, but unfortunately, it takes up all my time."

Necal Dust didn't seem all that exciting to Severo. His thoughts were interrupted when Elias, Norris, and Clive erupted into laughter. He twisted in his chair and stared at them.

Why are they smirking at me? Severo's knuckles turned white. *Elias better not be planning anything for this afternoon.*

Severo didn't think the principal would let either of them off with round two.

As he looked past Elias, he felt Vara's gaze on him, and his face smiled before his brain told him not to. She surprised him with an affectionate grin. His stomach flipped. He faced forward again, trying not to get his hopes up with these constant mixed signals.

"Good morning, class," said Professor Rose. "Today, we're going to start a new study. I'll be assigning everyone a new lab partner for this as it's important to gain new perspectives from others. The coupling will be as follows."

Just what Severo needed—a new partner. If he had to start studying now, where would that leave him?

Severo tapped his foot, waiting for his name to be called. Walt had already been partnered with Clive.

"Severo Arison and Vara Beautelle," Professor Rose announced.

Severo gulped, unsure if he was happy or not with this outcome.

"If everyone can go and sit with their new lab partner please, I'll announce the new assignment," the professor said.

Walt got up to leave, and with a look of discontentment plastered on his face, he glanced down at Severo.

"Catch you soon, mate," Severo assured him before Walt shuffled away.

"May I?" Vara asked, arriving at his table.

The over-polite formal chat is back I see.

"Be my guest," he said, overly sweet, and placed his hand on his leg. His knee had involuntarily started tapping off the table.

Stay cool.

Even in her plain cotton school dress she dazzled a room.

"Over the weekend, study up on chapter eight in your textbooks, 'The Life of a Sleacher.' Next week we will be visiting Purity Creek to have a look at these creatures in their natural habitat," the professor said.

After the announcement, merry chatter thrummed in the room.

"So, Vara. Maybe you could come by after school next week for a study session?" His leg was going again at a spasming rate.

The second she took to answer felt like hours. "Yes, that sounds good. When suits you?"

He didn't miss the rose-pink blush that glazed the apples of her cheeks.

Can she hear my heart beating?

"How about after school, on One? You could come for dinner, if you want. Our fairies make the best food, and I already know Cece will be happy to have you," Severo said, rushing out his words.

Vara's eyes sparkled. "Sure. Is it true that your fairies work with the head chef, Furio, at the castle?"

Severo relaxed. Finally, they were having a normal conversation. "Yes, that's true—hence, the reason we have the best food."

"Well, I think you need a second opinion. I'm happy to oblige."

As she finished saying this, her knee brushed his. His leg jumped, smacking hard beneath the table, and it split apart like a knife slicing bread.

The teacher ran over. "What's happened here?" she demanded. "Is everyone okay?"

Mortification settled over Severo. He bounded from his chair. "Yes, we're fine, but clearly this table wasn't holding up. I'll go and get another one from the stockroom."

As Severo left the room, Vara's soft tinkling laugh trailed behind him.

CHAPTER 22

Severo

The arena was set once again for Buzz Ball. Severo felt a tangible edge in the air as people arrived. The principal arrived first this time, no doubt to prevent a repeat of last week's event.

Vara and Clara walked in together, and Severo kept trying not to stare at Vara. Today was about Buzz Ball. She smiled at him, though.

We're making progress.

Niall walked in right behind Elias and joined Ben in the large expanse of bleachers. Had Niall been with Elias? Surely not.

A dark cloud settled over Severo as he avoided Ben's eye.

Cece entered through the tunnel with Gabriel.

Hmm. Do they like each other?

Last weekend, Severo had noticed them looking at each other, but Gabriel was so nice to everyone, the thought had left his mind. They were laughing, and Cece was bumping his shoulder. Severo's raw, brute muscles rallied up.

"Arlo. Can you round twelve players from our teams and get six ready for each side of the triangles? I'm thinking we'll add three potentials on each team. Once we start, I'll call the positions, and they can all stand on their dots." Severo rubbed his chin as Arlo nodded and skipped off.

Yeah, that would work.

The eighteen players would then be dispersed. Each team was made up of defenders, throwers, and scorers.

Players wore Boing Boots, specialized shoes that sprang the player upward when pressure was applied to the heel. Each player also wore a glove and virtual headset. The glove's trigger button could be activated when the thumb and index finger were pressed together. The fastest finger would draw the ball, and that player would become the ball commander.

When a person had ownership of the ball, it remained theirs. During a pass, the ball could be taken by anyone. The players could see everything on the virtual screen, and the aim was simple: to get the ball to the scorers and into the goal—a floating wooden barrel that moved of its own volition.

I hope everyone is ready to bring their game.

Severo had to look at her again. Vara was talking to her friends, but she was distracted. Not by him. She was looking at Ben. His stomach tightened then fluttered. He punched himself in the gut. His brain and heart seemed to be in a never-ending battle these days.

Focus on the game.

Severo lifted tables and set up the judging panel. All players were easy to identify in navy stretchy fabric, giving them more flexible movement during the game. Arlo handed out padded outer garments in lilac—essential for play. Elias stood cracking his knuckles and offered Severo a salute. He was being too pleasant.

Something is brewing. I can't believe I was once friends with that jerk.

Severo called the positions, and the two teams made their way to their allocated posts. Position one was across the middle and held by the throwers, highlighted in the headset in red silhouettes. The scorers held the second position, and their featured color was black. Lastly were the defenders and their outlines were light blue. Each player also had a number that floated in a circular bubble about their colors.

Elias and Arlo—the other team's captains—distributed the headsets and hand controls. The yellow ball stayed stationary until Severo activated it by throwing it in the air. The whistle blew. The crowd was soundless in anticipation. Gabriel and Cece were on the same side. Severo had appointed her the position of thrower, hoping it would be the safer option. She'd been unwavering about coming today. Gabriel was a scorer.

As always, gameplay was rapid and furious. Cece triggered the button in her glove, and the ball flew into her hands. She jumped and sent it sailing through the air to Gabriel. He pressed back on his boots, caught it, and sprang to the barrel, sending the ball sailing straight into the goal.

The first team to ten would win the game.

Severo's previous irritation turned to fascination. His sister just kept on producing new skills, and Gabriel's precision was on point.

Throughout the game, Gabriel scored the most points, aided by Cece who was hurling the ball from every angle. It was a good game, and Severo forgot that he was watching his friend and sister. The game ended seven to three, which meant Gabriel and Cece were on the winning team.

Severo, Elias, and Arlo conferred in a huddle.

"Arlo, Elias, as you know, we have three names to choose out of ten. I have two that come to mind judged solely on the state of play today. Being head captain, I'll have the final say. What are your thoughts?" Severo asked.

Elias stayed quiet, rubbing his chin. Arlo looked at them both and then said, "I choose Gabriel, Cece, and Erik. They all worked well together. Severo, you never told us you had an undisclosed weapon in the family."

"Hey, I'd no idea. Believe me, my sister is full of surprises. Before I state my names, Elias, can you tell me yours, please?" Severo waited, deeply curious.

Elias met his gaze with a bright smile. "I agree with Arlo. Those would be my choices. They played the best game, after all."

Severo held in his surprise. He had been sure Elias would vote for anyone but Gabriel.

His turn to pick. Cece was too good; he didn't have a reason not to choose her. This game got so rough sometimes, it would be hard to protect her, but maybe Striker could add an armor detail. "I stand in agreement with you both. Let's go and make the announcement."

Everyone was waiting.

"You all played well, and thank you for your participation today. The judging panel has reached a joint conclusion, and we would like to welcome our three new recruits. We have chosen Gabriel Johns, Cece Arison, and Erik Wallace. You will each be placed with your new team tomorrow at our practice game. Please be here mid-morning.

Well done, everyone." Severo concluded his speech with a clap of his hands.

Severo weaved through the crowd of players, making his way to Cece and Gabriel. They were hugging. His stride kicked up a notch. Now they were looking at each other in a way he didn't like. Severo barged right in between the two and put his arms around them.

"Hey, you two, so, well done and all that." He kept his hand a little bit tighter on Gabriel's shoulder than needed.

His face reddening, Gabriel pulled out of Severo's grasp and rubbed his shoulder. "I can't believe I got chosen. I honestly had no idea how today would go," Gabriel said in disbelief.

"You were amazing, Gabriel. A natural." Cece was googly-eyed.

"Right, Cece, time to get home. Gabes, see you at practice tomorrow." Severo pulled rather than escorted Cece out of the arena.

As soon as they stood outside the castle, Cece slugged Severo's shoulder. "Sev, you big oaf. Get your hands off me. What is your problem?"

"Nothing." Severo didn't care that she was angry. She was fifteen and too young for any romance nonsense. "I just thought we better get home, check on Mimi. She will be waiting for us."

Cece faced him with her hands on her hips. "Don't give me that; I can read you like a book. Let me guess, you saw me hug Gabriel after the game and decided I'm too precious and young to have anyone be within five feet of me?"

She wasn't wrong. "Look, I wouldn't exactly put it like that, but now that you mention it, pretty much, yeah!"

The red rant was coming.

"Let me tell you something, Severo. I'm my own person, and as much as I love you, I'll not let you dictate my life. You forget there are only ten months between us! Get your meat-filled head around that fact. I'm taking charge of myself, and moreover, trust that I can make the right decisions. To be frank, I find it insulting that you think I can't make up my own mind." Cece stormed off with her long, red curls darting everywhere.

Severo stood glued to the spot, staring after his headstrong sister.

SEVERO WAS THE DEEPEST OF SLEEPERS, JUST LIKE HIS MOTHER, BUT THAT night he couldn't shut his eyes. His sister hadn't said a word to him all night—even his mother noticed, but she didn't say anything. Instead, the fairies overcompensated with needless conversation.

He tossed and turned in his bed for hours, and just when Severo was about to drift off, he heard a shout.

"No, come back, don't leave again."

Severo jumped out of his bed and grabbed his robe. The sound came from Cece's room. Anger and worry fought for first place.

He threw open her door and dashed into the bedroom, ready for a fight, but there was no sign of anyone.

Cece shouted again. "I'll find a way. I'm so sorry—I love you."

Severo rushed to her bedside where she was writhing beneath the covers. Her eyes were sealed shut, trapped in a dream.

"Cece, wake up! It's me, Severo. I'm here, wake up." He shook her quivering shoulders and repeated his words.

Cece woke, shaking all over. Her eyes were tight with fear. When she came to and saw Severo, she burst into tears.

Scared by what had happened, Severo sank onto the bed and wrapped his arms around her. "Cece, what's going on? Tell me," he said, pouring comfort into his voice.

Cece took a shaky breath, and her panicked words came rushing out. "It's Father, Severo. He's alive…"

CHAPTER 23

Niall

N iall sat outside Vara's father's dress shop. A hopper sprang down the length of his black blazer, and he crunched it under the pad of his thumb and then flicked its remains. Hundreds of insects' lives had met their fate recently, but the darkness inside required more fulfillment. The waiting was taking its toll.

He scratched at his scabbed skin and peeled it, inviting the thrill that came with fresh blood.

He almost hadn't made it on time. He had an important task for Pixel and it kept him late. His chess club plans excited him. The ease of control was electrifying.

With *her* absent from his mind, frustration burrowed into his thoughts. It bothered him not knowing the game plan and being required to act without prior warning. Niall worked better with strategies, but he couldn't raise a dispute. He slumped and almost lost his balance as he grabbed for the flowered ledge outside the shop window. His dark clothing camouflaged him in the dim moonlight.

I need to be more careful.

Last week he discovered after hurting Ben's eyes that Ben could repel him and Gabriel was doing the same. Three times he had tried reading Gabriel's mind, and each time Niall had excused himself to throw up.

At least Clara is doing what she's told.

He only tolerated her because she served a purpose. Her power was strong, and that made it harder for him to control her mind.

Is her mind restoring the damage I'm trying to inflict? I can't have her telling anyone.

Vara was pacing in the shop, waiting for her friends. Niall tapped into his new aspect, and it was like he was right there, in amongst the tediousness.

The things I have to do.

Vara called for Prine. She answered, "Miss Vara, how can I assist?"

"I just wanted to check how the dress preparations are coming along?"

"All in order, I'm just finishing up my designs. I will bring out the options when your friends arrive. All the fairies are working hard this week. It's taken our mind off, well, you know."

Ha, yes, that was an interesting turn of events.

"I hardly know what to say. I'm sorry you have lost some of your friends. Prine, while I have you, is there any more news on The Vale breach?"

Prine flew right up to her ear and whispered, but Niall still heard.

So, Vara knew about The Vale breach.

"They still don't know who it is, but Master Niall is working hard for the king to find out."

He inwardly growled.

Why couldn't the fairies keep their mouths shut?

"Thank you, Prine, that's interesting. I'll call for you when my friends arrive."

This girl was no threat to him. She was just like the others—nosy with a taste for gossip.

Niall smelled the sickly-sweet scent of Clara's perfume before he saw her. He swallowed down the bile that threatened. He watched her enter with Cece. They hugged.

Pathetic creatures.

"Now that you have arrived, I'll call Prine for the big dress reveal." Vara clapped her hands, and her friends squealed.

Prine clicked her fingers and floating gowns of colored silks flew into the middle of the room. Niall rubbed the irritating sounds of "oohs" and "ahhs" from his ears. He couldn't watch anymore.

C'mon, Clara. Talk. She didn't.

Instead, he listened to the unconscionable chatter about the dance until finally, it came to an end. Niall drew back into the alley between the dress shop and the blacksmiths as the chime from the door rang out.

He slid off his black brogues and crept behind them. The shadows clung to him and the chill from the cobblestones radiated through his body. When they arrived at Vara's home, he climbed the towering tree with ease and slotted into a well-concealed nook.

Her annoying sisters answered the door and were hanging all over Cece. The redhead seemed to enjoy this. Strange the way they all behaved. The sooner this was over the better. He focused on their voices again. He could see right into Vara's bedroom. The three of them entered and sat on a large chaise lounge.

"Your little sisters are so cute. I hope I have twins one day. I love kids," Cece said.

"I can see that." Vara laughed but seemed distracted. Niall didn't care.

"Clara, have you any thoughts on your dress?" Vara asked.

"Well, I was thinking about all white, with a scooped neck and full, swinging skirt."

Good. Clara was talking.

"Wow, Clara, that sounds wonderful. You seem inspired."

"Niall always wears darker clothing so I thought it would make a nice contrast. I hope he will like it."

I won't.

"Oh, I didn't realize you liked Niall?" Vara said, sounding surprised.

"Neither did I, but after school the last few days, he's walked me home. We got on so well. He's so intelligent and very handsome."

Niall read Vara's expression like a book. Vara didn't agree, and he could tell she was dubious of him. *She should be.*

"Clara, would you mind getting us a selection of hydration juice from the kitchen?" Vara asked.

Niall sighed with impatience as Clara walked away in a daze. Bored, he turned back to the other two. Vara went to hold Cece's hands.

"Cece, what's wrong? I want to help. Whatever it is, you can trust me."

Niall perked up. *Did I miss something?*

"I wouldn't know where to begin." Cece appeared close to tears.

No doubt due to pointless romantic issues.

"Can I help?" Vara said.

Cece stood and wiped her tears as she paced. "That depends. How much do you know about visions?" She laughed with no humor and had Niall's attention now.

As Vara went to answer, Clara returned. "So, girls, what did I miss?" she asked.

"Oh, nothing much. We were just waiting impatiently to hear more about Niall. Clara, over to you. We want every detail." Vara smiled at Cece, and she returned it gratefully.

Hmm. I wonder what's going on?

"We've talked about anything and everything. I feel so dazed in his company though, I often forget what we've talked about. He'd been planning to ask me to the dance but is still happy that we can all go together. He asked me to dance exclusively with him that night. Isn't that amazing?"

"That's lovely, Clara," Vara said.

"Who will you both be asking to dance?" Finally, Clara was getting somewhere.

No one answered.

"You know, Niall told me that Ben has a huge crush on you, Vara, but still feels shy around you. I think Ben's planning to get closer to you at the dance," Clara said with a gloating smile.

Vara's eyes popped. "Seriously? Okay, that means a high-priority dress decision right now."

Good, Vara was where Alunattra wanted her. He'd heard enough. These girls were such simple creatures. Put a boy or length of fabric in front of them and they were deterred. He was doing what he was told. That was what mattered for now. He smirked.

They have no idea what I'm capable of. They will soon.

Niall climbed down and lurked in the tree's shaded groove, planning his next move. He would accidentally run into Clara on her walk home. He didn't like her. He understood the premise of attraction and was grateful it had bypassed him. The power trip that accompanied her obedience repleted him.

Only the Dark Princess had power over him, and he needed more of what she gave him. Her absence had started to affect him. Those two times in her presence had fueled him but the last two days he craved more power. Power that could only come from her.

He watched Clara leave but was drawn to the conversation happening at Vara's doorway.

"Cece."

Cece trotted back towards Vara's front door. "What's up, V?"

"I just wanted to say, I'm sorry we didn't get to talk more. I didn't want to bring it up in front of Clara in case you felt uncomfortable. Are you feeling better?"

Cece checked behind her.

The fool doesn't even see me.

Niall focused on her face for the first time. Dark circles decorated Cece's eyes. Intriguing.

"Honest answer, not really," Cece said, "but I'm working my stuff out and I have Sev. He's the best. It's not safe to talk here but maybe soon we can thrash it out. Thanks, though. These last few weeks have been odd, to say the least, but I'm glad to have you on my side. Sev said you're coming for a study session?"

"Yes, he even invited me for dinner, if that's okay?"

"Obviously. Hey, think of it as a second home. Oh, we have Buzz Ball practice after school, so do you want to come to practice? Then we can all walk back together."

"Sure, makes sense," Vara said.

I will need to stop that from happening.

Niall tried delving into Cece's mind as she skipped past, but frustration prickled.

It's not working. Again.

Niall yanked on some loose twigs till he heard a crunch, then crushed them in his palm. He didn't wince when the thorns broke his skin. This girl was of little importance to him, but he would keep what she said on standby.

He caught up to Clara instead. "Hi, Clara, what a lovely coincidence. I was just out for an evening stroll. Would you like me to walk you home?"

Clara blushed and slipped her hand in his. "Thank you, Niall, that would be lovely."

As they walked in silence, Niall resisted the urge to throw her hand away. He was keen to get back home. Ben was coming over for dinner.

"Niall, are you okay?" Clara asked.

"Yes, I apologize. I was waiting for the nerve to tell you how beautiful you look this evening." Niall kept up his shy pretense.

Clara hesitated at her front door, then leaned towards him and planted a kiss on his cheek.

"Goodnight. Thank you for walking me home," she said before she closed her door.

Niall scratched involuntarily at his face and glared after the girl who meant nothing to him. *How would it feel if Clara's neck was the branch I were to snap?*

CHAPTER 24

Ben

Niall's cottage sat smack in the middle of the village homes, off to the right of the gravel path. Tonight, it stood out. Bleak somehow.

Remember, it's Niall. Your best friend since your first day of school. No need to be worried.

The hydrangeas lining the roof's border were withered. Dying.

Ben gulped before gripping the door knocker with sweaty palms. No amount of pep talk calmed the internal storm brewing inside him.

"Ah, Prince Benjamin, please come in," Niall's mother said, taking his coat. "The fairies have prepared your favorite—braised lamb and minted potatoes."

Ben had never felt comfortable in Niall's home. It had all the bare essentials but was missing something. Warmth. He passed the kitchen worktops where device prototypes covered every inch of the surface. Proctor never stopped working.

"Thank you, Mrs. Smart. Is Niall upstairs?"

"Yes, he will be down in a minute. Come and have a seat at the table."

Is it just my imagination or does she sound more robotic than usual?

It was hard to tell. Mrs. Smart never really seemed present. Ben sat down as Proctor arrived and took a seat. The room felt colder.

Pixel floated a crystal goblet toward him. She clicked her finger and sparkling red grape juice filled the cup to its brim. Ben turned to thank Pixel, but the tiny fairy was gritting her teeth, and her gray skin darkened till it was almost black.

She looks like she hates me.

"Ben, it's been too long. Glad you could come," Niall said, taking a seat opposite him.

This just gets weirder. Niall was always formal, but the comment felt forced.

"Yeah, tell me about it," Ben said, trying to act natural. "Thanks for having me."

As they ate, Ben's discomfort grew. The silence made him squirm, and the small talk he tried to initiate came to nothing.

Why are his parents not speaking?

After dinner, Niall asked him to come up to his room.

"Bring your drink and dessert. We can have it upstairs. Pixel has made me a new game— I'll show you."

As they climbed the curved staircase, it felt like Ben was visiting this house for the first time. "Are your parents okay?" he asked. "Your dad normally talks more about his projects."

Niall turned, and Ben almost lost his footing. Niall's eyes darkened, and Ben wanted to look away.

"They're fine. Father is preoccupied with work."

It was more than that.

Has something happened to them?

Ben's body became warm. His head snapped up and his eyes felt like they were trying to stretch. Was his power trying to tap into what was going on? He shook his head, caught between wanting to know and not wanting to intrude.

Niall continued up the stairs.

"So, what's the game?" Ben said, trying to clear his now sore head.

"It's a board game," Niall said, entering his room. "I mastered Shriek a long time ago, so I thought it was time for a new challenge. This one's called Prediction. It centers around thought. You have to try and read what your opponent is thinking, and if you guess correctly, you win. First to ten points. Here's your playing piece."

Ben laughed as he took the piece of metal shaped like a small tree. "Well, that's hardly fair. You'll win every time. That's literally your gift."

Niall smirked. "You're right about that, so it can only be played with others that hold similar aspects. Like you."

I'm being put on the spot here. I don't want Niall to read me.

"Sounds a bit intense, Niall. I'd rather not. Let's just chill."

"How about one round, and if you don't enjoy it, we can get Shriek out?"

Is he testing me?

"Okay, fair enough. How does it work?"

"Sit down opposite me and cross your legs, like meditation. Then close your eyes. Think of something and I will try to guess what it is. It can be anything. I won't lie, but this helps me develop my skill to see if I can read people with their eyes closed."

I already hate this game. I like my mind to be my own.

Ben took his spot on the wool rug and Niall got into position.

What will I think of? Vara, Vara, Vara.

"Nope. I don't see anything," Niall said in a very clipped voice.

"Okay, so I get a point." Ben moved his piece on the star-shaped board. "Now it's your turn, Niall. Close your eyes."

Ben focused and tried again to search Niall's mind. He encountered an obstacle, like a brick wall, with a dark secret lurking behind it. Niall was shielding his thoughts.

He's cheating.

"I can't see anything either. Let's call it a tie. Get Shriek. At least we can get somewhere with that."

"Okay. Ben, can you go and open the window for me?"

Ben got up and strode toward the window. Although he faced the twinkling night sky visible through the glass, he could see behind him like he had eyes in the back of his head. His eyes stretched in their sockets and turned a one-eighty. This was new. His head felt tight but soothed by heat.

Don't react.

He didn't dare move as these new eyes watched in shock. Niall was pouring a vial of red liquid into Ben's drink.

CHAPTER 25

Vara

Vara stood at the coffee cart, watching students stagger through the open iron doorway. *Where is Clara?* No doubt late. Again.

Cece dug a playful elbow into Vara's ribs. "So, V, own up, which boy's it to be? The prince or the one I share a genetic pool with?"

Cece's question blindsided Vara.

I wish I knew.

"Do I have to answer?"

"Not at all but you can. As much as I love my bro, I'll try to show no bias. Consider this your safe space." Cece wiggled her finger, motioning to the small area between them. "I will add, Sev is my people, and as his sidekick, a word of warning: He's mush inside. Don't let the muscles fool you."

This comment made Vara feel worse. She sipped her treacle coffee, savoring the extra shot. She had to practice avoidance tactics with Cece. She'd known her for a week, but the girl was too perceptive. She could float from asking about Vara's father's satchel line to the intense inner workings of the island. She wouldn't change their budding friendship, though. Cece got her. It was refreshing. Vara moved the subject to safe territory.

"So, I'm trying to get my dad to create a new school dress code. What do you think?"

Cece beamed. "Finally. Anything to get out of these stuffy, unflattering dresses. And ask him to change the color. Pale lilac washes me out."

Vara laughed. She didn't mind the color but a cotton three-quarter length frock with no shape and a rope belt wasn't what she would choose either.

"Maybe we could have different colors?" Cece's eyes danced.

"I'll propose that. My dad is a design genius."

Cece bowed with a dramatic flourish. "That he is. Your dress for the ball—wow. The boys are gonna lose it."

Vara was torn. She wanted that to be true, but who did she want? She had feelings for them both. She'd been trying to work out if Cece liked Ben after their shared looks at lunch last week, but she didn't think so, even though Cece could sway anyone. Vara was just glad to see her in better shape. She was worried about her.

Vara leaned in toward Cece and brought her voice to a whisper. "How are things? Have you had any more visions?"

Cece shivered and looked around, jutting her head to the castle doors. Vara followed her gaze. Double the number of fairy guards were there. She felt her skin prickle. Yes, something was off. They couldn't talk here. Disappointed, she nodded back to Cece.

Vara drew in a sharp breath as Ben and Gabriel exited from the far hall. Severo was behind them but not with them. He didn't look happy. She glanced at Ben, then at Severo, and her stomach squirmed. She was glad she had stuck to just coffee.

"Gabriel, you got your game face ready?" Cece asked.

"I don't want your brother to hurt me, so I'm saying yes."

Everyone laughed, but a hint of awkwardness hung in the air, and it appeared there was more to it than her complex triangle.

I wonder what?

As they walked to class, Vara let out a deep breath, appreciating her new group of friends. She had no date for the dance, and her credibility was gone in school, but what she did have was this once impervious group that felt like a family.

These people are changing me, and I like this version much better.

Cece slid her arm through Vara's.

I need to make a choice.

So many people to consider with this one decision. She didn't want to tarnish the unshakable sibling bond Cece shared with Severo or the long-standing friendship with Ben, but inevitably someone was going to get hurt.

As Vara sat with Clara and Niall in the front stand watching Buzz Ball, her stomach churned, creating its own sporting event. When she spied Severo, her tongue stuck to the roof of her mouth. She wished time would move faster but pause at the same time. She wondered how it would be on her own with Severo. She quivered, remembering their almost kiss.

Then there was Ben, who'd sat right next to her at lunch earlier and been talking as if he hadn't been absent last week.

Where had he been anyway?

Sometimes it felt like months since the ceremony when it had only been just over three weeks. Ben had held her hand under the lunch table, and she'd wished they were alone. Whatever had caused this impulsive behavior softened her previous feelings. He seemed stronger somehow. She liked it.

"Vara, I hope we can get a dance together at the weekend. Maybe even more than one if I'm not pushing my luck."

"If you play your cards right, I'm thinking several." Vara winked at him, but the heat coming from Severo's stare felt like a burn. She couldn't look at him, knowing the pain in his eyes was real.

If only he knew what this was doing to me.

People always told her they envied the fact she could have any boy in school, but they had no idea how it felt to be on the receiving end of this torture.

She blinked back to the game, pretending to watch as she clapped her hands and cheered at the appropriate intervals. Clara and Niall talked to each other, sitting so close they would need to be pried apart. Jealousy stung.

Vara zoned in at one point when she noticed Cece staring at Gabriel from the sidelines. He'd just scored for his team. Cece had that all-too-familiar look plastered on her face.

She's into Gabriel.

Vara looked at Gabriel. He was smitten too!

How did I miss this?

Gabriel appeared lost in dreamy thought and tripped. Cece giggled. Vara glanced at Severo but he didn't notice. She wasn't sure what he would make of this. Vara was happy for Cece and Gabriel. She could picture them together.

As if her gaze created an electric band of connection, Severo's eyes swayed to hers, and she hoped her smile relayed her feelings, as confused as they were. His returned half-smile crinkled slightly at the corner of his mouth, and she wanted to soothe his dejection. She would have time tonight with their study session. She gulped.

The last whistle sounded, and Vara was like a child released from a disciplinarian as she quickened her step. She left Niall and Clara sitting where they were in their own world.

As she hurried toward the others, Elias approached Severo. They were both talking, and Elias laughed. That was an oddity, and it got weirder. Elias lifted his hand from his pocket to give Severo a high-five. Severo raised his arm to return it, but then he suddenly stumbled. His fingers clawed and rubbed at his eyes in panic before he crashed to the ground.

Vara stood stock-still, frozen to the world moving in slow motion around her. She barely registered Niall shouting for Clara to go get help. But that was when Vara saw him taking in the scene.

Niall's body language screamed concern, but his eyes swam with something else... victory.

CHAPTER 26

Gabriel

G abriel dropped the headsets he'd been collecting and sprinted to Severo's side, but he was too late. Severo was already unconscious. This large guy, who a month ago would not have recognized Gabriel in a sea of faces, who had been the biggest surprise of all among Gabriel's new friends, now lay convulsing.

The professors in the arena fled for help. Cece held Severo's head; strength poured from her as she smoothed his sweaty hair. Her eyes blazed with anger as she scoped the crowd, clearly searching for Elias. If he was still here, he was hiding. Gabriel reached for her hand, and she gripped his.

Gabriel felt crippled. When he loved, *he loved*, and this family had him.

I feel so helpless.

His hurt deepened when an anguished Vara stood frozen. Her eyes quavered, as if locked in a nightmare.

Why is nobody back yet to help?

"Vara, I'm going to get the king." Gabriel indicated for her to take his spot. Vara snapped out of her daze and rushed to Cece's side. Niall was standing in the distance. Expressionless.

I have to go.

Gabriel glanced once more at Cece, hoping to convey his feelings. She stared back, and in her eyes, various emotions swirled, fighting a battle with no winner. Gabriel got to his feet and ran faster than his legs were capable.

He left the arena and sprinted to the invisible gate, screaming, "HELP! WE NEED HELP!"

Tharmus appeared and descended the staircase. "What's the meaning of this interruption?"

Winded, Gabriel's words came out in staggered breaths. "Tharmus, you need to get the king and Ben. Severo is hurt. Please, can you find my mum and the doctor? Severo needs immediate attention. He's not conscious."

Tharmus went into action mode and activated the gate. "Come with me."

Gabriel was at the guard's heels, and when Tharmus moved with a purpose, he meant business. Tharmus halted at the hospital entrance.

"You, inform your mother and Dr. Lovett. I'll get the king and prince. Where is Master Severo now?"

"At the arena. Tharmus, be quick. And thank you," Gabriel said.

Tharmus looked at Gabriel and touched his shoulder. "Don't worry, your friend will be fine."

Gabriel found his mother at her desk, and she ran to him, looking him up and down.

"Mother, Severo is unconscious. I think something's harmed his eyes. We need Dr. Lovett in the arena now."

His mother swallowed, then raced into a nearby room, and returned within seconds alongside Dr. Lovett.

The doctor is so young. Will she know what to do?

Gabriel led the way, filling the doctor in.

"Has anyone informed his wishing fairy and family?" Dr. Lovett asked.

Gabriel hadn't thought of that but hoped the other adults at the game found Severo's mother. He knew only Severo could summon Striker, so he did the next best thing. "Fritzi," he said with urgency.

Fritzi appeared out of breath himself. "Master Gabriel, if this is regarding your friend, the fairies are at the scene. Miss Clara asked her fairy to round them up, and the professors rounded up the rest."

"Does Striker know?" Gabriel asked, as they reached the doors of the arena.

"Yes, I believe he's already there," Fritzi responded, staying close to Gabriel's side.

They had to fight their way through the crowd. For as long as Gabriel had been alive, no student had ever been rendered unconscious. He didn't understand why. Could Severo die? Everyone was there, and the king, queen, and Ben had created a semi-circle around Severo. The sea of faces was quiet; all wore tight expressions.

Gabriel joined Ben. "How is he?" His eyes drifted to Severo. His friend lay pale and lifeless. Gabriel swallowed the lump in his throat. He couldn't fathom how a person with such valor could look so vulnerable.

What can I do to make this right?

Anger ransacked his heart as he searched through the crowd for that despicable face—the one that had been behind years of his torment. There the menace lurked, crouched down behind the doctor.

Gabriel jumped up. "Stay away from him! King Vardez, he did this." Gabriel pointed to Elias. "He's responsible. Do something." Spittle sprayed from Gabriel's mouth.

The king's brows furrowed. More and more guard fairies appeared around the arena like they had multiplied overnight and several buzzed in a line before Gabriel. Families were huddled together. The king seemed unsure how to answer.

Is there more to this than just Elias?

Before Gabriel could get out another word to the king, Elias interrupted with a rote apology. "I'm sorry. Gabriel, you're right. This is entirely my fault. It was an accident. One I'll never forgive myself for. You see, I had in my pocket a product to take home for my mother to try. Necal Dust. It somehow opened in my pocket, and when I lifted my hand to give Severo a high-five, there was powder on my gloves. It's since melted my glove. Who knew this could be so damaging?"

Gabriel didn't believe a single word. "Liar, you meant for this to happen. Funny how you somehow knew not to remove your glove!"

Vara pushed her way to Elias's side, kicked him in the crotch, and started hammering her fists into his chest. Elias collapsed, holding his ribs.

"That's enough," the king commanded.

Gabriel watched a flutter of guard fairies swirl two rings around Vara's wrists, pulling her back. Vara did what Gabriel wished he had done. His eyes found hers, and they shared a sad, knowing look. Part of their team was down.

The king intervened. "Please, do not worry. We have everything in hand. Master Severo has a strong pulse and is breathing well. He will have the best of care." The king turned to face Elias. "Elias, go to the confine office now. We need to take a statement from you. This is a very serious matter."

Nothing in Elias's body language suggested any amount of remorse as he strutted off. Elias locked eyes with Gabriel in passing, and Gabriel saw something he didn't like. Elias had brown eyes. Eyes Gabriel knew all too well. They were darker than usual.

The king addressed the fairies. "We need to get this young man to the hospital wing now, and please, can you find Walt? I believe he's been manufacturing this. He will hopefully have some kind of antidote to this product."

Some of the fairies disappeared with immediate effect; the remaining ones banded together encasing Severo. Striker perched on his shoulder with a worried gleam in his eyes. The fairies spun in a giant circle, and Severo lifted off the ground in a bed of fairy magic. They worked with super speed and moved his body with delicacy and precision.

Gabriel was immobilized, horrified that a person could hurt another in this way. He watched his larger-than-life friend float away as he stood stagnant, rooted to the floor. His forearm tingled as an arm slid through his, and he turned, surprised to see the queen.

"Come, let me take you to your friend."

Gabriel looked up at this woman who he hardly knew, and the kindness in her eyes sent a warmth of serenity flowing through him. Her gift of Calm had not been exaggerated. He only then realized they were last out of the arena.

With the queen's aid, they followed the crowd soon after.

Norris and Clive sniggered at him as he walked past and mouthed, "One down, four left."

Gabriel lost his legs. The queen moved her arm to his waist, and he leaned into her. He was aware of a tiny buzz behind him. Fritzi. Gabriel couldn't bear anyone else getting hurt. This was all his fault. He'd tried to tell Ben before.

The queen held him firmly through the hospital wing's double doors.

Disinfectant hung in the air.

Gabriel spotted Ben first. He was situated outside a room, and he relaxed his shoulders when he saw Gabriel. The queen left Gabriel's side to join the king. Whatever she had done left a protective peacefulness over him, like medicine that worked long after the fact.

Fritzi whispered, "I'll leave you with your friends. Call if you need me."

Gabriel whispered back his thanks as Fritzi disappeared.

Ben stood there, tugging at his shirt. "They won't let us see him. Only his mother and Cece are allowed in the room. Gabriel, tell me what happened. I've already heard various versions. I don't get how anything could be strong enough to do this to Severo."

Gabriel's horror reflected in his friend's eyes as he explained what happened fifteen minutes earlier. The two then sat down on a wooden bench, defeated. Further words failed them. Gabriel saw Vara sitting on an opposite bench with her head in her hands. Gabriel nudged Ben, and he went to her side, placing his arm around her. Ben tightened his hold as Vara's body jittered with sobs.

How is Cece?

Gabriel desperately wanted to be there for her. He looked around the room as more and more people were arriving at the hospital. It was then that Tharmus strode to the center of the wing and boomed in his dulcet tones, "Everyone who is not a hospital worker, member of the family, or close friend, please leave and return to your homes."

Tharmus caught Gabriel's eye as he finished his command, and he nodded in kindness. Gabriel returned the nod, hoping it relayed a thank you. Nobody liked Tharmus, but Gabriel saw something in him that he suspected rarely surfaced.

He's not so bad after all.

The king and queen were the last to leave after all reassurances of an imminent solution were made. Gabriel panned his eyes over each of his friends; they were all lost in thought. He stopped, lingering on Niall's demeanor. He wasn't sure what to make of it. Niall was scratching at his arms and neck, and a puzzling expression contorted his face. Gabriel couldn't tell if it was worry or confusion that seized hold of his features. He walked toward Niall, and the way he shielded Clara—like an animal that needed to be tamed—perplexed Gabriel.

He had an idea. "Clara, I was wondering, maybe you could help?"

Niall tightened his grip on Clara's shoulder. "I already thought of that, Gabriel, but Clara has been having issues with her gift. It will take her a while to learn how to use it. It could do more harm than good. Isn't that right, Clara?"

Clara flicked her eyes from Gabriel to Niall before she lowered her head and nodded in agreement.

Gabriel stood silent for a moment. That could all be feasible, yet it also seemed too convenient. "Well, hopefully that will change. Your gift of Healing could be an asset." Niall's eyes bore into Gabriel. He looked away. "I just hope they know how to help Severo."

"It seems nothing like this has happened before," Niall said. "The doctor and nurses don't know how to treat it. This Necal Dust appears to have gotten into the bloodstream, and with it being so new, they don't have an antidote yet. It's poisoning him. The only thing they have in production is a goggle product, but it's not finished. Plus, that is a preventative, not a cure. Neither will be released for months. I don't know how Elias got hold of it to begin with."

Gabriel bristled. "How do you know all that? Has the doctor been out with an update?"

Niall's brow twitched, and he looked irritated with Gabriel—there was no mistaking that. "I have very good hearing. I heard it in passing," Niall said nonchalantly, glancing aside.

"When did...?" Clara started.

But Niall jumped in, saying, "Clara, would you mind going and sitting with my family? They must be very worried, and I don't want to leave. It would mean so much."

Gabriel watched this exchange in fascination as Clara concurred and then walked away. Bone-chilling goosebumps seasoned his flesh.

Gabriel only looked away as the doctor came out of Severo's room.

"Thank you everyone for waiting. Master Severo is heavily sedated and the pain is keeping him unconscious. The healing water from Purity Creek is cleaning his blood, and we're working with the laboratory team to develop a product that'll help resolve this issue with his eyes. We're hoping to right this within a few days."

"Are you telling us that Severo, in his current state, is blind?" Niall's shoulders relaxed.

The doctor raised her eyebrows at Niall. "Well, yes, technically that is correct, but as I said, this matter should be resolved quickly. If you can all make your way home and give the family some time on their own," she instructed.

"Should we at least go in and say something?" Gabriel felt desperate.

Ben got up from his chair, went to the room that Severo and his family were in, and tapped the door. Gabriel was right behind him. Cece opened the door a crack. Her eyes were puffy from crying.

"Thank you for waiting. You can come in and see him if you want," she said, her voice sounding deflated.

Ben walked toward Severo and took a seat by his bedside. Gabriel went to Cece and held her.

"Don't worry, Cece, it'll be okay. Nothing can bring your brother down. Stay strong." He pulled back and looked her in the eye, offering all the reassurance he could give.

"Exactly. I know that. It's messed up, though. This never should have happened. I mean, how did Elias even know about this product? I don't buy his story. I just wish Sev would wake up." Cece squeezed Gabriel's hand before going back to console her mother.

Gabriel moved beside Ben, and he expected Niall to follow, but he was gone. Striker was lying on Severo's shoulder, his wings spread affectionately. Nobody said anything, but the pain each one felt emanated through the silent room.

THE NEXT MORNING GABRIEL AWAKENED BEFORE THE MORNING LIGHT. Fritzi filled him up on coffee at the dining table without saying a word. "Fritzi, be honest with me, why hasn't Severo woken up?"

"I wish I knew. Nobody has had an eye injury before, and this Necal Dust contains powerful components. Blood poisoning has also been at play. It's not a straightforward injury. Products are never released until they are signed off with instructions for use. How this boy got the product, or even knew about it, is being explored."

"Please tell me Elias will pay for this." Gabriel's fists flexed.

"As far as I am aware, he's been suspended pending investigation," Fritzi said.

At least Elias couldn't hurt anyone else if he was confined to his home.

"How are you feeling this morning, Gabriel?" his mother asked, kissing the top of his head before getting a cup for her coffee.

"Much the same. Can I come with you?" he asked, giving his mom a pleading stare. "I want to check on Severo before school."

"Well, it will depend if Tharmus allows it. We can always try." His mother looked dubious, but he followed her out and walked with her to the castle.

Severo needed to be okay. Gabriel wondered for the umpteenth time why Niall had left without trying to see his friend. Ben kept staring at Niall yesterday at lunch.

I hope Ben is being careful around Niall. Gabriel knew Ben had been for dinner with Niall but didn't know how it went. *Can I even ask him about that? I don't want to be at odds with him again.*

The castle doors were open. He hadn't realized they opened so early. Maybe it was for the workers. On closer inspection, Gabriel realized it was for a different reason. Fairy Guard recruits perched atop the white curved bridge. More security. Where had all these fairies come from?

His mother gripped his elbow. "Wait here," she said before going inside.

His mother returned to buzz him in. Tharmus had come through again.

Gabriel moved through the hospital doors. Cece stood outside Severo's room, and she was crying. He ran to her. "Cece? What's happened? Is Severo okay?"

She nodded but couldn't speak. Without a word, she led him by the hand to Severo's bedside. He was sitting up with his eyes open. They looked red, sore, and the skin around his eyes was irritated.

"Severo, you're awake." Gabriel sighed in relief, biting back the happy tears that threatened to fall.

"Gabes, my man, is that you?"

"It sure is," Gabriel said, breathing easier at the sound of his friend's voice. "You gave us all a scare." His friend looked so weak, and although he was talking, he wasn't looking Gabriel in the eye. His eyesight still hadn't been restored. "It's so good to see you." Gabriel instantly regretted his choice of words.

Severo's pale lips formed a smile, and it livened his features. "Ha, I wish I could say the same, but hey, it's only temporary I'm told. For now, I'm loving all the attention," Severo said, a bit too sure of himself. "Has Vara been by?"

Gabriel didn't know, but Vara's soft voice tinkled behind him. "I'm here, Severo. I came as soon as I woke up. How are you feeling?"

Severo sucked in a deep breath. "You owe me a study session." He laughed.

"Well, what do you know, I preempted this and brought my books." And true to her word, she pulled out her Botany textbook.

"Vara, you need to learn how to take a joke!" Severo teased.

At this, Cece caught Gabriel's eye and indicated with a head tilt to leave the room.

Gabriel followed her out and closed the door behind him. "Cece, is there anything I can do?" He stared at the girl he was falling for. His fingers twitched, longing to wrap his arms around her. He felt utterly helpless.

"You're already doing it. Thanks for being here. Ben's been in and out as well, but I know Sev was waiting for Vara." Cece sighed. "What a mess. I swear if I ever get my hands on Elias..." Her sentence trailed off and every aspect of her clenched.

Gabriel stepped in impulsively to give her a hug, but she pulled back.

"I better get Severo some water and organize food. He must be starving." Cece laughed awkwardly before making her way to the nurse's station.

Cece was pulling back.

I get it. Severo comes first.

Gabriel told his mother to pass on his goodbyes and that he would be back on his lunch break. He made an on-the-spot decision to go and visit his father in Weapons and Devices. It was time to find out why they didn't have a cure for Severo yet. Walt had a permanent working space there.

Maybe he can help us?

As Gabriel crossed the walkway, that familiar tingle started in his toes till it covered his body.

My cloak is up.

Gabriel continued walking and pulled back when he saw Tharmus. The guard wasn't alone. Niall was by his side. They entered Weapons and Devices.

Gabriel closed his eyes and took a step forward, hoping he could move through the iron door. Not only did he make it through, but his bracelet didn't buzz when it should've been going nuts without clearance.

He fell in behind Niall.

CHAPTER 27

Ben

"Ben, over here."

Ben followed the whisper and saw the crack of a door open. He entered from the dark alley into the back of the cake shop.

"You do like your secret hideouts, don't you?" Ben laughed and Gabriel relaxed.

"You're getting to know me well. Follow me to the best booth in Landis."

Morning light teased through the bay windows, creating golden pools on the marble floor as they walked to the tucked-in table at the back. Before they even sat down, Lila was there, twirling her fingers. Fresh strawberries swirled into Gabriel's waiting glass followed by sticky, pink syrup and cold milk, topped with a plump cherry. All week long, Ben and Gabriel's morning routine had been in the hospital—this was a welcome change.

Lila did a double take. "Oh, it's you. I mean, sorry, Prince Benjamin. What can I get for you?" she blushed, and her orange skin brightened.

"I will go with your favorite, Lila. Surprise me."

Lila whirled so fast Ben's head spun. She floated a glass over from the hanging rack above the counter, and he watched as different ingredients flew from the cupboards: chocolate sauce, fudge pieces, ice cream, and whipped cream. His stomach churned, but he offered a beam of thanks, and she bowed. Once Lila had returned to her duties, he sprinkled the Conceal Dust.

"Thanks for your note," Ben said, spooning a dollop of cream into his mouth. "It's getting claustrophobic in that castle. Sorry, we haven't been able to talk. I owe you an apology." He couldn't look at Gabriel and kept his eyes locked on his ice cream.

"For what?"

Ben sighed. "You were right about Niall." Ben paused before meeting Gabriel's eyes, but his friend nodded without judgment and waited.

"Niall is up to something. I just don't know what. He spiked my drink at his house."

Gabriel's eyes widened, and he nearly dropped his spoon. "He what? Wait. Are you okay? What happened?"

"Nothing. That's the thing," Ben said, chewing his lip, "it was like I grew a new set of eyes. There was a throbbing heat in my head. When I turned my back, I could still see everything behind me. I faked a headache and left. So weird. My gift saved me, I guess. Like it knew before I did."

Gabriel shook his head up and down. "Instinct. Mine is doing it too. Our powers are preempting danger. Ben, why do you think Niall did that?"

"He keeps hounding me about my power," Ben said, holding his spoon idle inside his glass. "He wants to know how it works. My body always responds before I can form words and stops me from saying anything."

"Niall knew about Severo too," Gabriel said.

Ben looked up sharply. "What are you saying?"

"Only that he knew. I don't know how." Gabriel slid his ice cream glass aside and dipped his head in close. "He also mentioned that Clara is having problems with her power. It seemed suspicious. It's not just Niall, though. Too much is going on. At the arena, I saw it. Everyone is getting freaked. Guards are everywhere. What do we do, Ben?"

Heat filled him, making his power swell. *I'm getting stronger.*

"I've got this," Ben said. "If nobody is telling us the truth, then I'm going to find a way to get answers. I've had more dreams. The girl. She's so much clearer now. I can feel her, but something is separating us. The recent voice I'm hearing keeps pulling me out. Gabriel, the voice leads me to the Tree of Vulnerability. I know I'm there. I spoke to my grandfather, and he's given me a book. I'm not supposed to share it, but I had to tell someone. This book gives more isolated details about our Sovereign Dominions and part of my power can cause my body to project itself. I think that's what's been happening in my dreams."

Gabriel raised his eyebrows. "Does that mean you are able to be in two places at once?"

"I think so, but it's so unpredictable. I don't know how to stay put or how to pull back. The closest I've gotten to the tree, all I got was a jumbled-up sentence... 'You have the power and the eyes to see, with a few who will help you be, all you can be. Beware the stare, hate lies there.'" Ben scrunched his hands in his hair.

"I think we need to consider that this voice could be talking about Niall," Gabriel said, his brow furrowed. "He was in Weapons and Devices the other day when I was visiting my father. Tharmus and Pixel were there too. Niall's father took them through every device in production. I followed behind. Niall absorbed everything. Tharmus seemed kind of dazed. That can't be good."

"I hate to admit it, but I think your instinct about Niall was spot on. I guess I refused to see it out of loyalty. We need to be careful. I brought my grandad's book. I hope it might help you. You cannot let anyone see this."

Wide-eyed, Gabriel took the book. "No, of course I won't. Thank you. Is there only one copy of this?"

Ben nodded and filled him in on what his grandad said. "We better go and see Severo. I just wanted to have a chance to catch you up." Ben got to his feet and turned back to drink the barely touched ice cream float. He forced it down and gave Lila a thumbs up on the way out.

"Any change with Severo?" Gabriel asked on the way to the hospital. "My dad told me Striker has been sick with worry this week."

"Striker hasn't stopped looking for a cure. Walt is helping. Hopefully, they'll have something soon." Ben didn't want to consider any other outcome.

His grandad and father were coming out of Severo's room when they arrived.

"Ah, Benjamin, Gabriel. Your friend is filling up on Tweetles. He sure can eat!" his father said.

Grandad ruffled Ben's hair. "Severo is looking well. We will leave you to it. I'm off to meet with your mother. We'll send more treats down for you all later."

"Thank you," Ben said, glad Grandad was looking out for his mother. Things had been better with his father this week too. A pleasant change.

His mother had everyone working hard, and it seemed a welcome distraction. After days of observing her demeanor, he knew something was still wrong, but she was a closed book. Ben vowed to get to the bottom of it. If only Severo could be cured first. He was alert sometimes, asleep others. Niall floated in from time to time and stood at the back of the room, absent from the conversation. *I'd rather he was around so I can keep an eye on him.* Vara was there at times too. Nobody knew how to be. It was as if this one event had rocked each of them in very different ways.

Strangely, Severo was the only one that seemed like himself, but Ben knew it was a front. The frustration ate at him. He wished with every ounce of his being that he could've prevented this from happening to his friend.

I wish I wasn't so wrapped up in my own world all the time.

Ben couldn't begin to imagine how it must feel to lose your vision.

"Good morning, boys—oh, and girl," he quickly added as his eyes landed on Vara, who offered a subdued smile. Could it be that she was more beautiful today than yesterday? Guilt pinched his insides.

"Tweek," he called.

Tweek arrived, winked, then clicked her fingers. Hydration juice, lemon and strawberry pastries, and chocolate coconut squares popped into life along the window. She left Severo a special blended drink—a rock-solid twist and shake—along with more Tweetles at his bedside.

Ben smiled. "Thank you, Tweek." She placed a kiss on his cheek before leaving in a puff of fairy dust.

"Tweek has prepared a smoothie for the big man, along with a monstrous side of Tweetles, and for the rest, your morning coffee and cake." Ben handed the coffees out and left the extras on the window ledge for the others, still to come. Would Clara show up to have hers? She hadn't been around much. Ben shivered.

What is Niall up to?

"Sweet. Mimi and Cece will be back soon with morning rolls galore, but I'll take the Tweetles to start. I finished my last lot." Severo wiggled his fingers. "Fill me in on school this week. What's happening?"

"Not much really," Ben said, tapping his restless finger against his coffee cup. "Incessant talk about the dance mostly, and Walt was asking for you. I think he'd like to visit. He's working round the clock to help with a cure for you."

"Ah, yes, the dance. We need to finalize our plans." Severo pulled his knees up to his chest, tucking his sheet over him. "Anything to get me out of what I can only assume is an unflattering hospital gown!"

Ben scratched behind his ear. "Maybe it's best if we all sit the dance out—"

"Try stopping me from going," Severo interjected, folding his arms across his chest. A spark of his strength shined through the obstinate front. "I'm not letting this 'incident' spoil my fun. I intend to be there, and I'm going home tomorrow. Apart from the fact I can't see, everything else is working perfectly well! Tell Walt to come on by. I could do with talking to him. After speaking to the doc, I put two and two together. Walt was filling me in on Necal Dust in class, and it was as if Elias heard the whole thing. Who knows how? He was at the other end of the room, but it's too coincidental."

Silence fell in the room as Ben looked at Vara, then Gabriel.

Severo straightened up in his bed. "Why the quiet? Was it something I said?" he asked with a slight edge to his voice.

Ben peered through the blinds to check the hall was clear. "Sev, there's something I should have told you, but I just didn't think. Hold on a minute." Ben retrieved his Conceal Dust from a pouch in his satchel and sprinkled it along the edge of the room. Vara stared at him with her eyebrow raised.

Ben returned the Conceal Dust to his satchel and faced his friends. "Vara discovered that Elias has developed a way to hear distant thoughts, which means he can communicate with others out of his vicinity. Elias must have heard what Walt told you and went from there." Ben gritted his teeth. "What I don't know is how he got his hands on it!"

Severo's face reddened.

Is he angry? Does he know something?

The silence turned to tension as Cece and her mother walked in.

"Hey, team, grab a roll before Severo inhales yours! Ooh, coffee and pastries, thanks, Ben." Cece took a second to realize nobody was responding. Her mother remained unaware.

Cece blinked. "What did I miss?"

"Not as much as me clearly. Cece, will you show this lot out? I'm tired." Severo shifted, rolling over in his bed, abruptly ending any further conversation. His mother hurried to his side.

Severo knows I've kept things from him. Of course, he does. Some friend I've been.

The guilt dug deeper. "Severo, I'll come back on my lunch."

"Don't bother, I have a busy day planned."

Cece looked at them all in turn. "I think you guys better go. I'll walk you out."

When they got to the end of the corridor, Cece stopped and shot them a scathing glare. "Do you three wish to explain that?"

Ben hung his head, unsure what to say, and Vara and Gabriel mirrored the motion.

"My brother has been through enough this last week and what he needs is support. I don't really care what's going on but fix it, and fast. Come back when you're ready to do that!"

Cece's anger and frustration cut like a knife. Her words stung, putting Ben in his place, and deservedly so. The time to tell Severo had passed. He needed to know the whole truth.

As the bell chimed, the three of them sauntered to physics class without a word. Vara nodded as she took her seat next to Clara, still subdued.

Ben pulled his eyes away and turned to Gabriel. "Hide hut, lunch?"

"Just what I was thinking."

In Meditation, his second class of the day, Ben welcomed the smell of essential oils as he lay down on his soft cream mat. Flower tapestries hung around the room; the floor was the color of grass. It felt like lying in a meadow. He breathed in the calmative aromas. He needed some time alone with his thoughts. Life had always been simplistic—now it was full of complexities. Niall's signature scent of washed linen wafted over, announcing his close vicinity.

It was getting harder to act normal around him. Instinct told Ben to play it cool, though.

They both began their breathing exercises.

"How was Severo this morning?" Niall asked between breaths.

Ben swiveled toward his friend and felt the detachment reach a new level. Their eyes met. Ben tried to pry behind the layers. Telepathy was an advanced aspect of his gift but how to access it wasn't clear. He closed in on Niall's secrets, but before Ben could glimpse the truth, Niall blinked, and the grip was gone.

"He was in relatively good spirits, just tired," Ben said.

He didn't mention more. His own fatigue and consuming thoughts pressed upon him, so he lay back and centered himself. Niall said nothing else.

As he zoned out, the professor spoke to the class.

"Now breathe in, and out. Use this next hour to disengage and feel your inner strength." Her lyrical voice made the tension escape from his body.

The warmth radiated through him again. He remained calm, and it felt like part of his body was being peeled away. This was a first; instead of a dream, he was awake and aware.

Keep control. Keep control.

Thinking of what his grandad's book had said, he kept his consciousness tethered. As his soul detached, he saw the class of students before him—all lying still. He floated, weightless, just like he'd read in the book. The magic rippled through him. He connected to it, like he had wings to fly, taking the control. Ben was at one with his power as his soul led him through the castle to Severo's hospital room. Cece sat by his side.

She must have a study period.

They spoke in low voices, but their words rang clear as day. They had no idea Ben was there.

Wake up, wake up!

He didn't want to be here without them knowing. The guilt from earlier still festered. He tried to move, but his soul was in charge. His body might as well have been drowned in cement.

"Sev, what was that about with your friends earlier? I didn't want to ask in front of Mimi."

Ben tried to move his hands to cover his ears but again, in his spirit form, it couldn't be done.

"It doesn't matter. Just leave it," Severo replied.

"When have you known me to leave anything? Would you rather talk about Father? Because I'm all ears on that subject. It's not going anywhere. I had another vision by the way."

"Cece, you don't give up, do you?" Severo ground the heel of his palms against his temples. "Fine. You want my opinion, here it is. What you're experiencing is called dreams. You know, when you go to sleep and nothing's real. Look it up in a book. Father's not visiting with you. I don't buy it. You need to learn to move on. I have. And as for my 'friends,' they've formed some sort of hush-hush club that even has a headquarters."

Severo laughed with a bitter edge, and Ben would have squirmed if he could. "Not sure what the requirements are to join, but I don't fit the bill, or Niall it seems. Not stuff I've ever had to think about before and I hate being forced to now. To top it all off, my best friend and I are in love with the same girl. So what do you have to say to that, Cece, because now *I'm literally all ears*."

Cece gave her brother a blunt stare. "Wow, you're really lame, aren't you?" She nudged his shoulder and laughed. Severo hesitated at first but then laughed with her.

Come on, body, why won't you move?

Ben could have cried hearing this. It was like being tied down and forced to watch his worst nightmare.

If someone did this to me, I would hate them.

His friendship with Severo meant everything, and the speech he just uttered was one hundred percent justified. He'd just betrayed his friend. Again.

Ben would find a way to fix this—he had to.

Oh, now my body starts moving again?

His astral self was doing its own thing. He could still see his class; everyone rested in a meditative state. He drifted through windows until he wasn't in the castle anymore. Soaring over 'The Row,' he phased through a house and found himself on an upstairs landing he didn't recognize. Ben froze in midair as Tharmus faced him.

Is this where he lives? Come to think of it, where's Tharmus been?

He hadn't been hanging around Ben in the shadows lately.

Tharmus stood tall and at ease. Ben shimmered right through him, resisting the immature urge to taunt his father's head guard! He passed through a doorway and saw Elias pacing in what Ben presumed was Elias's bedroom.

So, Tharmus is guarding Elias.

He was muttering under his breath.

"Cancel the next wave of the operation. I need to lay low and wait. I'm in enough trouble. Besides, we have other things in the pipeline."

There was nobody else in the room with Elias.

Ben focused. A visible thread was connecting Elias to something. Ben's eyes projected out again, and he followed the link. Elias was talking to Clive and Norris.

Unbelievable. This is how his power works.

Ben listened further.

"Yes, but now is the time to act because you're not at school. They will never suspect you," Clive said.

Elias chuckled. "Since when are you the brains, Norris? I do have to agree, however. Maybe take it down a notch, though. Subtlety is key."

Elias had no moral scruples. At least Ben was forearmed this time. He would need to fill Gabriel in and look up Elias's gift in the *Book of Sovereign Dominions*. Maybe then they could stop any further attacks.

Ben was merely a passenger as he took to the clouds, flying at a falcon's speed across Pure Bay. Ben tried to resist—to pull back into his body—but to no avail. This time, there was no voice calling him, just an ominous force that pulled him against his will. He descended into the forest of nightmares. His feet landed in the withered grass, but he felt nothing. He turned toward the Tree of Vulnerability.

Silence.

His eyes were drawn to the barrier, which started to spark. Beams of electricity showered upon him, harmlessly floating through his transparent frame. As he stared at the bleak emptiness before him, black smoke started rising on the other side. The same raven smoke he saw before was stretching itself through the barrier. He couldn't move. The blackness elongated further and curled behind him. His eyelids would not close, and he was forced to stare straight ahead in a trance.

The black swarm sprang forward—within inches of his face. It curled behind his head. His All-seeing Eye saw everything. His body seemed far away, yet he felt the rapid pace of his heart, his breathing leadened in his chest. Distant voices echoed in his eardrums, trying to wake him from what was becoming a real-life nightmare.

Ben couldn't get back.

The intricate black threads churned and writhed, slowly forming blotchy, grotesque features. The only lucidity in this web of whirling smokiness manifested in its center mass. Red-rimmed eyes, and irises as black as coal, lurked there like a hungry beast. Below the eyes, a jagged hole emerged. Ben couldn't look away.

Spiked teeth protruded, and out of the mouth came the words, "You have finally come. Soon, Benjamin. Soon."

It was her. Ben was shackled.

Full, bruised lips formed and peeled back over the razor-sharp teeth that prodded the barrier. The face boomed an eldritch scream, splintering through Ben's soul.

His body recoiled, but the sheer force of the scream catapulted him out of the forest. Glass shattered, and intense pain sliced into his wavering unconsciousness. His eyelids fluttered, staring up at the room he'd just fallen from. The window was smashed to smithereens. Blood trickled from gashes scattered across his body. He shifted on the floor and winced. Heart-stopping pain pulsed from his leg; a bone jutted from his skin. Bile rose in his throat.

"Tweek," Ben moaned, feeling faint. She was there, her screams muffled, as if underwater.

He didn't want to lose consciousness. He couldn't go back there. That face would haunt him.

Other people were there with him now. He was being carried. His eyes grew heavy, and his vision darkened.

"Prince Benjamin, you must stay awake."

Tharmus is helping me? That's a first.

Ben zoned out again. He could feel the comfort of a bed below him. Sleep.

Yes, I need to sleep. I'm so tired.

"Get Orthos, Sleechers, and Scorchlings. Now," someone shouted.

Ben detached in his state of unconsciousness, floating up and out of himself. Reality crawled along as his broken body lay on the hospital bed. The sheets were splattered crimson. His mother and father arrived. His mother threw up all over the floor, and his father's legs gave way. Tweek nestled in his hair, sobbing.

My body looks deformed with all these broken bones.

His astral self was aware of a crowd gathered outside the room, but he couldn't tear his eyes away from what was happening right in front of him.

He watched as the doctor administered soothe serum through his body's veins. Ben was transfixed. The fairies, the doctor, and a nurse placed Orthos all over the protruding bones. His twisted leg sat unnaturally as well as several limbs in his body—all fractured. Pincers appeared from under the Ortho's shells and gripped the shattered bones, clicking them back together. Large brown dollops were placed on his body—Sleechers. They slid over his body and slurped up the excess blood before infection set in. Bright red Scorchlings seared the open tissue and healed the skin. It was like watching miniature fires expand and contract over his skin. There wasn't a trace of a scar. The nurse was spraying healing water all over his body.

I don't feel any of this.

"The prince is going to be fine," the doctor told Ben's parents. "It looks worse than it is. The good news is he got here in time. I'd like to give him a transfusion as he's lost a lot of blood. The fairies are retrieving that from the blood bank and will be here to do that soon. He'll need to stay here tonight for observation but should be fine to be discharged tomorrow."

His mother and father shared a doubtful look, but they both nodded their thanks. They took a seat on either side of Ben's bed and took his hands in their own. Ben couldn't feel that either.

My body must be numb all over.

"How could this have happened, Vardez?" asked Ben's mother.

He wished he could hug his mother in answer; she looked so fragile.

"I don't know. The professor told Tharmus he was lying perfectly still in meditation, and out of nowhere, he stiffened in distress as if he was pinned down. Then he..." His father stopped to catch a breath. "Twisted in the air before flying out the window. I'm just grateful Tharmus got him here in time."

His father's eyes glassed over. Ben wanted to tell them he was fine, but communication wasn't possible. They didn't say anything else.

The door opened, and his grandad entered. He stared right at Ben's astral form and gave a deliberate wink.

How's that possible? Can he see my astral self?

"Now, Ben," Grandad said, standing at the bedside. "You know you need to wake up. There's too much worry in this hospital wing. Be a good boy for your parents."

"Now's not the time for complacency, Father. Can't you see how distressing this is?"

Ben watched this exchange with interest. Two very different-minded men stood before him. One very set in his ways and one that took life in his stride.

That was the moment Ben became one again. He could feel his mother's gentle hand in his. He tried to open his eyes, but the effort took more energy than his body could give.

The doctor and fairies returned with the blood, and everyone was politely asked to leave. As the fresh blood made its way through his system, a whisper of his strength returned, but he still couldn't open his eyes.

In a matter of minutes, the job was done, and his family was back in the room.

"If I may," the doctor began. "What Prince Benjamin needs is rest, and my advice would be to return in the morning. It's unlikely he will wake before then, and I wish to encourage an air of positivity in his presence. Please return to your chambers and have some well-needed rest too. I can assure you your son is in the best possible hands and will be back to his usual self tomorrow."

Ben tried again to open his eyes without success. He felt his mother kiss his forehead and whisper, "You're all I've ever been able to have. I love you. Please sleep well, my Benjamin. I'll see you tomorrow."

His father squeezed Ben's hand and cleared his throat. "We'll be back tomorrow morning, son. We love you."

If Ben could've choked on invisible air, he would have. His father had never told him he loved him, and ironically, he felt annoyed that this was said while unconscious. However, that passed as the reality of the words hit home.

His grandad ruffled his hair and whispered so Ben was the only one who could hear. "My brave boy, we'll talk tomorrow. There is much to say."

And with that, the room went quiet.

BEN STIRRED WHEN HE SENSED MOVEMENT AT HIS SIDE. HE RUBBED HIS blurry eyes, registering where he was. His head hurt as fresh memories came rushing back. He winced and jerked to a sitting position in his hospital bed. Pain became a sidekick to every one of his muscles.

"Ben, can I do anything?"

Ben relaxed at the sound of Severo's voice. His friend sat in a chair facing his bed. "Severo, how long have you been here?"

"Oh, about as long as it took for everyone to leave. It's pretty late. I tell you, you do go to some lengths just to get a conversation with me." Severo laughed.

"Well, I had to do something to rectify the prize fool I've been." Ben searched Severo's gaze for signs of improvement in his condition but detected none. "How did you get in here anyway?"

"I walked."

Ben cringed.

"It's okay. I know what you meant. I've discovered the use of my other senses, and my boy Striker made me something cool." Severo pointed to his eyes.

Ben squinted at his friend; Severo's blue-green eyes appeared deeper in color. "What's that in your eyes?"

"I had an idea. No sarcastic comments, please. You know our Buzz Ball headsets? I asked Striker if it would be possible to make something that could sense people through heat spots, and he spent days in Weapons and Devices putting together a prototype. Sensor discs. I'll level with you, Ben: It's looking doubtful I'll get my sight back. The doctor says too much damage has occurred. These sensors can at least tell me where someone is in a room. Striker modified them to color coordinate so each person I speak to will have their own color. You're a dark blue silhouette. That'll make things easier, and Striker's already looking at ways to add more advancements."

A knot constricted Ben's throat, crippling his speech. Severo couldn't be cured.

"I don't need my eyesight to know what the silence means, Ben. Pity I can do without. Do you really think I'd let this get the better of me? Maybe you do, after all, it seems we don't know each other as well as I once thought."

Severo was right. If it was him, Ben wouldn't want that either. Ben took a breath, thinking of how to explain the last few weeks.

"I'm not sure where to start, but I'm going to do my best to get you up to speed. First, I need Gabriel to be here, though."

"Of course you do," Severo said with a hint of resentment.

Ben ignored him and called for Tweek. When she arrived, he said, "I need you to go find Gabriel and tell him to be discreet." Tweek left without asking questions.

"We need some food—I'm starving," Ben said.

Severo smiled at Ben's request and summoned Striker. "Can you oblige us with some fuel, little dude?"

Striker's body bumped his master's hand and spun in a corkscrew. Metal domes grew in size, and he glided them onto the trolley beside Severo's bed. Striker waved his hands and the domes rose, revealing bloomer bread filled with fresh cured meats and cheeses. He clapped his hands and two plates appeared. Striker filled them and floated them over to Ben and Severo.

"Before Gabriel arrives, I just want to say how sorry I am. It was not intentional. Life has been beyond strange since the ceremony, and today's events... I don't know what's real anymore." Ben shifted and the pain intensified.

"What can I do?"

"I think the soothe serum has worn off. If you have any of that, I'll take it." Ben tried sitting up further, then nibbled on a bite of the bloomer bread.

"Yeah, that stuff's the tweets. Check your wrist. There is a band with a button. If it's red, it means you can press it, and more serum will be released into your system. It only works when it's red, I'm told. Believe me, I tried pressing and pressing. The doctor was losing her head over it! Of course, that just made me do it more. Dr. Lovett is hot by the way, or so I remembered." Severo smirked then skittered a look to the far corner of the room. "Oh, hi Gabes."

Is Gabriel here?

"Gabriel?"

Am I really awake?

Ben blinked his eyes.

"Hey, Severo," Gabriel said. "How did you know I was here?"

"I was just showing Ben my new device. I can sense people through heat spots, and I chose yellow lemon for you." Severo's lips formed a broad smile. "So, Gabes, you can outsmart technology but not me!"

"Impressive, Sev," Ben said, marveling. "That could definitely be a useful skill. But, Gabriel, how did you get through the door and here so quickly?" Ben rubbed his tired eyes and pushed the red button on his wrist. The pain was soothed instantly.

"I was already near the castle. Let's just say, I've discovered new abilities, but enough about me. Ben, I've been freaked all day. They wouldn't let me in. Are you alright?" Gabriel paused for a second and looked at Severo, as though not sure if he should say more.

"I'm sore, but I'll be okay. Listen, I called you here because it's time to fill Severo in."

Gabriel's face showed great relief.

Ben shared all the events leading up to today—about both their powers and how their abilities had quickly escalated. He mentioned the Conceal Dust, the hide hut, how Vara found out about Elias, and lastly, he clued Severo in on his visions and dreams. He didn't tell them that he'd come face-to-face with Alunattra. He couldn't. Instead, he told them that he'd astral projected and lost control.

"Niall doesn't know any of this," Ben said before explaining Niall's unusual behavior. "We found out he's working with my father to find out who breached The Vale, but"—Ben paused—"I think it might be him."

Gabriel rubbed his hands on his trousers.

Ben shared a knowing look with Gabriel; it couldn't be denied anymore. They both gave Severo a nervous glance. Severo placed his elbows on his knees and brought his hands to his face.

Ben still hadn't voiced his thoughts about Cece. That was something he was going to talk to her about directly.

Could Severo's father still be alive?

Ben tensed watching Severo's face. It was blank at first, tight, then he bent his elbows to his knees and rubbed a hand through his hair.

"Hmm. That's a lot to take in, and I have questions—mostly about Niall, but at least I know now. Thanks for fessing up." Severo hesitated. "What I'm about to tell you might make more sense to you then, although let's not jump to conclusions. I discovered something unusual today about Niall when he came to see me."

Prickles roamed over Ben's skin as he waited on an explanation.

CHAPTER 28

Ben

Ben knocked on the ajar chamber door. "Mother, you needed me?"

"Yes. Oh, Benjamin, you look wonderful," she said with a delicate smile. "Navy's your color. When I think of what could've happened to you this week, I'm so glad you are well and home."

She hugged him so tightly it reignited the aches in his body, and he coughed awkwardly. *She's stronger than she looks.* His mother was making him more curious every day.

"Please, excuse me, it has been a trying week. Benjamin, go over your plans for the evening. I need to know where you are at all times."

Ben smoothed out his coattails and looked at his mother in exasperation. "You don't need to worry. I've spoken with Grandad, and we're working on gaining control of my power. I'm already feeling better about it. He's given me homework. Please, Mother, try to relax. I'm going to Severo's to meet everyone, and we'll all arrive at the party together. We need a night to switch off. I'll see you soon."

"Your father's in with Master Niall just now. Why don't you wait and go with him, so I know you're not on your own?"

"Yes, good idea."

Ben quickly left his mother's chambers.

Niall wouldn't try to harm my father would he?

Ben had read up on his father's power. The gift of Command was strong. Niall shouldn't be able to pull the wool over his eyes, but both powers were held in the top-tier bracket.

He went to find Niall. His father's study was a jaunt, and his legs were not complying. It didn't help that his breeches and boots clung to the remnants of his injuries. His clothes were not the only thing suffocating him; his mother hadn't left his side since his release yesterday.

He paced as he waited for Niall to come out. No voices drifted through the thick walls.

So much had happened over the past few days. Ben, Severo, and Gabriel had talked everything out but there was one issue: Niall. Severo said the other night that when he looked at Niall, his chosen color for him was gray, but the film that swam over his frame was fragmented. Not being able to look Niall in the eyes, Severo—for the first time—had felt uneasiness in his presence.

The three of them had sat till late studying the book. They looked up Niall's Verdo, Perception, and focused on a few areas.

1. *Over the years of cultivation, the user will be able to mold the minds of others to bend to their will—although the user will be able to perform this, it should only be carried out under extreme circumstances—an advanced skill that may never manifest itself.*
2. *The user will make others see what is necessary, not what is actual.*

"I think this is talking about mind control, but why would Niall need that, though?" Gabriel said.

Severo let out a long breath and tapped his feet. "Look, guys, I know Niall is atypical in the way he does things, but this is bonkers. And Gabes, you're right—what exactly would he need to control? I may jump to conclusions sometimes but this? Maybe we need to give him the benefit of the doubt or talk to him."

Like two sides of a token, Ben had known what was going through Severo's head. The difference now was the evidence couldn't be denied. "Sev, I said all this to Gabriel weeks ago but something's off. Something happened on the day of the ceremony, and I don't know what. All I'm saying is we need to be careful. If he's been the one to breach The Vale, something may have happened to him, but I've never felt like I could talk to him about it. So, I'm asking if you can keep this to yourself?" Although Severo couldn't see him, Ben willed his friend to agree.

"Fine, but can I just add being on the receiving end of not knowing what's going on is *not* the tweets," Severo said.

Gabriel jumped in, "We know, and I'm glad you know now, Severo. Let's all agree to be normal around him, and for now, we can leave it at that. If anything changes, we'll talk it out and go from there."

Ben and Severo agreed. Ben just wanted a night when his brain didn't feel like it was brimming over. Any time he thought about what had happened to him, his whole body started sweating, and last night's sleep had evaded him. He didn't want to succumb to his dreams.

"Ben, you brush up nicely."

Ben jerked his head up at the sound of his grandad's voice and spun on his heels. "Grandad, I swear you need a sounding horn! But thank you."

Since the incident, his grandad was never far away.

Is he watching over me or am I imagining things? Whatever Grandad is doing, he doesn't look as worried as everyone else does.

"Years of experience and observation has taught me well," his grandad said. "Well done on your meditations this week. Strength will ground you—keep that in mind. I wanted to see you off. Have a great time tonight. Do you have the magnets?"

"Actually, yes. They're in my pocket."

"I've had them for years. My father gave them to me. A pocket is always a good place for them. Anyway, good night, my boy. I have a meeting with your mother."

Ben could do with a cryptic code book. *What did all that mean? And another meeting with Mother?*

He said goodbye to his grandad as the door creaked open, and a duo of voices seeped into the corridor.

Ben drew his shoulders back. "My mother informed me you were here. Do you want to walk up to Severo's together?"

Niall smiled brightly and agreed.

"Benjamin, are you sure you're feeling well enough this evening?" His father held real concern in his eyes. Neither of them had known how to be these past few days.

"It's okay, Father. I'm healed now. I'll catch up with you at the party. Thank you for letting it still go ahead. Should be a fun night."

His father patted his back as he moved past him, and Ben felt the warmth of the gesture. The closest they had come to any kind of embrace.

"Ben, how are you really feeling after what happened in class? It all happened so fast, I'm sorry I couldn't help at the time."

Ben studied Niall. The concern was there but the feeling behind it wasn't. "It's kind of blurry. If anything, I've realized I need to hit the books and practice my meditation. As you could see, that's not exactly fine-tuned."

"It seemed to me that your body was experiencing astral projection. That's a superior skill, and I was surprised that you were able to achieve it so quickly after your ceremony."

How had he concluded that?

Chills crept in uninvited. Ben chose to lose that thread. "Maybe, although, it's all a bit of a blur. Anyway, enough about that. How are things with Clara?"

"Fantastic. I'm stopping by her door to pick her up, if you don't mind?"

Ben registered irritation in Niall's eyes but didn't know if it was because of Clara or him. "Yes, of course, that's fine."

They picked up Clara, and Ben watched as she slipped her hand into Niall's. Ben was sure he detected Niall flinch, but it was so fleeting, he wondered if he'd imagined it.

When they got to Severo's house, Cece answered the door in a navy chiffon swirling dress with a jeweled bask that caught in a 'V' at the waist. The skirt tickled the floor as she walked. Her terracotta curls were all piled up and decorated with baby's breath. She looked incredible.

Gabriel must be losing his mind.

"Come in, come in, the crew's all here."

As Ben walked into the living room, his eyes were drawn to Vara. She looked sensational in a high-necked, lemon floor length dress covered in a sheet of lace with a band of embroidered roses around her waist. So elegant. He gulped as she glided over to greet them.

"Ben, how are you?" Vara embraced him, albeit awkwardly. He didn't want her to let go.

"I'm fine, and can everyone please stop asking? Let's just have a good night. That's an order." He smirked and delicately brushed her hand. She blushed.

"Agreed. How about some punch for everyone?" Severo announced, appearing at the foot of the stairs. "Watch in awe folks." Severo walked with ease and filled cups for everyone. Calling them by name, he handed out the beverages with a huge smirk on his face.

Stunned silence filled the room.

"You're probably all wondering how I know who you are. Well, you're all in color to me now, friends, so don't think about pulling any fast ones." Severo lifted his glass with a grin. "Cheers," he said.

Ben stood conflicted between his friend's colossal strength and the knowledge that sight would no longer be in his future. Ben clinked his glass in awe of Severo's bravado. "I sure hope your fairies put this punch together and not you, Sev."

Severo laughed. "No need to fret, my man. Striker has me warned."

"Clearly, we girls are missing out on something. Brother, do you care to fill us in on whatever idiot story you're referring to?" Cece gave them each a pointed look.

Ben smiled, wishing he had a sibling. Severo and Cece had a real, close bond.

Severo teased his sister and then regaled them with the tale of the vineyards. Ben remained quiet as everyone laughed, feeling half-in, half-out of the conversation. The erratic pace of his heartbeat felt at odds with the levity surrounding him. This night was supposed to be about fun, but all he could think about was how to help his friends. A weight that got heavier by the minute.

My friends—they need me. We need each other.

He relaxed his shoulders and took a sip of his punch.

I also need to lighten up.

He caught Vara's eye and gave her what he hoped was an encouraging smile. She smiled back, but it didn't match the conflict in her eyes.

She's torn. I'll have a dance with her later—I hope. Severo deserves to know my feelings, but tonight is not the night.

Ben went to help Cece in the kitchen. "How is he really?" Ben asked, under his breath.

"Severo's not just strong on the outside, Ben. He's dealing. Here. Take this tray to the living room." Cece's lips pursed, and for a split second, he saw that same resilient look in her eyes, but something had changed. A note of determination, maybe.

Ben wanted to know what was going on with her, too, but directly this time—not eavesdropping in his astral form. Maybe all the strange events of late were connected? Cece was a tough nut to crack, but her strength on a mental level equaled her brother's. Ben found himself liking her more and more.

He tried to switch off as they all sat and talked. Gabriel went to sit by Cece, and she smiled warmly at him. Clara, he noticed, didn't say anything unless it was to Niall. Ben didn't know her well but this seemed odd. The white of her gown drained her already pale skin.

"Clara, how are you finding this school semester?"

She looked at Ben, alarmed, then Niall answered for her, "You're enjoying it, aren't you, Clara?" She looked at Niall and let out a breath, nodding in agreement.

"That's the good thing about Clara—we have so much in common, unlike you lot who've never studied a day in your life."

Ben laughed, but inside, unease stirred in his gut. Gabriel was right. Niall was doing something to Clara. It was obvious. Like a veil being lifted, Ben was no longer blind to the truth.

Was this what Niall tried on me? Is that why my eyes hurt so badly?

Like an insect eyeing its prey, Niall stared into Ben's eyes, and they both knew.

CHAPTER 29

Vara

Her mother's words played through her mind as she walked alongside Cece to the dance.

"I'm worried, Vara. Your father is too. We're relying on you. If you secure the prince before the courting, you secure our family's future safety."

If Ben chooses me, I'll be moved to the castle along with my family. Vara wanted her family to be safe, and the swarm of security around Landis suggested they weren't as safe anymore.

She shivered her thoughts off.

The dance. I can't wait to get on the dance floor, but who do I want to dance with first?

Vara was glad to see Ben back to normal and Severo in good spirits. They both were brave. A quality that she wanted in a future husband.

One lunch break, she'd gone in to see Severo and taken a seat at his bedside. She'd held his hand while he slept. "I'm here, Severo. I'll always be here for you."

As if her voice had triggered something, he opened his eyes and looked right at her. She could get lost in those blue-green pools. His gaze made her heart swell. His handsome face was untarnished aside from a slight color change in his eyes.

"Green. I chose green for you, my Vara." His eyelids closed again but with a tight grip on her hand.

She blushed when realizing what he had meant—that he could see her now in the form of a color. She loved that he'd chosen green. It was the color she was wearing the first time they'd properly spoken. He had called her, *his*. She had been too, at that moment. His suit tonight would look out of place on anyone else. The vivid bottle green with gold buttons, she felt sure was a private message for her. She loved how it fit every part of him.

I wish he could see how he looks.

She gulped and swallowed down her sadness.

Ben had promised her several dances tonight, and she hoped it provided the chance to talk with him. After Ben's freak accident, she hadn't been allowed in to see him; then the next day he was healed. Fate had been cruel this last week—first with Severo and then with Ben. It was clear there was more to the recent events and she wanted to know what.

She watched them all walking ahead. Niall and Clara were still stuck together, although something about it struck her as peculiar. Clara leaned into him like a crutch. It wasn't natural. She hadn't seen her friend on her own all week.

Am I just jealous? No, something is wrong with Niall. I should tell someone.

Out of the blue Cece said, "Don't ask me how he is, V. That's all anyone's asking. He's fine."

Vara flushed. "Cece, I wasn't going to. I'm happy to be silent. Just know you can talk about it if you want."

"Sorry, I didn't mean to bite your head off. It's been a rough ride," Cece admitted, casting a quick glance toward her brother. "Forgive my snarky remark."

"What is life without a little snarky remark here and there?" Vara grinned, linking her arm with Cece's. She leaned her head in close. "Are you at least looking forward to the dance?"

Cece looked at Gabriel with a cheeky side smile. "That I am. A night of fun and distraction is needed by all."

They walked the rest of the way arm in arm. Cece always had a way of putting things into perspective.

Maybe tonight will be a good night after all.

CHAPTER 30

Gabriel

G abriel resisted the urge to look behind him. A few weeks back, so many prospects seemed possible with Cece. Now, she was handling too much, and he wanted to be her friend first.

More if she'll allow.

Earlier in the week when he'd visited Severo, she'd still been keeping him at a distance. But when she smiled at him, all the tension had left his body. He was going to ask her to dance and had itchy feet in excited expectation. This also meant it was time to talk to Severo.

If only Niall didn't keep edging his way into Gabriel's thoughts.

I'm keeping my eye on him.

The most important thing was Ben and Severo were alive and well, for the most part. Severo led the way, walking confidently, keeping up the conversation. Gabriel swallowed the lump in his throat. Severo was stronger than all of them. He'd been studying Severo's Verdo this week, hoping the *Book of Sovereign Dominions* might indicate a solution, but it didn't. In fact, the one thing the book specified was that the eyes would always be vulnerable to harm. It also mentioned the person wielding the power of strength would have fortitude of mind beyond any other coping mechanism. The user would always endeavor to make others stronger in his presence. This was at play already, and Gabriel was inspired by his friend.

They soon arrived at the party. A large marquee covered the

grounds, and the dazzling glow of light lured them inside. Gabriel's gaze lifted, counting the numerous floating chandeliers that showered the dance floor with luminous light. Long tables sat around the edges, and at the very back, Gabriel spied the grand banquet table stacked high with enough delicious fare to feed all of Landis. The band was in full swing with a classic folk song. Many partygoers were already up dancing the well-known routine.

Gabriel and his friends claimed a long table with a decorative runner, which sported the most beautiful, embellished artistry, composed of gold stitched crowns and swords. Each one was a different color and embedded with the smallest of emeralds and rubies.

Gabriel breathed in the sights, finding it easy to relax in this environment. The canty music took the edge off. Gabriel tugged at his maroon suit jacket and undid the top two buttons. He noticed for the first time how perfectly color-coordinated he and Cece were.

A new couple's dance was beginning. "Cece, would you like to dance?" Gabriel's words left his mouth before he knew he was talking.

"Lead the way." She beamed, offering him her hand.

Gabriel slipped his fingers in between hers and felt like anything was possible. The music shifted to a slower beat, and he hesitated before putting one hand on Cece's shoulder and one at her waist.

"I don't bite, you know," Cece teased, as she laid her head on his shoulder.

Gabriel lost his breath glancing down at her. She smelled like the sunflowers in his garden. "You're beautiful, Cece."

She looked at him. With heels on, she was almost at his eye level. Rosiness formed in the apples of her porcelain cheeks, and she seemed lost for a retort. Gabriel noticed something in her eyes he'd not seen before—he'd been too nervous to look directly at her until now.

"Cece, is everything okay? You seem worried?" His concern increased when she remained silent. "It's been some week, hasn't it? Please know you can always come to me for anything. I'm a good listener." He tried to pass this off but grew alarmed when sudden tears gathered in her eyes.

"Please, excuse me. I'll be right back."

Gabriel didn't let her go, instead he led her by the hand in silence. The bridge was clear tonight, which meant the guard fairies were likely all at the dance. The castle doors hung wide open, but it was derelict inside. When he got to his hide hut, he checked to make sure nobody saw them before popping the panel.

Cece followed behind and whistled in amazement. "Every time I think I have you pegged, you do something to surprise me. What is this place?"

"Call it a place to maintain one's sanity. Up until a month ago, it was solely mine. Now Ben and I hang here, and Severo's just found out about it. It's a safe space if you want to talk." Gabriel sprinkled some Conceal Dust around the hut.

"And what is that?" Cece asked, folding her arms with a twinkle in her eye.

"Conceal Dust. Nobody can hear a thing. Tweek made some for Ben, and I've since inherited my own stash."

They both sat on the velvet cushions, and Cece tucked her legs under the chiffon layers of her dress. Gabriel waited patiently.

Cece bit her painted, petal-pink lip and met his eyes. "Gabriel, something's been happening to me since the ceremony. I've been having visions. Severo says it's only dreams, but he doesn't understand how real they are. I don't have my Verdo yet, so it shouldn't even be a possibility."

That's weird. First Ben and me, now Cece?

"What are your visions about?" he asked tentatively.

"My father. He's alive, I know it. But he's trapped. He's trying to reach me, but I don't know how to help him. I feel less than useless."

Cece exhaled, a mask of exhaustion wearing heavy on her face, and her head dipped into her hands. Gabriel couldn't bear to see her in pain. He lifted her face to meet his and feathered his hand over a loose red curl that caught at her chin. He found her delicate hand again. Cece laced her fingers through his, and Gabriel leaned down, gently placing the softest of kisses on her lips. Cece hesitated briefly then wrapped her arms around him and kissed him back. They both forgot where they were and took comfort in each other.

Gabriel pulled back, winded. "Wow, that was, wow."

Cece's giggle tinkled like crystal chimes. "Sorry, I didn't mean to attack you there."

Gabriel laughed as well, and his cheeks erupted with heat. His legs were numb. He tried, with great difficulty, to redirect his thoughts. "As much as I would like to relive this, well, forever, I think we better get back. But before we do, I just wanted to let you know I believe you, and I'm going to try and find out anything I can about your father."

Gabriel stood and Cece held out her hand. He gently pulled her up as she said, "I already know where he is."

Gabriel gulped, unsure he wanted to know.

"Alunattra is holding him prisoner, and I'm going to get him back."

CHAPTER 31

Severo

Severo blinked. His head ached sorting through the myriad of colors. It was going to take some adjustment. Vara's emerald shade of green dominated. She stood out. She always had. Its soothing effect was like lying in soft, fresh cut grass.

He plucked up the courage to ask her for a dance, taking extra care not to bump into the blend of colors around him. Talking to her didn't seem so daunting now that he couldn't see her, but he missed her lovely face.

"Vara, take pity on an invalid and come dance with me." Her bright green spark sashayed toward him, and he felt the warmth of her arm slide through his. He vaguely noticed Gabriel and Cece leave the dance floor. He would need to address that one again but, in all fairness, there was no nicer dude than Gabriel.

Ground rules though.

Severo held her tightly. "V, you look incredible as always."

"Did you get your sight back and forget to tell me?"

If anyone else had made that remark, Severo wouldn't have responded well, but with Vara, he knew she meant it to humor him. He held her tighter. "I don't need my sight to know you're the most beautiful girl in Landis and not just on the outside. That fact is imprinted on my brain."

Vara leaned in closer. Severo's heart quickened on the spot where her face now rested. He didn't know if Vara could ever feel for him the way he felt for her but this warmth upon his chest was a win for now.

The dance was interrupted by a bell chiming. As Severo and Vara pulled back from their trance, Severo saw King Vardez's gold haze shimmer to the podium. Like a reflex, he looked for his sister. Orange and yellow were back on the dance floor, and he noticed how well the two colors blended. This was happening whether he liked it or not. Ben's blue light hovered at the other side of the stage and Niall and Clara were intertwined in gray and purple. Severo was drawn to them like a swelling bruise on his skin. Niall's frame appeared like an animal with its prey. Severo shivered as the gray flame of color expanded and contracted.

King Vardez's silhouette raised his arms to command silence. "I hope you're all enjoying the evening. I won't keep you long, but I wanted to celebrate this evening with a couple of important announcements. An official notice is being handed to your families as I speak. The first regards the fairies of Landis. Whilst our fairies have their own lives and free time, the king's guard and I feel it may be best to institute working hours and weekly days off. We would never want our fairies to feel we're not grateful for how they make our lives better. This will begin immediately. On these days, we, the people, will be required to fend for ourselves, so that means some of us might benefit from cooking lessons."

Severo laughed along with the crowd. He was glad his house fairies would have days off, but he would miss Striker on those days.

"The fairies will leave all necessary supplies for everyone. Any emergencies, please come to me, the queen, or Tharmus. Secondly, I have the pleasure of announcing a forthcoming wedding."

The chatter swept through the crowd.

Whose wedding?

Severo dipped his head close to Vara. "Do you know who it is?"

"No idea."

Severo felt butterflies in his stomach as her hand grazed his.

"I want you all to know that our two chief fairies, Aristo and Perial, will be getting married this year. It will be the event of the season and now that the announcement has been made, preparations can be in full swing."

Severo brought his hands together to cheer with the rest of the crowd.

The dancing resumed, but Severo didn't join in. Fluctuating movement in the corner of his eye grabbed his attention. Niall was leaving with Clara by his side. Something about the urgency of their exit gave Severo an uneasy prod to his senses. He didn't want to cause alarm. Ben was nowhere in sight but luckily Gabriel was close by.

"Vara, I'm just going to check on Cece. Can we have another dance later?"

"I'll hold you to that. You could do with a few more lessons." Vara stood on her tiptoes and placed a kiss on his cheek.

Severo stood dumbfounded for a second, rooted to the dance floor. Touching his warm tingling cheek, he forced himself to march off and find Gabriel. He noticed his sister holding Gabriel's hand, and she dropped it as soon as he approached.

"Sev, you okay?" Cece asked in an innocent tone.

Do they not realize I can still make out what they're up to?

"Gabriel, a word." He led Gabriel away from the bustling couples on the dance floor and bumped around the edges of a large table.

"Severo, I was just dancing with your sister, but I—she's... well, you know—you're her brother. It's just, um, you see—"

"Gabes, man," Severo cut in, giving his friend a strong clasp to the shoulder, "you're giving me a headache. Honestly, I don't need my sight to see what's going on here, and I'll come back to that in a sec. The reason I pulled you aside is that Niall's just left, and he was all over the place. Something about it was off, too abrupt maybe. You can probably find Ben quicker than I can. Just thought you should know. And regarding my sister, hurt her, well, you know what I can do. That being said, you're not stupid, and there are worse people she could be attracted to. She's still fifteen, group dates will be fine."

Severo waited but couldn't gauge Gabriel's emotions. Unfortunately, his device couldn't detect feelings.

"Gabes," Severo prodded, jostling Gabriel's shoulder, "are we understanding each other?"

"Yes, sorry, Severo. I think you're right. I'll go find Ben to tell him, then I think I'll turn in. Can you tell Cece I said goodbye?"

"That's my boy, off you go. I'll tell her."

Pleased with himself, Severo meandered his way back to Cece and passed on Gabriel's message.

"What, he just left?" she said, enraged.

"Yes, but he's being respectful of my wishes. I may be blind, but I can still see things. I've given my permission for authorized group dates. Gabriel said to tell you goodbye."

"Severo, I swear." Her voice lowered like she was on the verge of growling. "Have you forgotten I'm sixteen in less than a month? I'm not having this conversation again. Argh!"

His sister's orange color flared like a sparked ember as she stormed off. Severo did not understand why she was so mad. A typical red rant. Knowing Cece would cool off, Severo went on the hunt for Ben to fill him in. He waded through the shades of colors until he found Ben's vibrant blue frame walking around the side of the castle—Striker had programmed his discs to outline bigger areas. To Severo, it looked like a technical drawing, white lines on a black page. He wasn't alone but joined by the color Severo lived to see—green.

Severo couldn't help himself and walked closer but kept a safe distance. He held back as he saw them stop, then watched in horror as Ben's frame wrapped his arms around Vara and bent down to kiss her.

CHAPTER 32

Niall

N iall bounded from the party but did a sweep with his mind. It was easy to leave, everyone was lost to their hormones. Something he would never understand.

I need to get out of here. Ben knows something.

He walked faster as he stared at the pathetic girl gripping his hand tightly. Clara was like a bug in his brain, and he needed to get her home. She couldn't be trusted on her own now—she'd seen too much, and her strength retaliated. She had caught him several times this week working his skill on various school peers. She nearly spoiled everything the previous week with Elias. Niall was constantly trying to reprogram her.

"Niall, can you take me to see Severo? I've been practicing my meditation, and I'm so attuned to my power now, I think I could help him. I don't understand why you won't let me go," she had said.

This is becoming a big problem. Something may need to be done soon.

Alunattra swept back into his mind and whispered, "Keep telling this girl her power has yet to develop and is of no use. Do what you must to make sure that does not happen. The boy is too strong and needs to stay at a disadvantage; it suits my plan better."

She had reappeared again throughout the week. Niall sensed when she was gone from his mind, it was because she couldn't be there for some reason. He itched to know why. He stopped, their minds still linked, but no thoughts came from her. He was shielding it from her again. It was like he could visualize the box in his mind reserved for his private thoughts. His mouth watered.

All his other cohorts were in place, ready to move when the time came.

Niall called for Pixel. "I need you to keep watch and make sure Clara doesn't return to the party."

"Yes, Master. I have something I can use to keep her sedated if you wish it," Pixel said in perfect obedience.

Niall wished it.

It won't be long now.

Alunattra had all the classified information on the weapons, and Pixel was trying to help him construct a device with the potential to penetrate the barrier. Niall knew there must be a flaw, he just couldn't find it. He had been to the barrier several times now at *her* request and studied it. It was exhausting but his determination was unwavering. If the barrier collapsed, then Alunattra could be pulled through to the other side, but he wasn't sure he wanted that now. What would be his role? Would he be her equal or would she want him to serve her? Could he be rendered useless?

Stress was on a revolving turntable that stopped and gnawed at his gut.

Niall hurried away from Clara's home and sprinted to The Vale; Alunattra had retracted again. He was only supposed to come here at her command, but he was done waiting.

Time was running out. He knew what happened to Ben. Alunattra's scream had rung through him, and he'd glimpsed Ben there with her. Ben had been terrified, and Niall had felt the thrill of it. No emotion stirred in him when he saw Ben lying in a pool of blood— much the same as with Severo. In a twinkling moment of clarity, Niall realized the depth of his hatred. He wanted Ben gone.

He had greatness, and his friends would not stand in the way of that.

His body swelled the closer he came to the forest. The power of being in her presence was what his soul demanded. Afterwards, new elements of his Verdo always evolved in him. The Forbidden Vale welcomed him like an old friend, and the twisted branches detangled for him to navigate easily.

As he reached the place where he could nourish his hunger, impatience set in again. He centered his mind and focused in the way he'd been practicing. She was not there, nor aware of his presence, but how could that be?

Niall focused harder, and a sensation from another reverence raked over him. He faced the Tree of Vulnerability and walked toward it. Unlike the feeling he got from *her*, this maddening itch made him want to claw his skin away, not in fear but strangled irritation. Something lay within this tree. As he crept closer, his skin burned, and he fell back in pain.

Does she know about this? Is this why there are times it's not safe to come here?

Almost instantly the instinctive thought disappeared, replaced with the familiar chilly tingle. Niall sighed in relief, already feeling the void fill inside.

She was coming. Niall felt her wrath before he saw her. His physical strength wavered.

"You come to me unannounced. I told you to wait for my command. You disappoint me, young Niall. You're merely my servant. You do not make the rules, you obey them. If you don't, you're expendable."

Niall cowered as her frame projected itself out from the barrier and pinned him down. Like a static shadow, the filmy barrier hovered inches from his face. This time, she was a spider of nightmares, creeping above him. Niall could not move. Her endless limbs coiled around him, pressing his body into the earth. His face burned as though disintegrating beneath the intensity of her stare. Her black eyes oozed from their sockets into his own like melted tar. His lashes wouldn't close, as if they'd been webbed in place, forcing his eyes to connect with hers. A pressure forced its way into his skull. She was trying to read his mind, but it wasn't working. Niall had her blocked. But it wouldn't work in his favor for Allunattra to think he was deceiving her.

Niall opened his mind. At the same time, he mentally pulled from her like a device needing to be charged and plastered a contrived expression. She did not respond but waited for him to speak.

"I understand," he said, keeping his voice level. "I needed to see you. My power's waning; I needed strength to continue. I'll not defy you again."

Alunattra jerked back from him abruptly.

"My queen?"

Her hiss reverberated off the barrier and the ground shook beneath him. "What do we have here? Who dares to challenge me?"

It took Niall a moment to realize it was not him being addressed. Alunattra scuttled along the barrier. Every scurrying step was a static pulse in Niall's ears as he followed her movement. At the other side of the tree, she pounced out from the barrier. Something landed in a thorny bush, and a voice cried out in pain. Niall peered closely as invisibility evaporated to reveal Gabriel.

Niall had the urge to inflict pain upon this irritant who was like an unpickable scab. Destructive ideas formed in his head as he strode like a predator towards Gabriel.

Gabriel's face drained of color, and Niall snickered.

"I'll let you deal with him, young Niall—a gift from me, and I will live vicariously through it. The perfect way to please me." Alunattra was inches from Gabriel's quivering frame. "So, you're the boy with the gift of the Mask, aren't you? Not so powerful now, child."

Gabriel winced.

Niall's skin prickled all over. As he inched closer, Gabriel shot up and closed his eyes. His invisibility took hold again, and he darted off. Niall screamed in defiance but wasted no time hurtling after him. Although he couldn't see Gabriel, a trail was left in his wake. The forest entered the fray, making it difficult for Gabriel to leave.

"He cannot be allowed back into the castle grounds." Alunattra's shrill voice screamed in his ear.

Niall sprinted. He was fit and spry. It worked in his favor. As he got to the edge of the forest, a rustle of leaves just ahead caught his attention, and he sprang. Gabriel was in his grip, and the invisibility shield came away.

"You were never getting away. The question now is, what do we do with you?"

"Niall you will not get away with this," Gabriel said, struggling against Niall's grip. "You're being controlled. Let me help you."

Niall laughed with mock humor. "It's comical to think *you* could help *me*. You have no idea what you are talking about, idiot boy. I'm not the one in need of help. I'm going to take you back to her now, so she can watch you die," Niall said, sneering.

As Niall gripped Gabriel tighter and prepared to move back into the forest, a loud voice commanded, "Stop right where you are and do not move."

Niall's body was frozen. Several figures marched toward him.

King Vardez led the way with Tharmus and the Fairy Guard. Niall realized why he couldn't move—the king had commanded it.

Think fast!

"Fix this, NOW!" Alunattra's words would have shattered him if he was a pane of glass.

"My king, I'm so glad you're here," Niall said, feigning relief. "I've found the perpetrator. Before you, I hold Gabriel Johns. His mind is full of lies and calculation, and I've put myself at great risk to extract him. I advise that this be dealt with immediately. His power of invisibility is already at play, to the point where he's almost able to shield his thoughts. Left to his own devices, he could be destructive to our world." Niall paused. "I also have reason to believe he's in communication with the dark side of the island. He must be stopped."

Gabriel tried to interject. "King Vardez, please—"

"Silence, you will speak no further." The king held his hand up and Gabriel's mouth shut.

Gabriel's eyes widened as he tried to speak but no words came out. Conflict appeared in the king's eyes.

I need to act fast.

"King Vardez, I'll return to the castle with you now, so you can take my full statement. This boy's had us all fooled, me included, which should be a statistical impossibility. He's highly dangerous. I think keeping him quiet shows accelerated judgment. Who knows who he may try to manipulate!"

The king was pondering something.

Niall grasped for *her* in the darkness, but she was gone. Knowledge came to him then like scales falling away. He hadn't imagined it; she didn't have complete control over him, and this fueled his power further. So many possibilities came with this realization. This time, the awed fear he usually felt lessened at the thought of her name. Their connection, and the power he received from her, was allowing his Verdo to mutate.

"Tharmus, Fairy Guards" King Vardez called. "Take the boy home and summon Vallore. We'll keep Gabriel confined so he cannot escape, and Vallore has his ways. Explain that the situation is top priority. The boy will stay silenced for now."

Niall stared ahead as they took the mute Gabriel away, and his lip curled with satisfaction. That would do for now until Gabriel could be permanently silenced.

CHAPTER 33

The Landis Tribute

URGENT NOTICE

*Many of you may not be aware that for some weeks we have
been investigating a recent breach of The Forbidden Vale.
Last night, this person entered The Vale for a second time,
and due to the help of a citizen, they have been
reprimanded.*

*GABRIEL JOHNS is now being held in confinement within
his own home, and the circumstances of his crime are being
monitored.*

*The Johns family is not to be approached or contacted, and any
person found trying to interact with the suspect will be
held fully accountable and answerable to the king and
queen.*

*The king would like to stress there is no further threat and The
Vale is being closely monitored. The barrier is being inves-
tigated by the hosts with your safety as the primary goal.*

*We have some exciting weapons and devices to share with you,
which will improve safety measures. The school will be
testing these out this week.*

Wishing you all a happy day Seven.

Regards,
The News Fairies under direct order from King Vardez.
Landis Tribute

CHAPTER 34

Vara

Urgent meeting to take place in the hide hut. Come alone. Tell no one and
meet inside the castle at the paneled corridor opposite the thinking benches.
First morning light before school. Burn this letter.

Vara read the letter on repeat and tightened her eyebrows. It
didn't make any sense. *What is a hide hut?* She tucked the letter
away into her slacks.

The thought of school filled her with dread. She had left the dance
early. What was supposed to have been an event to clarify her feelings,
had only added to her internal torment. Dancing with Severo had felt
like her very own safe haven; there was nowhere else she would
rather have been. When their hands had grazed, she felt something
ignite in her.

Life seemed to constantly interrupt the good moments. Ben had
surprised her with a suggested walk, but she never would have
dreamed he would kiss her. It was so out of the blue. She'd wanted to
talk with him about the day of his meditation class, hoping he could
pacify her unanswered questions. When she'd tried to bring it up, he
pulled her to him and kissed her with a strange urgency. At first, she
had been elated and kissed him back until he ran off without explanation. Kissing Ben was something she'd pondered a great deal, and it
was not how she'd imagined her first kiss with anyone.

"Darling, you're very quiet this morning. Too much fun at the party?"

Vara managed to curve her lips. "Yes, something like that. I didn't sleep very well."

Her mother's eyes glazed over as she sipped her coffee.

"No doubt thinking of your future prince. I remember my courting days like it was yesterday. Your father and I had our first kiss at a dance. He was always the only one for me."

Vara watched her mother with envy. *Well, I had my first kiss at a school dance too, yet not the moment of assurance I'd hoped for.*

All their house fairies appeared in rapidity at the dining table.

"There is a notice from the tribute with a message from the king," Prine said, giving Vara a worried glance.

Her mother shot up from her seat. "I better call your father and the girls."

Each member of her family looked as nervous as she felt. Her father's fairy moved his hands furiously as he produced the document in question. Everyone waited on edge as a tiny speck transformed into a sheet of paper.

Her father picked up the king's notice and read it out loud. Vara listened in shock. Panic jolted through her body. She'd just seen Gabriel. What could possibly have happened? This was some kind of mistake. She knew it with certainty.

"Vara. You know this boy—what's going on?" her father asked sternly.

"I've no idea but this information cannot be true. Gabriel's not capable of this. It must be a misunderstanding. I need to go and find out what's going on." Vara rose from her chair, and her mother pulled her back.

"Where exactly do you think you're going, young lady?"

Vara stared her mother down. "To see Severo and Cece."

Her mother didn't let go of her arm. "Oh, no you're not. You'll remain in your home, with your family, where it's safe. I don't want you outside, and I do not wish this to be spoken of in our house."

Vara clenched her jaw. "C'mon, Mother. You know things are happening in Landis. Why is everyone so willing to sit around and do nothing?"

"I will not be spoken to like that. Go to your room this instant."

"Gladly, and just for the record, in case you haven't noticed, something *is* going on. Try having your wits about you for once. Ignoring things won't make them go away."

Vara ran to her room and slammed the door. She couldn't remember ever having a fight with her mother but so much had changed, and her family was so void of reality sometimes.

Vara took the note out of her pocket again and read it. Then she destroyed it.

THE NEXT MORNING, SHE CREPT DOWNSTAIRS AND LEFT A NOTE FOR HER parents that said she was going to school early. They had barely spoken since her outburst, and she felt only relief not having to deal with them.

Vara had no idea what the cryptic letter meant or who sent it but maybe it was the only way to get some answers. Her hands were shaking, and her eyes darted everywhere as she walked. An audible scatter of stones behind her made her stiffen. She halted and turned. Severo and Cece caught up to her.

"We didn't want to shout in case anyone heard us. Did you get a note as well?" Cece asked.

Vara breathed out in relief. "Yes, I did. Have you heard any news? Do you know if Gabriel's okay?" Vara spoke to them both, but Severo didn't look at her. Her heart skipped a beat.

"Nope," Cece replied, tsking. "I tried to get out of the house yesterday, but my mother put her foot down. I know he didn't do anything. Gabriel is not capable of wrong." Cece clenched her fists.

"Sometimes people surprise us," Severo said under his breath, glancing in Vara's direction. Then he put his hands up when Cece's eyes squinted.

Was that addressed toward me?

"I agree, Cece. Let's go before anyone sees us," Vara said.

The three walked in silence. Severo had his hands buried in his pockets, closed off, and Cece was putting on a good front. Vara wanted to say something—anything to Severo. Their dance had meant so much to her, but he was acting strangely.

As they arrived at the castle's entrance, Ben was sitting on one of the thinking benches in the wood paneled corridor. Shoulders slumped, he walked over to meet them.

"What are you guys doing here?" Ben's eyebrows lifted, and he appeared as bewildered as they were.

The letter hadn't come from him then. Vara noticed Severo's hands ball into fists and his face reddened, which deepened her puzzlement. Her stomach squirmed.

Could he have seen me with Ben?

"We got a note," Cece said. "I presume you did too?"

They all stared at each other in confusion then a loud noise directed their gaze to the wooden panels further down. An invisible force was lifting a panel away and placing it to the side. Vara grabbed Cece's arm in fright.

"Gabes, you are one sneaky little dude," Severo said, chuckling.

Vara watched Severo swagger toward thin air.

Where is Gabriel? The gift of the Mask. It must be.

She couldn't see him anywhere. Severo stepped inside the panels and disappeared.

Cece laughed. "Lighten up, V. It's all good." Cece followed them and twirled her hand with a bow. "Tada. I give you the hide hut."

As Vara walked over to them, a firm hand squeezed her fingers.

"Vara, I'm sorry about the dance. You deserve to know everything. I want you to know everything. Will you give me a chance to explain?" Ben asked.

Vara's heartbeat quickened as she looked at Ben. *He needs me after all.* "Of course."

Ben kissed her hand and indicated for her to step inside.

Vara spied around in wonder. Large, plush cushions sat on the rectangular floor and a table rested against the back wall with steaming coffees and pastries. Speechless, she snagged a treat and took a seat on one of the cushions.

Gabriel materialized right in front of them, tired and unkempt in what looked like his nightwear.

Vara jumped again and dropped her lemon glazed pastry. Everyone laughed. Cece threw her arms around Gabriel and hugged him. A blush quickly colored her cheeks as she clearly remembered they were not alone. Severo cringed, then went to fill a plate with five different flavored pastries.

"Only five, Sev? You unwell!" Cece teased.

"I eat when I'm on edge." Severo passed a narrowed look at Vara. "Don't worry, sis, this will only fill me for five minutes." His cheeky grin was back in place.

Is he okay?

Gabriel asked everyone to sit before sprinkling some of that same dust Ben had in the hospital. He sipped his coffee, then took a deep breath and began. "Thanks for coming. If you can just listen to what I have to say and my side of things, I'll get you up to speed. Two nights ago, at the dance, I followed Niall after the party."

Gabriel looked at Ben, almost apologetically, and Ben's face was unreadable.

Why was Gabriel following Niall?

"I trusted my gut feeling and it was right. Niall went to The Forbidden Vale and walked right inside the dark forest until he reached the barrier."

"Gabriel, what were you thinking?" Ben said.

Cece jumped in, shooting Ben a pert look. "I'm pretty sure Gabriel asked for no interruptions. Go on."

Gabriel gave Cece the smallest of smiles before continuing.

Vara didn't reach for another pastry. She felt numb and rubbed some life back into her arms. *My whole life, I've barely thought about the other side, and Gabriel and Niall went there?*

"What was it like, Gabriel?" she asked.

Gabriel smiled and then told them all what happened in the forest. "And one more thing, a voice from the Tree of Vulnerability called for you, Ben."

Vara looked to Ben and saw a flicker of alarm wash over him.

"What happened?" Ben asked Gabriel.

"The voice said this inside my mind: 'Ben, you must leave. She's coming soon, I can feel it. When she's here, I'm not.' I spoke back and said I was a friend of yours, but the voice was already gone. Ben, I think it's the same voice you've been hearing. It must have sensed me and presumed I was you from your recent experiences. Whoever is hidden within is trapped, and I wondered if maybe this entity is blocking Alunattra somehow, and vice versa."

Someone gasped.

It's me. I gasped. How can this be happening? Our world is supposed to be safe.

Everyone stayed silent. Vara had no idea what was coming next.

Everyone's food lay untouched. She sipped her coffee and rubbed away the sudden chill grazing her skin.

"I watched Niall talk to Alunattra, and I'm not ashamed to admit I was terrified. I have never seen a creature like her. Niall, it seems, is acting on her behalf."

Vara listened, her eyes wide as Gabriel relayed all the information. *I wasn't wrong about Niall then!*

"Vallore appeared and sealed my room so I couldn't leave," Gabriel finished.

"Not to sound thick, but am I missing something? How are you able to be here and speak to us?" Severo said, sounding confused.

Vara had been thinking the same.

"That's the thing, my cloak—when activated—can not only walk through rooms and buildings, but it also moves through Vallore's seal. Fritzi, well, he may have broken a rule or two. Severo, Fritzi had Striker help him make this."

Gabriel retrieved a small tin and opened it. Everyone stood to look at what was inside. Some kind of firm but shiny substance, one side yellow, the other blue.

"I can't see it. You will need to describe whatever it is you're holding," Severo said, folding his arms.

Vara felt a sudden lump in her throat as sadness choked her. Severo was never going to be the same. It was easy to forget when he looked no different than before.

Gabriel's skin pinked, but he continued without drawing any more attention to Severo's words. "It's called Mute Balm. The blue side, when applied to my lips, will silence me and the yellow lifts it. Your fairy, Severo, is a genius, and he weirdly knows that I'm innocent. He made the yellow part. These tins are few and far between as they've never been needed."

"You rebel, you!" Severo sniggered. "That's Striker for you. Never ceases to amaze me, and he's always been a sound judge of character." Severo winked at Gabriel.

Ben jumped up and started pacing.

"Ben, are you okay?" Concerned, Vara went to him then turned when Severo inhaled loudly.

Ben crouched to his knees and ran a hand through his hair. "So let me get this straight, Niall is working with Alunattra and we think the captive voice is there, but only when Alunattra isn't?"

Gabriel nodded. "I believe so. When I read up on my power, it said that my power will expand my mind with great intuition, to see things others can't. I think that's what happened. Also, Alunattra wasn't pleased that Niall was there of his own volition. She must be very selective about what she's revealing. Ben, we have to figure out what to do. This is serious. Niall has every item in Weapons and Devices now memorized. I think he's trying to find a way to break the divide."

I've seen those weapons. What if we have to use them?

Vara lost the feeling in her legs, but strong arms broke her fall and caught her coffee cup. She molded herself into Severo. His eyes found hers and they glistened with pain. A hard look of betrayal flashed across his features and an angry glare settled. He let her go.

He knows.

Vara crumbled onto a cushion, her mind consumed with far too many thoughts. "I knew something was not right with Niall, but this? What will we do? Something bad is going to happen. I just know it."

"Vara, we now have information, and that's why I called you all here—we need a plan. Niall will know that my supposed silence will not be forever, so we need to move quickly. I have some ideas I want to run by you all, if that's okay, Ben?" Gabriel drained his coffee and waited for the go-ahead.

Ben opened his mouth to say something but staggered. He collapsed and started convulsing. Vara screamed in fear as Severo and Gabriel bolted to his side.

"What's happening to him?" Vara said to nobody in particular.

"I'll check his vitals, but we might need the doctor." Cece checked Ben's pulse and his breathing. "All good," she said in relief.

"Severo, his body is trying to move," Gabriel said, sounding worried.

"Don't worry about that. Ben is no match for me. I got this."

Vara watched in awe as Severo's powerful frame held Ben down in gentle firmness. There was no end to Severo's depth. Her feelings swelled again toward him.

I need to make things right.

This was all too much. An internal giggle burst out of her until tears were rolling down her cheeks.

Cece came to sit opposite her. "V, please, remember I'm your friend, and this is not personal." Cece slapped her across the face.

Vara stopped laughing and brought her hand to her throbbing cheek. "Ouch."

"Cece, was that necessary?" Severo asked, a sudden scowl contorting his face.

"Well, it worked, didn't it? We've all had a lot of information to process and losing our minds will not help, so, Vara, you're welcome." Cece grinned unashamedly.

Vara had to admit it did help her refocus.

Ben remained out. His body writhed, fighting to break free, but under Severo's hold, it wasn't going anywhere. Vara knew Severo would keep Ben safe.

Everyone stayed silent after that, willing Ben to come back. Gabriel said nothing more about his plan. After what felt like hours, Ben came to.

Gabriel was first to speak. "Ben, what happened?"

Ben let his ragged breathing return to normal before he sat up. "Firstly, Sev, thanks for keeping me grounded. Gabriel, I saw everything you just went through, like a flashback, but there's something else." Ben paused. "Severo. Cece. I saw your father. He's trapped in Obsidian Creek, and I may have an idea about how to get him back."

CHAPTER 35

Ben

en's startling news shocked his friends into silence. He was quivering after this vision, but with it came incredible clarity. Severo's stronghold had given Ben the ability to face his fears. This last week he'd been broken in more ways than one. He looked at Vara; she didn't look back.

What an idiot I've been.

"There's a lot to cover. Let me start at the beginning. When I blacked out, I was at the barrier. This happened to me before—last week in class. But this time, it was what Gabriel just saw, so Alunattra couldn't get to me. Niall was so clear to me in this vision."

Ben took a moment to wipe his sweaty hands on his breeches. Everyone was staring at him.

He took a breath. "In my astral state, it seems my inner sight is at its strongest. Niall—the Niall we knew—is gone. Alunattra is his addiction. He needs her but only because she accelerates his power. He has his own agenda, but they are using each other. It was very clear that this outcome for Niall was predestined. Alunattra lured him."

Ben saw Severo clench his fists and shake his head.

He's struggling with this as much as I am.

Ben kept going. "Alunattra's very hard to read. I was trying, but I think over time, I'll gain more knowledge. Niall is managing to guard some of his thoughts against her, and his mind control is strengthening. Honestly, I don't know if I can ever get my head around this." Ben's voice cracked, looking at Severo.

Severo exhaled. "In that one, you're not alone, but at least it's confirmation."

Ben swallowed. Niall was a third of their pack.

Would this ever sink in?

Severo was so strong, and Ben envied him, but the twinge of sadness refused to leave, and then there was Vara. Guilt set in as he remembered the kiss.

I need to talk to him. Severo deserves that.

"I know," Ben said, holding in his emotions. "I feel the same. I don't think there's anything we can do about Niall. He's dangerous, but we must all agree to act the same around him, and that goes for Clara as well. Niall is controlling her so use your words carefully."

Ben tried to give Vara a reassuring smile, but she sat strong and stoic. Her eyes were firm. Determined. She would make a good queen one day.

Stop thinking about Vara.

Everyone was waiting for him to speak. Again. "Eh, yeah, additionally, we need to guard our minds. Gabriel, Niall can't read your mind and neither can Alunattra. I saw them both try. Whether you knew that or not, you can deflect them."

Gabriel nodded. The pennies were dropping.

"With my power, I can do the same and, Severo, you will be safe as long as you keep your eyes averted when you speak to Niall. Cece, Vara, you will be the most vulnerable to him so be careful. We must all act normal and stick together."

"In all honesty, I doubt Niall has me on his radar. That can only be an advantage," Vara said, not displaying an ounce of fear.

"What she said," Cece added but got up and started pacing. "However, Ben, I don't mean to be rude but my father, now that we know where he is, I have to go and get him. How do I do that?"

Severo remained sitting quietly as if he was scared to find out the answer.

Ben shifted uncomfortably. *How would I feel if this was my father?* "Cece, I'm coming to that, but there is no 'I' only 'we,' and a careful plan is needed."

Remember, you're the prince. Keep it together.

Ben couldn't meet Cece's eyes. "I also need to admit something. I witnessed you having a vision about your father, and I wanted to talk to you about it before, but I didn't know how to. I didn't want to intrude."

Severo guffawed. "Wow, you're full of surprises these days, Ben, and that sounds like a contradiction to me. How could you not have told us this? Unbelievable!"

Cece folded her arms, staring at Ben with more impatience than anger.

Ben swallowed. This was never going to be easy, even Gabriel couldn't meet his eyes. Vara was a blank wall.

"I've no control over what's happening to me, believe me. I didn't ask for any of this. It's important we all act normal while we figure everything out, and I need time to tell you as much as I can before school begins."

When nobody voiced any objections, he continued.

"After my vision, my body moved past the barrier to Obsidian Creek, and that's when I saw your father." He held Severo and Cece's rapt stare. "He was in a cave, and he sensed me. He met my eyes for a brief second before he disappeared. Everything came to me, like a dream. All those years ago, Alunattra tried to tempt your father into the forest because of Danyall's power of teleportation and its lack of control at the time. He often neared the edge of the forest, and her voice kept luring him in. Eventually, he gave in to her power and went to the barrier."

Severo stamped his foot so hard, it cracked the marble floor. "How could he have been so stupid?"

"Aren't you listening, Sev? It wasn't his fault. Alunattra did this!" Cece yelled, her face turning red.

"Sev, Cece's right. She tried to brainwash him the way she did with Niall but, Sev, his mind was strong and his heart stronger. Danyall knew if he touched the barrier he would die and no harm would come to you both and your mother. When he did, his power took over and instead of teleporting to somewhere in Pure Bay, the connection to the barrier pulled him to the other side. Your father's been hiding ever since. Alunattra has stopped searching for him since she's never been able to catch him." Ben couldn't believe Danyall had survived all this time on his own.

Cece crumbled in floods of tears. Severo, Vara, and Gabriel huddled around her. Ben faced her and held her hands.

"Cece, I promise you, we're going to get your father back. Danyall has given me a clue. The barrier was weakened when he touched it, and I think there may be certain gifts that don't apply when it comes to the barrier." Cece didn't say anything, but she squeezed Ben's hands tightly.

"How can that be?" Vara asked. "Surely Vallore would only allocate powers that can protect us completely, right? If there are gifts that don't apply that would leave some vulnerable." Vara's eyebrows knitted together in a way that couldn't be comfortable.

Ben locked eyes with her. "Exactly what I've been wondering. Danyall's gift is top-tier and it made him an easy target for Alunattra. When Vallore blessed me, I tried to see behind his eyes. My power was already working, and I didn't know it. He's definitely got secrets. He was too strong and blocked me but perhaps Vallore doesn't decide our power. Maybe we do?"

"Makes sense," Gabriel said, pouring a fresh cup of coffee. "It would explain how we all have affinities before our ceremonies."

"Which also explains why we're told not to use our gifts outside of a controlled environment," Vara added. "If you think about it, that also means we have more control to do what needs to be done."

"Precisely." Ben smiled at Vara, and she blushed.

Severo shuffled his feet. "Ben, let's move, then. What's the plan? I'm ready, so let's do this."

Ben fist-bumped Severo's shoulder in response. "We need a bit of time. Alunattra can't find your father so that is a definite advantage. What I propose is a skillfully planned rescue mission, but I need you all to help. The voice told me a while back to pick who to trust and you guys are it. I'll need to try and communicate through my astral self. It may be the only way. Gabriel, we need to have another look at the book and study your Verdo further. That goes for all of us."

"What book?" Vara asked, her eyebrows raised.

"Ben's grandfather gave him a book that gives detailed information on Sovereign Dominions," Gabriel explained. "I've been studying it, but some of it appears in riddle form, so it's not cut and dry. Maybe we could meet again this week and see if our combined minds can decipher our Verdos?"

Ben nodded. "Yes, I agree."

"Ben, if I can just put forward a suggestion: How would you feel about asking our wishing fairies for assistance? I bet they'd be able to help."

"You literally took the words out of my mouth," Ben said, grinning. "I know I can trust Tweek, and I don't mean to sound condescending here, but how well do you all know your fairies?"

"There's no fairy as loyal as Striker. Look at the Mute Balm. Case in point," Severo said.

"Agreed. I feel the same, Sev." Ben looked to Gabriel.

"Fritzi is the one person I knew well until a month ago." Gabriel smiled. "He's friendly with Striker, and they both helped me be here today. I would say Fritzi's a safe bet."

"Vara, Cece?"

"I don't know," Cece said, her voice pensive. "I never speak about anything serious to mine, and I won't take a chance with my father's safety, so I vote no."

Vara's eyes snapped up as if she was just processing the conversation. "I agree with Cece and fairies gossip a lot. We need to be sure who we can trust. I love the relationship I have with Prine; she did tell me about Niall working with the king when I pressed her, but she's nervous, and I don't want to involve her in this."

"Okay," Ben said. "Let's summon them now."

Severo and Gabriel agreed, and the fairies were summoned to the meeting.

Ben called on Tweek. She took in the scene and squeaked in uncertainty, then rushed to Ben's shoulder.

"Tweek, Striker, Fritzi, things are happening, and we are out of our depth. We need your help." Ben quickly explained everything to the fairies.

"Oh wow," Tweek said before adding, "I've always wanted to go on an undercover mission. Ooh, we need a name, and I'll start designing our outfits. But I don't think the other fairies are needed. I'm sure I can handle whatever you need." Tweek glanced at the other two with petulance.

"If *I* may, I have the necessary expertise to assist in such a mission," Striker said with a crisp and studious voice. "I'm happy to take command. I know what I'm doing." Striker flew to Tweek, hovering over her.

"Are you a fairy to a prince?" Tweek rose to meet Striker's eye level. "Master Ben, tell him."

Ben stared up at them, fascinated. He never gave much thought to how fairies got on. Fritzi was just floating in silence, wearing a frown, as though not sure what to do. "Look, we all need to work together. We'll all have important jobs to do. There's no time for bickering."

Tweek and Striker twirled back to Ben and reluctantly agreed.

"Striker, is it true we're getting a new weapon introduction this week in class?"

"Yes, Master Ben, that's correct."

"Striker," Gabriel said, "Niall knows everything that is going on in Weapons and Devices. He's been spying. We also have reason to believe that Pixel, Clara, and Tharmus are under his control. Maybe others."

Striker cringed, appearing overwhelmed, but rallied himself. "I'll take that under advisement and try to investigate. It may be that the new equipment will be rendered useless. I can stall the training. Leave it with me."

"And with me," Tweek butted in. "I'll definitely be able to think up some ideas."

Ben tried not to laugh at the extremity of Tweek's enthusiasm. "Okay, that's great, thank you both. Moving on. Cece, I need to ask. When you see your father, are you able to talk to him?"

Cece, still glassy-eyed, snapped to attention. "Yes and no. He sees me, but he can't hear what I'm saying. It's so frustrating."

Ben understood her frustration, but he had a wild idea that could bring his friends answers. "Can everyone meet at mine on day Three after school? Severo, I need you to be an anchor for me and Cece." Ben faced her, and her keen eyes held steady with his. "I think if we meditate and focus, I could infiltrate your vision, and we could get a message to your father that way."

"Sure, whatever you need," Severo said without the slightest hesitation.

Ben relaxed, glad his friend was on board with his plan.

"We could try it," Cece said, shrugging, "but I've never been able to dream on demand. It's very selective. I shouldn't be able to do what I'm doing anyway."

"Well, it really is fortunate that you asked me to be here as I have just the solution." Tweek disappeared and then returned instantly, maneuvering her hands to bring forth a spray bottle.

Ben took the elevated product in his hands and read the label aloud. "Eelps Mist." Ben looked at Tweek expectantly.

"I made this for you, my prince, when you were a baby. It helped you drift off to sleep like that." Tweek snapped her fingers and then sent Striker a smug look.

"Fantastic, Tweek. Cece, this could work."

"Ben, do you think these visions I have will be connected to the Verdo I'll get?"

"In short, yes," Ben said, nodding.

Cece sighed in relief. "I've been wondering about that. Hey, I'm just glad to know I was right about my father. We need to get him back."

"Cece, I'm sorry I didn't listen to you," Severo said, squeezing his sister's hand.

"What else is new big brother?" She grinned up at Severo, patting his arm. "At least we know now, and we can do something about it. I just wish it could be quicker."

"I know, Cece," Ben said, "and thankfully all evidence suggests his power will keep him safe. I'll do everything I can in the next few days to have a starting point." Ben felt his power stir in his veins. It really was a part of him. Things were becoming clearer.

"We all must be at our best with our Verdos," Ben continued, tucking into a strawberry pastry. "Be meditating and building strength every spare minute you have. Severo, your new sensors, have you tested how far that goes?"

"Yes, pretty far. Striker, can you assign a color for my dad? It should give me a wide berth for detection."

"Absolutely, it will be done today," Striker said.

"Sev, that'll be an epic help, knowing where everyone is at all times," Ben said.

"Is there a way that we could communicate more easily with each other? Some kind of vibrating device maybe?" Vara suggested.

Striker's brow furrowed in consideration. "Very clever idea but not easy to do, Miss Vara. I'll add that to my list and see what I can do. Fritzi can assist me," Striker said.

"Have I suddenly become invisible?" Tweek flapped her wings with an irritated rhythm.

"If only," Striker muttered, rolling his eyes.

Tweek flew to Ben's nose. "Are you going to let him talk to me like that?"

Ben blinked before he went crosseyed and sighed. "Striker, I called the three of you here because we need help from all of you. Tweek will assist also."

Tweek stuck her tongue out at Striker, and he tilted his head in reluctant agreement. "Yes, Prince Benjamin."

"Which brings me to our big gun." Ben turned to Gabriel. "What exactly are your limitations when it comes to barriers?"

Gabriel sheepishly rubbed the back of his neck. "Funny you should ask. I'm able to go anywhere in the castle now—including the royal quarters."

This just reinforced Ben's previous thoughts.

Vallore has no idea of the depth of our powers. That must be why it's dictated for us not to use them...

Ben shook the thought away, glad of Gabriel's answer, but it did make him wonder what Gabriel had been up to.

Severo broke the tension as he bellowed a laugh. "Gabes, you are a sleekit boy but don't forget your magic won't work on me!" Severo flicked his gaze from Gabriel to Cece. "I'm watching you."

Ben smiled at Severo but didn't know if he could sense that. His friend was like oil to a squeak, smoothing any rough areas. He really wanted to talk to him.

"Are you able to cloak anyone other than yourself?" Ben asked Gabriel.

Gabriel shrugged. "Not sure, I've never experimented with that."

Ben stood. "Can you try it now?"

"Sure." Gabriel stood and downed the last of his coffee. "Any volunteers?"

Severo was on his feet. "Try it with me," he said with boisterous readiness. "That way if your shield tries anything, my body will deflect it."

"Good thinking," Gabriel said. He scrunched his brow, concentrating.

Gabriel's shield took form, and they all stood a little dumbfounded. It was like he was being erased before their eyes. *So cool.* Severo remained in clear view.

"I guess that one doesn't work." Severo slumped. "That could've been handy."

"Ahem. I may be able to help with that one also." Striker proudly took center in the room before sliding a gloating look in Tweek's direction. "It's risky for me, but I have my ways. I need some time, but I can modify your bracelets so that in close vicinity it would create a link band. The five of you would appear as one entity, allowing you to be cloaked under Gabriel's protection."

Fritzi gazed up at Striker with everything indicating hero worship; Tweek gave a dramatic groan.

"Striker, the definition of brilliance, everyone." Severo led the group in a deserved cheer for his fairy, aside from Tweek, whose stance reeked of hostility.

Heat filled Ben's head. An idea formed and he didn't hold back. "Gabriel, do you think your shield could penetrate the barrier to gain access to Obsidian Creek?"

Vara gasped and Cece hung her head. Severo beefed up his torso, ready for anything.

Gabriel gave a slow, pensive nod. "I don't know, but I'll try anything to help."

Cece went to Gabriel and curled up on his knee.

Ben knew this would be Gabriel's response. What he was asking of his friend would put him and everyone in danger.

Striker flew to the middle of the hut. "I might add at this point that what we are doing is breaking all the rules, but I am committed to the cause. I believe sometimes things must be tackled in alternative ways for the greater good. You have my silence and word on this."

Tweek and Fritzi came alongside Striker and gave a bow.

Ben's heart swelled, and he thanked them.

We're doing this.

"Give me these next few days to put something airtight into motion and we can go from there." Ben closed the meeting and told Gabriel to hang tight. For everyone's safety, things had to stay as they were for now. Gabriel nodded and left quickly. The school bell had just chimed.

Ben's eyes fell on Vara as she left with Cece. When he'd kissed her, the magnets had prodded his leg through the pocket of his breeches, and his mind filled with the girl who owned his dreams. But looking at Vara now, all he wanted was to fix everything.

Before he was tempted to run after the girl who scattered his emotions, a more pressing situation flicked like a switch in his brain. Ben tapped Severo's arm, and his friend paused at the hide hut's exit.

"Can you meet me in the library at lunch? We need to talk."

CHAPTER 36

Severo

S evero made his way through the morning, and for once, food was not welcomed.

I can't believe my father is alive.

It hadn't sunk in, and guilt swamped him for not believing Cece. His impatience was like an itch he couldn't scratch. He hoped Ben would have some answers soon. The Arisons, as a general rule, didn't like to wait for anything, and his father needed help.

It didn't feel like eight years had passed. He still remembered that day. His parents had been arguing in the morning, and when he'd arrived downstairs, his mother was crying. His father had already left and sitting on the worktop had been his identification bracelet. He had never shown up for his post at Weapons and Devices. With his gift of teleportation, everyone had expected him to return, but he never did. To this day, Severo hadn't asked his mother what the fight was about.

As he made his way to the library, his discs perked and highlighted everything. People had already forgotten he couldn't see.

I haven't.

Some days were harder than others. He missed seeing his mother's and Cece's face. Their outlines were at least detectable, but it wasn't the same. And then there was Vara. She burned brightly, but he longed to get lost in her chocolate eyes again. Anger took a front seat. Elias had got off lightly with everything.

Flashes of smaller lights filled his darkness. Fairies. Lots of them.

Nobody cared about Elias because there were bigger things to worry about. Severo was ready.

Bring it on.

As if thinking Elias's name summoned him, Severo's new instrument lit like a flame to a candle. He had assigned Elias the color brown, and his sidekicks were beige and taupe—indicative of mud and sludge. Elias was excrement and they were his flies.

They hadn't seen Severo, so he ducked behind a pillar. So it was true—Elias had been allowed back to school. No doubt down to his persuasive lies. They were leaving the library. Severo's fists twitched, but he held himself firm.

"What a stroke of luck with Gabriel. Are you sure you didn't do it, Elias?"

"Clive, I wish. If anyone asks though, tell them I did. At least he's taken care of. It's doubtful his luck will be changing anytime soon."

Norris's obnoxious laugh carried through the library. "Brilliant. What about the others?"

"Oh, I haven't forgotten about them," Elias said, his voice dripping with spite. "Ben will be tricky, but Vara and Cece—well, idiot girls won't be a problem, will they? I can't believe that ugly redhead had the nerve to hit me."

"Ha, you're just mad she never said yes when you asked her to the dance." Clive laughed but shut up when Elias punched his arm.

"Get your facts right, Clive. It was never about her, anything to noise up Severo and that weed Gabriel. Anyway, they'll get what's coming to them."

Severo shoved down the impulse to throw Elias over the walkway. He couldn't risk a house arrest now. No way was any harm going to come to his sister or Vara. He wouldn't let these leeches anywhere near them. He would need to tell Ben. Forearmed is forewarned.

He made to move but caught Niall's gray smoke. Severo let him pass. He wasn't sure, but as Niall descended into the bricked stairwell, it seemed like he handed something to Elias. Sight would be helpful right now. He watched Niall's gray shroud disappear into the stairwell. Could this really be the same person he'd known for eight years? Severo froze, remembering the first time he registered Niall.

His father had just disappeared, and Elias had been winding him up. He'd locked himself in a toilet cubicle. It was the only way to hide the tears that couldn't help falling.

He jumped when someone tapped the door.

"Hello, are you okay?"

Severo stiffened. "Go away."

He flung open the cubicle to find the prince and his sidekick—Niall, was it? All he knew was that Elias hated them. Severo glared at them, knowing his face was angry and tear-streaked. The prince was biting his lip and Niall had his hands in his pocket, as though not sure where to look. They didn't say a thing. Unlike Elias and his cruel words; nevertheless, Severo couldn't stand the pity.

"Can we help you? Do you want us to walk home with you?" Ben asked.

"No, I said go away. I mean it, and don't you dare tell anyone about this!" Severo brushed past them and slammed the bathroom door.

For weeks he'd kept to himself, waiting to hear the rumor that he'd been crying in the toilet, but he never did. One day, he sat beside Ben and Niall. Nobody spoke about it, but they'd been friends ever since.

Everything was different now.

I have to get my head around that.

He quickened his step to the library.

Like the beginnings of a painting, Severo saw the outline of rows of book stacks. Ben's blue mist was already waiting beside the largest one. He signaled with his arm, and Severo assumed to follow.

Severo walked in a straight line, his disks differentiating the outlines of different objects in his path. He took care to avoid bumping into anything whilst keeping up the act of being unperturbed. The musty mix of dust particles made his nose twitch as it dawned on him how little time he spent here. It smelled like books. He got why Gabriel liked it here. The air held an element of calm that relaxed Severo. Ben moved ahead and stopped at a circular table on a stand-alone island, then sprinkled what Severo now knew to be the Conceal Dust.

"Hey, Sev, thanks for coming."

"Ben, you can lose the formalities, we've been friends since we were eight. I know why you asked me here, so spit it out." Severo tried to read his friend's face but all he saw was a light blue blur. Ben stayed silent, and Severo grew frustrated. "Ben?"

"Sorry, you know I don't do feelings," Ben said, his voice sounding more awkward than normal. "I'm not sure what to say."

Severo cleared his throat. "How about I start you off? Landis is falling apart. My father is stuck and you're trying to find a way to get him out. You have crazy visions you can't control. A voice is talking to you. Evil is about to pay a visit and we're in love with the same girl."

Ben gave a nod. "I've always admired your ability to summarize."

Severo smiled a half smile but didn't say anything.

"I don't know how long it will take to get your father out, but I know we will. I haven't spoken to anyone else. I don't know if anyone would believe us. Not sure my father would even hear me, but I have a few ideas."

"Don't keep me hanging," Severo said. "What are they?"

"Well, the voice that I hear, I'm never sure when I'll hear it. I need to find a way to summon it. It's a risk going to Obsidian Creek as my vision confirmed—the voice will only be there when Alunattra's not. If I can find a way to communicate with it and your father, we could arrange for your father to be at the barrier when Alunattra's not. We may only have a small window."

Severo forced out a heavy sigh. "You're right, it's risky, but it could work. How are you going to contact the voice?"

"I need your help with that, Sev."

Severo could hear the doubt in Ben's voice. "So, you think because of our feelings for Vara that would stop me from helping you?"

"No, that's not what I meant at all. It's more I feel guilty for asking."

Severo made sure he was facing the outline of Ben's face. "Our world, for all intents and purposes, may not be ours for long. You should know me well enough by now that nothing would get in the way of helping you, especially as it involves bringing my father home. Just because we both have feelings for Vara doesn't mean we can't put those aside. This is bigger than our love life."

Ben paused, then chuckled. "When did you get so smart?"

"Hey, it's always been there." Severo smirked. "It took me losing my sight to finally see. I do want you to know that I can't ignore my gut. I've tried, but I saw you guys kiss. I honestly could have eaten you for breakfast, but I figured if it'd been me, I would've done the same thing." Severo shrugged.

"You're a better man than me."

"Finally, something we can agree on." Severo smiled.

"Life sure was easier when we were kids!"

"Life was easier without hormones, you mean!"

Severo and Ben chuckled in understanding.

"So. What's the deal with you and Vara?" Severo knotted his arms.

"I don't know. The kiss didn't go well. But, like you, I have feelings for her too."

Severo's heart thundered. It hadn't been what his limited vision had encountered then? Maybe he still had a chance with her. He was scared to let his heart hope but giving up was not in his make-up. "Okay. What now then?"

Ben nodded. "Maybe we're at an impasse?"

Severo felt like Ben was asking him for permission to proceed. "No. I think we state our case to Vara—inevitably she will be the one to decide. Until then, we both know how each other feels but allow each other the chance to win her over." Severo saw the contour of Ben's shoulders relax.

"So, you're saying we both express how we feel and let her choose?"

Severo blew an exasperated breath in his friend's direction. "Sheesh, are you really the one we're entrusting our world to? Yes, that's what I'm saying!"

"Okay, then, on one condition," Ben countered. "No matter what happens, we respect Vara's decision and remain friends anyway. Not to sound like a total wet blanket, but I've no intention of losing any more friends."

Severo pondered Ben's request. "I agree to your terms." He held his hand out across the table and they shook on it. "So, can we stop talking about all the feelings now?"

"Please," Ben said in relief.

"I just saw that cretin Elias and his lackeys in the hall. He's planning something. It seems you have him stumped, but I'm worried about Vara and Cece." The tension building in Severo's shoulders and neck piqued again.

"Not on our watch. Honestly, we've no time for stupid games. We will need to be on guard. My father just seems to ignore it," Ben muttered. "I don't think he can see past the peaceful world he thinks this is."

"This is a job for us, and after what Elias pulled with me, I would say he is not to be underestimated."

"I know, sorry," Ben said, "I didn't mean that. I wish we could find a way to get him off our backs for good."

"We'll keep close to the girls, and I'll keep my ears to the ground. Let's get back to the lunch hall. I want to check on Cece, and we also need to show face for Niall, which reminds me. I think, although I can't be sure, he just handed something to Elias. Have you spoken to him today?" Severo asked.

"Yes, I played him at his own game." There was a hint of craftiness in Ben's tone. "Do you think he's controlling Elias?"

Severo shrugged. "Who knows. I'm simply saying it looked suspect, but with no eyesight, it's impossible to tell."

Ben shifted uncomfortably. "Hmm, okay. Noted. Niall bought it this morning, though. Thinks we're all up in arms about Gabriel. I laid it on thick and even thanked him for helping my father. I didn't feel happy about it, but it needed to be done."

"I know what you mean," Severo said, feeling the weight of that truth all too well. "I can't believe how much our lives have changed. Can we meet before day Three? Cece and I are heavy on edge."

"My parents told me I'm not allowed to have friends over for a few days until the dust settles with Gabriel. Give me a few days to get a plan together. How're things with Striker?"

"He's saying much the same—that he needs time, but he already has things underway and said he will bring a progress report to the meeting, so I suppose we'll just need to wait." Severo contemplated all of this as he and Ben made their way to the noisy lunchroom. He tried not to flinch when Niall's gray dot came into view. It wasn't so mixed up today. He remembered what Ben had said about not looking him in the eye.

"Niall, man, how are you?" Severo greeted, maintaining a friendly veneer. "Can you believe that about Gabriel? Just when you think you know a person." As Severo sat, he couldn't see Vara or Cece's shadows anywhere.

"Yes, I'm as shocked as you. I'll be honest, I'd suspected something was wrong, but I didn't want to believe it. Clara, you were the same."

Clara nodded stiffly as if she'd been programmed.

Dividing his attention, Severo couldn't stop scaling the room and beyond for the girls. "Have you guys seen Cece or Vara?"

"I saw them this morning, but they haven't been here during

lunch. Maybe they went to the library," Clara suggested, and Severo gauged rigidity from Niall.

Severo felt Ben's gaze as he turned to him.

"I'm sure they're around," Ben quickly added. "No doubt Cece wanted some time on her own, especially with the news about Gabriel. Is she okay?" Ben asked Severo, clearly trying to act normal for Niall's sake.

"She's dealing."

Something is wrong.

As the bell rang, Niall said, "Should we all head to VDS? I hear that you, Ben, and the other new starts get to try out your skills today. Well, all but Gabriel that is. Such a sad shame, that."

Severo played coy when he side-swerved a glance in Ben's direction.

He must be seething right now.

Severo had no way to know. One more thing to remind him of his disability. He bit the inside of his lip to keep his mouth shut.

As they arrived at VDS, the bell rang, and everyone took their seats.

Severo kept looking at the door, but Vara did not appear.

CHAPTER 37

Niall

N iall held his composure, but inside, a restless desire brewed. What would Ben do with his power? Niall gnawed on his bottom lip, anxious to see it manifest. So far, nothing he had tried had worked. But today he was prepared. His pawns were in place. His teacher was under his thrall, primed and ready.

This morning had been a triumphant success. Deep satisfaction bubbled up within him watching the pathetic disappointment that oozed from Ben about his precious Gabriel. Niall had to stop himself from gloating in Ben's face. Everyone was so quick to believe his story, although he wasn't that surprised. His power was incomparable to others, especially with its new depths.

One day this world will be mine.

His body twitched with excitement. The king believed Niall for now. Vallore putting a seal around Gabriel's home didn't offer Niall reassurance though. The boy needed to be dealt with, one way or another.

Niall flicked his gaze around the students and homed in on Severo, who seemed distracted. *Why?* With his disability, he had become near impossible to read. It was something to do with his sister.

Why did he care so much? They're all fools.

Severo shot up from his seat. "Professor, may I go to the bathroom, please?"

"Yes, of course, Severo."

As Severo left, Professor Longwind pivoted to Ben, her straight hair unmoving. "Prince Benjamin, would you like to take us through the elements of your Sovereign Dominion, then maybe a demonstration?"

Niall fixed his eyes on Ben who flinched at the professor's request.

"What do you want me to do?" Ben said nervously.

"Well, I know your grandfather is your meditation supervisor," the professor said with a coaxing tone. "How about something he has helped you with?"

"Hmm," Ben murmured. "I still don't feel very sure. I'm meditating a lot, but I've not quite got a grasp."

The professor stepped toward Ben and gave him a pressing stare. "Niall tells me the aspect of astral projection has started to present itself, could you demonstrate that for us?"

Niall observed Ben. He squirmed like an insect was crawling around inside his clothing.

"If you like, Ben, I could assist you with this," Niall offered, adopting a pleasant facade. "After what happened the last time, I understand your reservations."

Ben finally looked at him, but Niall couldn't make out his thoughts. This was infuriating. Niall bit back his impatience as warm metallic droplets seeped through his teeth.

The creak of the classroom door announced Severo's return. He strode to the teacher's desk, and Niall heard with perfect clarity Severo's whisper to the professor, "I need the prince's assistance with a confidential matter."

Niall's irritation spread through him like an infection. He started scratching his hives as Ben left the room. He hated how no one questioned these things, although for him it did come with advantages. He wasn't about to let Ben and Severo sabotage his plans.

Niall leapt from his chair, disrupting the silence in the classroom.

"Where are you going?" Clara stared up at him in confusion, her eyes as wide as saucers. "We're in the middle of class."

He sported his fallacious smile, acknowledging the person who was now his eternal nuisance. "I'm needed, stay here. I'll be back before you know it."

Niall approached Professor Longwind, peering deep into her eyes. "I sense I may be of some help. May I be excused?"

The professor gazed back, under his thrall, and nodded without a word.

As Niall left the room, he closed his eyes and like branches of a tree, his mind scoped out his surroundings, homing in on people throughout the castle. Within a month, his power had accelerated, and he could perceive people beyond close vicinity. His perception pulsed like radar, tuning its frequency toward his targets.

Severo and Ben were still in the castle. All pupils were in class which made his mission simplistic. His friends were in the hallway outside the physics room. Niall took a gradual approach through the pillared halls, ducking below classroom doorways, remaining unseen.

"Are you sure Cece's not in class?" Ben said.

"No, I checked," Severo replied, a twinge of worry in his voice. "She never arrived either. Where are they?"

Niall kept close enough to hear their conversation. It was a bit strange that the girls were missing.

Could this be Alunattra's doing? How?

Grateful for the pillars' concealing width, Niall pressed ahead, trying to understand what was happening.

"We need Gabriel. He could help."

Confused, a nervous twitch battered Niall's eyelid as he took in these words.

"Yes, that would be helpful. Shame we're not talking to him, though," Severo said to Ben.

Relief flooded Niall. He'd almost thought Ben had double-crossed him. It was time to intervene and put on the concerned friend act. He left his concealment and hollered, "Ben, Severo, is everything okay? I was worried. Do you need my help?"

Ben remained quiet and his expression was difficult to fathom, offering zero clues.

Severo, however, spoke up. "Niall, Cece and Vara never appeared in their classes."

"Why don't I help you look? I'll do a walk-through of the castle and grounds to see if I can detect their whereabouts."

Severo's brow lifted with surprise, and Niall wasn't sure why. Was something else going on? Or was worry inspiring their unusual emotions?

The three of them agreed to separate and search, and as they went to do so, Tharmus alighted in his usual way. Out of nowhere.

"Of course, it's you three. Why are you not in class?"

Ben rubbed his temples in exasperation. "Tharmus, as always, you're the king of misunderstanding. Vara and Cece are missing. Perhaps for once, get over the eternal power trip and help us find them."

Tharmus turned a shade of puce. Niall sighed. All this time-wasting was aggravating him.

"Tharmus, I was just about to search the castle. Could I be of assistance to you?" Niall asked.

"Yes, Master Niall. Right away," Tharmus replied.

Niall bit back his smirk, knowing the guard would do anything he told him. The man was stupid. Niall almost laughed.

I've programmed him like a device.

When he was with Tharmus, the guard knew not to talk. Niall preferred the silence.

The mind control drained his body. He needed a boost soon. Pixel was invaluable; she hadn't found a flaw in the barrier yet but when she did, it would be the first step in breaking it down.

Niall could visualize when Alunattra wasn't there. His brain was now working from different compartments, like a tree with scattered roots. When she arrived back in his thoughts, however, it came with little warning and headaches were becoming commonplace.

Niall stopped. The girls were very close. He closed his eyes, allowing his mind to become a homing beacon. And there they were. Many feet below where he stood. In the dungeon.

Her voice swept into his mind like a raging fever. "Leave them there and don't allow anyone to find them, then come to me," Alunattra said.

CHAPTER 38

Vara

Vara's throat resembled sandpaper as she fought the urge to swallow. Nobody heard her incessant banging. Her wrists were red and sore. No healing came. She screamed. It was fruitless, and she now had an unquenchable thirst.

She descended back into the depths of the humid prison, away from the only glimmer of light, almost gagging on the rancid waft suffusing her nostrils. She crouched where Cece lay, placing a hand upon her chest, and was relieved to feel its rise and fall. Vara pinched her thigh to stay focused.

One minute they'd been walking together with their freshly brewed coffees when Vara spied out of the corner of her eye a strange hole in the marble floor. Cece bounded ahead, seized with curiosity. Vara followed on her heels, just as curious. They reached the dark opening, and a hard shove at their backs sent them spiraling down the musty crumbling steps, to the foot of the dungeon. Vara could still smell the remnants of coffee splashed upon her clothes.

Vara had bumped to the bottom unscathed after her clothes caught on a piece of protruding stone. Cece had not been so lucky. She lay twisted on the stone floor, her head surrounded by a pool of blood. A giant, festering burn was already forming on Cece's leg, and the fabric of her dress melded to her skin. Vara tried to peel the material off but it was no use. Vara grabbed a scarf from her satchel and applied pressure to the head wound, but she had nothing for the bubbling burn. The bleeding had at least stopped, but the longer they remained here, the more Cece was in grave danger.

"I'm so sorry, Cece, I know someone will find us soon. Stay strong. I've never met anyone with strength like yours. I promise everything will be okay." Vara sounded surer than she felt.

I wish I had some water.

Her raspy voice called for Prine again. Nothing but eerie silence. She knew now the rumors were true. Sovereign Dominions were useless here.

What if I never get out of here?

Her family. Severo. Ben. Vara promised herself that from now on life would be different.

Please someone find us.

Her teeth chattered, and she pulled her lilac hooded cape around her.

Who pushed us in? Was it Niall?

Vara gave Cece a comforting touch, then got to her feet and searched for a way out of this dungeon. The tiniest hum echoed in her eardrums. She tiptoed through the dark corridor. The further she traveled, the less she could see. Apart from the spotlight at the base of the stairs, there was no light, natural or otherwise.

Vara focused on that hum as she skimmed her hand along the dark, gray-stone wall. Each cell's iron door was closed and bricked in. There was a small opening above each doorway, but Vara could not see inside. The lack of light didn't help.

She stopped outside the cell producing the tiniest of thrums. The thick door had an alcove in the center. Vara tried to put her hand inside, but was blocked by a sheet of invisible glass. There was a small lock above the glass where a padlock hung. If something important was here, maybe someone would come soon.

The thought dissolved as Cece's weak moan drifted down the cell block. Vara touched the cold stone and worked her way back to Cece. Vara stiffened like ice. Cece's body was in the throes of a spasm. Tears flowed down Vara's dry, cracked cheeks as she cradled her friend.

"Cece, I'm here, stay with me."

Vara rested Cece's head on her lap and feathered her hand through her sticky curls. She sang to her and sighed in relief when Cece's breathing evened. Her friend remained unconscious, and the intensity of rapid eye movement made Vara's stomach clench.

Vara calmed her emotions and practiced meditation. She sent up a silent prayer.

"Please, help us. Keep my friend alive."

CHAPTER 39

Gabriel

G abriel lay tense in bed. Earlier this morning, he'd crept downstairs and seen his parents slumped over the dining table, food untouched, and not exchanging a word. He wanted to talk to them and almost lifted his shield, but he was supposed to be mute, in his room. They hadn't spoken to him since he was put under house arrest. His mother's shifts at the hospital had been moved to lates because of what happened, but today his parents were meeting with the king and council. Outside of the meeting with his friends, Tharmus was the only person he saw because the king had ordered intense surveillance. Gabriel got the impression Tharmus believed he was innocent.

Gabriel desperately wanted to leave the house. For some inexplicable reason, he had the most gut-wrenching feeling that wouldn't leave him alone.

"Fritzi."

Fritzi appeared immediately at his command.

"Any news?" Gabriel asked, sitting up.

"Why yes." Fritzi buzzed in a circle on Gabriel's palm. "Striker has been working round the clock, and he has some amazing news to share with you all at the next meeting. I have just come from Weapons and Devices." Fritzi furled his arms and let out a sigh. "Unfortunately, Striker and Tweek keep bumping heads. I've no idea why she has a problem. I think Striker is simply wonderful."

Gabriel smiled at Fritzi. He was the kindest fairy Gabriel had come across, always wanting everyone to get along and be happy. "I know, and maybe over time that'll change. I'm going to head back over to the castle soon. Have my parents said anything to their fairies?"

"No. I've been alienated in the fairy quarters. Nobody believes you are innocent, although I told them all this morning." Fritzi bowed his head as tiny tears escaped.

"It's okay, Fritzi. I know everything will work out. Trust me. I'm sorry you're getting treated badly. You come and hang out here anytime. Look, I even made you something while I've been stuck in." Gabriel pointed to the carved wooden structure at the side of his armoire.

Fritzi touched a hand to his chest. "For me?"

"All yours. I made it a while ago in woodshop and have just added the finishing touches. They cleared out my desk after, well, you know."

Fritzi floated over to the tiny carved house and flew through the open shuttered windows. All handmade furniture. Fritzi sat on the miniature chaise lounge.

"I love it," Fritzi hiccupped, his eyes glimmering.

Gabriel gave his fairy a wide grin. "Think of it as your second home, and hey, I needed a break from climbing the walls."

"Have you been climbing the walls? Is this a new aspect you've discovered?" Fritzi asked in disbelief.

Gabriel held in his laughter at his fairy's naivety. "Just an expression, Fritzi. It means I'm going crazy here. Why don't you head back to help Striker and Tweek, and I'll go find some halls to haunt." He paused, then added, "Another joke."

Fritzi gave a weak attempt at a smile before waving goodbye.

When Gabriel heard his parents leave, that was his cue to go. He padded his bed with pillows and dropped from his window to avoid the guard fairies stationed outside his room. His legs enjoyed the exercise after being holed up in his room. The crunch of gravel under his feet made him feel free, although he glanced over his shoulder to make sure nobody heard him. He was alone.

I wish I was soundproof too.

He would check in on the gang first in VDS, then surprise Cece.

Gabriel remained cloaked the whole time and slowed while walking over the bridge. The Fairy Guard was everywhere. Being light on his feet was a perfect art now. He glided through the open doorway without having to buzz in.

Demonstrations were underway when he arrived at VDS. Arlo's fingers elongated to reach an item across the other side of the room, distracting Gabriel until he realized that none of his friends were in class. The knot of discomfort deepened in his stomach as he moved through the halls.

Something's not right.

Maybe Ben was in his own quarters for some reason. But that didn't explain Severo or Vara's absence from class. And what of Niall? Gabriel hadn't seen him in VDS either. That fact sparked a riot inside his gut.

He shuffled toward the barrier to the royal wing, and the instant tingle that allowed him access hardly fazed him. Having done this several times now, it no longer seemed like a fluke. The halls were silent, and Ben was not in his room. The hide hut was the next place on his checklist, but he stopped at the base of the open stairwell that led to the roof terrace. Through the long skylight, Gabriel caught sight of the stone tower, the castle's topmost peak. A ribbon of white silk dangled from the tower's terrace. Gabriel held the metal railings as he climbed the stairs toward the flash of fabric. It was a tight squeeze. Unlike the enclosed stairwell that connected the castle levels, this was open and curved.

He stepped onto the veranda. This was the first time he had been here. Smooth stone lay beneath his feet. A sculpted stone balustrade fenced in the terrace and the tower pillar sat in the middle, tapering to the sky. Swirls of electricity sparked from the tip and weaved in and out of the clouds. The power center of Landis.

He tiptoed, not sure his gift would extend to the intimidating tower. He had never thought to explore it before but like everything else, he sailed through.

He looked to his right, and shock seized him. He clamped a hand over his mouth before he made an audible gasp. There, sitting dazed on the ground, was the queen. The tail of her dress grazed his ankles in the wind. She stared into space, tears absently falling—catatonic like.

Gabriel's veil threatened to lift when his emotional capacity dipped for a second, but perception was one step ahead of him. The queen would know about his supposed atrocities; however, if she needed help, he would locate someone. He turned to leave, and the queen whispered something he didn't catch. Had she spotted him?

When he focused on her face, she wasn't talking to him but searching into the skies above as she said,

"High Host Vallore,
I call to thee.
I ask that you
present to me."

GABRIEL FORGOT TO BREATHE AS HER BESEECHING REQUEST RESONATED with him. Vallore could be summoned. Gabriel repeated the words to himself to lock them in.

Vallore materialized. The white of his robes shone brightly, and Gabriel avoided looking directly at him, afraid of being caught or blinding his eyes. Vallore didn't seem aware of his presence; the High Host's penetrating gaze was fixed on the queen. Gabriel strangled his nerves, careful not to make a sound.

"You risk much by calling me," Vallore said to the queen. "We do not like to be disturbed for things out of our control. You're already suffering from the consequences of your actions and what has passed cannot be changed. You made a choice, and you will reap what flourishes."

With that, Vallore vanished, and the queen crumpled into a fetal position, crying a river of tears. Gabriel felt compelled to go to her and would have if not for a commotion in the halls below.

"Father, Father. We need help."

Gabriel descended from the tower, hoping the queen would be okay. He reached the lower hall, and to his surprise, Ben and Severo were now in the royal quarters. Their faces were etched with panic.

Gabriel's step quickened, and he fell in line behind them. Ben knocked on a door just as the king answered.

"Benjamin, are you well?" Concern permeated King Vardez's eyes. "Is it your mother?"

Ben shook his head. "No, Father, we have a serious situation. Vara and Cece are missing. They never appeared in their classes. Can you get the Fairy Guard to patrol?"

Gabriel felt sick. *Cece.*

The king pondered before answering. "Of course. The main guard is in our meeting quarters. I'm sure it's nothing to worry about, son. Maybe they've been requested for something, but rest assured I'll attend to this right away. Go back to your class for now and leave it with me." The king left in a hurry.

Gabriel recognized the resolved determination in Ben and Severo's eyes. They had no intention of doing that and neither did he.

"Gabes, I'm so glad you're here," Severo said, looking straight in Gabriel's direction. "We need you. Is there anything you can do? Something's not right."

Ben put his finger to his lips, silencing Severo, then indicated for them to follow him to his room.

When they arrived, Severo looked distraught, pacing like a restless animal, and Ben was pale.

"Tell me what happened?" Gabriel said, exiting his shield. "Do you think Niall has something to do with it?"

Ben was quick to answer. "On this occasion, I don't think so, but we can't rule it out. Niall is off with Tharmus now, but that doesn't give me any comfort." Ben's voice turned serious. "Gabriel, he has Tharmus under his thumb, and he was spying on us before. I almost gave the game away, but Severo spotted him on his radar."

Gabriel knew what they were thinking. "Could they have gone to The Forbidden Vale?"

Severo shook his head at the suggestion. "I know my sister. Although she can be impulsive, she's not stupid, and she knows she would need backup."

Gabriel mulled over Severo's words, not so sure. "Listen, I may be the only one safe enough to go there. I could check it out and hide if I see any sign of Alunattra. I do have an idea, though."

Severo's troubled features unscrewed enough to form a taut grin. "I had a feeling you might. Let's hear it."

"Severo, if you could ground Ben and be his anchor," Gabriel said, then directed his attention on Ben, "do you think your astral self could locate them?"

Ben's pained expression suggested he wished that had been his first thought. "Yes, I think so. We have no time to waste. Gabriel, make your way there and be careful."

Gabriel nodded and put his disguise in place.

He kept light on his feet, sprinting as fast as his legs would allow, pausing with a slight hesitancy when he saw the queen descend the narrow tower stairwell. She looked like her usual self, her complexion a healthy, fair shade. Gabriel didn't have room for further thought but vowed to speak to Ben as soon as he was able. At least she appeared well for now.

When he reached the ground floor, he made his way past the coffee cart and psyched himself up for what he needed to do. His feet came to a sudden lurch when he detected the voices he'd spent years hiding from. Force of habit deterred him, and he scurried into the shadows.

Elias, Clive, and Norris were laughing uncontrollably. Shielded, Gabriel approached them.

"I still can't believe you did that. How did you manage to get it open?" Norris asked Elias.

"Here's the thing," Elias replied, his face plastered with smugness. "My fairy happens to work on the king's guard. It was a breeze."

Gabriel watched Norris pale as he asked Elias another question.

"But what happens now? What if nobody finds them?"

Clive gulped.

"That, boys, is not my problem." Elias snickered like a nasty imp. "They have more than me as an enemy and it was due. Pathetic girls that think they're better than everyone can find their own way out."

Vara and Cece's disappearance was their doing. Anger burned in Gabriel's chest. Without thinking, he launched himself on Elias and pinned him up against the wall, losing his shield in the process.

"Where are they?" Gabriel snapped. "Tell me, and I won't report you to the king."

Elias sneered at him and made gestures to his friends. Thick calloused fingers gripped Gabriel's arms from behind.

Elias called out, "Slick."

Gabriel assumed this was his fairy. He struggled to get free, but Clive and Norris were strong, and their firm grip kept Gabriel bound.

"I need you to open the dungeon again for one more," Elias said, smirking with mischievous delight.

"Master Elias, may I ask if this is a good idea? If the king finds out, you and I will be punished."

"Slick, just do it. Gabriel is supposed to be on house arrest. The king needs to know what he's dealing with. I'm being of service to Landis here. Gabriel is the culprit, not me. I'll go to the king in a few days with our version of events and everyone wins. Ha, well, except them," Elias jeered.

"Very well, sir. As you wish," Slick said.

Gabriel couldn't believe Elias would manipulate his fairy like this.

He wanted to shout, but Clive's hand was firm against his mouth —and it smelled like sardines. He wanted to vomit. Elias moved aside, and Clive and Norris dragged Gabriel across the floor.

Gabriel's eyes widened as Slick opened a concealed trap door. Norris and Clive let him go as Elias pushed him into the depths of the dark hole.

CHAPTER 40

Ben

"Find them, Ben," Severo pleaded, standing nervously at Ben's bedside.

Keep control, keep control.

Ben slowed his breaths. "Just make sure you don't let me fly out my bedroom window."

"That was your problem the last time. I wasn't there. Go do your thing!"

Ben said no more and got into position, laying flat on his bedroom floor rug. Severo had a strong hold on him, and Ben felt safe. Recent meditation with his grandad had allowed him to reach his hypnagogic state more easily, and his essence departed quickly. He tapped into the corner of his mind that deepened his mental acuity, and he vibrated upwards, effortlessly.

Severo looked more hopeful than confident, and Ben knew it was up to him. He exited the castle and made his way first to each of their homes, more to rule that out. The townsfolk were everywhere. The sounding horn made a loud automated announcement, and the people were panicking. No wonder; nothing like this had ever happened before. It was chaos. The villagers were huddled in groups and doors were wide open throughout the neighborhood. Floating candles lined the village square and lit up the alleys, highlighting all paths.

The Arison home consisted of his friend's mother in an unresponsive state. She was being comforted by Leah—Gabriel's mother—and Dr. Lovett was also present. No sign of Cece.

In Vara's home, her parents held hands, sitting closely together with their twin girls, one on each knee.

Ben searched through each room.

Has Gabriel found anything?

Ben last saw Vara this morning at the meeting, so where could she be? She meant so much to him, and he needed to tell her. Was she with Cece? His need to help his friends compelled him to further his search. They had to be alright.

Ben breezed through the gardens, reminiscing the time they had been there.

It feels like yesterday, not four weeks ago. So much has changed.

Next, he checked the vineyards and the farm, followed by Purity Creek and The Crying Caves. Panic started to bubble within as the horizon over Landis announced the pending evening. Any minute his body threatened to become an experiment gone wrong. At least Severo had control of him this time.

They must be in the castle somewhere.

Hours had passed but Severo still held strong. Ben's spirit re-entered the castle, and he frantically searched high and low. Something niggled at him, like an answer on the tip of his tongue. He regained control of his thoughts and followed a path in his mind that revealed itself to him. The girls were close. On the ground floor, ahead of the coffee cart, and before the wrought iron entrance was solid marble flooring. Peering closer, Ben saw the outline of something underneath. The dungeon.

This must be it.

Ben floated below the marble floor, into the darkness, and down the decaying stone steps. He witnessed not only Vara and Cece, but Gabriel also. Cece was unconscious. Vara held her head in her lap, stroking her hair. Gabriel was checking Cece's vitals.

"Can any of you hear me?" Ben asked, hoping his voice reached them. "I'm here. I'll get help right away."

Gabriel turned and stared right at him.

"Gabriel, can you hear me?"

"Ben, I see you, our powers don't work down here. If you can get out, Slink, Elias's fairy, is responsible for opening the doorway. Your father will need to get the Fairy Guard to open it from the outside. Be quick. Cece is just holding on." Gabriel's voice broke as he said the last word.

Ben vanished back up the decrepit stairs, hearing Vara's voice briefly in the background. "Is Ben here? I don't see him."

Ben retracted from the dungeon without issue. He didn't know if he managed it on a technicality because his actual body was located somewhere else in the building but was glad of it.

As he sprang from his sleep-like state and back into his weighted body, Severo let go and Ben bolted upright.

"Severo, they're in the dungeon. It's located in the south hall, to the left of the castle entrance, near the coffee cart. Call the fairies. I'll get my father and Tweek to help." He gripped his friend's broad shoulder. "Sev, Cece is hurt."

Severo leapt to his feet, calling for Striker at the same time, and he fled with wondrous speed. Ben called for Tweek.

"Do you know where my father is?" he asked, steadying his legs beneath him.

"I do," Tweek replied, nodding. "He's called a meeting."

Ben marched toward the bedroom door. "Tweek, can you let him know Elias and Slick are behind it? Vara and Cece are in the dungeon, and so is Gabriel. We need to get him out without him being discovered."

Tweek had her tiny hands over her mouth in a squeak. "Right away. Striker has made something this week that could work."

"Great, Striker is with Severo. After you find my father, can you ask him for his help?"

"Of course. I'm so sorry, Ben. I hope your friends will be okay." Her strawberry-colored eyes enlarged in alarm.

"Thank you, Tweek. We're running out of time. Go, and I'll meet you down there."

As she vanished, Ben took to the stairs, dizzy and almost falling head-first. Thankful for the railing, he gripped it tightly. Severo was there at the coffee cart, as well as all his friends' fairies.

"The king is on his way with the guard, Master Ben," Tweek said, as she flew onto his shoulder. "They have reprimanded Slick, but no sign of Elias."

Striker bobbed before him. "Prince Benjamin, if I may. I have devised a potion that will grow and expand when dispersed. Anything it touches will be clouded over. I have not had time to test it, but it should work on Master Gabriel. I hope to get him out safely. I'll make sure to be first down there when the door is opened."

Ben hoped it worked. Everyone had something to lose here. "Thank you, Striker, I hope so."

Ben's father bounded across the marble floor with the Fairy Guard in his wake. The fairies gathered in a circle and performed a chant. The ground shook, and the hidden door cracked open with a loud creak.

True to his word, Striker was the first down, followed by the king and Ben.

Ben rushed straight to Vara, and Severo lifted Cece, cradling her like a small child.

"Vara, I'm so glad you're okay. Thank you for looking after Cece," Severo said before he sprinted for the hospital.

Ben put his arm around Vara and lifted her tenderly. "Vara, I don't know what I would've done if anything had happened to you. C'mon, you need to get checked over."

"Ben, I'm fine, I promise," Vara said with a brave face. "It's Cece I'm worried about. I want to stay with her. I think she's lost a lot of blood."

Ben squinted at the ground. Drips of red stained the stone—the evidence of Cece's head injury. He shivered and held Vara tighter. "Let's get to the hospital."

Vara gazed up at him with the look he had been waiting for, and he kissed her salty, sweet forehead.

The dungeon closed with a thud behind them, dissolving back into the marble floor.

"What happened to Gabriel?" Vara whispered. "He was with us. I've never seen anyone so frightened yet so equipped in a crisis. He was amazing with Cece."

"Striker told us he had something that would get him out safely. I'm sure he's already at Cece's side."

Ben wrapped his arm around Vara's waist and led her to the hospital. She leaned her head on his shoulder. Ben could feel her body stiff in his arms.

Just as they arrived, Vara stopped, and Ben turned to face her. Her eyes brimmed with unshed tears.

"Ben, I don't know where to begin," she said, her voice cracking. "I thought we were going to die. Cece first, then me. When Gabriel arrived, I thought we could get out, but he was stuck too. I think it was because he wasn't cloaked when he fell. You saved us. Thank you isn't enough."

Vara caressed his face and stood on her tiptoes. Ben looked down at her beautiful face, and his pulsing heart hammered through his skin. She wanted to kiss him.

With a new earnestness, he bent to meet her, and their lips touched softly. When she didn't pull away, Ben strengthened the kiss, and his hands found her lower back. He trembled with intensity as she tightened her arms around him. This time, hers was the only face he saw as he kissed her back.

CHAPTER 41

Severo

S evero's legs had never been so swift as he barged through the hospital doors with his sister encased in his arms. Déjà vu hit him like a blow to the solar plexus. Far too much time had been spent in this place.

A peach haze approached with haste. He didn't know this person. "Are you a nurse?"

"Yes, I am."

"Please, get the doctor. My sister is hurt badly."

"Right away." The nurse gestured for Severo to follow her. "Bring her into this room here. Fiora," the nurse called out, and a fairy appeared. "Find Dr. Lovett immediately. One of the girls is here in the hospital."

Severo laid Cece on the hospital bed and sat at her side. His sister's light dimmed, and he wished with all his might she would recover.

"The doctor will be here right away," the nurse said, her voice soft and caring. "I'll fix her medical tag to relieve her pain. I'm Constance. She's in good hands."

Severo smiled weakly at the nurse. He had no words. A tightness formed in his chest. He focused on Cece and gripped her hand, willing her to live. Although her mist wasn't as bright, her essence lingered like a firefly refusing to yield its glow. Cece was strong. She would make it. She had to.

"Severo, I'm here. Where is the doctor?" Gabriel sat on the other side of Cece, brushing his hand over her forehead.

"They're looking for her now," Severo replied, unaware Gabriel had been there. Despite his renowned strength, the weight of this was pulling him under.

Ben and Vara arrived next, and the slender length of green sat down right where Gabriel was.

"Ouch, Vara."

Vara sprang backward in surprise. "Gabriel, you need to stop doing that to me," she scolded. "At least announce yourself!" Vara moved to the end of the bed and pulled over a seat from an abandoned stack in the corner.

Under normal circumstances, this would have inspired laughter, but deafening silence was all that lingered.

"Severo, I'll go and round everyone up," Ben said, heading for the exit.

"Ben, wait," Vara said, shifting in her chair. "I have an idea. Could you find Clara first? Maybe her gift could help. I don't know why I didn't think of that till now."

"Of course. I'll be back." Ben turned and left the room.

Severo looked at Vara. "Thank you."

"I don't know what happened," Vara said, sounding disturbed. "One minute we were walking, then we were pushed. Severo, I'm so sorry I couldn't help Cece more. You have nothing to thank me for."

They were interrupted by the nurse, who placed Scorchlings over the festering burn on Cece's leg.

"On the contrary, miss, you just may have saved your friend's life. Her vitals are strong and applying pressure to the head wound caused the blood to coagulate, which made the bleeding stop. The doctor will know what course of action to take when she arrives, and I'll be back shortly with sealers to set the leg wound."

"See, I'm right," Severo said, using levity to force light into the room.

"Well, I suppose it was due," Vara replied, and Severo thought she was smiling. He wished he could see it. Her smile was like a summer's day, but he detected something else in her voice. Guilt maybe?

The doctor arrived and asked them all to clear the room.

Severo took a seat in the waiting area. Vara slipped in beside him and threaded her fingers through his. Severo removed his hand from hers and slid his arm around her instead, pulling her in like a child needing their comforter. He could have lost them both, two out of the three women he loved most in this world.

Gabriel started pacing. "Severo, Elias did this. He cannot be allowed to get away with it. His pranks are no longer pranks. People could've died. What do we do?"

"He needs to be locked up and the key thrown away. If not, I'll be liable for murder, and I'm not joking." Severo thumped his fist on the window ledge and split the wood.

"Agreed. We need to speak to Ben. It's time to change the dungeon rule to age 16, not 18."

Severo put his hand out for a high-five.

Gabriel returned it and whispered to Severo, "I need to go and speak to my parents. If she wakes, tell her... well, tell her something nice and that I said it."

Severo squeezed Gabriel's shoulder in response. From now on, he would support that relationship. Gabriel loved his sister. It radiated from him like sunlight.

The doctor reappeared. "Master Severo, may I speak with you privately while we wait for your mother?"

Severo nodded and followed the doctor to a private room. "What's happened? Has Cece got worse?"

"No, your sister's stable, but we're awaiting results from her head injury. We need to keep her heavily sedated for a few days. It has been several hours of blood loss, which will need to be replenished. We are a bit out of our depth. Unfortunately, the blood bank doesn't have her blood type. This sort of thing has never happened until recently, and sadly, blood is not something the fairies can produce."

Severo ripped off his sleeve and held out his arm.

The doctor gulped and laughed at the same time, then cleared her throat.

"Thank you, but I already checked your records—you're not a match. We will have someone soon. It'll help your sister tremendously. There's one other thing. Your mother is quite unwell, although not physically. Leah Johns and I were with her. She needs round-the-clock attention. It seems the trauma's been too much for her. Leah is bringing her here. I can assure you that physically she's well, but her mind appears to have had a transitory shutdown. We would also like to monitor her and keep her close. We will set up an additional room for you so you can be here with them both. Her family around her is what she needs."

Instead of plowing into the initial reaction of despair, this was the boost Severo needed to step up to the mark. He would stand strong and be the pillar his family needed. "Where they go, I follow, Doc."

Severo returned to the waiting area. So many colored spots were there now, including Ben, who had returned with Clara. Severo noticed Niall was nowhere to be seen. *Good.*

"Clara, Cece is in this room. Do you think there's anything you could do to help her?" Severo felt his heart flutter in hope.

Clara's body language was tense and uncertain.

"Clara, please," Severo said gently.

"Of course. I can try."

Severo watched her. Her light was trembling, and she rubbed her arms like she was trying to shake sand off her body. Niall had messed her up.

I need to get this girl away from him.

Severo stood as Clara approached his sleeping sister. He held the railing at the end of her bed. The doctor was right behind him.

"Excuse me, may I ask what's going on here?"

"This is a friend of ours with the gift of Healing, and we wanted to see if she could help Cece," Ben said.

The doctor's ivory mist shifted. Severo could make out her hands being placed on her hips. "Any decisions about your sister have to be approved by me. I'm still waiting for the fairies to return with the results, but I'll admit, it may be worth visiting this suggestion. You already know that for Clara to use her power requires permission. Miss Clara, if you can come with me to my office, I'd like to discuss this with you, the nature of what you can do and how it works. Your sister is in the best place right now with no cause for alarm. I need to make sure all protocols are followed."

Severo slumped, demoralized as the doctor left with Clara.

It's not right that we can't use our powers. It's so hard not to.

How many times had he used his strength accidentally and never been caught?

Ben must be right. We have more control than we're led to believe.

Vara moved quietly to his side as Ben nudged Severo's shoulder.

"Sorry, Sev, but maybe the doctor is right. We don't know much about Clara's power, and I don't think she does either," Ben said.

"And why do you think that is, Ben?" Severo said, and he didn't care how terse he sounded.

Ben said nothing back; Severo had plenty more to say.

"Our dear friend Niall is behind all of it. We need to get Clara away from him. The girl is a basket case and completely drained!"

Ben sat down and put his head in his hands. "We need the book. We need to know the depths of Clara's power and make sure it's a safe option... Tweek," Ben called, and his fairy appeared. "Can you locate Fritzi and relay a message to him?" Tweek nodded a firm yes. "Thank you, tell him we need the book as soon as possible, please."

They sat in troubled silence. Severo couldn't sit, though. What was taking so long? His sister was not waking up.

A flutter of candy pink wings announced Tweek's reappearance.

"Here is the book," she said, twirling her fingers into a spiral.

"Thank you, Tweek. Ben, get reading." Severo knew he was being rude, but he didn't care, and thankfully Ben said nothing. He really didn't give his friend enough credit.

"Gabriel also wanted you to know the Fairy Guard still can't find Elias. His family said he never came home. Gabriel thinks he's in hiding due to what he did. Slick's been put in the dungeon till further notice. One more thing: The king and Fairy Guard are issuing a decree to tighten security. Everyone is on edge. People feel the shift we've all been experiencing for months." Tweek's voice quivered, and her wings fluttered more rapidly.

"That worthless waste of space better stay gone," Severo spat. "He's safer that way because if I get my hands on him..." Severo didn't need to finish his sentence. "Ben, anything in that book?"

Ben glanced up from his reading, his finger on the page. "Looks sound, Sev. Clara's gift is a powerful one. It can only help."

"May I suggest we move into Miss Cece's room and have a private meeting?" Tweek said. "Striker has asked me to have you all together as he will be along shortly."

"Now is not the time for a meeting." Severo's frustration laced every word he spoke. "We're waiting on the doctor. You know what? I'm done waiting."

Severo marched with purpose along the squeaky-clean corridor, looking for the pearl-colored spot, and he thundered right into Dr. Lovett's office.

"Where are we with your decision about my sister?" Severo demanded. "Every minute she doesn't wake up is a minute she's not getting back."

Dr. Lovett let out a whimsical noise. It seemed as though she might be counting to ten in her head.

"Severo. Clara's been showing me how her power works. She's not tested it yet, so I gave her an experiment to carry out with my plant that was on its last legs, and I have to say, I'm impressed with her ability. I would be happy for her to try and help your sister under my guidance."

Severo stepped around the sizable desk, ignored etiquette, picked the doctor up, and twirled her around in a bear hug. "Well, let's do this, then."

Dr. Lovett tittered awkwardly, and Severo heard her smooth her clothes. Her office smelled like her: *lilacs.*

"Follow me," she said.

Relief washed over Severo until he sensed panic around him. Vara's voice shouted in desperation.

"Dr. Lovett, come quickly. Cece is having some kind of seizure."

Clara dashed toward Cece. The world stopped, and Severo held his breath as this girl he barely knew transferred her healing energy into Cece's convulsing body. Although Severo couldn't see it, his dark vision crinkled with little threads of light.

Cece's writhing orange form slowly relaxed. Everyone in the room released a long, collective exhale. Severo hadn't been the only one holding his breath.

It had all happened so fast. Dr. Lovett's hands were a thing of wonder; they seemed to be everywhere at the same time. He could hear the slurp of Sleachers and the crackle of Scorchlings on Cece's wounds. Tiny orange and red dots that glowed brighter in his vision as they worked.

"Severo, I'm not sure what caused Cece to seize today, but my expertise is leading me to believe it's from the head injury. Our fairy scanners detected swelling on the brain, which would be a normal reaction to an injury of this kind. I'll get them to do another check now. Her pulse has strengthened with Clara's aid, and I'm confident that'll reduce the swelling. What we need is blood for Cece. If you can wait outside, I'll be with you for an update very soon."

The softest fingers slipped into his own and guided him to a seat outside in the hall. Vara touched his shoulder.

"Cece's going to be fine. I've never met anyone stronger than her, well, except for you maybe," she said, breaking out a soft giggle. "Anyway, my point is, strength is in your makeup. Believe in your sister as I believe in you."

Severo looked down at Vara. Even though he couldn't see her eyes, he hoped that she thought he was staring right into them. Vara was the one with the real strength. She got him, she challenged him, she grounded him.

Ben cleared his throat. Severo had forgotten they were all there.

"Vara's right: Nobody can bring the Arison family down." Ben turned to Clara. "Thank you for what you did."

"Yes, Clara, because of you, hopefully there will be no damage to her br—" Severo cut off. He didn't want to finish that thought. "Anyway, my family thanks you for trying to help us." Severo rose to embrace her.

Clara burst into a flood of tears and fled the hospital.

Vara stood to go after her.

Tweek flew into the middle. "Vara, you must let her go. Severo, call for Striker. There's a small empty room at the end of the hall. Let's go in there and talk. I'll send Leah to check on Clara and sit with her."

Severo agreed with a reluctant nod and followed the rest whilst calling for Striker. His fairy took his spot on Severo's shoulder as he walked.

"Is my mother okay, Striker?"

"Yes, Leah just arrived with her. We thought it better to wait. We were hoping Miss Cece would be awake by the time she arrived." Striker's wings drooped.

"I hope she will be too." Severo wanted to hear his sister's voice—know for a fact she was okay. "The doctor will be back with the results soon."

They all walked into a clinical-smelling room. Like schematics on a smart board, Severo detected the object outlines of a large table in the middle with several chairs. As Ben sat, a Door Dot—a new alarm device—announced an arrival. Ben re-opened the door. It was Fritzi.

"I'm here to represent Gabriel. His father arrived home, so it's impossible for him to be here right now. His father won't allow it."

Tweek indicated for Fritzi to hover alongside her. "This meeting couldn't wait. Time is of the essence, and we need to gather our thoughts." Tweek floated to the middle of the room, her pink glow bright with gold edging around the wings. Striker had made the fairies feel so real to Severo.

"Ahem. I believe it's myself leading the meetings," Striker argued, folding his arms.

Ben broke the tension. "We don't have time for this. What's this all about?"

Surprisingly, Tweek kept quiet, bowed her head, and let Striker speak.

"Thank you, Tweek." Striker was equally surprised. "This last week, Tweek, Fritzi, and I have been working round the clock and observing things on the down-low. Firstly, I wanted to say, we've been reading the book and trying to determine hidden meanings within the Sovereign Dominions. We can confirm some interesting findings. Clara's power has threads of depth and can heal completely if the damage to a person is not absolute. In other words, if caught quickly enough, that said person would fully recover. The power must be used to develop proficiency, so it may be diluted as Clara hasn't practiced it yet. I believe, Severo, that Cece will be back to normal in no time. However, the quicker she receives blood will only aid her recovery further."

Striker took a breath. "I've made what I call a Chip Connect." Striker held something tiny up in the air.

"Wow, what is it, Striker?" Vara asked, as they all gathered closer to look.

"This should be a way to keep you all connected and by extension, allow you to be masked under Gabriel's guard."

Severo had almost forgotten they still had a mission. His family was hanging in the balance. Cece would want him to do everything possible to help get their dad back. "Shall we test it out?"

"Yes, I have every reason to believe it'll work," Striker said. "It's not been authorized, but I have made it so that when it touches each of your bracelets, it will be completely absorbed in, therefore, unde-tectable. We'll test it when Gabriel's able to join us. I also needed to say that the three of us"—Striker indicated to Tweek and Fritzi—

"have devised a product to mist the barrier. I used it tonight to extract Gabriel from the dungeon and it worked astonishingly well. It's a liquid. One drop will expand in size and when applied, Alunattra will not be able to see to the other side. Gabriel will still be able to move through the barrier but it's risky. If she can't see you all, you can't see her either."

Ben perked up. "What about me? If I time it well enough, I could astral project to the other side, and I'll know if we can make it."

"Yes, that's an option, but reading up on Alunattra's power, I assume she may see you, even in your astral form."

Severo listened in amazement. He couldn't believe his fairy had figured all this out.

Ben's head swiveled towards Striker. "Right! It already happened once before, but she can't harm me in that form. I'll just need to be quick and careful!"

"This brings me to our next observation," Striker continued. "Elias's unique ability has slipped under our radar. Judging by the recent displays of his accelerated skill sets, I'm led to believe Elias can hear for miles. Through progression, his gift will lead to telepathy but that'll come in time. I don't think he's aware of this, but you must be careful. That boy has shown what he's capable of, and I would go as far as to say the signs indicate he has sociopathic tendencies."

"Tell me something we don't already know," Severo said, slamming his fist on the waiting room table. It shattered into splinters. "Oops."

Tweek and Fritzi swiftly dealt with the shards of broken glass and worked to regenerate it as Striker continued, not fazed by Severo's outburst.

"Lastly, our biggest threat on this side of Landis is Niall. His power is in accelerated development and goes far beyond the realms of a photographic memory. Mind control will not only work but over time will cause damage and destruction, leaving any victims in a vegetative state. Servants merely to carry out his will. Clara, Tharmus, and Pixel are at massive risk right now. I believe Clara is being manipulated as she's a source of good for our world and that'll be a threat to Niall. If he can control everyone, he can rule. I'm sure Alunattra knows this and Niall, although an asset to her right now, would no doubt be her first target should she discover a way to break through the barrier. What we don't know is whether Niall suspects this. He's under her control and in turn, her presence and technique of transcendence will only make him more lethal."

"He's tried things on me and Gabriel. Have any of you felt differently around Niall?" Ben asked.

Vara spoke up first. "Honestly, I don't think he's ever looked in my direction."

"I'm fine. I suppose it's just as well I can't see to look at him," Severo said. Unsurprisingly, nobody found this funny.

"What about Alunattra? Did you find out any more about her in the book, Striker?" Ben asked.

Striker's color seemed to shrink. "Yes. Yes, I did. It seems any person she manages to get a hold of, by touching them, will not only die, but it will transfer any existing abilities over to her."

CHAPTER 42

Niall

Niall was high on adrenaline as he made his way to The Vale. He ditched Tharmus on the way, with instructions to arrange a meeting with the chess club. It was almost time to act. Hopefully, Vara and Cece wouldn't be found, and the search would act as a very necessary distraction. It was Gabriel that needed to be disposed of; he was the imminent threat. And Clara too. But that would just be fun for want of a better word.

As Niall waded through the sludge, he didn't care that he was muddied to his knees. Alunattra had summoned him and maybe that meant she was ready. He shuddered in anticipation of the power that would soon fill him. These sly acts gave Niall the freedom to explore avenues he never would have thought possible.

An audacious thought teemed within his mind. Maybe Alunattra would answer to him one day.

The sooty swirls of darkness kissed his cheeks as the monster within rippled to the surface. His feet glided to the one place that mattered now. He scratched at his skin as he waited and waited.

Niall saw the curl of her dirtied claws first and wondered what it felt like to use them to tear and devour. She was in her human form and although contemplative, her eyes locked on him, and he felt like he was submerged in icy water on the verge of drowning. He didn't like it.

"This night has been unexpected." The screech of her voice made him want to rip his ears from his skin.

Alunattra drummed her long, bone protruding fingers inches from his nose. "As it turns out, serendipity won, and it seems I didn't need you to come after all. You've failed. The girls have been found and your charge, Clara, has partially healed one of them."

Niall's jaw dropped. "How can that be?"

"I have a very willing new source, and he doesn't ask ceaseless questions. I have waited to see what you'll do but as it turns out, very little." Alunattra tutted. "Such a shame too."

Niall had been feeling untouchable, but uncertainty now plagued his mind.

Who is helping her?

"I came to tell you that Pixel is close to finding a way through, and I'll dispose of the girl as well as anything else you require. Please." His pathetic plea sat on his dry tongue like a piece of tainted food.

Alunattra flung her limbs out from the barrier like an animal launching at its prey. The barrier didn't prevent her putrid breath from devouring his face. Niall stood stagnant, awaiting her next words.

Alunattra took one of her fingernails and sliced the length of her cheek. Her blood congealed on her gray skin. "Time is running out for you."

She evaporated before him.

Niall scanned the woods and stopped when he sensed one of his pawns. Elias. He was hidden somewhere, but Niall's mind couldn't locate him. Alunattra had double-crossed him. This changed the gameplay. He had work to do.

Niall stomped away from the barrier fueled with hateful determination. Silent fury took hold as he left this time, unfulfilled. Niall powered his way back through the sinuous forest with a purpose. He needed to make Alunattra think he was on her side.

Niall returned to the village, his mission consuming his thoughts. An onslaught of anxious people clogged the cobblestone streets, getting in his way. Clearly, the village had been awakened to the events of the day, and the people were more than a little frenzied. Their murmurs were a clamorous buzz in Niall's ears.

His hand moved to his pocket to check if the vial Pixel had made earlier was still there. It was. With relief, he knocked on the door and waited for an answer.

The door opened, revealing Clara's mother.

"Good evening, Jeanie. I was hoping to take a walk with Clara."

Jeanie's eyes were drawn to Niall's, and she stood connected to him as if through magnetism. He had her attention now and his way into her mind.

"You'll allow this, and from this day forward, if anyone asks about Clara, you'll tell them she's homeschooling and not to be disturbed for the foreseeable future. May I speak with your husband?"

The woman made a swift pirouette, and Niall watched with delight as his instruction was carried out beautifully. For most people it worked flawlessly. When the father arrived, Niall performed the same command on him, then the fairies as Jeanie went to get Clara.

Clara's blotchy red face looked frightful.

"Clara, I'm so glad you're well," Niall said, adding a drop of relief to his tone. "Has there been any word on Cece?"

Clara peered into him, and he flinched at her stare.

Am I too late?

He focused on the blue irises of her eyes and worked harder to ingrain his command. "Come and take a walk with me. The village is crazed, and it'll do us good to get some fresh air."

Clara's hands were jittery, but she closed the front door and fell into step beside him.

They remained silent. Niall took her reluctant hand and led her through the busy village. Those that were aware of them turned, and he redirected the people in their path. How could Alunattra have thought to dispose of him? Did she not see what he was capable of? And then it struck him, the obvious slapping him right across the face. Of course, she did. She saw what he had done with Elias.

New ideas unfolded in his mind.

The castle swarmed with frantic search parties. Niall tapped into his perception. They were looking for Elias. They would never find him. Alunattra could have him; the boy was weak, and he had served a purpose.

With the castle now behind them, Niall said to Clara, "Remember the story Severo told you about us boys in the vineyard?"

This seemed to relax her, and she smiled. "Yes, the one at the cere-mony party?"

Good, this reaction was what he had hoped for. "Well, I thought we could blow off some steam and have a little wine of our own, what do you think?" Niall put on his most endearing face, knowing its intensity would be hard for anyone to side-swerve.

Clara didn't blink, as though lost in his gaze. "I've always wanted to try wine." Clara's hand ran the length of the grape-covered greenery.

Her robotic way of answering played right into Niall's checklist. He placed a hand inside his satchel and pulled out two wine glasses he had retrieved from his parents' cabinet. If Alunattra had been paying attention, she would have seen his scheme required measured steps.

He bent over the barrel of wine, hovering his hand over the brass tap. "Can you pick a few grapes from the vine, and we can place them on top?" He curved his lips upward. "I want to remember this night forever."

Clara obeyed. Before he poured the wine, Niall took the vial from his pocket with practiced ease and emptied the contents into the shimmering glass. Scarlet red wine, the color of blood, trickled and coated the edges. He poured one for himself and handed Clara her crystal flute.

"Cheers, Clara. Thank you for making my year the most interesting one I've had yet."

She reddened and they both sipped the delicacy together. Clara's cheeks flushed as she gave a marveled gasp. "Wow, that's delicious."

Niall agreed wholeheartedly. Clara drank some more.

"Niall, I have enjoyed our time together, but I feel now might be a good time to step back. I'm still young and I wish to focus on my studies."

The wine was making her bolder. Niall found this all very humorous. "Why yes, I think you may be right."

Clara let out a breath of relief and then her hand went to her throat.

"Clara, are you okay?"

She coughed. "I don't know, I..." She coughed again. "What's happening?" She fell to her knees as her breath came short. Bloodshot eyes rose to meet him. She said between gasps, "What. Have. You. Done. To. Me?"

"Whatever do you mean?"

Clara's face turned crimson, and her eyes bulged from their sockets. She couldn't speak anymore. Her veins popped, and her rigid body faltered. Niall continued to drink his wine; his spirit electrified by the scene before him. White frothy foam bubbled from the corners of her mouth, and he stared down at her convulsing body with ecstatic fixation.

Her body stopped mid-spasm until every ounce of life had left her. She lay motionless in between two maintained grapevines.

Hmm. So that is what that feels like.

He expected more, not this anticlimactic sensation.

After he dragged and disguised her frail, dead body into the vineyard cabin, Niall strode towards the castle with a lightness of step. With blood on his hands, the urge to spill more prodded him with impatience.

He listened.

Did she see that?

His mind remained quiet. He summoned Pixel. "Where is everyone?"

"In the hospital wing, Master. Your friends are in a meeting, and the doctor's trying to locate a blood donor for the injured girl."

Pixel whispered some new, very interesting information. Niall was pleased with her.

Niall's mind clicked like the last piece of a puzzle as he walked straight into the room of the peaceful sleeping girl. He knew what he needed to do.

"Can I help you?" the doctor asked, turning to face him. She looked tired and helpless. This port of play would be...fun.

Niall locked in her line of sight. "No, but I believe I can help you. You're in need of a certain blood type. I'm a match and I'm here to anonymously donate." He smirked. "Anything to help my friends."

CHAPTER 43

Alunattra

H e killed the girl.

Alunattra watched all of it through Niall's eyes. The goodness that radiated from the young girl made something twinge inside of her.

What is happening to me? Is it a fluke or are there others like this girl Clara?

Alunattra tried to push it from her mind, but she couldn't keep one thought from pushing its way in.

Him. The prince. He's good.

Whatever way she looked at it, Niall needed to be disposed of.

He thinks he's outsmarting me. Fool.

He was now giving his blood to poison another. His heart of evil would not stop. He was strong—too strong.

At least Elias is mine now. Another very human thought entered her mind. *And he can't harm anyone anymore.*

The power from the tree sang from its branches and it pained her, like a wind to the gut.

No, no, no, no, no. I don't want to be silenced, I don't want you here. Why haven't you stayed dead? Go away.

She was back. She was there, and her voice sang out from the tree. "Enough, get back to your prison."

It was still the same, all these years later.

The high-pitched voice was like nails clawing at her skin. It had clung to her like a second skin for the entire time she'd been trapped in this place. Alunattra sank deep into the soil. Stuck. She was back in the dungeon, two hundred years ago with flashbacks of the same voice that taunted her now.

"You were born evil, Mileah, you can't ever run from me. I'm a part of you. As you live, so do I. This island is coming for you… daughter."

CHAPTER 44

Ben

Ben's eyes hurt to blink. The exhaustion of the day overwhelmed him, and rest beckoned. With their meeting adjourned, they went to check in with Cece and the doctor before this horrible day came to a bitter end.

The whole group sauntered towards Cece's room as the doctor approached.

"Severo, I was just coming to find you." She wore an elated smile. "We had an anonymous blood donation—same type as Cece's—and your sister is stirring. I believe she'll want to see a familiar face."

Severo brushed past the doctor and threw open the solid oak door in a hurry to reach his sister.

Ben was right behind him, relief washing over him like a waterfall. Cece's eyelids fluttered as she strained to open her eyes.

"Water," she croaked.

Tweek was already on the task, floating a translucent plastic cup toward Severo. Striker perched on Severo's shoulder, and Fritzi must have left to tell Gabriel.

Severo cradled an arm around his sister, helping her into a sitting position before raising the cold, fresh water to her lips. Cece took a loud sip, and her relief was obvious.

Ben hadn't wanted to think of the possibility that she wouldn't make it. Severo, as strong as he was, could not have sustained that, none of them could. Too many things were going wrong, and it was a relief to clasp onto the good.

A nurse appeared with thick, feather-filled pillows and padded them around Cece.

"Cece, I…" Severo began, words failing him.

"Don't, big brother." She stopped to catch a breath and struggled with her sentence. "I'd rather not have your giant tears soak my fluffy pillows." She smiled weakly, and he squeezed her hand.

Ben added with humor, "Yeah, nobody wants to see that."

A bubble of laughter filled the room, and Ben breathed easier. So did his friends.

Cece looked at each one, full of appreciation, then panic clouded her already pale face. "Where's Gabriel?"

Vara slotted into the empty seat on the other side of Cece's bed. "Gabriel's fine. He kept us both alive. Because he's still on house arrest, he had to get back, but he said he'll be here soon."

Severo reached across the bed for Vara's hand, and she took it willingly. Jealousy and guilt wrestled inside Ben's chest like a match of tug of war. He screwed on a cool expression, hoping no one spotted his inner conflict.

"Gabriel said to tell you, he's always here even when you can't see him. A bit sappy if you ask me, but there it is," Severo said, returning to his usual self.

Cece searched her brother's face, and her eyes softened. "So, what did I miss? I want to know everything."

"So do I," a quiet voice said.

"Gabriel, you're here." Cece was beaming, and she tried to sit up.

Gabriel let his cloak fall.

Ben felt awkward looking at the two of them. This bond they shared sparked something in him that he couldn't put his finger on. Shaking the unwanted feeling away, he moved to open the window, welcoming the cool, night air as it grazed his clammy face. Ben caught Cece up on current events.

Cece shocked them with her next words. "I saw my father when I was sleeping. He didn't see me. We need to get him out, but he's hanging in there for now. Realistically, how long before we can get it done?"

Ben wished he had an answer for her hopeful eyes but, thankfully, Striker answered for him.

"It will need to be a weekend day, on the fairies' day off. I'm still working with a few prototypes, and I need more time. We need to test the Chip Connect."

Before they could do that, a dazed Tharmus burst through the door. "Children, you need to be in your homes. NOW."

Tharmus pulled Ben back as he went to leave. "Not so fast. Your mother is waiting for you. No detours."

Ben was too wiped out to respond. He'd forgotten about Tharmus. It suddenly dawned on him that Tharmus wasn't at his heels these days. Niall's doing no doubt.

He knew where his mother would be, in her sitting room where she spent so much of her time. Over the years, this book-brimming room always carried an air of peacefulness. When he was little, he used to climb the ladders and swing the length of the shelves. These days, Ben went there just to think. He slipped open the door and his mother was there in her tweed-covered armchair. A book lay open on her lap, but she was looking out the moonlit window.

"Mother, you wanted to see me?"

She rose from her chair and beckoned him over. As his mother embraced him, she breathed in his scent, and Ben pulled back in concern. His mother's eyes glistened.

"Has something happened? Please, I know something's wrong, and I feel everything is falling apart. I want you to tell me."

Fear made a brief appearance as her tight lips prepared her words. "Benjamin, my son. Life is not always as it seems and sometimes we need to feel what we're feeling. You'll be faced with all sorts of choices in your years, and you'll not always make the right decisions. On occasion, this can work in your favor but not always. Choose your path wisely, as taking the wrong one can leave a part of your being behind."

With that, his mother kissed him and before she left said, "Don't forget."

Ben saw a glimmer of truth behind her eyes. Whatever weighed on her, seemed to be some sort of mental affliction. She looked away before he could see more. With his mother's calming air, he was left staring after her, mystified as she walked away. He still had no definitive answers, but her resigned confidence suggested all was well, physically at least.

Not all things can be cured by magic I guess.

His legs felt like dead weights as he gripped the metal railing on the climb to his quarters. There was no sign of his grandad or his father. No doubt working on this decree that had been spoken of. What was to become of them all?

His brain was overloaded. He had some pina drops and swallowed them without a drink. His head molded to his pillow like a maternal embrace and sleep found him.

"I HAD TO COME AGAIN," SHE SPOKE.

They were sitting opposite each other, crossed-legged in the darkness, closer this time, but there was still no way to touch her. The outlines of her face were clearer again.

Dialogue still didn't come even though he tried to form words. The silence comforted him in a way he had never experienced, and even in this dream-like state, this girl held that missing piece his heart craved.

"*I feel the same,*" *she said.* "*I know what I need to do now. I will come soon.*"

A vibration in his ear jolted him awake.

"Finally," Tweek said, exasperated.

Ben tried to evaluate his surroundings. He was in his room. Everything was blurred and then it wasn't, as a wall of scattered fresh memories broke upon the inner workings of his mind. He wished to return to his dream. The girl. Goosebumps prickled over his tingling skin, and he tried to etch her image within.

Is she coming here? How?

Tweek nibbled his ear.

"Hey, stop that." Ben shooed off his fairy. "Give me a second, will you? And use your Door Dot like you're supposed to—outside, and not to wake me up!"

"They were made because rules are slipping. I follow rules. It was a slip of the hand. Your grandad is requesting to have breakfast with you. He's been waiting for ten minutes. Did you take some of my Eelps Spray?" Tweek wagged her tiny finger and tutted.

"No, Tweek, I was just tired. I'm on my way."

It wasn't even light yet. No wonder he'd still been sleeping. The stained glass above him twinkled as the morning light teased its way through. He hadn't seen his grandad in days and hunger pangs took hold. It may have been a day since he had eaten anything.

Ben opened the breakfast room door to the aroma of freshly baked bread and the tempting smell of bacon. The trolley at the far end was laden with various delights.

"Ah, my boy. Grab a plate then come sit."

Ben smiled warmly at his grandfather and wondered how much he knew about the present goings-on.

"Your parents are still sleeping," his grandad said before biting into a strip of bacon. "The king's decree will be arriving at everyone's breakfast table this morning, and your school lessons will be done from home for the remainder of this week. The same for your peers."

Ben's look of panic couldn't be hidden. How would he see his friends?

"Benjamin, I'm somewhat attuned to what you must be feeling. I advised your father to do this. I'll be your teacher this week and might I say that I'm very relaxed about a lot of things. I know perfectly well what's going on and that very soon, our world could be in a spot of bother. I hope to help you and your friends. I know your friend Gabriel is innocent."

Ben, a bit stupefied by this revelation, continued stuffing his face like there was a famine. Ben got lost in the deep-set lines that sprinkled his grandad's face, each one showing a wealth of experience. Ever understanding, Grandad bit into a sticky bun, allowing Ben to process this information.

Like a fountain that never stopped pouring, Ben relayed every emotion, hardly breathing between speaking. A feeling of transference lifted his soul as the last sentence somersaulted out.

"I know," his grandad said.

Typical. Grandad Bay didn't often say much, but when he did, it was of value. Ben's muscles relaxed. He finally had an ally he could fully confide in.

"I've organized for your friend to be here this morning."

"Which friend, Grandad?"

"I'm already here, Ben," Gabriel answered, dropping his cloak.

Ben's bewilderment increased, and he took his next bite at a slower pace.

There was a twinkle in Grandad's eyes as he wiped his fingers on his cloth napkin. "When I discovered what was going on, I had a private meeting with Mr. and Mrs. Johns, and they were more than relieved to find out Gabriel was innocent. That being said, Landis needs to remain under the misconception. All meetings will be held here. I've already used the Conceal Dust, so we're protected. We have an additional issue you may not be aware of. Alunattra has recruited another. Elias Tassey. I followed him when he fled and witnessed Niall go into the forest also. Though I don't know if Niall is aware. Elias, I imagine, has been brainwashed into submission, whereas Niall is becoming the master of his own mind. If your old friend manages to either dissolve the barrier or get to the other side, it will only be a matter of time until destruction pulls apart our world. We cannot allow that to happen."

Ben sat there with his mouth falling open. He had no idea his grandad had been conducting his own investigation into these matters.

"Grandad, I don't know what to say." Ben paused. "What do we tell Father?"

"Leave your father to me. I'll tell him when the time is right. I've already spoken with your fairy team. I'm up to speed with their objectives and all we need is a few days, then we can meet and plot our endgame."

For once, Ben was relieved to be rendered useless. All this pressure had taken its toll.

"May I add something?" Gabriel asked, staring at the ground.

"Why yes, of course." Grandad gestured for Gabriel to continue. "The floor is yours."

With shaky hands, Gabriel poured black coffee into a porcelain mug before settling at the other end of the long rectangular table.

"Ben, your mother," he began, the steam from the coffee diffusing around his serious face, "I know you've been concerned about her well-being. Yesterday, when we were searching, I found her in the tower. She summoned Vallore and asked for his help. Vallore refused to help her and told her she would reap her own consequences. I have no idea what it meant, but I thought you should know."

Ben scooted his chair back and approached the large bay window. The sunrise was now in full bloom.

"There's something happening to her, but she won't tell me." He hung his head. "We spoke last night. She seemed well, and whatever it is, she's made her peace with it, it seems. I couldn't bring myself to question her further. It was like I was intruding on her privacy. Grandad, do you know anything?"

"On that, I cannot say." Grandad rested his chin on his hands. "You both will understand when you get older. We all have battle scars. The mark will always be there as a reminder, but how you deal with them will determine your future."

Ben shivered as déjà vu took hold. His mother's speech seemed oddly familiar now. He would lay this matter to rest. "Grandad, when will we meet?"

"I propose a meeting at the end of the week, under the pretense of a back-to-school lunch. I'll relay this to your friends."

Gabriel awkwardly bowed, and Grandad gave him a friendly squeeze on the shoulder.

When Gabriel left, they sat in comfortable silence, letting the warmth of the sun graze the room. Ben's parents entered together. His father, although dressed in his kingly attire, looked aged. His furrowed forehead read like a map that led to nowhere.

"Good morning, son. Father."

Ben's father took his seat at the head of the table, and after his mother gave him a kiss, she sat opposite his grandfather.

"Young Elias has not been found," Ben's father said with a tired sigh. "This will give me and the Fairy Guard time and space to search efficiently. This is a temporary measure, and we hope to have everything resume as normal next week."

"Okay, Father. Can I request a visit to the hospital this morning, though? I'd like to check how Cece is and see if Severo and his family need anything."

"Just this once. You need to follow rules like everyone else."

Only once? How would that work for four days!

His father continued, "Please tell the Arison family, if they need anything, they have but to ask. Also assure them, when Elias is reprimanded, the situation will be dealt with severely."

That's if Elias ever comes back.

Ben finished his breakfast. Preoccupation was evident in the room, and Ben was happy with that. At least they were moving forward, and his grandad was going to help get Danyall back. Severo and Cece would be so relieved.

The girl from his dreams popped into his mind like an unforgettable event, and then he was there with her again.

She reached out her hand, and he responded by doing the same.

Ben blinked, not sure what was real anymore.

Did I blackout?

Confliction centered within him surrounding this unknown girl who somehow made him feel like there was more to his life.

She's not here though. Vara is.

Vara wasn't just beautiful, she was strong willed and kind. She would make a great princess.

Ben hadn't heard the voice from the tree for some time, but he knew not to be blasé about it. He knew, like morning and night, it was coming.

Keen to see his friends in the all too familiar hospital wing, he marched through the double doors. Leah was at her desk, and she winked at Ben in acknowledgment. He winked back, glad they knew of Gabriel's innocence. Happiness seemed to be overflowing from Cece's room, and the laughter made Ben feel like he'd just had his first taste of chocolate.

"Ben, what took you so long?" Severo said with a teasing grin.

"I was starving."

Severo's chuckle vibrated off the walls. "That I cannot condemn you for."

"We need to know what's happening, Ben. We're ready. Have there been any developments?" As Cece asked this, her eyes were fevered with intensity.

Ben rubbed his eyes before resettling them on her curious face. He decided not to tell them anything till the meeting.

Cece's darkened irises returned to bright green. What had he just seen?

CHAPTER 45

Vara

Vara paced in front of her window, looking at the bright white castle that shone no matter the time of day. The Landis three-striped flag stood tall like the topper of a cake, shimmering in the wind. The early evening light dawned on each home.

She wished she could see her friends. It had been two days since the king's decree.

I hope everyone is okay.

Her mind raced from one frightened thought to the next. The island that once comforted her no longer felt safe. Lights were on in every home, but no doors were opening. Everyone was shut in as if a dark terror threatened their safety. When she gazed at The Forbidden Vale, a smokiness billowed in and out of the forest like it was preparing to strike.

Alunattra is real and she is coming.

Vara moved to her three-mirrored vanity, feeling helpless and wanting to be with her friends.

I hope we can get Severo and Cece's father back before it's too late.

Her restless nerves crawled up and down her arms. What she wouldn't give for a distraction—anything to occupy her anxious thoughts. She fixed her powder-blue silk sheets, retied the lace that hung on each pillar of her four-poster bed, and slumped into her rocking chair.

I wish there was something I could do.

Hours scraped by before Prine announced herself with her Door Dot. Prine had been doing school lessons with Vara the last two days. Vara had undertaken all her required work, but Prine must have sensed Vara didn't want to talk and gave her space.

Vara opened the door for Prine and smiled with a sad fondness.

"Miss Vara. Your parents require your attendance downstairs."

Vara closed the door without saying a word. Her usual vivacity had been snuffed out with her inefficiency to function. She wanted to run from her thoughts, yet she stood by as they mocked her.

Ben. Severo. At least she'd been spared from having to face them. Procrastination was a very close friend of hers. Her kiss with Ben had been so spontaneous, and Vara hadn't resisted. She owed him her life. She wanted to hold him and not let go.

That kiss should've been our first kiss.

They'd got lost in each other and it felt good. They both had a need that was satiated, but was it for the right reasons? She had thought of little else. Severo—it was too painful to think of him. Whatever way she looked at it, she'd betrayed him.

Vara made her way to the kitchen. Her mother and father were laughing about something, and the twins' immaculate frilly outfits were covered in their evening supper. She took her seat at the oval table clothed in her cream house dress, as she had nowhere to be. The table was set to perfection. How could her family continue with such ignorance? Each one of them dressed to exception, oblivious to what was going on. She grabbed the coffee pot. The smell teased her nostrils, and she drank, not caring that the heat burnt her tongue.

"Good evening, sweetheart, how did your lessons go today?" her mother asked.

"Fine." Vara filled her mouth with gravied chicken. She didn't mean to sound bitter but lashing out was her only comfort.

Her mother ignored her, and her father stood. "The new decree came earlier. As of day Five this week, the village will resume all business and schooling as normal. The curfew in the evenings will remain for the time being. You will go to school and come straight home."

Vara slumped. "Father, what about Elias? Has he been found?"

"Well, no, it doesn't seem so. There are rumors, however, that he may have found his way to The Forbidden Vale. Security has been tightened and there are guard posts running the length of The Vale. It seems doubtful he will return. The king also decreed that should a crime of this magnitude occur between the ages of sixteen and eighteen, a sentence would be carried out in the castle dungeon. If Elias is found, he will be arrested."

"Good, I hope they find him and throw away the key." That creep deserved it.

"Vara, dear," her mother said, her lips downturned. "I know you have been through an ordeal, but your dramatic air is unbecoming, especially if you are practicing princess etiquette."

Vara couldn't sit there any longer. She pushed her plate away. "I'm going to my room."

It was clear her parents thought her an unsolved mystery as they returned to their conversation.

It's not their fault though. I'm the one who's changed.

There was a tap on her shoulder. "Vara. Wait, sweetheart. Can I have a word?"

Guilt flooded Vara as she looked at her mother. Her confidence had been replaced with uncertainty. Vara hugged her.

"Vara. Your father and I have never felt fear as we did when we discovered you were missing. No parent should have to go through that. You were right too. We haven't been aware of what's going on. Or maybe we've ignored it."

They sat at the top of the stairs. Her mother's eyes were glassy. Vara held her hands.

"I suppose we haven't had to worry all these years. Life has been good to us. We don't want for anything. Nobody has but now it's different. I see new sides to people. It's unsettling. I need to protect my family. *You* need to protect your family. Now more than ever the princess plan needs to take shape. If you marry the prince, we will all be able to live in the castle. I know strange things have happened recently, but the castle is the most protected place in Landis."

Her mother stopped and burst into tears.

Vara swallowed and stroked her mother's cheek. "I don't want you to worry about that, Mother. I promise I will look after our family. Trust me."

Her mother sighed, wiped her tears, and kissed Vara's head. "We love you very much. I know you'll do what's right.

She watched her mother go back down the stairs. They had never spoken so openly.

I will not disappoint my family.

Vara opened her bedroom door. She shivered.

Someone's here.

She reached for the nearest thing she could find... her hairbrush. She swiped it from the vanity and tried to appear threatening.

She heard a giggle... Gabriel.

He let his shield down and she relaxed. "You seem to be making a habit of sneaking up on me."

Gabriel's face tinged with color. "I'm sorry, Vara, I had to stay cloaked to make sure I wasn't caught. Sorry if I gave you a fright. I certainly don't want to meet the wrath of your hairbrush."

Vara laid her brush back down and laughed. It felt so good her cheeks hurt.

"I came to give you this note from Ben."

Gabriel handed over a cream piece of parchment with her name written on the front in gold font. She caressed it with care.

"Thank you, it's really good to see you. I feel like I've been going mad."

"We all have. None of us have been allowed to see each other, but I have my ways."

Vara sighed. *Oh, to be invisible.*

"Everyone misses you. I've barely left Cece. I'm sorry I didn't come earlier."

"Is Cece okay?" Vara asked, anxious for an update.

Gabriel's brows were furrowed. "Yes, she's in full health again. Mrs. Arison is still getting back on her feet after the shock, so they're all staying in the hospital. There were also a few things I needed to pass on to you. Ben's grandad has joined us and has been working with the fairies. We're meeting on Five for a luncheon in the breakfast room in the royal quarters. I think we're almost ready to fly."

Vara gulped but was glad to know these last few days hadn't been wasted.

"I better get back."

"Gabriel, wait. How's Severo?"

Vara tried to keep casual but knew she was failing. What was worse was the heartfelt sympathy in Gabriel's gaze. *I don't deserve it.*

"He's well. I think he misses you. Goodbye, Vara, see you soon."

Gabriel was gone, just like that, dissolving before her eyes. Vara went to her chair and removed the red wax seal with the purple and yellow Landis logo.

Vara,

I wanted you to know I'm thinking of you. I haven't forgotten about our date. I just wish you were here. There is something I wanted to ask you, and I would have asked you in person but that hasn't been possible. Would you be my girl? I know it's not courting month yet, but my parents have given their blessing, and you can count this as my first letter. All I need is your answer. I can't wait to see you. Day Five can't come quickly enough. And I can't stop thinking about our kiss.

Ben.

Tears pricked Vara's eyes.

My first love letter and what a lovely one.

She re-read the letter again, admiring the beautiful feather quill strokes of his handwriting. Ben saved her. He'd proven his loyalty and thinking about their kiss made her stomach flutter. She cared for him deeply. No matter what happened, Ben and Severo both owned a piece of her heart. She hesitated. Her time was up.

She knew who she was going to choose.

CHAPTER 46

Severo

S evero hunched over the small table in the hospital's waiting area. It was the only part of this place that gave him peace, and it helped that it was full of floral bouquets. The room smelled glorious. It was late as he put the finishing touches to the letters he'd been writing for a while now. He laid his quill next to his ink pot and sighed, touching the bundle of folded paper. He was grateful Striker had created a new ink that appeared in fluorescent yellow. His fairy had given him a ribbon too, which he tied around the package in a perfect bow. He couldn't see it well, but he felt the rough paper and smelt the ink that penned his words.

Now that Cece had recovered, Vara owned his thoughts. He needed her to read the words held in his heart. Romance had never been his area of strength, but it wasn't even about that. He loved how she wasn't scared to stand up for herself or call him out when he needed it. She mirrored him. He loved her and these letters were the easiest way to explain that. It was remarkable how the words had fallen from his nib.

I get to see her in two days.

Cece's nurse breezed into the room in her calming peach mist. Severo tucked his private thoughts away into his satchel.

"I noticed you never drink coffee, so I brought you a rock-solid twist and shake," she said.

Severo's mouth watered imagining his first sip of the smooth, bright green drink. "I think we may be kindred spirits." He beamed. "Do you know I inspired this drink? I have Nilla under my thumb."

"That makes sense. You are what I would call inspiring," the nurse said boldly.

Severo shifted at this unexpected flirtation and deflected. "Don't you ever sleep? You've not missed a beat these last few days."

"Seldom if ever," she answered. "Thankfully, my Verdo allows me to function on little rest, and Dr. Lovett always has things for me to do."

Severo couldn't remember what the nurse looked like. Was she much older than him?

"Do you mind me asking what your Verdo is?"

"Not at all, it's Surgical Acumen. It may sound boring, but I showed an affinity for it before my ceremony. It allows me to evaluate any medical need and know instantly the necessary procedure. One aspect is having a clear and open mind that can sense a need prior to action. I don't think I have worked harder than this last month. I seem to have an element of calm, and I take sleep when I can as I don't really get tired."

That explained why she was always there. "You are something else, nurse. How long have you worked here?"

"I finished school last year, but I was interning before that. I started the day after I graduated."

I was right, not much older than me then.

"I don't think you get enough credit," Severo said. "Thank you for everything you have done for Cece, my mother, and me. You and the Doc."

"You will always be Dr. Lovett's biggest regret." A tinge of sadness entered the nurse's voice. "She wishes we had spoken with Clara straight away and you could have been cured."

Severo felt the urge to go to the nurse. She seemed so sad. He felt rotten that he didn't even know her name. He nodded instead. "Look, I've made peace with it now, and funnily enough, it has added some very useful attributes to my skill set. Promise me you guys will not hang on to this. My life is complicated enough."

"I promise to try. I've been meaning to speak to you for a while now, but there was never a right time."

Severo shifted in his seat, not sure what to say.

Fill the silence.

His head snapped up, as something he'd been meaning to ask sprang to mind. "The doctor never told me who donated blood, do you know?"

Severo could feel her warmth of expression as she got to her feet. "I don't. It's anonymous for a reason, I've been told. Don't be a stranger, Severo. You know where to find me." Before she left, she turned back to say, "I'm Nurse Constance by the way, but you can call me Connie."

Yeah, she was definitely hitting on him. His stomach stirred. She wasn't Vara though. Not even close.

His mother was sleeping soundly, so he went to check on Cece. The pungent smell of disinfectant made his stomach squirm. He couldn't wait to leave this hospital and relax in the comfort of his own bed. The mattresses here were so soft, his back was breaking.

As he entered the room, Cece stopped talking. Severo looked around the room, but he couldn't see anyone. Gabriel's mist hadn't appeared either. That was weird.

"Who are you talking to, Cece?"

"Sev, I would say you need your eyes tested, but we all know that would be pointless. Obviously nobody," she said with a snarky tone. "I was just running things over."

Was it his imagination or was that remark a little bit close to the bone? "Are you ready to go see Ben?"

She nodded but kept her back turned.

Severo searched her orange light for any clue that something was off, but she was vibrant. "Cece, are you sure you're alright?"

"You know what? I feel better than I ever have."

If that was the case, why did Severo feel so unsure?

CHAPTER 47

Ben

B en opened his bedroom door. Cece and Severo were there.

"Thank you both for coming," Ben said. "Get in before we're caught." He had just returned from a late stroll through the royal wing. All was quiet with no guards in the vicinity. Most were patrolling the front of the castle and its perimeter. Still, what they were doing was risky.

Two days to go. This had better work.

"What do you need us to do?" Cece said.

"Severo, if you sit in between Cece and me, you can keep us grounded while we go under. Cece, spray some of this on your face." Ben held up a small vial and handed it to Cece. "It will put you under instantly."

Severo stiffened. "Ben, are you sure that's the safest option?"

Cece was already spritzing her face with it. "Done," she said before falling onto the cushion Ben had laid out.

Ben followed and waited until he could pick up Cece's essence. He entered the vision and saw what she saw. Danyall was there. A cape of shriveled black leaves rested over his gaunt body—his broken shoes, held together with tightened twigs. Danyall shivered in the darkness, and he sat higher up, away from the murky stream of water that ran through the base of the cave.

Ben got closer and he saw a flicker of light. A small fire burned. Ben gulped when he saw what Danyall was roasting. Worms.

Danyall jumped. "Cece, is that you?"

Ben could hear Cece but couldn't see her.

"Yes, Father, it's me. I don't know if you can hear me, but my friend Ben, the prince, is here, and he wants to talk to you. Don't be scared."

Danyall had the slightest suspicion in his eyes as he looked around the cave. Then he saw Ben.

"Mr. Arison, I am a friend of Severo's and Cece's. They led me here. We are coming to rescue you two nights from now. Stay strong till then. Is there a way we can get you out safely?"

Danyall's voice was hoarse when he spoke. "Sometimes she goes into a state of trance, but it's never for long. Mostly she has forgotten about me. I could teleport near her. I'm good at building fires, although it's always here. If I make one in the open space that could create a distraction."

"Yes, that sounds like a good idea," Ben said, nodding. "Make sure it's after the last light. Keep hidden and safe. We will see you soon."

"We love you, Dad. Stay strong. You've got this."

Ben felt Cece's essence leave, but he wasn't ready to return yet. He floated for the first time over Obsidian Creek. Dark clouds knitted together above him with not even a crack of light coming through. It was difficult to see anything. The ground beneath him was swamp-like, interspersed with flat pieces of land covered in black, shard-like dead grass that looked like they could break skin. He stopped.

Facing him was another structure, cave-like but chiseled to resemble a small fort. At the highest point, coal-like spirals served as edging. Deadly.

Ben took a breath and floated through the wide doorway. Hundreds of spiders scattered as if sensing his presence. His heart raced. Alunattra was there. Elevated in the air before him above a glass throne. Her body hung limp like a doll. In a trance, like Danyall had said.

He knew he shouldn't, but he moved closer. Although her eyelids were open, her eyes rolled back, darting from side to side. She was fighting this.

Her eyes stopped moving. They opened.

For a split second, their eyes locked.

In a panic, Ben jerked back into his body. That was progress from last time.

Did she see me?

There was no way to know for certain. Ben was glad to be back, and that Cece was too. Seeing Danyall like that was hard to watch.

Cece must be feeling so many emotions right now.

Time to get this done.

I hope this all goes to plan...

CHAPTER 48

Gabriel

G abriel fidgeted. *Has anyone seen Niall this morning?* He started to sweat.

Tomorrow. It's all going down tomorrow.

Cece walked down the south wing steps with Severo, appearing half-demented as her eyes evaluated every inch of the coffee cart and its surroundings. Gabriel's heart burst with empathy as he paraded over to her and slipped his hand through hers. She exhaled. Anxious thoughts boiled up again.

Gabriel melded through the barrier as Severo and Cece buzzed their access. Cece's grip tightened the closer they came to the breakfast room. As they entered, she whispered to him, "Don't leave my side."

Everyone was there and Gabriel didn't want to draw attention, so he wrapped an arm around her in answer.

Ben's grandad was at one end and Ben at another. The fairies were moving the finger food and hot drinks to the middle of the table. Tweek had placed a tablecloth down and then directed a silver paper plate to each seating place. Gabriel salivated as a crystal platter of all kinds of sweet fruits lay right in his eyeline.

Severo whispered something to Vara; she blushed but looked guilty. Gabriel looked at Ben, and he was squirming in his chair. *Hmm?*

Cece moved her chair, so it was as close as possible to Gabriel. He laid an arm over her shaking shoulders. Something was not right. She should have been getting better.

"Thank you all for coming," Baylor said from the head of the table. "I can confirm the room is secure and there will be no interruptions. We finalized the details this morning. Our three fine fairies here have agreed to exchange their day off and take the place of the guards."

Ben clapped and directed his hands toward the fairies, and everyone applauded them.

"Before we go over the itinerary of events, I'll pass the reins to Striker with no further ado."

Striker flew to the middle flanked by Tweek and Fritzi. Gabriel had barely seen his fairy; he'd been working so much. Gratefulness clung to him.

"Firstly, I would like to test your Chip Connects. We're very much relying on this part to work. This should give us the inference we require."

"Striker, we don't all have genius in our blood," Severo said. "Can you dumb it down a bit here?"

Tweek laughed with the others, and Striker gave her a cross glare. Fritzi held a blank look on his face.

"What I mean to say is," Striker said, clearing his throat, "in order to reach a satisfactory conclusion, this part needs to be carried out without error. Gabriel, if you can move to the middle of the room and the rest of you, can you gather 'round in a circle."

Gabriel waltzed toward the open space in the center of the room. Baylor closed the large curtains, and Striker extracted five tiny gold specs that enlarged before them. Every spec found its way to those standing in the circle. Amazed, Gabriel watched the spec touch his bracelet and absorb itself into the plastic. The only evidence of its existence was a slightly bulbous jut on the underside.

"Okay, so what happens now?" Gabriel's nerves throbbed.

"Now, I want you, Gabriel, to press the prominent part of your bracelet."

He did.

Striker flew to the side. "Now lift your shield whilst keeping your finger in place and the rest of you press your buttons."

They all followed suit.

He could feel his friends like static electricity on his skin. It was weird. "Striker, I know I'm covered, but is it working with the others?"

"I can assure you it is. I can't see any of you. Excellent, that can be ticked off the list."

"If Gabriel doesn't know if it's working, how can we be sure on the night? What if there is a malfunction?" Ben asked what Gabriel was thinking.

Striker added with a tight smile, "If all of you stretch your arms out behind you, then tell me what happens."

Vara jumped. "Ooh, I can feel a buzz on my fingertips."

"Me too," the rest said in unison.

"Anytime you have reason to question its function, trail your fingers around the outskirts for confirmation. As long as your buttons are pressed, the shield should extend as you move." Striker enunciated each one of his words. "Any further questions?"

"Yes, once the button is pressed, is there a time limit?" Cece asked.

"Once activated, it will be in place till the button is pressed again," Striker replied. "Like an on/off switch. I'll add at this point, if any of you press the button after it's activated, it will bring the shield down for all of you. Extreme care is required here."

Gabriel wondered something. "Will the three of you be coming with us?"

The red rim of Striker's silver wings deflated as he replied, "Unfortunately, we can't. The edge of The Vale is the furthest we can go. Alunattra lost her fairy a long time ago and strives for that kind of power. If we were to enter, we would run the risk of being utilized, or worse, killed like our friends were. Fairy magic is something she's used to manipulating. There are many dangers in the forest, and while we can do great things with our skills, we can't risk getting too close to her power. We would never compromise your safety."

Baylor interjected, "There's much more to discuss but first, please eat. Nourishment is of utmost importance this week. Don't forget to pile on the fruit—it's the ultimate brain food."

Gabriel was glad to get a quiet moment. "Cece, what's going on? Please tell me."

"Gabriel, I wish I knew." Her eyes drooped with frustration. "I spoke to Dr. Lovett, and she says I'm experiencing an after-trauma condition. I keep having blackouts, but it's almost like part of my mind is not my own. Not to sound like the pathetic girlfriend, but it's better when you're here."

The word he had longed to hear for so long. Gabriel's heart skipped a beat.

"Girlfriend?"

Cece blushed. "Hey, you know me. Subtlety is not my thing."

Gabriel's heart sang as he brought her hand to his lips, wishing they were alone so he could hold her. She was going to be fine. Strength was in her blood. He tucked a wave of her hair behind her ear. "Cece, you can't expect to recover mentally right away. What happened to you was serious. I'm right there with you, always. You're not alone."

Cece clung to him, and her wild hair shaped the curves of his face. He loved her. He knew that with certainty. She was his everything.

"Cece, have you seen Clara this morning? I think we should thank her and make sure she's away from Niall."

Cece leaned into Gabriel's chest. "Vara and I went to see her earlier. Her parents are homeschooling her and said she's not to see friends just now. I'm going to try again once this is over."

Gabriel hugged her tighter. This week had been tough for everyone. He hoped Clara was okay. At least she was safe at home.

As they stood side by side, another exchange in the room drew Gabriel's attention. Severo's hand was deep in his satchel as if to retrieve something, but Vara's words stopped him in his tracks. Whatever she said must have been crushing; heartbreak was written all over his face. Vara's eyes were glimmering as she stood and placed a kiss on his cheek.

Nobody needed an explanation for the obvious. Gabriel hoped Severo would be okay. To own the truth, Gabriel had always assumed Vara would choose Severo, but who was he to decide?

Baylor gathered them back to the breakfast table, and they sat down with nervous suspense.

"Now for the main reason I called you all here today. Listen closely because this is what I propose."

Gabriel listened to the plan. It was now in place. No going back.

Gabriel's head hurt as they all left the room. He caught Ben's arm. "Have you seen Niall today?"

"Just once. He's not here. I saw him leave toward The Vale this morning."

CHAPTER 49

Ben

An abrupt hammering brought Ben out of his daze. Worried, he darted to the door. It was Tharmus. Before Ben could even be angry Tharmus rushed in with something cradled in his arms.

"Close the door."

The urgency of this request made Ben do exactly that.

As Tharmus placed this wrapped bundle on the ground, a dark gray blanket unfurled to reveal a frail-looking Clara. Shivering, she looked around the room first, then focused on Ben. Relief flickered across Clara's bloodshot eyes and she jumped up, stumbling towards Ben.

Ben jumped back, his eyes widening. What in Landis was going on? "Tharmus? Is she okay?" Ben tentatively moved toward Clara, who had now flopped back on to the floor, out of breath.

"No, she's not. None of us are." Tharmus paced back and forth.

"Ben, Niall knows you're coming. He left me for dead after poisoning me. My body healed itself, and Tharmus happened to find me on a security patrol. I got a glimpse into Tharmus. Parts of his inner brain were starting to deteriorate. I healed him."

Ben stared at Clara in sheer disbelief. *What?*

He slowly sank to the floor, his mind reeling. Niall poisoned her? He shuddered, pulling his legs to his chest. He knew Niall had changed but murder? And Clara? Bile rose in Ben's throat.

Clara scooted over to him. "Now that my head is clear, I see how my gift kept trying to restore my mind, but with Niall constantly at my side, brainwashing me, I kept faltering. Niall doesn't know I'm alive. Even my parents' minds have been tampered with. They think I'm alive and home-schooling. I'll keep it that way for now. To keep them safe." Clara gave a weak smile. "Tharmus and I stuck to the shadows this week. We couldn't risk Niall finding out. Plus, the poison was strong. It's taken me a while to... recover. He has converted others, and we are trying to do damage control, although two of his chess club buddies—Arlo and Eloise—can't be accounted for tonight."

Stunned, Ben looked at these two people who'd barely registered on his radar. "Clara, what must you think of all of us? You deserve better. I should've protected you."

That's why Clara wasn't at school yesterday. I should have stopped this.

Clara smiled knowingly. "Ben, we can't change the past. We're new friends, and friendships are not cut and dried. You have to navigate the curves. When you hold steady, you know there's a foundation to build on. Now, go and do what needs to be done. You can make amends when you return."

Tharmus further surprised Ben by saying, "What can we do to help?"

Ben could've been crowned king of underestimation right there as guilt floored him. He got them up to speed. "Can you both remain here and alert? Striker has programmed our new Door Dots to work at a ridiculous sound level. If you hear anything, inform my father and the guards."

"Absolutely, Prince Benjamin," said Tharmus. "You have my discretion and trust."

The guilt burrowed deeper as Ben held his hand out to Tharmus. "Thank you."

Tharmus took it and grasped it firmly.

"Both of you stay in here. My room is protected. Keep safe. I don't know how to thank you."

"Don't. Just come back alive. All of you," Clara said.

Ben stood anxiously on the other side of his bedroom door. A familiar cedar scent lingered in the air around him. Gabriel. Ben's All-seeing Eye was stronger again. "Hi, Gabriel."

"I must be losing my touch," he said with a chuckle.

"Not at all. I'm learning to reach for help from my available senses." Ben stretched out his hand and patted it on Gabriel's invisible shoulder—at least that was his aim. "Maybe less cologne next time," Ben sniggered.

Gabriel gulped, shuffling his feet. "Good point. It's not great if people can smell me coming."

"I was only joking with you, but we need to go. Niall is waiting with company. Enough is enough. This needs to end. Now."

Ben could hear Gabriel fidgeting. He bumped his friend's arm. "Don't worry, at least we're forewarned."

Ben and Gabriel pressed their bracelets and Ben slipped under Gabriel's cloak. The hall was devoid of sound as they kept to the shadows. They came to an abrupt stop as his parents exited his mother's study and walked hand in hand right past them. The first inadvertent test had passed. Hopefully, everyone else had managed to get to the meeting point.

Ben still couldn't believe Gabriel could guide him through the doors of the castle without opening them, but to his utter amazement it worked. It made his stomach feel queasy and left him more than a bit lightheaded. They crept behind a full, flowing cherry blossom tree in the gardens. Their friends were there. Vara had a large bag at her feet with the supplies and Grandad held a tall, slim container. Severo and Cece were huddled together, and the three fairies were talking, perched on a tree branch.

"Good, you're here," Tweek said with a sigh of relief. "Everyone, take a hooded cloak. It will help you—the Barrierettes blend into the night."

"The Barrierettes?" Severo scoffed through the last bite of a sandwich.

"Don't listen to him, Tweek. I like it." Cece nudged her wing and Tweek twinkled.

"Okay, crazy names aside, let's do this," Severo said, true to form.

Ben thought of something. "What about any additional guard fairies?"

"Covered," Tweek said, then gave a sly grin. "I may have slipped them some of my special brew."

Striker stifled an impressed giggle and Tweek looked shy.

"Benjamin, a word." His grandad pulled him around to the back of the tree. "I had this made for you. It should have been gifted to you for your birthday, but it's taken a while."

Ben took the case from his grandad and its heavy weight surprised him. He unclipped the leather clasp. Inside lay a silver sword, its handle rippled gold. Mesmerized, he stared at the bound material wrapping the hilt. It bore his engraved initials. Ben gripped his hand around the hilt, and the sword felt like it belonged there. A shiver of strength breezed through him.

"Thank you, Grandad. I love it."

"You're welcome, my boy. Something else to keep you safe." Grandad's voice broke a little as he squeezed Ben's arm.

They walked back to the group. Having Grandad there strengthened him. They were as ready as they would ever be.

Ben took the lead with his friends behind, and his grandad and the fairies were to his side. The night air shifted to a biting wind. Rain sprinkled overhead, pitter-pattering around their feet. But as they neared The Forbidden Vale, the rainfall plummeted with more intensity as though it were throwing a tantrum. The fast-moving anthracite clouds merged into one giant, angry mass, but Ben and his group remained dry and untouched under the protection of Gabriel's shield.

Ben worried for his grandfather, but as he thought this, Tweek buzzed and produced above Grandad a floating windbreaker. She was getting the biggest treats tomorrow.

On their arrival, blades of tethered smoke protruded from the woods. It seemed to be coming from the Tree of Vulnerability. The forest was waiting.

They formed a circle at the rim of the forest, and Severo held Ben while he went under. He'd mastered the practice and lifted from his body more easily. His astral self soared above the thrashing trees and hovered to the ground at the Tree of Vulnerability. The briefest of movements revealed Danyall, crouched low behind a large rock, knee-deep in the thick murky soil.

"Danyall, is she near?" Ben whispered.

Danyall's head craned around the large stone, and his sunken eyes met Ben's gaze. He didn't look well.

"She's distracted, the way she gets sometimes, but it won't last long!"

"We're all here to rescue you, including Severo and Cece. Keep hidden and don't move."

Danyall thanked Ben with a humbled nod, and one lonesome tear escaped in slow motion down his dirtied cheek. He was too weak.

Ben left Obsidian Creek and continued his hunt through The Vale, but there was no sign of Niall. Moving back to the Tree of Vulnerability, Ben noticed frantic movement within the realms of a nearby tree. In his astral state, he slithered over to take a closer look. A pair of embedded eyes peered out. Eyes he would know anywhere. Elias. As Ben delved into them, a flashback with evocative images clarified everything that had gone down. Niall had recruited Elias to hurt Severo, and then Alunattra had taken Elias for herself.

Ben gazed at what he thought was discolored tree bark. It was an elbow tangled through layers of the tree. Ben noticed other fragments of body parts woven through the tree shaft. Elias was lost, his spirit stolen. Alunattra had drained his body. He was a puppet with a useful skill. Alive but dead.

Ben was grateful Elias couldn't see him, as now they would need to avoid this particular tree. He willed the voice to speak to him. When nothing happened, he approached the Tree of Vulnerability. Comfort enveloped him. The voice returned and words rang in his ears.

"Why are you here?" the voice asked, frightened.

"I have someone I need to rescue, and I need to know if Alunattra is here." Ben wished he could know who this was.

"As long as I am here, she is not. If you must come in, do it quickly, but Alunattra is not the only one you have to fear," the voice said.

"We are shielded and plan to stay that way. Can you hold firm?" Ben pleaded with the voice.

"I wish I could guarantee that, but I don't make the decisions. Be quick, she is distracted now. Make sure you keep shielded or you will be discovered."

Ben withdrew back into himself.

Four pairs of eyes gazed at him with expectation.

"Gabriel, you cannot let this shield down," Ben said, sitting up. "Severo, I can't find Niall. Can you be on guard for him?"

Both his friends held up their palms, and they met in the middle for a triple high-five.

"We know Niall's here, and we can assume he's armed," Ben said. "Severo, he won't see you coming with your skill, and hopefully, as long as Alunattra is out of the game, we should go undetected when cloaked. Vara and Cece, do you have the barrier mist?"

"I have it securely in my satchel, and Vara has everything else," Cece replied. "Us girls will apply the mist as soon as we're safely back over."

Striker ticked a non-existent list. "Do you all have your amended Door Dots?"

Ben lifted it from his pocket as did his friends.

Ben turned to his grandfather. "Don't come in with us. I know you planned to, but I need you here with the fairies to run the second wave."

Grandad's lips twitched in proud amusement. "Alas. No longer a boy but a man. One day soon your role as king will suit you well. Be safe, my boy."

Ben hugged him tightly. They didn't need any more words.

"Time to go." Ben led his army into the twisted forest, using his sword to slay the branches. It was heavy but sliced a clear path with ease. The elements still raged, itching to break through their shield. Thick, slimy mud tried to encapsulate his feet as every muscle pulled against the grain, holding strong. Ben detoured to avoid being exposed in any way to Elias.

The voice said, *"You don't have long. She will be here soon."*

As they approached the barrier, Ben whispered commands to the group. "Severo, here is your father's identification tag. Put this on his wrist and get him to activate his button so we can get him out safely. When we are back on this side, Cece and Vara will apply the mist."

Ben felt sick as he prepared to move through the barrier with his friends. Shreds of doubt clung to him. He hoped it worked. With precaution, he inched forward until the buzz of the shield met the forbidden screen.

This all-powerful barrier was supposed to be untouchable. He paused.

Nope. Just do it.

Ben stepped forward.

The first thing he noticed was the smell. The Vale smelled bad, but Obsidian Creek was putrid. His stomach curdled, and he wanted to vomit. His leather boots settled into the sludgy soil. His hopes accelerated as they passed through to the other side.

Ben patted himself down and turned to his friends. Not a scratch on them. He squeezed Gabriel's arm. They had done it. Everyone let out a deep breath. Ben lingered on Vara. She smiled in relief. He smiled back. He also noticed Severo standing so close to her and Cece that he looked like an attachment. Cece nodded and gave Ben one of her c'mon-already looks.

The sludge turned into swampland. As they walked, it got deeper. The rocks where Danyall hid were close. Just a little further.

They made it. Ben pointed Danyall out to Severo and Cece. Cece gasped, cupping her hands to her mouth. Her father lay with his head barely above the water, struggling to keep his eyes open. Cece splashed so fast, she was immersed in the foul water. Severo gripped and steadied Cece, lifted Danyall, then placed his bracelet on and pressed the button. Ben wished he could call for Tweek, but that was not an option.

"Hold on to him," Ben said, plodding forward and reaching Danyall's side. "We need to get back through. Is he breathing?"

"Just," Cece replied, opening the supply bag. Tears fell as she wrapped her father in a warm blanket.

Vara rummaged in the supply bag. "Cece, here. This might help." Vara handed over a dropper and some hydration juice. "After you told me how your father was, I brought everything I could think of. This will be easier."

"Thanks, V." Cece placed the dropper into her father's mouth, and his eyes flickered as he drank it. Severo held Danyall with ease.

They all waited, knee-deep in sludge.

Ben flicked his head. "Come on, let's get back to the barrier."

They were almost there. The circle huddled together and waded back to the other side. Ben squeezed Vara's hand in triumph before she let go and started misting the barrier with Cece. Only a small portion was covered; hopefully it was enough to make them undetectable from the other side and get Danyall out of the forest. Alunattra was nowhere to be seen.

She still needs to be defeated.

All at once, Ben caught Severo's whisper.

"Niall. He's here," Severo said.

What? I've not been focused.

Ben closed his eyes. Niall had been there all along—watching everything. Ben saw it. Niall had used barrier mist to keep disguised. It was dissolving before his eyes.

Ben didn't have time to react, his feet were pulled from under him. Niall's fingers gripped Ben's ankles, and his torso was dragged along the thorny gloom of nettled grass. The shield had come loose. His arms were being tied up with a rough rope. He squinted at the sound of a fairy hissing. Pixel was here too.

"Ben," Gabriel shouted, rushing toward him.

Niall moved fast, throwing a sheet of blue expanding plastic that swallowed Gabriel's form, pinning him to the ground. One of the new weapons—Ticplas.

Gabriel yelled to the others. "Go, now."

Vara, Severo, and Cece used their Door Dots and shot up high above them—an aspect Striker had added—and Severo held tight to his father.

Niall's wicked laugh made Ben wonder how they could've ever been friends.

"Your friends are inconsequential. I have what I want. Your inefficiency to carry out a plan is remarkable." Niall sat on a nearby rock with Pixel poised and ready.

"We were once your friends too." Ben tried to move, but Pixel was hovering in front of his face, her hands outstretched in a trance. She'd used an enchantment.

"That's not relevant now. Your ability, Ben, is wasted. You're simply not smart enough to use it. This is the beginning of the end for you."

Niall retrieved something from his shirt pocket and placed it on the ground. That something grew to take form. Eloise, the school gossip.

Niall clicked his fingers and Pixel feathered hers, clearing the transparent cloud of barrier mist away and revealing Arlo. Niall knew it all.

Ben looked at Eloise and Arlo. Their eyes were black, vacant, and they stared at Niall, entranced. Arlo moved his legs stiffly and crouched beside Gabriel.

Ben clawed furiously at the thorns that surrounded him till he felt the rope fray, then tear. Warmth erupted from the raw, flayed skin. But his body felt strong. His mind connected to his surroundings, and he could see a way out.

Ben knew what to do. With practiced focus, he zeroed in on the tree that loomed over Niall. His mind pried loose some of the dark wet leaves.

How can I be doing this?

The leaves moved with force and plastered themselves over Niall's face, temporarily blinding him. This distracted Pixel, and she went to help Niall. The enchantment was broken. Ben didn't have long, and this new action had winded him.

I can move things with my mind?

The book... A bullet point popped into his thoughts. *After practiced meditation, your mind can evaluate situations and create a way out. Therefore, manifesting the answer.*

Ben felt the skin at his wrists rip further as he broke free. He sprinted toward Gabriel, keeping an eye on a thrashing Niall, who was scraping his fingers at his face. Pixel was frantically trying to assist. Like stretchy dough, Arlo's fingers sailed from where he stood to peel the leaves from Niall's face.

Ben tried but failed to release Gabriel from the layers of plastic and now Eloise was like an ant, crawling all over Ben's face. He caught her at the side of his ear, pinched her between his fingers, and cast her away. She took full form again as a tree broke her fall. She slumped to the wet ground, unconscious.

"Ben, go!" Gabriel yelled, flailing beneath the plastic. "Make sure everyone else is safe."

"No, I'll not leave you."

Behind him, Niall seethed. "What a touching moment." Then he launched himself at Ben.

Everything happened so fast. Ben and Niall grappled at each other, rolling in the sludge, kicking, and striking with their fists. Ben's eyes were doing that weird thing again, where he could see everything. A familiar face emerged from the trees.

Severo.

Severo crept up behind Arlo. He pulled Arlo's extended limbs and tied them around a tree. Severo then lifted the sheet of taut plastic off Gabriel with swift ease.

At the same time, Ben became free. His grandad was there, and he had pulled Niall off Ben. Grandad threw Niall out of the way. Ben heard Niall wince as he landed on a thorny bush.

Grandad ran to Ben. "My boy, you're okay." Relief washed over his grandad's face and Ben rose to embrace him.

Niall was back on his feet and rampaging towards Ben. Incensed, he grabbed hold of the back of Grandad's overcoat. Niall was too quick as Ben tried to catch up. Instead, he watched Niall lift and hurl the man who was Ben's champion into the barrier. The last thing Ben saw was his grandad smile at him with eyes full of love.

Ben's guttural scream reverberated through the forest as his grandfather was instantly incinerated. All that remained was floating ash.

Shock flooded Ben's veins, immobilizing him. The air in his lungs evaporated, and he couldn't breathe. His gaze remained fixed on the reverberating spot where his grandad vanished into oblivion. He was too deadlocked in horror to fully register Gabriel charging toward Niall. He closed his eyes and felt himself sinking into a black void.

"Ben, where did they go?"

Is that Severo?

Ben couldn't think. His heart was drumming against his ribcage, pounding in his ears. It was all he could hear. Nothing else.

"Ben!" Severo shouted, shaking him. "We need to get Gabriel. He's gone. So is Niall."

"Gone?" Something inside Ben flinched. No, not Gabriel too. "Where?"

"I have no idea. Let's press our bracelets," Severo suggested.

Ben looked down. His bracelet was missing. Struck dumb, his brain clicked and he rose to the occasion.

"My bracelet is gone. Severo, help me. I'm going under."

Ben let his body fall, and he separated before reaching the ground. Gabriel and Niall were on the other side along with Pixel. Pixel had some sort of glowing band tightening around both of Gabriel's arms and legs. Something similar lay over his lips.

Ben knew Niall couldn't see him—that was his saving grace. "Gabriel," Ben whispered.

Gabriel arched his eyebrows and struggled with no use.

"I'll get you out, I promise. Go along with Niall. Shield and fall back hard to activate your bracelet when I nod. Severo will click his and pull you back through."

Gabriel's face was pale, his eyes rimmed with panic. He was trying to tell Ben something, but he couldn't make out the words.

A weird rustling noise, then a thumping instilled terror, and Ben pulled himself back just in time.

Alunattra.

Her blades of hair slithered and probed her way toward Niall. He fell to his knees in a pathetic mess. She was armed with her offspring flowing from her like a spider sheath.

We're running out of time.

Ben thumbed back into his body and pulled Severo in behind the tree. This was not a safe space to talk or think.

Can Elias see us?

He reached into his satchel and pulled out a small notebook and pen and wrote something down, displaying the words to Severo.

Ben sat cross-legged with Severo holding down his shoulders. This gave him the strength he needed as his mind stretched and pulled with all he had. He focused on Gabriel who was not able to move a muscle. Ben willed Gabriel to move and fall backward, activating his bracelet.

"Now, Sev!"

Gabriel started to drift towards the barrier. When he got close, Severo pressed his button and dived around Ben to pull Gabriel back through. He was caught, bound by Alunattra's spiders who wove their webs around his ankles. Gabriel jerked, positioned between both sides. Alunattra swerved, then scuttled at an exceptional pace. She tried to slam into them, slashing with her sharpened hair. Severo pulled hard and freed Gabriel. Ben watched in horror as Alunattra sliced Gabriel's hand from his body. Blood splattered in every direction.

Gabriel's scream drilled into Ben's brain. His stomach turned, but he clamped a hand over his mouth, swallowed, and forced down the rush of bile. His friend needed his help.

Gabriel's scream turned to a soft whimper, and his eyelids fluttered shut. He was losing consciousness. Ben tore his shirt and made a tourniquet.

"Severo, get him, Eloise, and Arlo back! Call for Vallore—we need his help. Alunattra is too strong. If we go over there, then she will be able to come back with us. We can't let that happen. Hopefully, Vallore can do more than a barrier reinforcement this time. I'm right behind you."

Severo didn't question him and left with Gabriel on his back and Eloise and Arlo tucked under each arm.

The barrier mist dissolved, and Alunattra bore her blood-red eyes into Ben. Her grotesque limbs battered at the barrier, attempting to reach him. They stared hard at each other. For a fleeting second neither moved. Her hand rose and her fingernail pierced the barrier. She sneered.

Ben gulped. She was coming through. The events tonight had finally weakened the barrier enough. Without thinking, he pulled his sword from his belt buckle and lifted it high into the air. Although he had never held one, his body knew what to do.

He circled the air and the sword cut off her finger. Alunattra pulled back and growled.

He wasn't scared. Hatred fueled him.

They locked eyes again. Ben struggled to understand what swirled in Alunattra's eyes. He tried to look deeper, but a headache was already swelling in his skull.

He waited, ready to take her on, but an icy cold breeze made his bones shiver. Blinding white robes illuminated before him. Vallore.

The High Host's eyes radiated with intensity, his stare lethal. "You think you've won, Mileah. Never. My sister still whispers to me. I will always be one step ahead. I will never let you die."

Alunattra let her hand drop. Blood spurted from where her finger used to be. "And yet, you are only here because someone summoned you. If they hadn't, I would already be walking this world."

She was right. Ben had been thinking that for a while. Vallore could be outsmarted.

"I told you once before: You know nothing. You will never be a match for me."

Ben kept his eyes glued to their exchange, unperturbed by the rain soaking his garments. Ben sensed there was more to this. Maybe Vallore wasn't able to kill Alunattra for some reason.

Alunattra stood back. She wasn't angry or resigned. Her eyes held strength. Determination.

Vallore lifted his withered palms and Alunattra's head fell back as her body rose off the ground. Vallore's fingers sparked with what looked like lightning. He flung his fingers out and waves of light struck Alunattra. Her body convulsed and drooped as power was sucked from her. Vallore stopped and stumbled. Alunattra landed on the ground, enraged, and took her chance to grapple at his wrists.

The flames from their fingers repelled each other. Vallore hurled her body away, hard and fast. She darted into the sludge of Obsidian Creek. Vallore's fingers sank into the earth, creating a new barrier. It sparked and electric blue light flickered over the filmy forcefield, spreading until an explosion of light covered the barrier. Ben stumbled away, watching Vallore in a trance. The barrier rose higher, right through the clouds.

Alunattra swept into the air, muck dripping from her body. She didn't speak but never once did her defiant eyes leave Vallore's. Ben saw something in Vallore's eyes. Fear.

Vallore twirled his robe and was gone. He didn't acknowledge the fact that Ben had witnessed this altercation. So many unanswered questions.

Ben stood and faced Alunattra again. The barrier had been restored. But for how long? When he looked at her now all that filled him was hatred. Especially as he saw Niall, cowering in the distance. She came closer. They both were inches from each other.

"I think you should know that what happened today is all your servant's doing." Ben's eyes floated to meet Niall's uncertain gaze. "He's your problem now."

Alunattra flicked her head to Niall, providing the tactical distraction Ben hoped for. The need for death surrounded him like a toxic fume.

Niall shrank back as his queen rested her icy stare upon him.

"*You.*" The word hissed from her mouth like a curse.

"Let me try again," Niall pleaded on his knees. "I'll do anything you ask. All I do is for you. All for you."

"What a touching moment," Ben said, bitterness spewing from his throat. The very sight of someone he once called "friend" groveling at that monster's feet sickened him to his marrow.

Alunattra's creatures detached from her veined body and scuttled toward a petrified Niall. Ben zigzagged his way out of the treacherous forest and didn't look back. Rip-roaring screams echoed in his ears. Niall was a murderer and would get what he deserved; it was the only consolation for the devastation in his heart.

Ben collapsed at the edge of the forest. All the fight drained from him like melting wax. His father was there, along with Tharmus and Vara. His father picked him up in his arms and Tweek came to rest on his shoulder. Ben fell into an entranced, exhaustive state.

CHAPTER 50

Alunattra

Alunattra stamped her feet into the ground. Mud rippled like a giant wave over the marshland. If only Vallore had not been summoned. It was the boy with the shield. Gabriel. He called Vallore. She'd heard his chant as he wavered in and out of consciousness. How had Gabriel managed to get through the barrier? Whether he knew it or not, that act had allowed her her chance, but now it was all for nothing. The boy ruined everything, and now his hand lay before her. A trophy from this night.

I will find another way.

At least she had Niall where she wanted him. A poisonous weed that would not be allowed to spread. She cocked her head, staring down at the boy with contempt.

"Please, don't kill me," he begged, squirming beneath her spawn. "I can be of use to you. Now that we're together, nothing can stop us."

Spit fell from her sharp incisors. "No, Niall. We failed. Like I did so long ago. Killing you would be kind. No, you will remain here to rot like the prisoner you are, and I will gladly stand by and watch."

Alunattra swirled her fingers, and her legion of spawn pinning Niall down flocked back to her. She released lightning bolts from her fingers until they shocked and curled around Niall. He screamed in pain. She flexed her fingers, and his body flew through the air into an open cave. Alunattra clicked her fingers, and the cave came together, trapping him inside.

She screamed a message to him.

"I will leave here one day and find this other world, and you, Niall, if you're still alive, will be left to the wrath of your friends."

CHAPTER 51

Ben

P ain filled every crevice, including Ben's eyelids he tried to open. His mother and father were at his bedside. He was glad to be in the warmth of his bed. Everything came flooding back and Ben sat up too quickly.

His mother laid him back down like he was the most precious ornament. "Do not move. You are covered in bruises, and Miss Clara will be here soon. Everybody is okay and being cared for."

"Gabriel?"

"He's going to be fine, son."

Ben searched his father's face, needing to know that was the case, and was met with genuine truth.

"Father... Grandad. I'm sorry."

Ben crumbled as the floodgates opened. His mother sat up on his bed and pulled him in, cradling him like a newborn baby. His father gripped his hand.

After what seemed like hours, Ben's hiccupped breathing quietened, and his father spoke softly to him. "Your grandad was a brave man, Benjamin, and loved you more than life itself. He went out gallantly, fighting for what's important: Family. I expect he must have known his time was coming. He met with me yesterday and requested I give you this when the time came."

The smallest of tears tapered down his father's cheek as he handed Ben the letter. "We'll let you have some time on your own."

Ben's mother rose in agreement. "We'll be right outside."

With gentle perfection, Ben unraveled the letter. A new lump in his throat formed as he read the words written in his grandad's hand.

MY BENJAMIN,

The day you were born will stay with me long after I die. Your inner strength glowed from your tiny, wrinkled body. Know that you were loved every day of my life. Just like you will never leave me, I will be there by your side always. Be strong and brave and do not be scared to make difficult decisions. Err on what is right, not what is easy, and always be kind, as hatred is for the weak.

YOUR LOVING GRANDPA BAY.

CHAPTER 52

Vara

Vara breathed in the scent of roses. She loved weddings. Aristo and Perial glowed as they clasped hands, then held their breath until they said, "I do."

The first grand fairy wedding. Pure Bay was alive in celebration. A large canopy floated in the sky above them, with the edging trimmed in lace. Snow white linen adorned the tables, ready for the feast to come. It was perfect.

Is this what my wedding will be like?

She skirted a glance at Ben and wondered if he was thinking the same. He smiled down at her, and she cuddled into him. Still, she fought the urge to sigh.

It didn't feel like two months. So many lovely dates with Ben, yet she couldn't stop staring at the dance floor. Severo and Constance were dancing double time to the music and their laughter flourished over to her. It looked like more than friendship to Vara. Her life was mapped out and she was content, for the most part, yet she couldn't help questioning how it would be if she had made a different decision. It didn't matter; her family was overjoyed with the match and so were the king and queen. Something she told herself every day.

She had to look. Severo must have felt her inquisitive stare and returned it with a conflicted expression. She broke away and excused herself. After splashing cold water on her face, she said to herself in the mirror, *You have made your choice and it was the right one.* Deflated, she made her way back through the crowd and guiltily slipped her hand into Ben's.

CHAPTER 53

Severo

S evero meandered his way to the large table of food to fill his insatiable appetite. Connie was engrossed in conversation with Clara, who was now a weekend intern. He watched Vara's emerald mist walking away from the crowd and his instinct was to go to her but he didn't. She had made her choice and he loved her enough to respect her decision. He touched his satchel in relief. The letters were still there. Like a security blanket, he always kept them with him. He couldn't bring himself to throw them away. Maybe one day.

"Ahem, Master Severo."

Severo raised his eyebrow at his fairy's frantic wings. "Ah, Striker, I wondered where you'd disappeared to. You having fun?"

Striker's red glow burned brighter. "Well, yes. Yes, I am. I thought I might have a dance. I suppose it would be rude not to."

"Good on you." Severo watched his fairy fly over toward Tweek then bottle it, only to find him seconds later doing the same thing again. Finally, his fairy worked up the nerve and the two floated to the dance floor.

Well, how about that.

His happiness escalated, feeling his sister's joy in Gabriel's arms. Gabriel watched over her like a guardian. Cece was definitely altered, but for the most part, her spark was back in full force. She just needed time.

Life had been strange, having his parents together again. His mother slowly opened the prison gates she had locked herself behind, and they were learning to love and trust one another again. His father hadn't uttered a word since his return but was trying his best to fit into a life that wasn't his anymore. They were all adjusting. His parents were smiling and tripping all over each other as they tried to dance in time to the music. Severo laughed.

It's good they have each other again.

He sighed, wishing he could have a partner. Connie was lovely, but his heart belonged to another. Regret partnered longing as he pulled her in for a hug and imagined holding Vara instead.

CHAPTER 54

Gabriel

Today was a good day. Gabriel held Cece tighter. Her laughter sounded like a song.

"Don't damage another limb."

Gabriel beamed, pulling her closer, albeit awkwardly. He smiled at Clara who waved from across the dance floor. Clara had healed him, but he was left with the shadow pains of what once was. He wasn't sure he could get used to being without his right hand, but he tried to focus on the good around him. Cece looked beautiful in a bright, orange floor-length dress that clung to his legs as they danced. Every day he hoped to see improvements, and today she was bright.

Cece had turned sixteen and her ceremony would take place soon. Gabriel watched her often and worried about her as she was still suffering from the turmoil of these last few months. She was getting counseling which seemed to be helping a little. Sometimes a vacant look appeared in her eyes that made her seem distant, but it had been over a week since that'd happened. He made it his mission to protect her at all costs.

Fritzi flew to Gabriel's shoulder and hung his head, looking a bit down in the dumps.

Gabriel poked his fairy. "You not dancing, Fritz?"

He sighed. "No. Maybe later."

His fairy flew off, lingering around Striker who was dancing with

Tweek. Gabriel did a double blink. *Poor Fritzi.* Hopefully, he would find a companion one day.

Their circle had changed, and repairs had taken some time. All five of them spent most of their time together and were occasionally joined by Constance—or Connie as Severo called her—and Tharmus. Most were coupled up, but friendship was at the head.

Gabriel hated thinking of the negative but so many things still niggled him. For now, he chose positivity. They had each other and they had their lives. It had been a lucky escape and not one he ever wished to relive.

Every now and then, his thoughts flickered to the far side, where the contained darkness still seemed a present threat to him. Battle scars. Hopefully now they could all move on with their lives. Everybody had lost so much. He leaned into Cece and embraced her, basking in her calming warmth.

CHAPTER 55

Ben

B en smiled, wishing his grandad could've been alive to be here but knew on some level he was. He squeezed his partner close and gazed into her beautiful chocolate eyes. Ben had been dating Vara for the past month and they were highly talked of. Courting month was almost here, but he already had his princess. Being the prince had its advantages.

After the fight with Alunattra, many things happened, and they all had issues to work through.

The change in his parents was irreversible, but the loss had taught them to embrace and appreciate life. Their relationship as a family still needed a lot of nurturing, but Ben welcomed this work in progress. His mother finally seemed free from the weight that had pinned her down. Maybe he didn't need to have all the answers.

A buzz of merrymaking pulled Ben from his thoughts as the fairies led a procession across the dance floor, with Tweek taking front and center. All her peers were in awe that she had concocted a takedown. She thrived on her tale of the Barrierettes which had caught on as she hoped. She looked over and flapped a winged hello. Ben blew her a kiss. None of them would be here today without the devotion of their fairies.

Ben glanced over at Gabriel embraced in Cece's arms. The two of them were inseparable, but his friend now had a missing limb, lost forever to Obsidian Creek. On that night, Clara had been wonderful.

She and Tharmus had helped tremendously in the rescue operation and rounded up others whose minds Niall had compromised. Eloise and Arlo had no recollection of what happened. Ben would never forget it. He was even warming to Tharmus, something he could never have predicted.

Ben was drawn to the couple who glided over every inch of the dance floor: Severo and his partner, Nurse Constance—the young apprentice from the hospital who was so smart, she had finished school early. Severo insisted they were just friends. Sensing Ben's gaze, Severo cocked an eyebrow and indicated to the girl in his arms with a grin on his face. His friend finally had come round to him and Vara being a couple. He wanted Severo to be happy, knowing full well he was responsible for clipping that. His collar felt tight.

Aside from the loss of his grandad, which was a wound he felt would never truly heal, his world had returned to normal. After that catastrophic night, Vallore had impacted the outskirts of the forest. It was impossible to enter it now. Ben was present with his father the day after the fight. When they spoke to the High Host, there was no mention that some of them had managed to penetrate the barrier. Vallore had the power to destroy, and Ben knew he had to keep Gabriel, himself, and the others safe. His father had concurred.

That day, Ben had got a glimmer into Vallore. For some reason, Vallore could not kill Alunattra. But Ben knew *he* could. His sword had injured her. There was power in it. He would be armed and ready if there was a next time.

They all had studied their powers more and discovered, once granted, the gifts remain that of the keeper. It felt good, like extra protection.

Many village recruits surrounded the barrier now on a shift rotation, and Striker had created protective armor for them to keep the dark voices out.

Niall's parents were the only two people allowed to be excused from today's grand event. They were still not coping with the knowledge of what their son had done and struggling at the same time with his loss. The people of Landis had not been so easy on them, and Ben wasn't sure the hostility would ever die down. Elias's family was the opposite. They knew he was lost to the forest, yet they lived their lives in ignorance and refused to be tarred by the sins of their son.

Pixel was presumed dead.

Ben smiled, an action of late that made an occasional appearance. He bent to kiss Vara's floral-smelling hair and sighed with contentment. The voice from the tree had not called out to him, and his visions of the girl from somewhere else appeared to have stopped. A niggle jabbed at his side, but he cast it away.

Ben tried not to wonder what happened to Alunattra. He hoped the quiet meant they could all live happily once again.

I'm happy. I'm happy. He'd come to repeat this on a regular basis in the hopes it remained true.

His parents moved to the podium hand-in-hand, stronger than oak, and his mother caught his eye as she smiled around the room. His father raised his glass in a toast to the newlyweds, and the celebration ran into the small hours of the morning.

Epilogue

I t hurt to blink, to move. She had to. Her soaked clothes clung to every inch of her skin. She tried to stand but her legs wouldn't comply.

I must be dying.

Someone was there, though. She felt a hand on her forehead. It was warm. She wanted to open her eyes but sleep beckoned her.

"You're going to be okay."

That voice. It was familiar.

I'm safe now. I'll just sleep for a little while.

SUDDEN WARMTH FLOODED HER BODY. SHE JERKED AWAKE. HER BLURRED vision cleared and that was when she saw him. The boy from her dreams.

"It's you," she whispered.

His knitted brow softened as he smiled with a sigh. "And it's you."

Landis Readers' Guide

Are you ready for more of LANDIS? Check out the Monarch website for the LANDIS Reader's Guide. This free educational resource is perfect for educators, librarians, homeschools, small groups, and readers who want more of Shelly Mack's world!

www.monarcheducationalservices.com

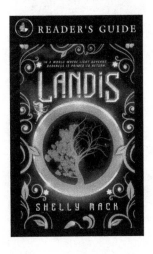

Acknowledgments

The seed for Landis began with a bedtime story and grew from there. In 2020 I decided to follow my lifelong dream of writing a novel. Frazer, Olivia, Gracie, Mum, Dad, Bruce—my team, thank you for always helping me reach for the stars and for being my biggest fans. I wouldn't be here today without your guidance, expertise, love and support. A shout-out to Jo and Kirsty for always being there.

A special mention to my brother Bruce who helped design the cover. Your talent astounds me everyday. Thank you so very much. I love that you get to be part of my book in such a big way. And thank you to Saii for the additions to the cover.

I want to thank my publisher, Dr. Jennifer Lowry for believing in my story and characters, and for understanding them the way I always intended. You have made this Scottish girl's dream a reality. My faith is everything and I spend a lot of time praying; when Monarch called, I got my definitive answer. So proud to be part of your team of wonderful authors and a special thank you to the lovely Ashley White who brought us together. To the inside team who refined and shaped Landis; Kayleigh Merritt; Kelly Martin; Jessica Eddy and Stephanie Cotta [my very own Yoda]. I'm sending you all a virtual hug. You have made me a better writer and I've learned so much. Thank you.

Stephanie R. Graham, you started me on a path I will never leave. Thank you for your wisdom and expertise but above all, your friendship.

The first person to read and finish Landis was my friend Bryan Minto and even when it was miles from being what it is now, you loved this story and it gave me so much encouragement. Thank you Louise Grant for reading and loving Landis, can't wait for you to read this version. To my other alpha readers for your support and comments in the early stages, it helped more than you can possibly know.

Elysia Nates, my fellow author and friend across the miles, we will meet one day to have our well-talked of hot chocolate. Thank you for your friendship and kindness. Sending love to you.

Thank you to my wonderful friend, Nicole Harkness, you are my very own Jiminy Cricket. You champion all that I write and keep me going. I'm so blessed to know you.

To my writing critique partner, Jess, I'd be lost without you and all I can say is, I'm glad I have unlimited calls. You make me stronger. Thank you.

To Marisa Noelle and Emma Finlayson-Palmer, thank you both for the help you gave me at the beginning, It got me on the right path. I value you both so much and I am so grateful for your input.

Thank you in advance to those who read Landis. I hope you love it. Don't give up on your dreams. Believe and they will come true.

About the Author

Shelly Mack is an author of children's books, including picture books and young adult fiction. From a toddler through to adulthood, books have been a permanent part of her day-to-day life. Her children and faith inspired her writing. Shelly wants to keep books alive in a world that needs escapism and wishes to bring joy to her readers through her books.

As well as writing, she runs a 'Meet the Author' programme on Instagram, which has been a great addition to her author career. Shelly is a full-time writer living in Scotland with her husband, two girls and two cats.

Also By Shelly Mack

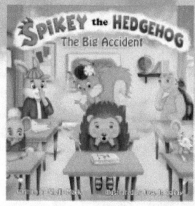

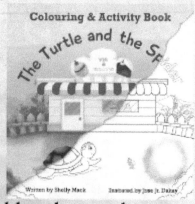

www.shellymackbooks.co.uk

Our Monarch Collection

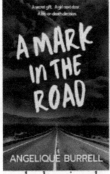

Printed in the USA
CPSIA information can be obtained
at www.ICGtesting.com
LVHW041204041123
762715LV00024B/43/J

9 781957 656267